A novel

IT WON'T ALWAYS BE THIS GREAT

Peter Mehlman

All characters in this book are ficticious. Any resemblance to actual persons, living or dead, is purely coincidental.

Bancroft Press
P.O. Box 65360
Baltimore, MD 21209-9945

(phone) 410 . 358 . 0658
(fax) 410 . 764 . 1967

bancroftpress.com

ISBN
978-1-61088-135-7 (cloth)
978-1-61088-138-8 (mobi)
978-1-61088-137-1 (epub)
978-1-61088-139-5 (audio)

Cover Design: Siori Kitajima, SF AppWorks LLC
Interior Design: J. L. Herchenroeder

Printed in the United States of America

A novel

IT WON'T ALWAYS BE THIS GREAT

Peter Mehlman

CONTENTS

FRIDAY, THEN AND NOW

I.

When did being me become a full-time job?

I know, it sounds unseemly to imply that you never considered yourself self-absorbed but, before the events I'm about to describe, I'd never given it any thought. So there you go, right? Maybe not.

Either way, everything changed last December, and it's important for you to know right off—I haven't told this story to anyone, not even God.

The fact is, until the flight down here, I planned to take it to the grave. I was never someone to jump into people's laps and spill my guts, and I'm even less so nowadays when everyone blabs everything, a trend that kind of makes me sick. I don't know, maybe there's not enough attention to go around anymore, with twelve billion people or whatever the wall-to-wall population of the world is. New people keep cropping up with their own little lives. It's like, I go to a crowded restaurant a mile away and don't know anyone. And these are people living the exact same life as mine. Ten miles away and the total strangers don't even look familiar.

You know, as long as I'm in confessional mode, sometimes when there's a news report of some natural disaster killing ten thousand people, part of me is thinking: Good. Gravity needs a break.

Well, not *good*, really. I'm not saying mass tragedies are good. Mass, personal, small group—all terrible. But for the sake of squeezing more years out of the planet, maybe these things need to happen. Some economist even said as much. Veblen, I think. Or Malthus? Like I know. I dropped Econ 205 after the midterm. Anyway, I'm just saying, I can't believe there's enough grain to cover St. Patrick's Day, let alone Asia.

It's weird, but I think about the end of the world a lot lately. I'm no big environmentalist, but there are what? Ten animals in the world not on the endangered species list? The Nature Channel shows these ferocious polar bears doing their baffled doggy paddles to the next studio apartment-sized iceberg and it's like: *Damn! When's our turn on the list?*

Funny, those nature shows go on and on about an endangered species and then show footage of fifty of them at a time. You don't know what to believe.

Anyway, like I said, I was okay not telling anyone this story, and I'm sorry if telling you in particular seems indulgent. Other people might see it that way, but other people aren't here, so tough luck.

It all started on a wickedly cold Friday. It's funny; I remember feeling like I just wasn't in the mood for myself that whole day. My typical ruminating, reviewing, and regretting, leading to conclusions that are all wrong . . . I just wanted to dodge myself from the moment I woke up. That's why I wound up staying late at work. The best way of getting out of my own head was to hang out with Arnie, the chiropractor who shares office space with me. Podiatry and chiropractic actually mesh nicely as far as mutual referrals go, but it's even better because Arnie is such a great guy. You'd love him. I mean, he's nothing like you, but still, the guy is a total riot. At around four, after our last patients, we had the funniest conversation in the history of the world. But it ran past sundown, so I was forced to walk the two-and-a-half miles home.

Now, don't for a second think I observe Shabbos. So why would I have to walk home if I work past sundown on a Friday? Here's why: My little Long Island town has become flooded with Orthodox Jews. Some were brought up Orthodox. Others reached a certain age, took stock of their lives, came up empty, and hit up God. I can only guess at the reasons, but I swear, it took hold like a virus. The streets, the schools and, most significantly, the retail establishments on Stratification Boulevard were full of people casually walking around in yarmulkes as if they looked totally normal. Stratification is a seriously high-end shopping area, but it's silent on Friday nights and Saturdays. Some idiotic rules get chiseled into a tablet for some guy and his poor blind brother to fetch at the top of some mountain in the Mideast and 5,000 years later, it costs Americans a ton of income. Fucking nuts!

Anyway, at the western end of Stratification is a four-story glass professional building, headquarters of yours truly, DPM. Now, the Orthodox don't overtly give you shit if you're not one of them. But (BUT!) they do throw their economic weight around. If your store is open on Shabbos, regardless of your religion, you will be frozen out of Orthodox dollars. Right now, maybe forty-five percent of my patients are Orthodox. I don't wear a yarmulke or have a mezuzah on the door, but they're okay with that. It's like: *My feet hurt, so what you do in the privacy of your own office is your business/shame.* But if they saw me driving home on a Friday night, then I'm just shoving it in their faces and they'd take their feet elsewhere.

Look, Commie, as clichéd as it sounds, I have a family to support.

That morning, Alyse had specifically reminded me to leave work before sundown, so I had to call her from Arnie's office to tell her I blew the deadline. "Alyse, Jesus, I'm sorry. I got to talking to Arnie and lost track of time."

"That's fine, hon, as long as you don't mind walking home. Take your time."

Alyse was in a lenient state of mind due to a fairly major parenting lapse she'd made that day. Not that she usually has me on a short leash. Or any leash. Alyse is great.

"I'll leave in a few minutes."

"Whenever. Say hi to Arnie. I love you."

I paused.

Alyse said, "You can give me the not-alone version of 'I love you.'"

I laughed and said, "And you're a really good person."

That's a thing Alyse and I have done since college, when ending all phone calls with "I love you" seemed like a great idea. Now the kids say it at the end of every call too. With cell phones, it's like eighty-five 'I love you's a day. It's nice, I guess.

I hung up and Arnie smiled. "'You're a really good person?'"

I explained the code and Arnie said, "My ex-wife ended most calls by slamming down the phone. Then again, she was the kind of woman who could hang up on you in person."

I laughed and vetoed the idea of asking about his current wife's phone habits, but Arnie did it for me. "Fumi doesn't even use the phone." he said, shaking his head. "She's scared of germs even though they'd all be *her* germs. What a nut. You know, I used to think the dumbest thing you could do was marry an ugly shiksa. But marrying an emotionally volatile Asian girl? What the fuck is the point of that?"

After getting my breath back from laughing my ass off, I said good night to Arnie, threw on my coat and gloves, and started walking home.

The town's hoity-toity stores line the south side of Stratification Boulevard. The sidewalk is generously wide, maybe twenty-five feet until you hit the curb, where there's diagonal parking, a two-lane eastbound road, then a grassy island before you hit the westbound road. North of that is a park with benches and swings and trees. It's pretty nice, actually. Spacious.

So I'm walking east along the stores, mindlessly looking at the windows. The Commerce Committee hypes the diverse joy of the season so, along with menorahs and dreidels, the stores all had white Christmas lights framing their windows. A faintly ecumenical Winter Wonderland.

With the wind chill, it was Minnesota out there, so hardly anyone was on the street. One demented jogger. A bag lady in an alcove whom I heard say, "I can't find anything in this house." Two non-local women wondering why the shops were closed. A forty-ish guy glaring at his Bernese as it sniffed other dogs' urine on a hydrant. *Anyone you know, Rover*? The guy yanked the leash and disappeared down a side street. Otherwise, it was just me, chugging home.

I won't go into it, but a few weird/annoying/troubling things that day kept trying to seep back into my head. Instead, I chose to think about my talk with Arnie. Some of what he said before the stuff about Fumi was so funny, I laughed aloud right there on the street. I felt good.

I. Felt. Good.

So, knowing me, Commie, you can guess that my high spirits had a narrow sell-by date.

Marching sprightly along, I reached Nu? Girl Fashions, a store for tweens that's a retail gold mine for the owner, Nat Uziel, one of the town's more prominent Orthodox Jews, whatever that means. Maybe he sits courtside for the High Holidays, I don't know. But more relevant, he was one of my long-time patients. Even more relevant, so was his daughter, Audra, a freshman at Columbia whom I'd seen that morning. She was one of my favorite patients, but I'd said something kind of stupid to her—the kind of little thing I torture myself over forever. I won't go into it, but suffice to say, as soon as I saw Nu? Girl Fashions, I thought of my idiotic comment and muttered under my breath, "Oh, come on! Let me forget my crap for one minute!"

With a real sense of defiance, I turned my back to the store and bolted ninety degrees to cross the street and continued my walk on the grassy island dividing Stratification Boulevard. *Get me away from everything that reminds me—*

On my second or third step on the grass, my left foot landed on something lying on the ground. My ankle jackknifed, the joint lurching to such a grotesque degree that my ankle bone touched the ground while my sole was still on the object I'd stepped on. I fell to the ground, grabbed my foot with both hands, and waited for the wave of nausea I knew was coming from the fifty times I'd rolled my ankle playing basketball. There was a delay before the pain set in. My next thought was: *That's it. I'll never play hoops again.*

It took a good two minutes before the pain eased enough to let me swallow and stand up. With all my weight on my right leg, I looked around, hoping someone would pass by and give me a lift home. But the area was still deserted and spooky.

Knowing me, you can imagine how my mind started spinning, recounting all my dumb mistakes and lousy luck leading to that moment. *If only I'd have gone straight home instead of talking with Arnie, which forced me to walk home along stores that, anywhere else, would be open and full of people who don't give a shit if you drive on Friday night . . .*

I treated myself to maybe thirty seconds of wheel spinning before finally looking down to see what protruding tree root or wayward rock I'd stepped on. It was so dark, I had to bend way down to see. It wasn't a root. And it wasn't a rock.

It was MOSSAD KOSHER HORSERADISH.

A wave of pure, livid adrenaline shot through me. I picked up the bottle, wheeled around, and committed the first real crime of my life.

I threw a bottle of horseradish on a beeline through the upper pane of glass above the sign for Nu? Girl Fashions.

I shattered the storefront of Nat Uziel's pride and joy along with the way-too peaceful monotony that had become my life.

II.

I later learned the shattered pane was fourteen feet high and twenty-eight feet wide. Chunks of screaming glass rained down on the street like crystals off a gaudy chandelier.

Then it was quiet again.

Instinctively, my left hand reached into my pocket for my phone. My right hand moved, my fingers all ready to dial 911 and own up to my crime like the dyed-in-the-wool mensch I am.

But wonder of wonders, Commie, my head swiveled around: still no one on the street. I looked back at the store: two old, low resolution security cameras—they looked like the boxes you'd use to watch an eclipse—were aimed down at the front door, blind to my position. I looked at my gloves, which covered my fingerprints. Then it was like my head said "no" to my hands.

Instead, I let go of the phone, turned, and walked away.

Vetoing my hands as they were about to confess, scanning for witnesses, casing out security cameras, excluding fingerprint evidence, fleeing—all of that happened in a flash. Amazing how adrenaline cranks down time and lets you notice a million details. On the other hand, it totally blinds you to the shit storm dead ahead.

I limped pretty fast, but not too fast. I went maybe three-quarters of a block when I noticed that the security alarm from the store was blaring. Weird. I hadn't heard it, even though, I later learned, it activated the second the window shattered. Suddenly, the pain in my ankle spiked. The swelling bulged out my sock. I walked another block and realized I'd never make it home that way, so I started to call Alyse to pick me up. But just before I hit HOME on my speed dial, I hung up.

Commie? You won't believe this. I didn't call home because, if I became a suspect, the cops could dump my phone records, triangulate and pinpoint where I made the call, and boom: strong circumstantial evidence. Did I mention that I watch a lot of *Law & Order*?

So I told myself, *Keep limping homeward*. That put the song

Homeward Bound in my head. Trembling and scared, I started singing *Homeward Bound* to myself. Then I got an idea for a new version: *Homeward Bound and Gagged.* I actually laughed thinking I should call Paul Simon. I mean, boy, who can explain the brain?

After another few minutes, I was silhouetted by headlights coming from behind. I turned and saw a car with a taxi sign on the top. I decided I was far enough away from the scene of the crime and hopped on my right leg, waving my arms. The cab stopped.

The driver, a boxy Greek guy in his late fifties, had his head under a beanie and some knock-off version of an iPod.

As I hobbled into the backseat, he asked, "Are you okay, man?"

"I sprained my ankle really badly."

"What?"

He took the pods out of his ears. "Sorry. You okay?"

"I sprained my ankle really badly." Then, seeing an opportunity to bolster my alibi, I added, "I tripped over a tree root about twenty yards back. Maybe thirty seconds ago. Thanks so much for stopping."

"Hey, I'm a cab driver."

"But I doubt you expected to pick up a fare around here."

"No. Truth is, I just dropped off a fare from JFK and got lost trying to find the parkway or I would've never passed by."

"Well, your wrong turn is my good fortune. I live nearby. I'll be happy to give you directions back to wherever you want to go."

"Deal."

Halfway through the drive, two police cars, sirens wailing, sped in the opposite direction. The driver looked back at them in the rearview mirror and said, "What could be happening to make them cause such a racket on a cold night like this?"

When he said that, it hit me that he hadn't heard the alarm when he passed Nu? Girl Fashions. Drowned out by the knock-off iPod. Beautiful.

I checked my pockets for a slip of paper to write directions for the cabbie. Nothing. I pulled out my wallet and—oh, get this—before I even opened it, I thought: *I really need a new wallet*. In the immediate wake of my first felony, that was my thought.

It's so easy to retrieve your mundane, event-free life. Scary.

While I was scavenging through my wallet, the driver said, "What's this maniac doing?"

I looked up, didn't see anything, and didn't ask. I'd had enough intrigue for one night. But keep this "maniac" in the back of your mind, Commie.

The cabbie stopped in front of my house. I gave him ten bucks on a six-dollar fare and, finding nothing in my wallet, wrote directions to the highway on a torn-out page from a *Sports Illustrated* I had in my attaché case. Then I hobbled—

Not that I like *Sports Illustrated* anymore. The way they conduct those snarky anonymous polls of athletes turns me off. "What NBA player would you least like as a teammate?" "Who's the most overrated player on the PGA Tour?" As I see it, it's all just malicious gossip under the guise of a survey.

But I'm not going to get into that now.

Arnie subscribes to it in the office.

I hobbled out of the cab.

"You should get some ice on that ankle, sir."

"Believe me, I will. Have a great night."

Turns out, his night was more than he bargained for.

Oh Jesus, Commie. Alyse is calling me. I swear, the phone is like having one of those house-arrest things around your ankle. I'll be right back . . .

III.

Hey. Sorry about that. Alyse is in Tribeca looking at apartments and wanted to ask me something about flooring. As if I know anything. We came into some money—which is actually part of the story I'm telling you—and we're pretty set on moving back to the city. Charlie is at hockey practice, but Alyse took Esme with her so of course I had to talk to both of them. This girl Harley Binder, a friend Esme had a falling out with—also part of the story—suddenly friended her on Facebook. "Daddy, do you think I should let bygones go and accept?"

I just told her to trust her own instincts. I swear, the Internet's made the world so fat with etiquette, it just wears me out. Last summer, I had a thought: *I have over three hundred Facebook friends but have only spoken to maybe two hundred people in my whole life.* So I pretty much stopped looking at it except to keep track of this cop I'll tell you about later.

Anyway, when I finally hung up on "my girls," I went downstairs here to the cafeteria to get coffee and started thinking about this story I've started telling you and, well, I just don't think I'm doing it justice. The whole episode was kind of life-changing and, I don't know, maybe it's because I've been carrying it alone in my head all this time, but I'm just all over the place with it. Also, it involves you to a degree and, I hate to say this but, even though we're great friends, I realized I'm kind of assuming too much familiarity between us. Let's face it, Commie, it's been a long time since we've been super involved in each other's lives.

So look, I'm going to double back a little, just to the start of that Friday, okay? It'll help you get the full picture of what happened and give us a chance to catch up.

Well, a chance for *you* to catch—I mean . . . Sorry.

My God.

By the way, Alyse sends her love.

IV.

You don't know Alyse too well. When I met her, you'd been kicked out of the frat and I'd become one of those weasels who gets a girlfriend and vanishes. I'm sorry for that and for being lax about keeping in touch. I was bummed you missed my wedding, but that's no excuse. Not that you missed anything; even calling it *my wedding* is a joke. The minute I handed Alyse the ring, her parents mobilized into wedding planning as if they'd given birth to Princess Caroline of Monaco instead of Alyse Epstein of Nassau County. For all their preparation, they could have planned an invasion of Russia. Instead, it all led to one moment when I stood on the pulpit in my Calvin tux in front of two hundred guests listening to the rabbi's stand-up act when suddenly, I had a thought:

Jesus . . . I'm not even hungry.

Yes, that's what I thought at the biggest moment of my life. Another thing I've never told anyone until now.

I wound up not eating at the reception. Nothing. I couldn't compete. Packs of sixty-five-year-old diamond-studded yentas sprint to the Viennese table like Marion Jones and—poof!—the catering hurtles down those begging-for-mercy digestive tracts. It's the sort of thing that makes you start dreaming of those Vegas weddings where you grab a chunky Verizon techie from Iowa as your witness and get the whole shebang over in a blinding two seconds.

Anyway, Alyse. In the first days after my bottle throw, she kept asking me, "You're so spaced out. What are you thinking about?" I ducked the question a few times before saying, "I'm thinking about what to say the next time you ask me what I'm thinking." Alyse rolled her eyes, called me a "fucking idiot," and that was that.

Maybe you don't remember Long Island girls, but it's okay when they call you a fucking idiot. If they're truly mad, they calmly lay it out in (weirdly) clean, (suddenly) unaccented English. And, believe me, it's their civility that can really broil your mind. Not that Alyse is like that. She's totally cool. Really.

Amazing how different our wives are, huh? I think they'd get along really well if they got to know each other, but they are from different planets. And it's not just the obvious stuff. But I gotta say, Commie, I do like that Southern humidity in Danielle's voice. It makes me imagine her father being a preacher or something, although, when I told my mother I was coming down here to see you, she immediately said, "Don't kid yourself. There are plenty of Jews in Charleston. And they're *very active.*"

So far, you're the only Jew I've seen and you're not too active.

Sorry. Bad joke. Awful.

I'm just saying, the girls down here seem like aliens who are anatomically identical to Earth girls. Like that nurse downstairs with the colorless hair and the bouncing crucifix. How exotic would it be to be married to a middle-American girl fully loaded with Jesus and two weeks' vacation time? My mother used to say, "Marriage is hard enough without intermarrying." Of course, she was wrong. It's harder to be married to someone appropriate. The disappointments are built in. I once told my ex-rabbi that most divorces are due to irreconcilable similarities. He disagreed, but who cares? I always thought he wanted to shtup my wife anyhow.

In a way, Alyse and I intermarried. We grew up fifteen miles and ten income tax brackets apart. Her family was all cocksure. Mine had this underdog mentality. Those are bigger differences than buying into Jesus or not.

Don't get me wrong. I don't mind being Jewish. The values, the cultural shit, all good. The God business I could do without. But hell, make up five reasonable superstitions and you can start your own religion. What amazes me is that we still throw around the word *Gentile*. Jews make up .0001 percent of the planet, yet we insist on having a word for everyone else? Even the WASPS who own America are merely *them*. And the way we snicker at how they drink on sailboats with their emotions all plugged up their marble-shitting assholes—shouldn't *we* aspire to that?

My dad used to say, "Jews wear their emotions on their sleeves and WASPS wear their sleeves on their arms." Not bad for a seafood wholesaler from Yonkers, huh? Not that my father was America's Jew or anything. He was like us: Get your Bar Mitzvah money and end it. When I was a kid and we'd be sentenced to an hour at shul, he'd elbow me and say, "Baruch atah, I'm annoyed." Then he'd call the cantor a "Hava Nagila Monster," and I'd just lose it.

The last meal I had with my father before he died was at JG Melon's on 74th and Third. He left a 12% tip, so I slipped the waiter an extra five. I shouldn't have done that. It's bugged me ever since.

Anyway, Alyse and I used to belong to a reform synagogue called B'nai Zion. So reform, we called it Jon-B'nai Zion. I hated it but kept quiet. Then, at a Yom Kippur service as a guitarist played back-up for the Torah reader, Alyse said, "There should be a sign out front: B'NAI ZION: WE MAKE JUDAISM LOOK EASY." Soon after, we let our membership lapse. Holiday-wise, we're pretty much down to Chanukkah. Even Passover got old: our kids singing *Dayenu* like it's the Jewish version of *99 Bottles of Beer on the Wall.*

V.

Alyse and I struggled to have a baby for years. I used to tease Alyse that she had "hamster-bearing hips." Then, sure enough, three miscarriages. Not that her hips caused it, but it was awful. Three heartsick morning drives from the OBGYN's office with a thousand Pampers boxes bulging out of every garbage bin we passed.

Jesus. So much goes on with women's bodies, but somehow they outlive men. Makes no sense to me.

Charlie came just as we thought Esme would be an only child. We stopped at two because, let's face it, having a third kid . . . now you're just trying to get attention. Anyway, the miscarriages gave me time to come up with some fathering rules, like never tell people, "We have a *little boy.*" It's a fucking baby. They're all little. Never go on about how the baby slept through the night. It's like waking up screaming in the middle of the night made no sense. And never ever go on about how I love baby poop because "it's from *my child.*" Guys become dads and turn so subversively boring, but I never forget that no one really gives a shit about anyone else's kids.

Okay, Alyse and I *did* go ga-ga over Esme for a while, cooing like idiots, loudly asking our infant what she wanted at Starbucks, believing there should be a movie about our quest for a baby. But we got a grip pretty soon and started mocking ourselves, coming up with titles for our baby movie. *Journey to the Placenta of the Earth. Afterbirth of a Nation.*

Anyway, I was a pretty confident father until my kids started having their own opinions and I started worrying that they'd think I was a schmuck. Why? No idea. But I found myself trying to make a good impression on my own kids, although I think the last of that feeling went away due to this story I'm telling you.

I should mention that the headline events of the story got some news coverage. People still talk about it, mainly because no one knows I touched off the whole thing. It's kind of thrilling having this secret. One crumb of world history, all mine. It gives me a little high. Losing that high is why I never told Alyse. Any comment she'd make would change a story that's so vivid in my mind. It's a precious thing at a time when most of my past has gone all blurry.

I took a gut course at Maryland on the Baby Boom where the professor said we'd always be cool because we'd always be the bulk of the population. Like when we're eighty, kids would want iron-on wrinkles so they could look like us. But now, any coolness I felt in college is so distant, I can't even relate to that version of me anymore. I look back at college like I look back on, I don't know, Patti Hearst joining up with the SLA: a chapter in someone else's life story. I attended Maryland, but I don't *feel it* anymore. And I've tried, Commie. I was once in DC for a podiatric conference (a lot like the one I'm attending here this weekend) and stopped in at College Park so I could literally sniff around campus for a familiar smell to make me feel like a sophomore again, with fresh legs and a shiny future.

Even driving around now, I scan the radio for songs that might take me back. Any song off *Yellow Brick Road* gives me a warm shiver—until some honking prick in a shark-faced BMW jolts me back to the God-knows-what of now. *My Little Town* reminds me of the GE clock-radio my aunt bought me. (Hey, remember how my aunt sent me ten bucks for my birthday and then, a month later, I got mono and she sent me fifty? You told me to tell her I had leukemia. Maybe it would be worth a few grand. Jesus.)

Then there's *Hello It's Me* by Tod Rundgren. The memory tied to that song has stayed with me to the point that—

Well, forget it. That's . . . no. It's grotesquely personal.

Commie? Hello?

I guess I'm an asshole if I don't tell you now. Okay: When I, you know, pleasure myself, it's always to the same girl. Jenji McKenna. She was from Hagerstown. Great body. I barely remember her face, but in September of '76 with that crazy-hot Maryland humidity, we were together at a pool. *Hello It's Me* was playing as I sat with my feet hanging in the deep end. Jenji held my legs to stay afloat. Somehow, her left bikini top slipped down exposing her whole nipple. She didn't realize it, so I leaned over and covered her up. She just smiled and said, "Thanks." You never know when a moment will stick in your head forever, huh? Usually, I'm an unreliable witness to my own life. But that moment is so vivid, I've been doing my business to Jenji, and only Jenji, ever since. Imagine: I'm *a monogamous masturbator*.

Kind of pathetic. Although, the volume of scenarios I've dreamt up for this one girl all these years? I beam her through time from the frat house to my podiatric office. *"Oh yes, Doctor! Yes!"*

By the way, contrary to Jenji's ecstatic moaning, I don't refer to myself as "Doctor." Never have. Most podiatrists are Dr. Blah-blah. Some even have license plates like PED DOC, as if the next driver's gonna honk and yell, "Can you squeeze me in at ten?"

Then again, my path to podiatry wasn't the same as theirs.

The thing is, Alyse's Uncle Monte got me into podiatry school without my taking even one science course at Maryland—not chem, not bio, nothing. Monte was a guy who reached a point where he had to decide between the American dream or full-time alcoholism, so he split the difference. He liked working with wood, so he started designing barstools. Somehow, it caught on—mail-order, retail—until he was bought out by a home furnishing chain. A bazillion dollars later, he developed a bunion the size of a stuffed cabbage, had surgery, and was so blown away by this procedure that's done eighty-five million times a day that he endowed The Carnegie Hill Podiatry School. Of course, it's in Hell's Kitchen, but whatever. Long story short, I got in without taking the boards or even filling out an application. It was like joining a fucking health club.

I guess if Monte had been saved from drowning by a dolphin, I'd probably be at Sea World carrying a bucket of dead herring right now. But you know what? I happen to be a good podiatrist. I finished in the top 19th percentile of my class. Or the lower 81st, as Alyse says. She's pretty funny. Anyway, if you had a foot problem, I wouldn't hesitate to refer you to me.

Granted, I may not be doing what I was put on this earth to

do. Maybe I was meant to help the world in a bigger way. But then again, the idea of leaving the planet a better place than you found it? How the fuck do you do that? The planet was a mess when Mother Teresa found it and a bigger mess after she died. So, screw it. If not for my kids, I wouldn't give a shit if the world ended tomorrow. At least I'd feel like I wasn't missing out on anything.

That was a little self-absorbed, huh? My inner censor is really enjoying its first day off. Anyway, Commie, you worked to make the world better. I wonder if you think you made an impact. If, of course, you *can* think or do anything that keeps up someone's enrollment in the human race.

I read on one of those ridiculously cheery medical websites that some doctors theorize that even in your . . .

"And in this corner, from the Persistent Vegetative State of South Carolina . . ."

Sorry. The website suggests trying to stir emotions, so I thought maybe making you laugh—or pissing you off—would help.

Jesus, who came up with that term? It makes it sound like you're so damn persistent that you just flat out refuse to wake up. Do they call it PVS? I swear, if I have to learn one more acronym, I'll be right there with you.

Good God.

VI.

Anyway, the second I met Alyse, the dice were loaded. We got serious pretty fast. After all the gold chains Alyse dated in high school, her parents loved me. I seemed like the kind of earnest kid who would try to support their daughter with a career I was actually interested in.

Well, I showed them.

As you recall, I was a journalism major. Remember that semester when I wrote sixty-six articles for *The Diamondback*? Which, by the way, was the top-rated student newspaper in the country that year. Man, I loved making twenty-five calls to get the truth about some story. I read *All The President's Men* and then saw the movie about five times.

During spring break, senior year, I decided to tell Alyse my plan. I rehearsed the whole speech in front of a mirror: I'd apply for jobs as a reporter in several mid-size cities. For a few years, we'd have to live in Omaha or Tucson or Louisville while I built up enough clips to get a job at the *Times*. I was going to tell her how journalism tapped into my inquisitiveness and wide-eyed wonder, qualities of mine Alyse admired. I was going to tell her that all the great things I'd accomplish wouldn't matter without her.

I took her out to dinner at Gusti's in Georgetown. Alyse called it *Dis-Gusti's*, but that's not important now. She'd just gotten back from spring break with her family in Barbados. You remember how tan girls got before SPF? Well, she was not only crazy tan, but she actually *smelled* like the Caribbean. So, at dinner, inhaling that scent, I was like: *How am I having dinner with this girl, no less dating her*? I remember looking at her thin brown fingers. Most girls at Maryland had stubby fingers with livid red nails. *Brr*. Alyse never gets manicures. I still look at her hands.

Anyway, there I was, dizzy in love with my very own Hawaiian Tropic girl. I'd decided, God knows why, to tell her my plans after the appetizers arrived. But after the waiter took our order, Alyse went off script like people always do.

"So honey, what's the big thing you wanted to talk about?" she asked.

I derailed right then and there.

"Well, while you were away, I thought a lot about what I want to do after graduation, you know, and I realized . . . *I have no idea.*"

At that moment, my future shifted into Alyse's navigation system. I know that sounds bad. I've met other guys in the same boat and for them, it has been bad. But me? I don't share their daily fantasies of dipping my wife in cement and tossing her in the Long Island Sound. I like Alyse World. I've never wanted to escape it.

And let's face it, everything in American life pushes guys toward escape. When Gwyneth Paltrow gets married, pulpy slobs from coast to coast feel palpable disappointment as if they'd truly had a shot with her. I wonder if Cindy Crawford ever sees some middle-aged guy and thinks, *I've probably ruined his life*. All those fantasy girls staring at you from every magazine rack . . . Arnie recently said to me, "I've never met Jennifer Aniston, but I feel like I'm already tired of fucking her."

Kind of mean but, at one time, you'd have laughed at that. You had some laugh. From anywhere in the frat, I could hear . . .

How the hell could this be?

You know, listening to myself here, I'm wondering if I used to spin my wheels like this back in college. Probably. The world always struck me as too complicated. I used to have that stale thought about living a simple life as a fisherman. But then I realized that, while the average fisherman waits for a striped bass to bite into a perfect rectangle of squid miraculously floating in the middle of the ocean, he's probably plotting the perfect murder just like everyone else. Maybe it's the brainless fish who's lucky. At least he's not having panic attacks from swimming out too far. I say that because I once had a run of panic attacks where I couldn't even drive on a highway. I tried lots of cures I didn't believe in. Yoga, meditation, acupuncture. Finally, I ate shit and became a poster child for Zoloft.

Those dull yellow pills made me feel more like me than I'd ever felt before. The doctor said my serotonin receptors were off so that anything potentially life-threatening, like driving, set off my fight-or-flight instinct. Now I see the guy twice a year for ten minutes and happily fork over $120. Alyse thinks I should change my AOL address to Email Zoloft.

Anyway, let me move it along here and get back to that Friday. Thank God, right?

Alyse snaps awake at 5:30 every day as if she's got a job on an oil rig. I should mention that she does work and make money. She's an agent for unknown visual artists. She displays their stuff on a site called Arteteria.com. She has a great eye. Or so I hear. I have no taste in art. Zero. Picasso seems all whacked and random while some seascape hanging in a Best Western blows me away. I said that to Alyse once and she looked at me like I was the nut who put a hammer to *The Pieta*. (That made it more interesting in my eyes, but whatever.)

So, yeah, Alyse gets up at 5:30 and I get up at seven, but the solo ninety minutes in bed aren't restful. I feel guilty that she's up and functioning while I'm just lying there. I tell myself not to feel guilty, that I make a nice living, that I'm a good father. But still, *I am just lying there.*

Like I said, I felt good from hoops the night before. It's weird. Some nights, I feel like I always did, quick and smooth. Other times, my body doesn't come to the gym with me. But that night, I blocked a few shots by thirty-year-old pishers, blew by them with crossover dribbles—

Jesus. A good rationalization just hit me for staying in bed after Alyse gets up: Between me, the kids, and her destitute artists, these are probably the best ninety minutes of her day. So really, I'm doing her a favor. Why didn't I ever think of that before?

Anyway, I get out of bed and slog downstairs to the kitchen, kiss Alyse, which, from what I hear, very few husbands do in the morning, but out of love or superstition or whatever, I do—grab *News-*

day and a coffee and plop myself down in the breakfast nook. I read about the pathetic Knicks. Fuck 'em. Ever since they fired Marv Albert, I've loved seeing them lose.

After about fifteen minutes, I humped it upstairs to wake up my kids. Esme is twelve and, I swear, I'm scared to go in her room.

Scared. That's a bit much. I'm *tentative.* Esme's at that tween age where there's a whole world in her head I don't want to know about. Let's just say I try not to think about how my friend Joey Annunziata felt up both Dana Sanders and Erica Hiller at my bar mitzvah reception. Imagine: I invite this Catholic kid and he winds up groping two different little girls while I stand with my grandfather as he machetes a loaf of challah. The American Jewish experience in a nutshell.

Anyway, Esme's room is at the end of the hall, part of an add-on we did a few years ago. The Mafioso contractor, Bennie Liotta, did an amazing job for a price (again, I just don't want to know *how* he did it). Anyway, I crack open her door a tiny bit and call out, "Ezzie!" The name Esme was Alyse's idea. At first, it sounded like Pig Latin to me, but I got used to it. Charlie was my idea. Solid name, no?

Only her foot stuck out from her comforter, a turquoise bracelet around her tiny ankle. "Ezzie?" I wait until I hear her say, "I'm up!" to enter. Then I watch her eyes open, big, dark pools like that actress who shoplifts.

Charlie is eight and so innocent it kills me.

"Charlissimo, what happens when you snooze?"

Charlie, all croaky, said, "You lose," then asked what the Knicks did last night.

"Speaking of losing, 116-85."

"They suck."

"Yes, but try not to say 'suck' around other adults, okay?"

"How about 'they blow?'"

"Not so great either. How about 'They stink?'"

"I don't love it."

The first time I picked Charlie up after he was born, I actually whispered to him, "We are going to have *so much fun.*" A gurgled bubble came out of his mouth, which I interpreted as, "Definitely." For a while, he was a bad sleeper, but when he was like, six months old or so, I started keeping a radio near his bed and I'd turn on games for him, especially when the Yankees were playing and, I swear, he'd fall right asleep. It was so cute. During the off-season, I actually played tapes of old games. Toward the end of that phase, when he was around two, his eyes would get heavy in bed and he'd say, "*Yankees . . .*"

Actually, another funny thing: For a little while, Charlie was wetting the bed and was real upset about it. So one day, I told him I'd gone through a bed-wetting phase too. I didn't, but I wanted to make him feel better. Charlie's jaw dropped. "Really, Dad?"

And I said, "Yup. And that was before wetting the bed was cool." I think that was the first time Charlie ever got a joke. And guess what? He never wet the bed after that. So you see, I don't parent by the book, baby. In fact, when some TV parenting guru advised reading to your kids at four months old, I thought it was so stupid that, one night, I read aloud to a four-month-old Esme from *In Cold Blood*. Alyse laughed her ass off.

Anyway, back to Friday. I made the kids pancakes. Charlie scarfed 'em down. Esme complained about carbs. Her metabolism races like a Ferrari, and her legs look like twigs in her UGGs, but still she's on fat patrol. Raising a daughter is a logistical nightmare.

Meanwhile, through all of this, Alyse was on the phone with one of her artists, a twenty-three-year-old Balkan immigrant living in Brooklyn with the obviously fake name of You-ey Brushstroke. I'm serious. Y-O-U hyphen E-Y Brushstroke. Alyse said he's a "talented nut." He'd had a scholarship to RISD, where he made a collage of his dorm room door, ripped it off the hinges, and turned it in as his freshman project. After they explained the concept of private property, he moved on to public property. He stole twelve stop signs, welded them into a bouquet, and under each STOP, he spray-painted the words, GROOMING FLEAS. What did it mean? No idea. But sometimes now, when Alyse or I get nit-picky, one of us will say, “Stop grooming fleas.” Anyway, when You-ey was expelled, the project was written up in an art journal. Alyse read it and immediately contacted You-ey.

“You-ey, that sounds amazing! That’s true. Everything in the city *does speak* . . . Where did you get the YIELD signs? Actually, don’t tell me . . . Hauling all that here on the Long Island Railroad? Today? Okay, why not?”

Charlie and I looked up like: *That whacko is coming here*?

Esme whispered, “Mom, I want to meet him!”

Funny. Even in a tiny little family. Cliques.

Alyse covered the phone and whispered, “I have a feeling I’m going to make a fortune off this guy.”

Anyway, we got the kids off to school. Public school because I wanted my kids to meet a black person before they turned thirty. Alyse went along with me out of some vague kids-of-the-people populism.

Hey, am I sounding all negative about Alyse? Because that’s not the case. The truth is, I feel weird having so few complaints about my wife. I mean, shit, the average guy I know? If his wife was one cup size smaller, he wouldn’t have married her in the first place.

Okay. So. As I went upstairs to get dressed, Alyse said, “Remember to try to get home before sundown. It’s don’t-piss-off-the-Orthodox night.”

Once, I did piss them off and learned my lesson.

VII.

About nine years ago, I was sitting on a bench eating a takeout cheeseburger and reading *American Podiatry Magazine* when, suddenly, I see this bony kid in a yarmulke gawking at me. It doesn't dawn on me then that cheeseburgers are inherently unkosher, and the kid, maybe fourteen, is so skinny that I finally just say, "You want a bite?"

I know. How stupid am I? Still, my heart was in the right place. I actually held out the burger to him. The kid looked at it like it was radioactive and said, "Aren't you Jewish?"

That's when the whole non-kosher thing landed on my head.

More accusingly, the kid repeated, "Aren't you Jewish?"

Waving the burger, I said, "Not according to your definition."

Well, this kid's legs went liquid for a second, and then he just bolted.

That night, I told the story to Alyse and she winced. "You know, he'll probably tell people what you said."

"So what?"

"So what" turned into an office visit from . . . Nat Uziel. Years earlier, a toe on his left foot had gone rogue and started climbing over the next one. I had to perform a procedure—*perform* (as if it's a ballet). Anyway, I had to break the toe and realign it. The procedure went fine, Uziel thanked me, and even offered me a discount at Nu? Girl Fashions. Now, I assumed some other toe flipped out, but when he came into my office, he just looked at me coldly and said, "Not according to your definition."

I did a full-body spasm. "That's why you wanted to see me?"

"Yes, that's why I took the ferry from my vacation home in Fire Island to see you."

Lamely, I said, "Wow, word really gets around, doesn't it?"

"The boy you rebuked with your vicious barb was my son, Jason."

Until my mind hit the brakes on the words *vicious barb*, I went into full defensive panic mode. Then the absurdity of that exaggeration grounded me.

"Look, Mr. Uziel, I'm sorry, but I don't feel my statement to your son was vicious. Pointed, perhaps, but not vicious. Just visualize the situation: I was quietly eating my lunch when, out of the blue, a total stranger asked me if I was Jewish. Frankly, with the way the world is, I was offended by the question."

"Why? Obviously it was a Jewish boy asking the question."

"I don't see why anyone of any faith has the right to ask me that."

"Can you see why a sensitive, religious young man would be taken aback at the sight of an older Jewish man eating a cheeseburger?"

"I wasn't wearing a yarmulke or a Star of David. And I was reading the *American Podiatry Magazine*, not the Talmud. So he couldn't know I was a Jewish man eating a cheeseburger unless he was an expert in racial profiling. So no, Mr. Uziel, I don't see why he would be taken aback by the sight of a man eating a cheeseburger."

Shockingly, Uziel considered my point, so I threw him a bone.

"That said, your son is at a vulnerable age in a complex world, and it does him no good to be on the receiving end of a barb, vicious or benign, from any adult. If it would help, I'd welcome the chance to see him and offer a secular but sincere apology."

Uziel slumped and said, "I think it would be best if I let him know that you are a good man regardless of your eating habits. But I appreciate the offer."

"Well, if you fail to convince him, my offer stands."

"I've never failed at anything."

I swear, he said that. *I've never failed at anything*. That statement provoked me a little. So when Uziel got up to leave, you won't believe what I said to him: "You can pay at the front desk."

He glared at me before being embarrassed at not getting the joke. A weak smile and he was gone.

I fought to concentrate on my next patients. My head was buzzing because, let's face it, confrontations like that are so rare. And the fact that I dug in and stuck it to him! Uziel intended to rip me a new one, then tell me my practice would be boycotted by his people for life. Instead, he wound up explaining to his miserable kid that I was actually a good person. On top of that, he later brought his eleven-year-old daughter Audra to my office with a case of recurrent plantar's warts.

I was wound up, so instead of going right home, I drove around replaying the event in my head and feeling warmly smug. I even came up with a more realistic golden rule: *Do unto others just slightly worse than you would have others do unto you.* I intoned it aloud in my car while burning onto the Grand Central Parkway, where I made the mistake of actually analyzing my emotions.

It dawned on me that I was in a blind rage and had been since hearing those two words: *vicious barb.* My calmness with Uziel: resentment. The fact that I was so (unusually) articulate in talking to him: fury. "You can pay at the front desk?" Pure pissed-off-itude.

Well, anger is not my thing, and suddenly my head started swimming. I looked down and saw I was doing 92 miles an hour. Heat surged into my face, sweat popping. My throat constricted. It was my first panic attack, although I didn't know it at the time. What I did know was that I had to get off that road, but I slowed down so abruptly that a car rear-ended me. A BMW, of course.

Oddly, the collision killed my panic. That's how screwed up I was: A car accident *calmed me down.* When the BMW guy cursed me out, I just said, "Look, I'm a good guy and I'm sure you are too. Why don't we do what we have to do and not kill each other?"

Well, get this: By the time we finished exchanging information, the guy apologized and confided in me, "My mother killed herself four years ago. My father called me this morning asking if he could sell her suicide note on the Internet. I'm just saying, I've had a shitty day and I'm sorry for losing it like I did." So, I—

Oh, me? No, I'm just an old friend . . . Do you attend to Mr. Moscow all the time or . . . ?

. . . Well, thanks. You have a nice day too— Whoa! Watch your step!

Jesus. Guy almost did a header right into the heart monitor. You know, I still find male nurses a weird concept. You'd think they'd come up with a more PC term for these poor schnooks.

Okay, let's see. The kids eat, go to school. I threw on a cashmere overcoat that Alyse had gotten me from Barney's for my forty-fifth birthday and checked the pockets for gloves. (I lose gloves every other day.)

I left for work, but as I got in the car, I had this tiny nagging feeling eating at me. When I feel like that, I literally have to stop and ask myself: *What's bothering you*? I rummaged around my head until I tracked that morning's angst back to when Alyse said about her psychotic artist, "I have a feeling I'm going to make a fortune off this guy." Yes, I'm embarrassed to say, the thought of Alyse making "a fortune" bothered me. I know of a few divorces owing mainly to the wife out-earning the husband. After the husbands took their wives to the cleaners, they were ostracized from cliques that sucked to be a part of in the first place. I read somewhere that men who earn less money than their wives tend to die younger. It makes sense—all that stress and crippled self-esteem. But I told myself it didn't make sense for me; I was still the breadwinner in the house. The kids have iPhones, we take vacations to Paradise Island, Disney World. Who paid for all that?

Finally, I told myself: Stop. Thinking. About. Crap.

I tuned to WINS hoping its latest version of horrible news would wipe out my puny fretting. There was a report on gangs in Cincinnati who target Prius drivers for car-jackings. Since the Prius makes no noise, it had become the car of choice for drive-by shooters. *Eco-murder. Love it.*

But then there was the next story, Commie: a report on how rich people clone their dogs so they can basically have the same dog forever. That was the first time I heard about the cloned Australian Shepherd who bit a toddler's pinkie off at the knuckle and ate it. Sound familiar, Commie? The maimed kid, the dog imprisoned in some shelter, the lawsuit against the Korean veterinarian . . . ?

Well, just thinking about the lengths people go to trying to control their little lives—money, time, travel—and it never works out.. It kind of put another wet towel on my post-basketball buzz, which pissed me off. I started thinking: *If only I got dressed two minutes earlier, I'd have listened to rock and roll on the radio and missed what Alyse said about making a fortune and missed the clone story and I'd still be on my high right now.*

I flicked off WINS, turned to a classical music channel, and scolded myself: *When you feel good, just keep the fucking world out of reach.*

VIII.

I go through that kind of thought processes all the time, recounting the pinballing events that lead to depressing moments. I've tried telling myself that maybe those little events delayed me enough to miss crossing paths with some drunk driver running a light. Maybe those moments *saved my life*. But theoretical stuff like that doesn't work for me, not on any gut level anyway. Sometimes I do my event recounts aloud with Alyse right there. She laughs and I feel a little better. Once, she described me as "inwardly mobile."

By the way, that morning, I did not take note that the cloned dog story took place in Hilton Head. I want you to know that. Right here in South Carolina.

I pulled into the office parking lot during what I assumed was the final movement of a symphony by Dvorak. I figured it was the final movement because it was getting a little loud. That's the extent of my musical knowledge, even though my parents did splurge to take me to Young People's Concerts with Leonard Bernstein . . . (My mother: "You need culture.")

I went back to Philharmonic Hall exactly once as an adult. Alyse and I lived on the Upper East Side after college, in the building that was used as the exterior for where *The Jeffersons* moved on up. I loved the city. Alyse worked in an art gallery, so I got to go to parties with lots of chain smokers floating above reality, discussing airy philosophies. I think pretentiousness is underrated. It's being down-to-earth that makes people boring. What I miss most about the city is the privacy. Not like suburbia where, God forbid, you're depressed and take a walk past all the French doors with everyone peering out: *Gee, Margot, does he look suicidal or what?* In the city, you pass the same people in your lobby every day and never acknowledge their existence. It's the peak of civilization.

Anyway, Arnie and I arrived at the office the same time that morning. The only difference is, he came straight from one of his martial arts classes. He's a black belt in something. (Like I can keep track of those Asians and their nutty belts.) Arnie likes to say, "I can kill a man with my bare hands and, someday, I hope to do so." I believe him. He's tall, All-American looking, and always incredibly fit.

Still, every time I think I have problems, I think of Arnie and take comfort. For his first marriage, he did "my civic duty and married a nice Jewish girl from New Rochelle." He also cheated on her forty times before her friends did a kind of yenta intervention, as if it were crucial she knew what a sap she'd been. After a divorce and a few of years of Olympic-level dating, Arnie married Fumi. She's smart and beautiful but, wow, what a nut! It isn't just that she refuses to leave the house without wearing a surgical mask, or that she eats virtually nothing but French toast, or that she has a compulsion to spit in elevators. She also likes to scream at Arnie for no reason. She'll show up at the office and go ballistic. Patients forget their bulging discs, hop off the table, and scurry out.

For a while, they separated. Arnie moved into an apartment in town, so he was paying a mortgage, rent, and alimony. He was verging on some dicey financial straits when he hit on an idea to drum up more business; he became Orthodox. Well, sort of. He wore a yarmulke, hung out at the Orthodox synagogue and, without ever joining, regularly engaged the rabbi about Jewish philosophy.

That rabbi, Mel Schwachter, is a good guy. If you met him on a tennis court and he was wearing a baseball cap, you'd assume he was Reform. He talked to Arnie for hours and put forth a highly sensible and forgiving theory to explain "the Asian woman." The thing I remember about the Rabbi's theory was that he quoted a Bob Dylan song: *I'm tryin' to get as far away from myself as I can.* Rabbis love quoting Dylan. In a heartbeat, they'll throw over the Talmud for *Blood on the Tracks*.

Anyway, Arnie promised to join the synagogue as soon as his finances allowed. The Rabbi would say, "Whenever you're ready," and Arnie would say, "Thank you, Rabbi." Then on Friday afternoons, Arnie would leave work early, make a show of stopping in the synagogue to say, "Shabbat Shalom," get in his car, drive to the city, toss the yarmulke in his glove compartment, and meet a few friends for sweet and sour pork on Mott Street.

Sure enough, Arnie got a slew of Orthodox patients without ever even having to join the synagogue. He said it was a case where bullshit talked and money walked.

That morning, one of Arnie's patients in the waiting room was bent over like he'd petrified trying to tie his shoelaces. He laid open a copy of *People* on the floor to read it. I guess it kept his mind off the pain, reading about whatever actress adopted a Rwandan baby that week. Amazing how these starlets get on these famine-stricken country adoption lists like the poor kid is a Mike Jacobs bag. *Mike* Jacobs? Doesn't sound right.

Whatever. Arnie and I share a receptionist named Sylvia Hoskett, who is, I swear, so nondescript I couldn't help a police sketch artist draw a reasonable likeness of her even though she's been working for us for seven years now. But she's a great receptionist and takes the job very seriously. Once, Arnie said, "I wonder if it's fun to be so squared away all the time."

My first patient of the day was Audra Uziel. Remember? I mentioned before that her father brought her in with plantar's warts when she was eleven. Now she was eighteen, a freshman at Columbia. I'd seen her two or three times when she was a tween. Plantar warts are very common in children, caused by the human papilloma virus, the same one that causes herpes but in a different manifestation. They can be treated with topical medication, cryotherapy, or surgical excision. Some people try a homeopathic ointment from the outskirts of science, but it's crap. I had treated Audra when she was eleven but, by fourteen, she was back in my office. That was the first time she'd come alone, which didn't surprise me. I'd seen her father a month earlier, and when I asked after Audra, Nat shook his head and said, "Audra is very independent. *Too* independent." Among other examples, he said that she "wanted to dress immodestly."

Imagine that scandal in the Uziel home, huh? Here the guy

makes a killing selling hot clothes to little girls, and when his daughter wants to be on the same playing field as his customers, he puts the lid on her. And, believe me, this wasn't a case of the hot eighth grader who realizes that anatomy is destiny and wants to put the sexy merchandise in the front window as much as possible. Audra was a plain-looking fourteen-year-old. Longish face with flat, pale skin, and kind of short teeth that made you want to reach in with a pair of pliers and pull them down further from her gums. But I guess all fathers think their daughters are gorgeous and Uziel was no different. He didn't want her turning into Miley Cyrus or Hannah Montana (whatever her real name is). I can't keep that shit straight.

That said, Audra and I had gotten along well since the first time her father brought her to the office. As you can imagine, most kids assume podiatrists must be freaks to devote their lives to the stinkiest body part. Oh—you'll love this—you know those scented cardboard pine trees you see dangling from mirrors in taxis? Well, when I get a child in for the first time, I hang one of them around my neck. Then I say, "You think I can treat your stinky little feet without something that smells nice around my neck?" The parents usually laugh, so the kid decides I'm funny too. With Audra, it was the opposite. Eleven years old and she got the joke immediately. Her father? Nothing.

Now, that first time she came in without her father when she was fourteen, I was happy to see her, but a little bummed that her warts had come back.

"So, Audra, your stinky feet are acting up again?"

"Actually, no," she said. "My feet are fine. I'm here because I wanted to apologize to you."

"Apologize? For what?"

"My family. Duh?"

"Duh? Well, I guess I'm seriously duh because I don't know what your family did to precipitate an apology."

Audra smiled. "Precipitate. I like how you said that word. So official and professional-sounding."

"I'm an official professional in the foot-care field. But, even with all my expertise, I still don't—"

"My idiotic brother badgering you on the street because you were eating a cheeseburger?"

"Oh, that?"

"Yeah, that."

"That was about six years ago, Audra. He was just a boy at a stage when he was a little too serious about stuff."

"A *little*? You think? You should see him now. He's got the beard, the black suit, the whole accessorized fanaticism."

"He's gone ultra-Orthodox?"

"More like ultra-Taliban-Orthodox. He's living in Crown Heights. I see him once a month when he deigns to come to the house for Shabbat. I say 'deigns' because, in his eyes, our 'merely Orthodox' home may as well be a mosque. But he comes because he loves my father for setting him on the path to devout lunacy."

"Does he try to convert you?"

"No. I'm too far gone. He sees me as an eighth grade whore."

When she saw in my face that I was fishing around for a reaction, she pressed her case.

"And then my father has the nerve to come to your office and give you shit for defending yourself against his whacked son?"

"Audra, take it easy. Don't get worked up."

Again, she smiled. "You think because I said 'shit,' that means I'm worked up?"

I had a thought at that moment: As soon as kids realize they're smarter than their parents, growing up becomes infinitely more difficult. Audra was in for a tough road.

I took a breath and said, "You're a smart cookie, Audra. And you know you're one of my favorite patients. Not that 'my favorite patients' is an overly competitive category."

She laughed out loud at that one, reminding me of the time she'd laughed aloud at my old air freshener joke.

"Well, you're my favorite care-giver, and I have a collection of them now."

"Really? Why? Are you okay?"

"I think I'm better than okay. But my father doesn't agree, and you know how when people make a lot of money, they think their opinion is more valid than everyone else's?"

Wow.

"Well, my dad has various health professionals refereeing our difference of opinion regarding my well-being."

"What's your dad's opinion of your well-being?"

"He's not sure. But, seeing as I just want to be normal, he assumes I'm not normal."

"Normal? Meaning 'not Orthodox'?"

"Among other things. He even brought me to an endocrinologist thinking maybe my problems were glandular. It would certainly be easier to explain me if my non-existent problems were not only real but somehow physical."

"Have you tried explaining your reasons for your—I don't know . . . Secular leanings?"

"I can't. I don't want to hurt him."

"Well, that's thoughtful, Audra, but he's probably stronger than you think."

Audra slumped and looked off to her left, where my joke of a diploma from podiatry school hung on the wall. I glanced over at it and thought of how my remote-controlled life had led to another strange moment. This one took the form of sitting with a teenage girl and having one of the most adult conversations I'd ever had.

Without taking her eyes off the diploma, Audra said, "Would you be surprised if I told you my dad didn't have a bar mitzvah until he was forty-two?"

"I would, um, yeah, be very surprised. Shocked . . ."

"That's how un-Jew-y he grew up. He hardly set foot in a synagogue until the baby who was to be my older sister came out stillborn. That's when my father put on the yarmulke he still wears today and became Orthodox. And when I came out fifteen months later, my father gave God full credit. So, I can't really tell my dad that the tragedy in his life happened to him, but not to me. And I can't ask him, if he got to have a childhood without the eyes of God bearing down on him, then why can't I? He's not that strong."

Nat's statement flashed back to mind. *I never failed at anything*. I did mention that, right? The day Nat, calm as a Mafioso, confronted me over my zinger aimed at his son . . . he was a mess like everyone else.

IX.

I looked at Audra, lost in her own little dilemma. She'd confided a lot to me and I sensed her beginning to feel as though she'd overstepped. I said, "I guess our dads went in different directions. Mine was bar mitzvahed at the normal age, then dismissed the religion. He died less than a year ago and, just before the end, a rabbi came to his hospital room, but my dad waved him off and said, 'Religion is for people who can't accept that this is all there is.' I loved him so much when he said that. In fact, when he died, one of the nurses told me he was in a better place, and I said, 'No he's not. Yesterday he was in New York. Today he's dead.' My dad would have loved that."

Audra looked up with a kind of wonder and said, "I wish *I'd* said that! Can I steal it?"

"It's yours," I said.

"By the way, I'm sorry about your dad."

"Thanks. The night before he died, someone at the hospital stole his wedding band. And I keep wondering if, in his drug-clouded state, he felt the ring twisting off the finger where it had been for 52 years, and if he thought, *I knew I should have sold the damn thing*."

Audra laughed.

Then I had a thought: "Audra, how did you know about the thing with your brother and the cheeseburger? You were like eight at the time."

"My mom told me the story a few days ago, after I asked her when my brother became such a freak."

I guess I looked stricken because Audra quickly added, "Oh, don't worry. My mom wasn't saying that you sent him spiraling to Crown Heights. She just included that one thing on the timeline of his anti-social highlight reel. I know it happened a long time ago, but just imagining that scene on the street bothered me so much. And I know this is sooo teenager-y, but I really wanted to apologize to you. I told my mom, and she said, 'If you feel like apologizing, do it.' See, I can talk to her about this stuff because, even though she does the Orthodox thing, I don't know if she believes in it or if, between my father and my brother, she just never knew what hit her. I don't ask because . . . let's just say I live in a fragile household."

At that point, I cut off my intimate look inside the Uziel family because I'm someone who can look away from car wrecks. "You know what, Audra? I accept your apology. Obviously you feel an apology is merited, so I'll respect your judgment."

"Good," she said getting up. "Now, if you'll excuse me, I have gym."

Audra never came to my office again throughout high school, although I did bump into her once at a smoothie joint where she told me her father had suffered a mild heart attack. I was surprised because he'd been coming to my office once a year for eight years and had never once mentioned any changes in his health. Not that pushing around his flanges would affect his heart. But I asked the question like I'm supposed to and he didn't come clean.

Now Audra's in her first semester at Columbia. Commie, didn't you apply to law school there? Whatever. So, this morning, she comes to my office wearing no make-up, a long skirt, bulky sweater, and woolen mittens. She wasn't "immodestly dressed," but she definitely looked different from her fourteen-year-old days. Her face didn't seem as long, her hair was short and stylish, and even her teeth somehow looked like they'd figured out where they ought to be hanging in her mouth.

She gave me a hug—a generation of compulsive huggers, these kids today—and said, "You been away? You have color."

"Oh no, it's probably endorphins from basketball last night. I had a great night."

She nodded like: *Still playing hoops? Not bad.* Then she took her mittens off, and I saw a ring on her left hand.

"Audra, are you engaged?"

"Huh? Oh, the ring. No, I just wear it to keep guys from hassling me. Lots of girls do it. It's jewelry as repellent."

She glanced at one of my hanging Bose speakers that wafts out the pre-programmed music I pay for every month like an idiot. It was a song by Gwen Stefani. I said, "I love this song, but what does that mean, '*I ain't no Harlem Black girl?*'"

Audra cracked up. "It's not 'I ain't no Harlem Black girl,'" she said, wheezing with giggles. "It's 'I ain't no *holla back girl.*' Oh my God! That is so funny!"

"*Holla back girl* . . . What the hell does *that* mean?"

"It's *so* not important." Then she shook her head and said, "You know, even at your age—not that you're old!—but you still make an effort to be cool. I like that you do, but at the same time, I would love to reach an age where I don't have to be so compulsively up on everything."

"I gotta say, I think '*Harlem Black Girl*' is a better lyric."

"Well, if you ever bump into Gwen . . ."

"I hear her husband's Jewish."

When I said that, Audra stopped smiling. Drearily, she mumbled, "Score. Another assimilation three-pointer for us."

"You know your basketball."

I sensed that treatment, as at our years-ago last appointment, was not going to be happening.

Audra shifted in her seat and said, "Last week, I saw you and your wife at The Flotilla Café. She's really pretty."

"Thank you. Why didn't you come over and say hello?"

"You really need the image of my plantar warts over dinner?"

"I'm sure I wouldn't have had flashbacks of your pre-adolescent feet."

"Actually, I liked just watching. Your wife was talking about something for kind of a long time and you seemed so attentive."

"She represents artists and she was telling me about this lunatic Balkan client who, by the way, may be visiting my house today, which doesn't thrill me."

"Wow. That's incredible."

"What?"

"You instantly remembered what the conversation was about! That's amazing. I mean, don't you ever look at other couples and see how they zone each other out, nodding and picking at their food? Or worse, neither of them talking at all? But you still really listen. That's so rare. You really look like you have a wonderful marriage."

Audra's eyes reminded me of how Alyse looked at me when we first started dating. That crazy Wow-this-girl-may-be-into-me feeling. And now 850 years later, there it was again. I felt a big hairball of self-esteem blow through my office.

So, what did I do with that feeling? I'll tell you what I did. I maimed it by saying an unbelievably stupid thing: "Well, Audra, looks can be deceiving."

I swear, I literally saw her expression go from whatever it was—sweet admiration, I guess—to disillusioned nothingness. I mean, before I knew it, I was saying, "Have you been wearing unusually high heels?"

A life-affirming discussion morphed into a professional foot care appointment like that, and then she was gone.

X.

When I heard the front door of the office close behind Audra, I went quietly beside myself. *How could you say something so stupid? Looks can be deceiving? The girl's obviously dating someone and in love and worrying if the feeling can last and looking to you for reassurance and you give her "looks can be deceiving"? What a fucking idiot.*

Over the years, I've managed to say more than a few stupid things like that. When I was in my twenties, I was a faux pas machine. Alyse swears I wasn't, but I'm more tuned in to my own stupidity than she is. And besides, I've always been ultra-careful around her because, no matter how long we've been together, I've always guarded against blowing things with her. I'm *still* guarding against blowing it. So, most of my faux pas happened out of her earshot, when the censor in my head was taking a break from the high stakes game of my relationship. But still, on the rare occasions that I still do shoot off a doozy, I can't help torturing myself over it. I go over it and over it, thinking about the way it should have come out in the first place. Then I'm like: *When are you going to learn to think before you speak*?

Before my next patient, I drummed up one rationalization to tide me over for a while: Talking to Audra made me feel like the twenty-one-year-old me who said stupid things for a living.

Anyway, I barely remember the rest of my patients from that morning until Rick Burlingame came in. He's a Wall Street guy and rich enough to hardly ever go near Wall Street anymore. I guess he spent most of his time at the gym because he had veiny biceps bubbling up under his skin. He's about 45 or so, that age when being muscular starts looking sickly. What does it say about a society that tells guys to turn their love handles into rock hard abs? Don't love handles sound nicer than rock hard abs?

Anyway, to make an annoying story short, all that gym time gave him a case of athlete's foot so bad it made me consider amputation.

I gave him the standard topical treatment—thank God for rubber gloves—and said, "Rick, I have two words for you: Flip-Flops." He laughs and says, "I know. What was I thinking walking around a locker room barefoot? I'm such an idiot."

There's something endearing about a person who calls himself an idiot, so I said, "Hey, from the ankles up, you look fantastic."

You won't believe what he says in response.

"Looks can be deceiving."

I swear to God.

Rick leaves and my suppressed agony over Audra does a total jail break. I mean, I told you about how bugged I was about the cloned dog, so you can just imagine . . .

I stop again, like I did in the car, and say to myself: *Why is this bothering you so much?* But, this time, the self-help pep talk doesn't pay off. I am bothered. Saying something that stupid trumps my self-forgiveness machinery.

If only I'd gone upstairs two minutes earlier, I wouldn't have heard what Alyse said so I wouldn't have had some unjustifiable bug up my ass about her so I wouldn't have been even subconsciously thinking the looks of my marriage were deceiving so I wouldn't have said looks are deceiving to Audra so I wouldn't haven't given a second thought to Burlingame saying looks are deceiving so at this moment my life would be moving along in its normal state of whatever.

Like I said, that's how my mind races. Eighty miles an hour on the wrong side of the highway. You'd think I could come to some kind of peace treaty with myself, but no, no, no.

I tried cooling my jets by drifting over to Arnie's office. His life was insane in such a concrete way, so maybe he could unknowingly talk me down by simply describing the experience of waking up with his multi-polar wife that morning.

Arnie was just finishing up with the hunched-over guy. Wait, what am I saying? It was a different guy. Jesus. Forget that.

Actually, this patient—I remember now—was a fireman. Excuse

me. A fire*fighter*. I'd seen this guy waiting to see Arnie many times before, so I guess he had some kind of chronic problem. Arnie introduced us and, nodding toward me, said, "Captain, if your feet ever start going to shit or you burn off a toe in some warehouse fire, here's your man." The firefighter cracked up and left.

When the firefighter was a safe distance away, Arnie added, "Poor guy comes in twice a week."

"What's wrong with him?"

"He's got back pain that's all in his head."

This I liked. What could be better for me at that moment than to hear about someone who's legitimately worse off than me? A bit too excited, I asked, "Why do you think it's in his head?"

"Well, the pain comes and goes with no identifiable causality." Arnie smiled. "You like that health-speak? Causality?"

"That was very impressive, Arnie. You should be on *CSI*."

"Yeah. Or a real doctor. Anyway, aside from the phantom causality, a little amateur psychology tells me it may be all mental. See, that guy's a major fireman and–"

"You still say 'fireman?'"

"Yeah, why the fuck not?"

"No reason. Go ahead."

"Well, this guy has medals and commendations up the wazoo. I'm mean, he's done some seriously heroic shit. He single-handedly saved this guy from King's Point—a super-rich guy who was smoking in bed because his wife was out of town. Poor guy gets a weekend furlough from his marriage and all he wants to do is whack off and smoke? Burns down half his house. This was in spring of '01. Anyhow, the guy is so grateful, he gives the fireman his house on Martha's Vineyard for a week. Of course, he's only grateful to a point; he doesn't give his savior the Vineyard house during the summer—that's peak-season. He gives it to him for ten days *after* Labor Day."

"So, the fireman was there during 9/11."

"Exactly."

"I think I see where you're going."

"Yeah. This guy invites some of his army buddies from all over the country to this house on Martha's Vineyard, where they fish for blues all day and drink all night. They're so wasted they don't hear about the attacks until the next morning. Three-quarters of his firehouse is dead. He was the biggest hit-the-beach guy in the outfit, so he knows he would have died. But instead, he spent September 11th half a mile from the Kennedys. Not that he saw any of the Kennedys, but you get what I'm saying. Survivor guilt."

"Yeah, it makes sense."

"I guess," Arnie said, though he shrugged doubtfully. "Personally, if I were him, I'd be the happiest guy in the world."

"That's probably a key difference between a chiropractor and a fireman."

"Exactly. And chiropractors don't die in the line of duty."

"Well, there's that."

"Although I would have been pissed that the rich asshole whose life I saved gave me his Vineyard house off-season."

"Shit, I'd have given the guy the July 4th weekend."

"Damn straight."

Then—and this is so weird, Commie—Arnie shakes his head and says, "Speaking of rich assholes, I heard something so fucked up on the radio this morning about these people who cloned their dog."

"I can't believe you said that! I heard it too and it really bugged me."

"Of course it bugged you. Idiots throwing money at problems that aren't even problems."

"Right. Like with enough money, you can control shit."

"Not to mention the fact that one of the biggest problems with dogs is that they don't respond to money."

"That's true too, but—"

"I can't even control my wife with money, and these people are trying to buy off *dogs?* You know, I actually offered to pay Fumi to see a psychopharmacologist?"

"What do you mean, 'pay' her?"

"I told her that if she'd go to a shrink and try some medications, I'd pay her. You know, like a salary. On top of all the money I already give her to blow on nothing every day."

"So, is she going to take you up on it?"

"She's said she might—might!—think about it."

"Maybe you should offer to pay her to think about it."

"Don't laugh," Arnie said. "I wish marriage was like being a pro athlete, where you could have an opt-out clause."

Right there, in that moment, I knew Arnie was my best friend. Talking to him was just so much fun. So unrestrained. And, really, what the hell else is a best friend but someone who you have an easy time bullshitting with? It wasn't the first time I'd had that thought about Arnie, but I'd never totally put myself out there with him. I don't know why. Maybe some vague thing about separating church and state: There's work people and non-work people.

But, actually, from time to time, Alyse and I would go out to dinner with Arnie and his first or second wife and we always had fun. Once, Arnie had us laughing until we almost threw up because he wanted to start a TV show called, *Live from the Chiropractor's Studio*. He would have a different chiropractor on each week in front of a studio audience of chiropractic students. It was the best double date I ever went on, but then we didn't get together again for over a year. For some reason, I'm just unmotivated when it comes to cultivating friends.

Most of the people Alyse and I socialize with are girls she grew up with and their husbands. We only have one or two couples from Maryland that we get together with, and even that's only like twice a year. Maybe. Otherwise, I'm a perennial "and guest," and always careful to make a good impression . . . It never ends. Not that I have a bad time with these people, because I don't. You, eat, drink, talk, divvy up the check, over-tip, get in the car . . . talk about the other couples, assess their marriages, debate who's starting to look old/fat/miserable, pull into your garage, and call it a night. Not so bad.

Besides, Alyse enjoys it, partly because I'm quietly funny and great at seeming like I give a shit about everyone else's lives, and partly because Alyse is so much prettier than the other wives that she's always the star of the meal. (Well, that part is just my theory, but I'm probably right.)

Even though I get along well with the other husbands, I never hook up with them on my own because I'm not into golf. All they do is work, golf, and play husband. They don't even have a goddamn poker game. Alyse thinks I should get into golf because I'd be so good at it. But other than playing the occasional indifferent round, I pretty much hate golf. Well, the game itself is okay. It's golfers I can't stand. I mean, you get these dumpy guys who could never put two dribbles together on a basketball court, and suddenly they turn forty, take up golf with a vengeance, shoot in the eighties, and it's like: Oh, suddenly *you're* an athlete? Please. Every time they take their twelve practice swings and mumble their one "swing thought," I just want to drag them off the tee to a basketball court, back them down in the post, and wipe the floor with them. *I'll give you a fucking swing thought.*

Arnie doesn't like golf either, though he's great at it. He just has a naturally perfect swing and he actually is a great athlete. He once said, "I don't know what the big deal is with golf. It's such a cake sport." And, sure enough, with no lessons and no practice, he consistently shoots in the mid-seventies. In the summer, he'll play once or twice a week purely so he can advise his playing partners to swing harder. No matter what might be going on with some guy's swing, Arnie says, "Swing harder." Why? Because if they take his advice, they'll usually wind up in his office later that week. How great is that?

XI.

Anyway, I don't know how I got sidetracked into this discussion of golf and my social life. Although some of the couples I was talking about *do* come into play in the story I'm telling you at such a ridiculously slow pace.

Let's see . . .

I was feeling better just talking to Arnie but, of course, he had another patient coming, so I had to skulk back to my office. I had two more patients before lunch and then I called Alyse. Here's another thing about a long-lasting marriage: She picked up the phone, I said "Hi," and she said, "What's wrong?"

I think people know their spouses better than they know themselves. Your own mind is trickier—harder to get hold of.

"Oh, nothing really. I just said something stupid to a patient and you know how that kind of thing bugs me."

"What did you say?"

This is probably unbelievable to you, but I didn't see that question coming. I felt shitty, so I called my wife, and that was as far as I had thought it through. Really, I didn't even think it through that far. The call was all reflex, my fingers dialing on their own, the rest of me following along in mindless lockstep.

"I just had a teenage girl in and we were talking about something as I treated her for a nasty ingrown, and—I forget how we got on the topic—but she was telling me, like, about how her boyfriend criticized her a lot about her weight, her hair, her make-up, you name it. Then she talked about how she spent a lot of time watching other couples and how she noticed that they all seemed happier than she was and, like an idiot, I said, 'Looks can be deceiving.'"

Alyse didn't say anything. I thought maybe we were cut off.

"Alyse?"

"Yeah, I'm here. Go on."

"That's it."

"That's it? That's what you're upset about?"

"Yeah. I just feel like I thoughtlessly disillusioned this kid."

Alyse made her little chuckle sound and, before I could whine about how I didn't find it funny, she said, "Look, it's sweet that you're so sensitive about these things, but don't you think you may be overrating your impact on this kid's life? You're not her father. You're her podiatrist. Just because you gave her a less-than-idyllic view of the world doesn't mean she's going to wind up a spinster with cats. You told her looks *can be* deceiving, right?"

"Uh huh."

"Okay, maybe it would have been nice if you told her that one day she'd meet the perfect guy and live happily ever after. But you didn't. You said what you said—which, believe me, was nothing compared to what she sees in the movies and on TV. I promise you, she'll forget what you said or bury it under all the crap she finds out on her own. So, just let it go. I mean, really, you've got to give yourself a break. You're not perfect."

"I'm not?"

"No. You're so fucking close, though."

I laughed. The sound of Alyse saying *fuck* in a joking context just rocks against her whole personality.

"Thanks, honey. I feel much better."

"No, you feel *a little* better. By Monday, you'll feel much better."

"Something to look forward to."

It wasn't until I walked out for lunch that I came clean with myself: I had been flirting with Audra Uziel—a woman less than half my age. When that realization hit me, my right leg wafted in mid-stride, my head and shoulders drifted back, my eyes closed, and I just stopped. If I had to pinpoint the precise feeling that shifted my whole body into neutral, I'd say it was embarrassment. The sheer, limitless idiocy of flirting with this girl!

Looks can be deceiving.

Oh, really, Doc? Tell me more. Your insights are so meaningful to me and I just want to hear more and more and take you back to my dorm room.

HOLY SHIT!

I promise you, Commie, I'd not only never cheated on Alyse, but the thought had hardly ever even crossed my mind. No, Commie, Jenji doesn't count. That started before I met Alyse, so she's been grandfathered in. Oh, sure, I see a gorgeous girl somewhere and do the split-second Jimmy Carter lust-in-my-heart two-step. But I don't dwell on it, and I certainly don't seek it out. It's probably been ten years since I've even leafed through the *Sports Illustrated* swimsuit issue. Like I need that shit. I don't want to pursue hopeless longing, and I could do without it finding me. I was in a Chinese take-out a while ago when a high school girl walked in with the sickest body I've ever seen and wearing this tight retro t-shirt. Sloping up and down this girl's Hall Of Fame chest were the words: McGovern for President. I was somewhere between dying for this girl and wanting to ask where she got the shirt. I mean, it was a cool shirt and I would have liked to get one. But I didn't ask for fear of her thinking I was just staring at her tits. That's how conscientious I am about not dealing with all the—

Look, look: I'm not a monk. I did wonder for a second if this kind of girl knows what effect she has on men our age. Does she realize that if she took her McGovern shirt off and gave some guy like us two minutes of free play with her breasts, she'd pretty much launch us back to the premature ejaculation age and make our lives complete? As you'll see, there's a connection to that thought with something that happened later that day. But, overall, just thinking that was no big sin, right? It was just a thought. More sociological than anything.

Commie, I know you. You're thinking: *Yeah, sure. Sociological*... But it's the truth. Look, my life as it is has just enough other shit in it to keep me interested, you know? My attitude is: I married my dream girl. Put a check mark next to that line of our nation's checklist for idiots and move on. I see guys our age out there—divorced, whatever—still looking for "the one." I mean, really, what fifty-year-old still has the energy to pass himself off as perfect?

So, God knows what hijacked my head and made me look at Audra—a girl that the nineteen-year-old me would have liked—and dip my fifty-one-year-old toe in the water.

Why?

I just couldn't get over my stupidity.

I thought to myself: Jesus Christ, at a certain point, the government should just send you an ID card officially proclaiming: YOU ARE OUT OF THE GAME.

And that, Commie, brings up another coincidence.

XII.

Well, technically, maybe not a coincidence. More like an appropriate segue to the next part of that day.

See, the government-issued YOU ARE OUT OF THE GAME card led me to a thought about a patient named Ruth Kudrow, who is 82 and who not only has a crush on me, but actually hits on me every time I see her. I swear, she is shameless to a degree that only someone in assisted-living can be.

I have three assisted living places I visit every other month or so. It kind of depresses the crap out of me but, frankly, it brings in a lot of money. I won't go too deeply into this, but old people need to have their toenails clipped regularly or all kinds of bad things can happen. Plus, it's hard for them to reach their toes. Plus, the toenails are often hard and erose. *Plus*, you have a segment of the elderly with diabetes, which bumps the need for podiatric attention through the roof.

Actually, one of my diabetic patients at the Briar Hill Assisted Living Center is my absolute favorite patient. His name is Carolina Lewis. And, no, he's not my favorite just because he's 81, black and, according to Met Life, has been dead for twenty years already. He's my favorite because he's got a life story that you wouldn't believe: As a young guy, he snuck away from working at his father's junkyard in Texarkana, drifted up to New York, took the Civil Service exam, and wound up a big deal in the Small Business Administration. He tells great stories every visit. I love him. (And, in case you were curious, his mother was from Asheville, North Carolina, hence his name.)

Anyway, suffice to say, each pair of dilapidated feet I treat counts as an office visit. So, yeah, it's a lot of money.

Unfortunately, Ruth Kudrow is also warehoused at Briar Hill. Before my visits, she bathes herself in a perfume you could smell from Cuba. When I work on her feet, she intentionally leans over to flash cleavage so gaping you could lose a Hyundai in there. She must think her cleavage can override the sight of her feet, but she's so far off *she's not even wrong*. I mean, this woman's feet are so gnarly, they can only be described as the end of the world. You'd think the pavement had been walking on *her* for 80 years.

So, over lunch, I constructed the following ridiculously harsh, SAT-style analogy: Ruth Kudrow is to me as I am to Audra Uziel.

How's that for beating yourself up?

By the way, women like Ruth having the hots for me is nothing new. I'm, like, the ultimate attractive guy to unattractive women. I'm the last person to detect someone having a crush on me, but I have noticed several super-fat women with the hots for me. It's as if I can only get the hint from women who outweigh me.

The amazing upshot is, when these women meet Alyse, they get angry. Like: She's too good for him. He deserves me, and no better. *At best, me.* The coincidence in all of this is that, as I finished my lunch, I got a text from Sylvia reminding me that I was scheduled to go to Briar Hill that afternoon. Perfect. I formulated the Audra-Ruth Kudrow analogy, and now I have to actually go and see Ruth Kudrow. I could swear I felt the last crackle of electricity from basketball short out in my legs.

I listened to sports radio on the twenty-five-minute drive to Briar Hill. The frothing host, Artie Something, had just come back on the air after his mother died. First caller: "Artie, sorry to hear about your mom. What is wrong with the freaking Jets' offense?"

Sports radio makes me regret steering Charlie toward being a sports fan. Life as a fan exposes you to an endless horde of other fans that, eventually, just makes you feel like you're sitting in the dumb row at school. When I was a kid, Knicks fans seemed so sophisticated. Now it's just Spike Lee whooping up 20,000 pea-brains. And I don't want to get into my theory right now about America's fall reflecting the majesty of Willis Reed to the clunky Formica-handed Patrick Ewing. I mean, why can't Charlie grow up on the sheer beauty of an Earl Monroe or the mysterious god-like Walt Frazier? Hell, one morning, I looked over at my sweet boy as he read the box scores, only to see his eyes drift off while reading an article about the coach getting accused of trying to bang team employees. What do you do?

WHAT. DO. YOU. DO?

You know, I think we're lucky to have grown up in an America that had a trace of innocence even if it was all bullshit. The next bunch after us, those mopey Gen-Xers, got gypped out of any hope thanks to Watergate being the first thing they remember. They didn't even get the thrill we felt from seeing that jowly psycho resign. Now people our age flail away trying to bless our kids with some semblance of a childhood, but the filth these kids see by the time they're eight? *"What's non-consensual anal penetration, Dad?"* Charlie, Charlie, Charlie. If only he could be gassed by the same illusions we had: building strong bodies twelve ways; putting a tiger in your tank . . . But no. My sweet boy, all giant eyeballs and kooky hair, has to make the leap to, *Well, Charlie, that's when someone doesn't want to but gets fucked up the ass anyway.*

All that said, I listen to sports radio because, if I'm not in the mood for music, what the hell else is there? The political call-in shows are unbearable. Even listening to people I agree with wears me out. These callers have opinions they're too afraid to tell anyone they know, but they pick up the phone and spill it to the whole fucking world.

Did I already go off on people and their opinions?

Anyway, I got to Briar Hill around two-thirty. In the main building, I checked in with Rico Pena, a Puerto Rican guy about our age who's been working there so long, they gave him the title of Executive Attendant. He moved to New York at 13, but his Spanish accent keeps getting thicker. "Hello Mistah Feets!" I told him not to call me Doctor, so Mistah Feets is what he came up with. I kind of like it.

Actually—and this is funny—Arnie hired a Panamanian nanny, Delmy, to take care of his only kid, Ross. She called him, "Dr. Arnold" and for years, Arnie would say, "The whole 'Dr. Arnold' thing makes me feel like a plantation owner. I don't need her treating me like I'm her master, when she's the one raising my fucking kid."

Well, one day when Ross was like eleven, Arnie says, "Get this: Yesterday I asked Delmy to take Ross to soccer practice, and she says, "'I'm too busy, Arnie.'" Can you believe that? "'I'm too busy, *Arnie*?'" Who the fuck does she think she is, calling me Arnie? Soon this Latina broad will be telling me to go wash my dick."

For the rest of the day, Arnie was psyching himself up to fire Delmy. He was worried about telling Ross but, when he did, Ross just said, "I don't know why the fuck you kept her around so long."

Anyhow, back at Briar Hill, Rico greeted me with some news: "So, Mistah Feets, your girlfriend had a mini-stroke."

Knowing exactly who he was talking about, I said, "Who are you talking about?"

"Mrs. Kudrow, mang."

"Oh, man. How is she?"

"Eh. She's a little foggy, you know?"

Barely containing myself, I said, "Will she even recognize me?"

"Maybe yes, maybe no. Yesterday, I see her and she says, 'Good morning, Yitzak.'"

"Yitzak? Who's Yitzak?"

"I don't know. Maybe that was her husband's name."

"Her husband's name was Herb."

"Look, mang, she called me Yitzak. Tomorrow she may call me Osama. She's pretty verklempt."

He saw me smile at his use of Yiddish and said, "I been saying that for years. Saturday Night Life."

"Live."

"Right. Anyhow, lotsa folks here like hearing me use Jewish words. Mitzvah, shiksa, kosher. Hazzer. Schvartzeh."

"That's great, Rico. Try not to say schvartzeh to Carolina."

"Oh no, Mr. Lewis don't mind. He laughs when I say it."

Rico goes with me on my rounds to move things along. The less mobile residents tend to talk a lot. If they keep me too long, Rico has no problem playing the heavy.

XIII.

That day, I buzzed through my first six seniors, with Carolina Lewis on deck. You're probably wondering what Carolina was doing in a Jewish facility. Actually, it's not officially a Jewish facility. It's just happens to be on Long Island, so it works out that way. Not to mention that it's pretty pricey as far as these places go. Carolina got a healthy government pension, so when it came time, he liked Briar Hill best. He didn't care that it was mostly Jews.

Carolina shook my hand like we're good friends, which I'd like to think was true. Unfortunately, diabetes has left him nearly blind, arthritis has him moving in slo-mo, his blood pressure ping-pongs crazily, and he's had a painful bout of shingles. "Man," he said with a tubercular laugh, "they should trade me in for the nineteen-year-old model." An amazing guy. Close to extinction.

Speaking of diabetes, Carolina looks a little like Jackie Robinson. Handsome, white hair. Robinson was more intense with those eyes, though.

Anyway, Carolina and I catch up a little and Rico, who knows I like talking to Carolina, goes outside for a smoke. Then, as Carolina puts his feet up for me, I notice that, on the counter of his kitchenette, there's a skinny bottle of horseradish. The blue label has white block letters: MOSSAD KOSHER HORSERADISH. I turned to Carolina and said, "You like horseradish?"

Carolina laughed and said, "Oh God, not for me. The people who make the stuff came by and gave out free sample bottles to everyone."

"I like it on gefilte fish."

"Be careful. That stuff is hot enough to make a fish grow its scales back and jump off your plate. But if you want it, help yourself. I was going to give it to Mrs. Kudrow, but—"

"Rico told me about her. That's a shame."

"Doctor told me I'm overdue for mini-strokes. No way around it. I'll tell you, I got a lot of stuff comin' that there's no way around."

We had a moment of dead air, so I started tending to Carolina's feet. Then, out of nowhere, I started telling him the whole story about Audra.

Maybe his mention of the 19 year-old model made me think of her. I don't know. But I gave him the true version of the story.

You really looked like you have a wonderful marriage.

Carolina listened intently.

Well, Audra, looks can be deceiving.

I stopped and Carolina said, "That's it?"

"That's what my wife said. Although I didn't tell her that it was the look of *our* marriage that I said might be deceiving."

"And you feel bad about lying to your wife?"

"Yeah. But I feel worse about disillusioning the girl."

"Man, you can do a job of screwing your head into the ground."

"You have no idea, Carolina."

"Look, as far as your wife is concerned, you threw a little white lie at her about something you said that, from hearing how you've talked about her in the past, you didn't really mean in the first place. No need to get all soul sick there. Marriages live and die on white lies. When the white lies end, the marriage goes with them. As for the girl, if I know anything about girls that age—and I don't. I mean, who does?—but, if I did, I'd say if they don't hear what they want to hear from adults, they go looking elsewhere for advice more to their liking. While you're here doing your post-mortem on something that happened with this girl hours ago, she's probably nine moves down the chessboard by now."

"Kind of a mixed metaphor there, Carolina."

"Yeah, well, I'm self-educated and never got around to literature class."

"You're totally self-educated?"

"I went to a tiny, segregated grade school down in Texarkana with a kindly white lady reading aloud from *Heidi*. Talk about tuning out. Later on, when I realized that reading and writing might have its advantages, I educated myself."

"*Heidi* was such a piece of shit."

"I refused to read it on principle."

I got to clipping Carolina's little toe. It was so dry and brittle, I felt like I could snap it off like the lion's head on an animal cracker.

"Did you tell your wife a lot of white lies?"

"I was never married."

"Really? Handsome, successful guy like you?"

"I grew up smack in the middle of three brothers and five sisters. I needed some alone time, though I didn't plan on a lifetime of it."

"And how do you feel about the expression *white* lies?"

Carolina cracked up. "It's just like a million other expressions. The white lie is innocent, so I guess the black lie is guilty. They find out that a pork chop is actually healthier than a steak and they start calling it 'the other white meat.' It never ends, man."

Rico came back, reeking of cigarettes. "Ready to roll, Mistah Feets?"

"Rico, my work here is done."

Carolina said, "You feeling better? Did my opinion or insight or rationalization help you out at all?"

"Yeah, Carolina. It helped a lot."

"Sure? You sound like one of those weight-of-the-world guys."

Rico inspected my face. "He's right, man. You got tsuris."

Carolina engulfed my hand again and I gave it a firm shake before leaving his little home. It felt like the temperature had dropped another ten degrees. I buzz-sawed through the next few pairs of feet before trudging over to Ruth Kudrow's. The normal dread I felt going to see her, wondering how low-cut her dress would be or whether she'd ask me to dump my wife and move in with her, was missing that day. I remember having a sick thought: *One woman's mini-stroke is another man's peace of mind.*

Ruth was wearing a wool sweater under a bathrobe. No makeup, no perfume. Just Ruth, old, blurry-eyed and, most notably, silent. *A big improvement*, I thought with a stunning lack of guilt. I'd once had a thought that Ruth looked a little like Barbara Walters, or what Barbara Walters might have looked like if she'd never decided to do something with her life. Now the resemblance was gone. Ruth's demeanor had a docile flatness that seemed barely human. She was like one of those detectives on TV who view gory crime scenes with no more emotion than they'd have looking for their keys on a kitchen table.

You know, Commie? I should maybe fix you up with her.

Okay, look. Can I just apologize in advance for every ridiculous, tasteless joke I make for as long as I'm here?

In pleasant silence, I attended to Ruth's feet. Unfortunately, my mind took one of its strolls over to the nearest minefield. I was bugged by something Carolina had said.

"You feeling any better? Did my opinion or insight or rationalization help you out at all?"

That one word. Rationalization. Why did he throw that one there? Was Carolina giving me an unbiased exoneration from my guilt or just a rationalization I could live with? I hovered over poor Ruth's feet, my hands working without conscious commands from my head, totally consumed with what Carolina said.

Opinion or insight would've been a justification for not feeling like shit. But a rationalization implies that I need to ease over something truly wrong. Shit! Why did Carolina have to use that word? If only I had worked on his feet faster, I could have just taken his original assessment of what happened and felt okay about everything. If only Rico didn't need to smoke, he'd have pushed me to work faster, and I'd be fine now. When will I learn? If someone says something that makes me feel good, just end it right there. God damn—

Ruth suddenly pulled her foot back. I looked up at her. With the blankest expression I had ever seen on a human face, she said, "I have never taken a man's penis in my mouth. God, what a life."

Commie, if there's a moment to wake up, this is it.

When I thought about it later—and there was no choice but to think about it later because Ruth shorted like nine of my brain fuses—it felt like she didn't even gauge my reaction to what had to be the most gripping start to an autobiography of all time. *God, what a life,* hung in the air for a thousand years, her eyes pointed my way without looking at me. It was one of the most chilling moments of my life. Even Rico whispered, "Mein Dios."

Mini-strokes are tricky. Maybe she didn't totally know who I was, or maybe my face sparked an involuntary motor response that tripped off something that had been on her mind for a long time. Or maybe she was perfectly lucid but too depressed from her neural jolt of grim reality to care what she said.

I didn't know what to say, so I said nothing. Zero. I gently pulled back her foot and finished my work. Every click of a toenail sounded like a blast from a twenty-one gun salute. After the last one, I mumbled something like "Take care, Ruth," and left.

I felt shitty about not responding to her in any way. But who can be expected to hear that and be unruffled enough to serve up an appropriate bromide?

Rico momentarily made me feel better. As we headed to the main building, he said, "Mang, I thought I'd heard it all here, but that poor Mrs. Kudrow freaked me out."

"Yeah," I said, "it's terrible. Just terrible."

Then Rico said, "You think she wants to shtup you, mang?"

So much for feeling better.

XIV.

I got in the car and my call-Alyse-and-tell-her-what-happened reflex kicked in. Esme picked up the phone and started talking to me without saying hello. Fucking Caller ID has torpedoed the whole social contract of the phone call.

"Daddy, I have to whisper because Mommy's crazy artist, You-ey Brushstroke, is here."

"He's crazy, Esme?"

"Maybe. He kind of freaked me out."

"Why's that, honey?"

"When I was alone with him—and it was just for, like, a minute—he said something so random and weird to me."

"What? What did he say?"

"He like, looked around at all the stuff in our house and said, 'You bagel-biters really know how to make money.'"

Christ. It never ends.

"Daddy, isn't that anti-Semitic?"

I paused for a second to drain the well of any alarm from my voice—*Jesus Christ, my beautiful little girl who made her own decision not to have a bat mitzvah because, God bless her, she feels like a full-fledged deliriously happy and free American, as opposed to a persecuted minority latched to its screaming history who gets exposed to anti-Semitism in her own home. Why?* Why?—"Well, Ezzie," I said, "it may *sound* anti-Semitic but, you know, You-ey is from a different country and sometimes foreign people say things that they don't mean or intend to sound bad, but it just comes out that way because English isn't their natural language. And also, sometimes their rules of conversation are different. You know, it's a cultural thing. Like remember in that book report you wrote about when you go to Singapore, they get mad if you spit or chew gum?"

"You mean, You-ey doesn't, like, understand the rules here, so he said something a normal American would keep to himself?"

"Exactly! Ezzie, you're so smart. How did you get so smart?"

"I have a really smart daddy?"

"Good answer, honey. So, don't worry about You-ey. I'm sure he's very nice, just a little different. Now, can I talk to Mom a sec?"

"Okay. I love you."

"I love you, Ez."

Alyse got on the phone and, still bottling up any hint of an APB in my voice, said, "Alyse, is *everything* under control over there?"

"Yeah. You-ey clashes with the decor a little, but yeah, all's fine. Why?"

I told her what Esme said and could almost hear vital organs rising in Alyse's throat. In a quivering whisper: "Oh my God. I can't believe he said that. I'm sorry."

"It's okay. I explained it to Ezzie and she's fine. The guy's a mild anti-Semite but who's not? Besides, he wouldn't do anything really bad because you're his only hope for any future income. So just relax and send him on his way gracefully. I was going to stop at the office, but I'll come right home."

"Okay." Then, "Shit, I'm such an idiot."

"It's okay. Should I stay on the phone?"

"No, it would look weird talking to him, holding the phone. I'll just make him leave. I can do it because I think he's smoked enough pot to make him pretty harmless."

"That's not so comforting."

I hung up and started driving fast which, of course, goosed the images of my panic attack phase, so I went into my calm down routine: dropping my shoulders, telling myself to breathe, and visualizing the Zoloft dutifully handling crowd control throughout my nervous system. I turned on the air conditioning to keep me alert at the wheel. I settled down just enough to start thinking of past *Newsday* headlines about families being murdered in their homes. You know, the kind of stories that can really spice things up on Long Island. I pulled over and reached down to call 911, but not before thinking: *At least I don't have a name like Buttafuco.* Of course, the second my hand hit the phone, it rang. Scared the shit out of me.

Alyse, breathless, "You-ey just left."

Exhale.

"How did you do it?"

"I decided to, I don't know, confirm his worst impulses by telling him I had to go to the bank and make a big deposit and then buy a dozen bagels for the weekend."

"Jesus, Alyse."

"I know, I know. But when I got off the phone with you, I went from panicky to pissed off in like two seconds."

Can you believe that? Panicky to pissed off in two seconds.

"Anyway, I reassured him I'd promote his art. He thanked me and left."

Alyse sounded a bit cocky about how she handled things, so I said, "And Esme?"

"She's fine. Look, honey, I never should have let him come here. Jesus. I'm sorry."

You know, Commie, parenting is like basketball. A game of runs. One parent goes on a streak of doing great things with the kids while the other screws up. Suddenly, there's a double digit margin in the "who's fucking up the kids less" game. Then it switches to the other way around and comes down to the last minute, whenever that comes, when the kid opens his college acceptance letter or you find a vial of meth in the kid's drawer. I don't even know if meth comes in a vial, but I like being ahead in the parenting game because there are so many other areas of my marriage where I feel like I'm thirty points down in the fourth quarter and Alyse is smoothly dribbling out the clock.

Alyse tried to steer away the conversation from her parenting crime, saying with mock cheer, "So, how was the rest of your day?"

I stopped myself as I was about to tell Alyse about Ruth Kudrow. *Quit while you're ahead.*

"My day was . . . a day. I'm going to stop off at the office and hustle home before sundown."

"Okay. I'll go check on Esme."

"Good."

"I love you."

"I love you too."

You know what, Commie? I'm going to give you a free pass on the thoughts I had driving back to my office.

They weren't much, really. Just middle-aged fantasies about torturing You-ey Brushstroke to within an inch of his life as if I were Jack Bauer from *24*. I started imagining myself walking down the street knowing I could kill anyone I passed with my bare hands. And, frankly, I do have a short list of people I'd like to kill. (Really, if you don't, you haven't lived much of a life.)

I only went back to the office to tell Arnie the story about Ruth Kudrow. If I wasn't going to tell Alyse, then I was going to have to share it with *someone*. Arnie was finishing up with a TMJ case. The second the jaw-clicking patient left, I said, "Arnie, do I have a story for you."

XV.

Upon hearing Ruth's epic statement, Arnie's face went blank. Then, as if the offices were bugged by the KGB, Arnie whispered, "That's what she said? That she'd never had a dick in her mouth?"

"Well, she said penis."

"Holy shit. How old did you say she was, ninety-six?"

"No, no. Eighty-two."

"Whatever. So what did you say to her?"

"Nothing."

"Nothing? Sure. That's what I would have said. Nothing."

"Actually, I felt bad. I should have said something."

"What? Out of the thin air, a semi-lucid battle-ax says she's never blown a guy and you think you should have had a good comeback? Jesus Christ, you should fill out one of those organ donor cards and leave your guilt to science."

"Well, thanks for saying that. I had the same thought, but it feels better coming from someone else."

"Glad I could help. That's maybe the third time in my life I've ever said the right thing."

The truth, Commie: Can you see why I think Arnie is basically the greatest guy in the history of the world?

Arnie then dissected the whole story like he lived for this kind of thing. "So, an old lady in a home has regrets about sex."

"I guess. The 'God, what a life' line sounded pretty, I don't know, rueful."

"Giving head seems like a fairly realistic goal. Even at 82, it's not too late. There's a guy out there for every fetish you can think of, and about forty million you can't."

"The devotion people have to their perversions is scary."

"I assume this Ruth is a widow?"

"Yeah. She told me they were married 47 years but slept in separate beds for the last ten . . ."

"Wow, she's full of too much information."

"She once told me her husband was on 'tranquilizers' and was a crazy hypochondriac. She told me about how she once took him to a doctor for a paper cut."

"She probably signed a Do Not Resuscitate form on him."

I paused a second before adding, "The funny thing is, Ruth was probably a pretty hot number as a young woman."

"That could be the source of her regrets. She was in her prime dating years before pussy was even popular."

"Nice, Arnie."

"In a way, you can see why blow jobs were on her mind. There's been lots of talk about 'the act.' It's not some secret thing only done by sluts anymore. It was a compromise for girls who didn't want to put out when we were in college. Nowadays, you hear all about how kids don't even count it as sex. And they have these fantastic rationales like 'friends with benefits.' It's an accepted practice with its own label. Ruth probably spent the last ten years in waiting rooms reading magazine articles about this stuff and feeling like she missed out on all the fun. It's everywhere: That show *Boston Public* had an episode about girls giving blow jobs like it was a pat on the back. For all we know, twelve-year-olds are sucking each other off in games of Spin the Bottle."

My face curled up like a chow's.

Arnie caught himself. "Not to imply that Esme is . . ."

I laughed. "Of course not. Although, I'll tell you, some girls hit puberty at nine these days. How do you deal with *that*?"

Arnie grinned, "First, you gotta lower the age of consent."

Laughing, I said, "I can't believe I'm laughing at that."

"Don't worry, you got time before Esme, you know . . ."

"Develops a hankering for big hairy—?"

Remember before, when I told you I didn't want to be a cliché father? This was another example. I'm not worried about karma sticking it up my ass for making a dicey joke about my kids. Hell, when Esme was a baby, a guy I play ball with asked me how she was doing, and I said, "She's great. Walking, talking, great boobs—just like her mother." I was a little stunned I said it, but I didn't feel bad about it. A bunch of years later, I even told Alyse the story. She found it funny, thank God.

Speaking of Alyse, Arnie asked, "Did you tell Alyse the Ruth blow job story?"

"No. I was about to, but I think I'll hold off. She'd find it really sad."

"It is sad. But Ruth's regret is nothing out of the ordinary. Let's face it, maybe one in ten million people wind up feeling like they've had a satisfying sex life."

Oh man, Commie, here goes. I'm going to let you in on another thing I've never told anyone in this whole wide world.

The truth is . . .

You know what? I changed my mind. I'm not going to tell you this one. I'm just . . . not.

XVI.

When the Ruth discussion finally ran its course, I realized that Arnie hadn't done his usual Friday thing, leaving work early to *Shabbat-shalom* everyone at the Orthodox shul and then go in to the city for Chinese. When I asked him about it, Arnie grimaced and explained, "My last talk with Rabbi Schwacter didn't go well."

"Why? What happened?"

"It's so stupid," Arnie said. "We were discussing different views of God, and I guess I got too comfortable because I joked about how odd it was that the Christian God had only one kid."

"What's wrong with that? It's funny."

"Tell me about it. It was so funny, I didn't even notice that the rabbi wasn't laughing. I just kept going, joking about Jesus' percentage of body fat; how the Jewish God has a surprising lack of business sense. Finally—finally!—it hit me that Rabbi Schwacter was scowling like he knew my whole conversion deal was bullshit. So, bottom line, I'm avoiding him and the Orthodox crowd a while, hoping any damage I did just blows over."

And that's when I realized it was past sunset, called Alyse, and started my fateful Friday night walk home.

Actually, Commie, I'm going to take a break here and grab a little lunch.

You need anything?

It would be really funny right now if you said, "I'll have the turkey club." Like the big Indian guy in *Cuckoo's Nest. Ahh, Juicy Fruit.*

Okay, I'll be back soon.

XVII.

This might surprise you, but when you throw a bottle of horseradish through the window of a retail establishment, things happen pretty fast. Alyse came into the den holding the phone. She had her hair in a ponytail and was wearing a tiny black tank top with white Converse All-Stars and peach sweatpants by Juicy. I know they were by Juicy because the word "JUICY" is on the butt.

Commie, why didn't we think of that when we were in college? Could you imagine how much money we could have made back then by simply coming up with the idea of billboarding girls' asses? Even if we'd just put a big U on the left cheek and a big M on the right, we could have made a fortune. Ass-vertising!

Frankly, it's your fault. I was never entrepreneurial, but your family was. How much did your brother rake in scalping ACC Tournament tickets? Two grand? Three? I can look it up. I still have a portfolio of my clips from *The Diamondback,* and the story I did on your brother's scalping is in there somewhere.

I guess, looking back, I shouldn't have used his name in the story. Not that he said he was talking off-the-record. Plus, I took notes right in front of him in the dining hall. It wasn't like I took three cabs so we could talk on deep background in an underground garage. In the long run, getting expelled worked out pretty well for him. And I'm glad we patched things up.

Okay, Alyse comes in looking just so beautiful—maybe or maybe not more penance for her parental screw-up with Esme. By the way, Esme was having dinner at her friend Harley Binder's house, so the floor was open for further discussion of the You-ey incident. I could have brought it up, but I didn't. I also could have just closed the case by telling Alyse it was no big deal, forget about it. But I didn't do that either. I was just sitting on my lead in the parental competence basketball game. Plus, as you can imagine, I was a little preoccupied.

"I just got off the phone with Meri Katzen. You won't believe this: Someone threw a bottle of horseradish through the window of Nu? Girl Fashions."

I was lying on the couch in the den with my foot propped up on pillows, my ankle surrounded by two bags of frozen peas. In the high-thread count warmth of my fully-alarmed and conscientiously appreciating home, I felt safe enough to seem only mildly curious about the horseradish news from Meri Katzen. Yenta. Meri's an interior decorator constantly moving swatches of gossip from home to home. She's so full of news, Alyse and I call her Reuters.

"Horseradish?" I said. "Who threw it? A disgruntled ex-employee?"

"I guess that's possible. But Meri said they suspect anti-Semitism."

"Why?"

"It was that Mossad Kosher Horseradish."

"That's so weird. I saw a bottle of that in Carolina Lewis' kitchenette today."

"It's not so weird. That's one of their promotional strategies, just giving it out to synagogues and nursing homes and whatever other Jewish-leaning places. The other marketing scheme—and the reason they suspect anti-Semitism—is that they won't sell their product to anyone they view as anti-Israel. Meri told me that, on their website, they list 62 countries they won't do business with."

"That's all?"

"I know it seems low." Alyse shook her head. "Like a Palestinian on the Gaza Strip is saying, 'Gee, I wish I could get my hands on a bottle of that horseradish.'"

That was actually a pretty funny comment, but I only said, "Ah-huh," and that's when, as I mentioned before, Alyse asked, "What are you thinking about? You seem distracted."

"Oh, nothing. Just my ankle and if I'll ever play hoops again."

"You'll play. Just ice it tonight, go ice/heat, ice/heat tomorrow, then hit the gym and rehab it. And soon you'll be back on the court screaming in agony from your next ankle sprain."

"Sounds like a plan."

"Excuse me?"

Sounds like a plan.

Alyse and I have this bug up our asses about expressions like that. If someone says "Been there, done that," Alyse wants to squeeze their head. She really went nuts recently when a jewelry store opened on Stratification called *Bling!* "Can you believe it?" she'd said, her strong coffee eyes bouncing, her perfect pink lips suspended in disbelief. "*Bling*! Don't white people realize that by the time they learn a hip-hop expression, it's too late? I feel like going in that store and asking, 'Excuse me, do you know what's going to be in this space when you go out of business next month?'"

The funny thing is, Alyse would actually do it. She's not only funny, she's got cojones.

"What I said was: 'That sounds like a good course of action.'"

"Right. I thought that's what you said."

I laughed a little. Even if you don't feel like laughing, you have to give it up to your marriage's little inside jokes, don't you think?

"By the way, Meri and Ira are joining us tomorrow night."

"How did that happen?"

"She asked if we wanted to have dinner and I told her we already had a reservation so she invited herself. She even called the restaurant and changed the reservation."

"Ah-huh." My mind was a somewhere else. Alyse knew it.

"Still thinking about the end of your basketball career?"

"Oh, no. I was thinking about Nat Uziel. The cops must have pulled him out of Shabbat services to tell him about the horseradish."

"Mm. Maybe he'll walk over there and the broken glass will do something bad to his feet."

"That would be great."

"No reason we shouldn't benefit from some alleged anti-Semitism."

"Alleged? So it may not be anti-Semitism?"

"I just said 'alleged' because of your investigative journalism background."

I looked up at Alyse. It was a little odd she'd say that. I wasn't sure if she knew that my ideas of being a reporter had been scrapped for her. Maybe she always saw that as one of the conversational no-fly zones in our marriage. Actually, it was the only one.

Well, that's not true. We never really bring up relationships we had before we hooked up. "Hooked up." Another expression to lose.

We probably don't discuss other relationships because she had so many more than me. In all—

Forget it.

Anyway, where was I? I was lying on the couch and—

Look, it stands to reason she would have had more exes than me. First of all, what guy wouldn't have wanted to date her? For God's sake, people tell her she looks like Phoebe Cates! After *Fast Times at Ridgemont High,* Phoebe Cates became Miss Jewish Universe in perpetuity. People ask me what my wife looks like and it would be so easy to just say "A less Asian-looking, five-foot-five, more delicate version of Phoebe Cates with a slight bump on her lightly freckled nose and a cleft in her chin that seems to vary in depth from week to week." But I just can't do it. It would sound like bragging. Shit, it's not like I designed her face. Anyway, that's what she looks like. So, of course, she left a trail of bodies behind her. One of her exes, by the way, wasn't Jewish, and I get the feeling the breakup demolished him more than all the rest. I think vaguely knowing your wife's past, rather than in detail, can save your life.

Another reason she dated so many guys is because that's what kids do in suburbia. Especially upper-middle class suburbia. Maybe because there's nothing else to do, and there's no daily tussle with the outside world to distract them. But, by the time they get to college, these kids are black belt masters of dating. You and I used to talk about this at Maryland. How we couldn't believe that clunky, unathletic Long Island or Pikesville or Mainline Philly guys with C averages and nothing but preset, black-hole futures in their fathers' businesses, had no trouble asking out the hottest girls. But ultimately, the answer is simple: It's what they do.

For me, stockpiled in twenty-four-story Electchester Towers with cab driver fathers and switchboard operator mothers, old couples, widows, even a smattering of blacks, girls seemed a million times stranger than they do now, and I still find my own wife totally inexplicable at times. I don't know. I took the bus to school with the *eleven hundred* other kids in my graduating class. I took the bus home, carrying a reserve quarter in my pocket in case some "hoodlum" asked me for money (my mother: "If they ask for money, just *give* it to them."). I threw down my books and played basketball. Every day. Girls were on my mind, but really not on my schedule.

You know, one afternoon during my junior year of high school, I was playing ball and, suddenly, in the middle of a fast break, I just stopped in my tracks, looked at my friends, and received a thought from heaven: I gotta get out of here.

And that's how I wound up going away to college. One moment of clarity without which I wouldn't be in this hospital room right now, I wouldn't have met Alyse, and my kids would look like someone else entirely.

Shit, even as a junior at Maryland, it probably took me more resolve to ask out Alyse than it took Rosa Parks to sit in the front of the bus. Of course, Rosa Parks had righteousness on her side. All I was doing was asking out a girl I'd done little more than stare at across a PSYC 401 lecture hall for half a semester. Why's it so hard sometimes to do what you know is right?

The first time I talked to Alyse was after class one day just outside Zoo-Psych. I had a Coke in my hand from a vending machine when we practically walked right into each other. I said hi and was about to boldly introduce myself when I fumbled the Coke, spraying it along the bottom of her shredded Levis. I felt sick but managed to say, "Those *were* nice jeans." She laughed, which was a huge relief. I was caught off-guard by her voice, kind of girly and feathery. Eventually, I bucked up and said, "Look, I'm going to fail this class because I spend all the lectures looking at you."

You know, I'm fairly sure she still has those jeans. Or maybe she cut them down to shorts. Not important.

On our first date, I took Alyse to see *Play It Again, Sam* at the Student Union. A smart move. I was so nervous, I let Woody Allen break the ice for me. Alyse loved it and thanked me for getting her to see it. Afterward, we walked through campus to Route One and wound up getting coffee and dessert at the Howard Johnson's. Can you believe it? But, there we were, under the orange roof, when four nuns came in for a late dinner. I assume it was a late dinner. I mean, who the hell knows what kind of hours they keep? Alyse and I eavesdropped on their conversation because neither of us could even imagine what nuns talk about. I whispered something like, "Isn't the convent like a dorm where they get free meals?" And Alyse says, "Maybe HoJo's is running an All-You-Can-Eat Fried Clams For Celibates Night." Naturally, I was a bit unnerved by Alyse saying anything even loosely related to sex, so I forced a laugh and said, "I thought their whole lives were devoted to God and whacking kids with rulers." At which point, Alyse asked me if I believed in God. Without skipping a beat, I said, "No, I don't believe in God and I tell Him so every day." I don't know where that came from. Maybe I was a little imbued with Woody. Alyse laughed out loud.

"That's hysterical! What a great answer!"

It was the first time I got a big laugh out of her, and I won't get into the whole pseudo-cool analogy about your first shot of heroin—as if anyone was less likely to try heroin than me—but it was a feeling I wanted for the rest of my life.

Then, on top of that, when I dropped Alyse off at her dorm, I said to her, "Well, there it is, Alyse. There's your date."

She thought it was so funny, she called me at the frat an hour later at like 1:00 AM to tell me she was still laughing about it.

Don't get me started on how many dates it took to kiss her, not to mention . . .

Hey, I just had a funny thought. Let's say you got really great tickets to an NBA game and you went to sit down and Rosa Parks was in your seat. Would you have asked her to get up?

Commie!

Christ, that's the kind of hypothetical question I used to crack you up with all the time. Remember how, in the middle of the night, we'd be bullshitting and I'd hit you with a crazy scenario like that?

Wake the fuck up, Commie.

Okay, so I was lying on the couch with my ankle propped up in frozen peas. While Alyse and I talked, I half-watched a TiVo-ed episode of *Law & Order SVU.* That poor Detective Benson was still trying to figure out how to live with owing her existence to her mother's rapist. And that Mariska Hargitay makes it believable. You know her mother was Jayne Mansfield? The shit people live with.

Out of nowhere, I hit the pause button and said to Alyse, "As long as we have two couples, why not make it three? I can ask Arnie if he wants to come along tomorrow night."

I turned to see Alyse looking at me as if we'd never met. At some point, her sweat pants had lost the string in the waistband, so she rolled them down to her hips, exposing an inch of creamy brown flesh on either side of her sloping innie bellybutton. Alyse never wore overtly sexy clothes and wasn't one of those mothers who turns forty and starts dressing sixteen. Aside from her choice of me, she has taste. So this unconscious but nevertheless rare sight of skin was, well, you know, it distracted me. What I'm saying is, I liked it.

I shifted on the couch and said, "What's wrong?"

"Nothing. I'd love to have Arnie and Fumi come. I'm just surprised you suggested it. Pleasantly surprised. Maybe your ankle pain flicked on the social director part of your brain."

"Or maybe it was throwing a bottle through a store window."

XVIII.

Just kidding. I didn't tell Alyse I threw the bottle. Or the two detectives who came to the door.

And no, I'm not kidding about the detectives. I'm lying there doing cryogenics on my ankle and admiring my wife's midriff when the doorbell rings. Alyse asks who it is and I hear, "It's the police, ma'am."

For the first time since I'd started having panic attacks, my fight-or-flight response kicked in for an appropriate reason. *I must have missed one of the store's surveillance cameras. They digitally saw someone throw a bottle through the window, brought it to the lab, enhanced the picture, printed it up, canvassed the neighborhood, showed everyone the photo, and the guy with the Bernese fingered me. Holy shit! I can't even run. My life is over. Everything. It's all shot to hell. Alyse, Esme, Charlie . . .*

Detectives David Shelby and Dennis Byron followed Alyse into the den. Like Lee Harvey Oswald in the movie theater, I froze, hoping they'd miss me. I could barely listen to what they said.

". . . minutes ago, a cabdriver named Nick Geragos was stopped for driving up a one-way street. He said he was lost, then recounted picking up a man a little after five on the 600 block of Stratification Boulevard and taking him to this address. Are you that man, sir?"

Lying on my back, I looked up, and the cops seemed humongous. I must have looked stricken because Shelby, the tall, balding, affable cop, chuckled and said: "Excuse my partner. He could be talking to you or Hannibal Lecter. He'd sound the same."

Coldly, Byron said, "Yeah, sorry." He looked like Perry Smith from *In Cold Blood*, a compact guy with a short fuse.

I sat up. My fear of being busted mixed with an urge to seem hapless, so I said all stuttery, "No, don't apologize. *I'm* sorry. See, I rolled my ankle on the root of a tree, that's why I flagged down the cab and I play basketball so the injury freaked me out that I'd never play again and I watch too much *Law & Order* so, with all that, *and* two detectives here—look, don't listen to me. I'm an idiot. What can I do to help?"

Shelby laughed out loud, but Byron just clenched his jaw. He didn't even smile when Alyse playfully nudged him and said, "Maybe you should cuff him, bring him downtown, and tune him up."

Alyse watches *Law & Order* with me a lot. It's something we love doing together.

It wasn't overly warm in the house, but Byron removed his sport jacket. He had on a blue short-sleeve shirt and mud green tie. He threw the jacket over his left shoulder as Shelby said, "A store was vandalized by a thrown bottle and since the cabbie picked you up in the vicinity of the store near the time of the incident, we took a flyer thinking you may have seen something."

As Shelby finished his gentle explanation, I saw Byron glance at Alyse's midriff. His look gave me a tiny chill, but so much other stuff was filling my head, I didn't dwell on it. Alyse went to the kitchen to whip up some coffee. Shelby said there was already talk of an anti-Semitic motive behind the crime. I said, "Why would an alleged anti-Semite throw—did you say it was a bottle?"

"Yes. A bottle of horseradish."

"Red or white?"

"Excuse me, sir?"

"I was asking whether it was red or white horseradish, but I guess that's not important."

Byron looked at me like he was dealing with a total moron, and I guess he was, but he didn't have to be such a prick about it. Then again, Commie, can you believe I asked if the horseradish was red or white?

"Anyway," I said, clearing my throat, "what anti-Semitic statement is made by hurling a bottle through a store window?"

Detective Shelby said, "The store owner is Nat Uziel and—"

"Oh! Nat's a patient of mine. I'm his podiatrist."

"So maybe you know that recently he became a big muckety-muck in some organization that deals with bonds for Israel."

"Israel Bonds?"

"Sounds right."

"So it could be less anti-Semitism than anti-Zionism," I said. "Either way, it doesn't narrow down the choices very much, does it?"

"No," Byron said. Or more accurately, grunted.

"Did anyone look at surveillance camera footage?"

"Not yet," Shelby said, "but odds are that won't help because, according to one of the CSI guys—do you watch those shows too?"

"Not really."

"Me neither. Truthfully, since *NYPD Blue*, I stopped watching all cops shows. Anyhow, according to Crime Scene, the bottle was thrown from at least fifteen yards away—out of camera range."

Alyse brought in two mugs of coffee and seventy-five varieties of sweetener. Shelby sipped his black. Byron threw in three sugars and drank like he'd just been rescued from an avalanche.

Then there was a creaking on the steps leading upstairs.

Charlie, after an hour of Wii, came down and, when I introduced him to the "police officers," he got this look I could feel in my own cheekbones. "Dad, what's wrong? What did we do?"

"Charlie, nothing's wrong. These two nice officers just wanted to ask me a question about an incident they're investigating. Unfortunately, I didn't see anything."

"Why 'unfortunately'? Isn't it better to not see anything?"

Commie, does that sound like anyone you know? Love that kid.

Doing my best Ward Cleaver, I said, "Charlie, we want to help the police do their jobs. We're the good guys and the police are also good guys. So we all have to help get the bad guys."

I glanced at Byron and caught him checking out that inch of skin over Alyse's sweat pants. I don't want to say I'm clairvoyant but, right then, I knew this cop was bad news.

Charlie said, "I have a sister too. Her name is Esme. She's having dinner at a friend's house. That's it. There's just four of us. No one else lives here."

"Charlie," Alyse said, motioning toward the civil servants downing Italian roast in our private home, "these men are detectives, not census takers." Then to the cops, "He learned about the census in school recently."

Then Charlie says to the cops, "They take the census every ten years to see how many Americans there are on Earth."

Alyse and I turned to each other like: *Don't look at me. He's your kid.*

Shelby said, "Well, we've intruded on you folks long enough."

But Charlie, regaining his sense of homeland security, said, "No, you can hang a while if you want."

"Charlie," I said, "the officers aren't going to catch any bad guys here. They gotta hit the streets."

Charlie said, "That's so cool. Do you make a lot of money?"

I looked at the cops with exaggerated discomfort and said, "Why do kids just love asking embarrassing questions?"

At which point, Byron gave me a look and said, "Why is that an embarrassing question?"

I said to myself: *What is this guy's problem*?

Shelby interceded, saying, "Charlie, your question wasn't nearly as embarrassing as our salaries."

I laughed too hard, Charlie laughed too soft, and Alyse laughed just right. Then, when the cops started leaving, Byron did another weird thing: As we shook hands, he turned his wrist in a way that flexed the muscles along his arm. He looked at his ripped arm, then at me. Who knows, maybe it was a macho weight lifter/cop move.

Alyse and Charlie escorted the officers out. I listened to the muted good-byes, the door opening, clopping steps, the door closing, an engine starting up, tires spitting gravel, and finally the return of our family's hum of residential bliss. Right then, an odd idea began brewing in my head. Fear of being caught mixed with queasiness about Byron which mingled with a dash of criminal thrill. All three blended into a strange feeling of defiance I'd heard about in other people. It freaked me out, but I went with it. Raising my fist in the air, I said under my breath, "*Pigs off campus.*"

XIX.

Maryland was no Berkeley, but I think there was some tear gas on the mall before we got there. We missed the campus riots and all that. One of my TA's told me it was all an excuse to blow off classes. I don't know what my excuse was.

Remember that day at the end of senior year when I bumped into you on the mall and you were livid because you got a B in Bowling? What was it? You bowled something like a 250 the first day of class but got a B because you didn't improve over the course of the semester? Your only B in four years. Sorry I laughed so hard.

Actually, I'm not sorry. Looking back, you have to admit it was funny. I honestly thought you might kill that professor.

Professor. As if the guy had a Ph.D. in Bowling.

You want to hear how much Esme is her mother's daughter? The Binders dropped her off after dinner around nine, nine-thirty. Poking around for signs of any residual damage from Esme's encounter with You-ey, Alyse and I asked about her dinner and she said, "Mrs. Binder kept asking me if I wanted spinach. I said no, 'No, thanks,' but she kept asking. 'No spinach? Don't you like spinach?' I swear to God, it was like The Spinach Inquisition."

I mean, not to be one of *those* fathers, but that's kind of genius-level stuff.

Of course, the main effect of the joke was that it eased Alyse's mind. It gave her reason to think Esme wasn't traumatized by You-ey's flash of Jew-hating. At least not for the moment. God knows what a kid does with something like that. Does it just roll off her back or stick in the memory banks waiting for a peak moment of vulnerability in life to pop into her consciousness and turn her into a paranoid schizophrenic?

I remember reading that schizophrenia usually surfaces in the late teens or early twenties. Jesus, how depressing is that? It's hard enough to keep your kids alive for the first eighteen years of their lives, not to mention sane and functional. Then, out of nowhere, your happy, slang-talking, well-adjusted kid is sitting in a dorm room and starts hearing voices? Come on! By fifteen, you should be allowed to declare that your kid's officially not defective. But no, the walk through the minefield never ends. Hell, the mere fact that a kid is born anatomically complete feels like something you'd need Penn and Teller to pull off. For that, you're rewarded with a day of ragged relief, then you spend six or twelve months watching a human blob, during which you're scared shitless about SIDS every night or wondering all day if you've spawned a vegetable. Then the kid starts smiling and you get a breath knowing you defused that pipe bomb before, one day, you float a freshly baked brownie in front of the kid's nose because you're supposed to keep their senses stimulated. And when the reaction isn't what you hoped, you start looking for signs of Asperger's or—

You reach a point where you imagine being grateful if your kid grows up to be merely a total asshole.

Jesus Christ. I took like eighty-five varieties of first aid classes. I can do CPR on a goddamn rhino, and I still feel impotent when it comes to keeping my kids alive. My parents raised me in total ignorance. I never buckled a seat belt until I was, what, twenty-two? And yet, here I am.

And here you are.

The whole point of it all—I don't get it. Sometimes I just think I'd be happier without being fully informed about anaphylactic shock. They come up with so many new afflictions that when one of our friends' kids is diagnosed with one, I actually get a tiny tinge of envy. At least the dread of what seems all but inevitable is over with for them.

That sounded idiotic but you know what I mean. It's like before my father got sick, I used to vaguely envy friends who had lost a parent. At least they'd been through it and survived. I told my father precisely that near the end, and I think it comforted him. He was worried about me, knowing I take things in the hardest way possible. When we talked in the hospital, he had so many machines attached to him making dull techno sounds, he kept saying, "I can't hear myself think." So one day, I lowered the volume way down on two of the machines. I mean, shit, I'm *something* like a doctor, right? In those few minutes, we had a great talk without getting maudlin. Or even overly serious. My dad was a pretty philosophical, realistic guy, and whatever regrets he had, he just accepted them, so I accepted them too.

That's probably letting myself off the hook a little too easily. I fed Alyse the same assessment, but the fact is, I preferred to merely estimate his regrets as opposed to soliciting them. I didn't ask him how he felt about his time on Earth because, ultimately, my own version of the truth was less haunting than the prospect of his. And shit, I'm the one who has to keep on living. You can't prepare for the death of your parents but, I gotta say, I tried. For the last, oh, ten years of my dad's life, my mind regularly detoured to his or my mother's death. Usually, I tried to figure out: What would be the best sequence of dying? It was obvious if my mother died first, my dad would have been lost, so I guess that panned out.

Panned out. Listen to me. My mother is, knock on wood, healthy. The fact that she's trapped in a never-ending state of heartbreak . . .

Jesus, Commie, is it possible to depress the shit out of someone in a persistent vegetative state? Another thing for the researchers to look into. Whatever. I'm sure you're thrilled I woke you up to hear this. Woke you up. Well, you know what I mean. Maybe I did wake you up. Maybe this is you at peak attentiveness.

Anyway, just bear with me a second while I wrap up this thought. I remember telling Alyse that my dad and I had a meaningful dialogue before he died because—I don't know if you felt this way—there's a ton of pressure to have THE TALK. I wasn't outright lying to Alyse, but it wasn't the kind of dialogue I was implying we had. At one point, my dad said, "I'll tell you, death is a no-win situation." I looked at him trying to figure out what he meant and he just said, "I thought you'd get a laugh out of that. That's a funny line! Heck, you should call Bartlett's."

Then I did laugh. I was like, "Sorry Dad, I thought you were saying something profound."

And he says, "God, no. Who am I, Nitschke?"

"I think it's Nietzsche. Nitschke was a linebacker for Green Bay."

"I know, I know. It was another joke."

"Wow, you're on a roll."

After that, we were just laughing away. In fact, after I hooked him back up to the machines, I asked him if he'd had anything to eat, and he says, "We have nothing to eat but fear itself." To the day he died, my father could get teary-eyed over FDR.

I'd say the only moment my father looked sad before he died was when he looked around his hospital room and quietly said, "You know, I don't believe in God. But that doesn't mean I want to constantly be proven right."

That line haunted me for a while. Shit, it still haunts me.

Jesus, I'd love to not be able to hear myself think.

Okay, enough of that. Let me get back to the story.

Actually, one more point. My dad mentioned Nietzsche? It really annoys me that the absolute dumbest people I know all quote that one line of his about whatever the hell you survive makes you stronger. I mean, it's bad enough these morons try so hard to sound smart. But I don't even think it's true. Shit. You ask me, whatever you survive makes you doubly terrified of it the next time you see it.

XX.

Anyway, sprained ankle, ba-da-ba-da, the cops visit the house, ba-da-ba-da-ba-da, Esme gets home from dinner with the Binder family. Okay:

Esme got home, told us all about the dinner using the words "random" and "like" at a steady but unalarming pace. So, she seemed okay. She said the Binders talked a lot about Israel over dinner, mostly focusing on the wall they built to keep out "crazy Arab suicide bombers." I made a mental note: When the kids go to someone else's home, it would be nice to get an advance look at all potential topics of discussion. Esme, God love her, said, "Mr. Binder asked me what I thought, so I said, 'I don't know . . . a wall? It's so random and like, lame.'" Then she added, "Harley got kind of mad at me for disagreeing with her father."

Did I mention that Alyse dated Harley Binder's father, Gil, in high school? She dropped him before the prom but they stayed friends. I don't like him—at minimum he's felt up my wife—but we've always been cordial. He does have good taste in women. I like his wife Janis a lot. She wears sixties clothes, believes in reincarnation even though Gil went Orthodox about fifteen years ago. She didn't go along with him but she accepted it. Except she won't allow him to wear a yarmulke if they go out on Saturday nights with friends. People make arrangements, Commie.

Anyway, Charlie told Esme about the detectives like it was the coolest thing that ever happened and she acted interested. Esme relates to Charlie more as a child than a brother. They get along pretty well, though Esme once described herself as "an aspiring only child." Alyse and Esme are like best friends—with their own codes and inside looks—which probably had a hand in Alyse committing the You-ey mistake. I'm glad they're close, and hope they stay that way, but what are the odds? Mother-daughter relationships are hardwired, hair-trigger booby traps. I already see moments when Alyse acts like a mother and Esme wants a friend, and vice-versa.

Or maybe that's just serve-by-the-slice psychology. All I know is, when my daughter draws out the word *Mom* to four syllables, I usually grab Charlie and get lost in assists and rebounds.

That night, the whole team was together, milling around the father with his frozen ankle. Charlie and I had ice cream, Alyse and Esme pecked at sorbet, and we gabbed and laughed for probably 45 minutes as the TiVo patiently waited for its go-ahead to resume unscheduled programming. In the middle of this Kodak family bliss, I wondered: *Did I commit vandalism or merely malicious mischief? I'm a first offender, so even if I get caught, I won't get any jail time. Then again, I'm not going to get caught. I'm going to get away with it. This will be my little secret, and remain so until—*

"What are you thinking about?"

Alyse saw the clouds in my eyes and asked the question for the umpteenth time.

"Just that I should call Arnie about dinner."

"That's what you were so lost in thought about?"

"Yeah. Why? Not interesting enough?"

Alyse laughed and said, "No, that's fascinating, honey. You have such a rich inner life."

To which Charlie asked, "What's an inner life?"

To which Esme said, "Don't worry, Chuckster. You don't have one yet."

To which I said, "Ezzie."

To which Esme said, "Just kidding, Chuckster. An inner life is just the stuff that rattles around in your brain. You know, random things you, like, think about without saying them out loud."

To which Charlie said, "Oh. Then I have an awesome inner life."

To which Alyse said, "I'm sure you do. Now pack up all your lives and take them upstairs to bed."

To which Esme said, "Nice segue, Mom. I'm going to sleep too. I'm totally wiped."

Fifteen minutes later, Detective Benson was stopping Detective Stabler from beating the crap out of some perp who enjoyed dressing like Princess Leia after raping and murdering women. (After? Jesus.) That reminded me of Arnie talking about how there's a person for every perversion, and so I called him to ask about dinner the next night. Arnie checked with his wife, and said, "Count us in."

"Good. The other couple is a yenta interior decorator and her corrugated aluminum executive husband who fights in Civil War re-enactments one weekend a month."

"Perfect," Arnie said. Then he whispered, "By the way, Fumi went to see a psychopharmacologist. Totally on her own last week and again yesterday. She didn't even tell me. I just saw a prescription bottle and she goes, 'Oh yeah, I saw a doctor in East Meadow. What of it?' Can you believe that? After begging her to see someone for months, she 'what-of-it's' me."

"Hey, just be happy she went."

"Yeah. A wife without thermonuclear mood swings. Suddenly that's my goal in life."

"It's important to have goals."

I told Arnie about my ankle, and you'll love what he said: "Look, if there was no such thing as professional courtesy, I'd say, 'Make an appointment and I'll fix your ankle up like new.' But since there is, and I wouldn't make any money off you, I'll tell you the truth: There's nothing I can do to help. You have ice in the house?"

Again, I ask you, Commie: How cool is Arnie?

Moments after hanging up with Arnie, Alyse came downstairs and said, "Well, Esme is convinced that pretty much everyone she hasn't met in the entire world is a rabid anti-Semite."

I lurched, sending the thawing peas falling off my ankle. "What? Really? She said that?"

Alyse smiled. "Actually, no. Not really. She didn't say that. I just felt the whole You-ey situation hanging over us, so I thought I'd prompt a discussion."

"Or you're hoping that talking about it will alleviate your guilt."

"Well, there's that."

"Alyse, don't feel guilty. Don't feel guilty or stupid or irresponsible. The fact is, I'm glad the 'You-ey situation' happened."

"You're glad?"

"Yes, I'm glad. I feel like the kids are a little too sheltered. Not that they need to be thrown into the deep end of the pool of life, but knowing there's a whole world beyond cozy Long Island is good."

"It's sounds like this is something that's been on your mind."

"Maybe. I don't know. Sometimes I just think we, and everyone we know, are insanely over-protective. I honestly don't think the world is as scary as we lead these kids to believe. Maybe that's a dangerous point of view and I'd probably kill myself if, God forbid, I lived to regret it, but still . . ."

At this point, I kind of realized that these thoughts were coming out of me on their own. From where, I don't know. Strange road for me to follow, but I kept going.

"Shit, Alyse, there are ten times more murders in the fictional New York of *Law & Order* than there are in the real-life New York. But the kids still get nothing but fear shoved down their throats without the backing of any firsthand experience. They need to touch the stove for themselves to know if it's hot. Look, I don't know what I'm saying exactly, but I'd really like to take the kids to the city more. Let them blow off their worthless, bullshit homework one night a month and take them to dinner and a Broadway show on a goddamn school night. I think I'd really like it if, in a year or two, Esme and maybe a few friends could just—"

I put my hands up to change the direction of my speech. Alyse pitched her head forward and I just kept plowing on:

"Look, when I was fifteen, I had a really good friend from summer camp, Glenn Shenker. He lived in Port Washington. One Saturday, in the fall or early winter, he calls me to tell me his parents are taking him to the city and do I want to meet up with him? I hop on the E Train, get off at 14th and 8th, and hang out with the Shenkers in the Village. Later, his father piles us in a taxi, gives us tickets to the Knicks game, and drops us off at the Garden. We sit in great seats. I mean, I was used to being up in the blue, and these were way down in the orange, right on the foul line. During the game, Glenn tells me a story about another friend from camp, Howie Mazen, who lives in Oyster Bay. One day, Howie throws up during trig class and is allowed to go home. He goes in his house and walks in on his mother sixty-nining Howie's piano teacher—"

Alyse comically put her index finger up and said, "This story will eventually relate to how we raise our children, right?"

"Eventually."

"Okay, just checking. Go on."

So Glenn tells me the story and for the rest of the game, you know what I'm thinking? I'm thinking: *What does sixty-nining mean*? I mean, I'd heard of sixty-nine and knew it was something sexual but wondered what the hell it meant. You know, specifically. Now, based on how Glenn told the story, he clearly knew what sixty-nine meant, so I was also thinking: *Why does he know these things and not me*? I decided it was because he grew up on Long Island, and kids out there are just way farther along in their knowledge of girls than I am as someone growing up in Electchester.

It really bugged me until—until!—after the game, when we're leaving the Garden, and Glenn asks me if I can walk him down to Penn Station so he can get his train home. I thought that was a little weird, but I was like, fine, whatever. Then, after getting his ticket, he asks me to wait on the platform for the train with him. That's when I looked at him holding his ticket and saw that his hand was trembling. I swear, you'd think he was holding a fucking tarantula. I realized he was terrified of being in New York City. Can you imagine? I'm a few minutes from getting on the F train to Jamaica and he's scared of waiting with two hundred white people for the cushioned seats and air-conditioned comfort of the LIRR.

So, between Glenn's grasp of sixty-nining and my total fearlessness in the greatest city on Earth, who was sheltered and who wasn't? You see my point?"

The story percolated in her head, then Alyse looked me and said, "You were fifteen and *didn't know what sixty-nining meant?*"

"Not really the point of the story."

"I know. I get the point of your story."

"So, what do you think?"

"I think you're totally right. I agree with you."

"Really?"

"Yes. Not that I've thought about it before, but, now that you mention it, yes. We should expose them to more. As you were about to say when you so rudely interrupted yourself, I think Esme and her friends should go to the city by themselves by the time they're, say, fifteen or sixteen."

"Or fourteen."

"Or fourteen. Not to go clubbing or anything. Just during the day to a museum or shopping or whatever they do."

"Right. When we lived in the city, remember those girls on the crosstown bus, those tiny little ballerinas with their feet pointed out at weird/cute angles, going to Lincoln Center or wherever? They looked so sophisticated and worldly and independent. I think I like that."

"I like it too. I'm glad you brought it up. I wish you'd bring up stuff like that more often."

"I wish I would too, but I have to wrack my brains just to find it. I mean, this whole overprotective thing. God knows where it came from or what caused it to come out."

"Look, I don't want to take credit, but what caused it to come out was me being a shitty parent."

"You're not a shitty parent." Smile. "Not all the time."

"Uh huh. And you actually figured out what sixty-nining meant *when* again?"

I smiled in a way that implied an answer juicier than the truth. That's what I do. I try to appear fascinating to my wife. It's my life's work.

After that moment of toothless provocativeness, I said, "You know, Alyse, if we got an apartment in the city and spent weekends there, the kids could stay in school here but also experience life in the city."

Alyse nodded, "They would live like kids whose parents are divorced."

"Right. Imagine having all the benefits of being from a broken home while still having your parents together."

"And just think of how smooth the transition would be if we did get divorced."

Even before Alyse said that, I saw the smile that always comes before she's about to give me shit. I can't handle divorce jokes even when I know they're just jokes.

"I hadn't really thought it through that far, Alyse."

"I'm glad." Then Alyse looked down and said, "Shit, I can't believe I had my sweats rolled down like this in front of the cops."

Instead of mentioning Byron's glimpse above her sweats, I said, "Stop grooming fleas. Lucky them, I say."

An hour or so later, I was in bed reading a book about doctors screwing up operations they've done a thousand times, and missing blatant indicators of various diseases. I was drawn to the book after my father died. Not that he would be alive and hitting tennis balls today, but I know his doctors screwed up. He went in for a simple angioplasty that lasted four hours. He wound up never leaving the hospital. When he left home the morning of the angioplasty, the last thing he ever said in his own home was, "I'm thinking maybe we should sell the Acura." During the last drive of his life, my mother told him she would make him spaghetti and "a nice shrimp cocktail" that night.

So, clearly, something in that hospital didn't go according to plan.

XXI.

Is it weird that I would want to read about doctors screwing up after their screw-ups shortened my father's life? I mentioned before that I'm someone who can look away from a car wreck. But when the wreck happens to me, I'm interested. Not that long ago, I rented this great movie called *The Sweet Hereafter*. It was about the aftermath of a school bus crash in a small town. A few nights later, at yet another dinner with three couples, everyone was horror-stricken that I'd watch *that* movie. All these *When Harry Met Sally* morons said shit like, "How could a parent of young kids watch a movie like that?" Maybe I'm the moron, but I wasn't ready for that kind of response. Luckily, Alyse was, and said, "He can watch it because the accident that killed several kids was fictional. Having kids should change your life but not your taste in movies. Did you stop flying after *Airport 1975*?"

It was beautiful. Alyse really stuck it up the asses of her lifelong friends and their mopey go-along-with-anything husbands.

As I continued to read in bed, Alyse came out of the bathroom in her sweat pants and nothing else. With her hair bunched up over her head in that way that girls can do faster than we can tie our shoes, she went around the bedroom doing her little preparations for bed. I made it look like I still had my head in my book, but really I was watching her.

Well, just seeing her blithely, mindlessly doing her activities, putting this here, that there, remembering something needing to be done the next day and jotting it down—she's a lefty and holds a pen cocked at this arthritic angle—the goddamn cutest thing in the universe.

All these years of marriage to the same girl and I never get over the mind-blowing sexiness of her absentmindedly walking around topless in front of me. Does she know she's putting on the greatest show on Earth? I have no idea, and I don't want to know. Why sully my membership in the only private club I've ever belonged to?

Lying there, in my little sliver of the American dream, at the end of a pretty long and weird day, I put my book down on the night table and tried not to think about my ankle, my crime, Audra Uziel, the cops or, especially, Ruth Kudrow.

SATURDAY THEN

I.

Commie?

I hope it's not too late. It's what? Ten-thirty-five.

PM.

God knows what kind of Circadian rhythm you're on. I was thinking before about that woman in Florida who had the same thing as you. They tossed Bush into Air Force One to stop the doctors from removing the feeding tube. Everyone on the news going on and on about the feeding tube, the feeding tube, the feeding tube. You'd think the Carnegie Deli was catering her coma.

I shouldn't judge. I know your wife is still holding out . . .

By the way, Alyse sends her love. I spoke to her before. And the kids. This is kind of funny: I told you how Alyse and I have the kids saying "I love you" to us and each other at the end of phone calls? A few hours ago, Charlie said it to his friend Ari Weprin. They've known each other since pre-school, and now they're working on a class project together where they have to build something—I don't know what. Probably a pipe bomb or something. Anyhow, after they finished discussing it on the phone, Ari said, "See you tomorrow" and reflexively, Charlie said, "Okay, bye, I love you."

Apparently, Ari had a brief brown-out then and said, "What did you say?" Charlie told me he explained to Ari about our family custom and how he'd just kind of spaced out on who he was talking to and apologized. I guess Ari bought it because Charlie laughed about it.

My mom thinks all this "I-love-you-ing" diminishes the meaning of the phrase. Score one for her, I gu—

Oh shit, excuse me. That banquet dinner's killing me.

Some banquet. Podiatrists can be pretty annoying when they're sober. Imagine what they're like when they've had a few and then have to listen to an entrepreneurial peer talking about his latest book on how foot, ankle, and back problems are skyrocketing due to flip-flops. Can you imagine someone getting a book published on that subject? Norman Mailer should have written a book about flip-flops. Even he could have figured out that a slice of rubber with no arch might not be great for an obese American public with a shockingly high rate of flat-footedness. *The Executioner's Fallen Arch Song* by Norman Mailer.

What was that guy's name, the murderer from *The Executioner's Song?* Forget it. I'll never remember.

So. If you're wondering, the night nurse was cool with me breaking visitor's hours to talk to you some more. I don't know how cool you are with it, but I know I'm a good two hours from falling asleep. I only go to one or two of these conventions a year, but when you've been married your whole adult life, even a couple of days of flying solo can feel disorienting. Arnie tells me that, when he's driving, sometimes he'll see the Best Western just off our exit of the highway and dream of checking in under a fake name and sleeping for a week.

Me? I'm like a goddamn orphan who just wants to be nestled in routine. I can't stand holidays. Even Sundays bug me. Any day with no mail somehow gets on my nerves.

But it's now Saturday in the story I've been telling you. As Esme would say, "Nice segue, Dad."

By the way, Esme once asked me, "If you don't have enough money to stay in the Best Western, is there a Second Best Western?" I think she was eight at the time. Kid's a genius.

Alyse got up at five-thirty the next morning, or so I assume. After sleeping right through to eight, I'm feeling pretty fresh. At the time, that didn't seem significant.

Actually, even now it doesn't seem significant.

Anyhow, I hobbled downstairs, my ankle in shades of yellow

and purple that even Ralph Lauren never put together. I kissed Alyse, who smiled in a kookier way than I was used to and pointed to an article from Newsday she'd circled with a red Sharpie.

Sharpie. Now, *there's* a company to invest in, huh?

Anti-Semitism Suspected
In Long Island Vandalism

The piece reported little I didn't already now. In fact, it said a lot less than I already knew. The only new tidbit was a comment from Nat Uziel: "It's deplorable that such senseless expressions of bigotry can still happen in this day and age."

Isn't it incredible how just about everyone who comes face to face with a reporter these days can morph into a press secretary?

The article concluded with Nat saying there would be a rally outside his store at noon on Saturday.

"Can they have a rally on Shabbat?"

Alyse shrugged. "I guess if they don't drive to the rally and they don't use a microphone during the rally and keep it restful."

"Maybe they got some kind of waiver."

"A waiver? From who?"

"Good question. It's funny that the Jews don't have a pope, you know? Someone calling the shots. I guess Alan Greenspan is as close as we get."

"Pope Alan Greenspan. Pope Eggs Benedict. Not too comparable."

"No, I guess not. But then again, Jews don't really need a pope. All of us—Reform, Conservative, Orthodox—we're good at making up rules as we go along."

Alyse almost smiled, but her face stopped at, "Isn't this is a lively discussion for eight AM?"

I grabbed a coffee and said, "We should go."

"Go where?"

Alyse is usually somewhere between two and fifteen steps ahead of me, so I was a surprised by her question. "To the rally."

She looked at me as if I'd said, "You should drink Drano."

I said, "Why not? How often do you get to see a pack of psyched up Jews go off on alleged anti-Semitism? In fact, we should take the kids. Expose them to their God-given right to paranoia now, so they can reject it at a younger age than we did."

I know, I know. I sounded like someone else. As if my usual inhibitions flew through the glass with the horseradish.

"That ankle sprain really set something off in you," Alyse said, wanting to believe it. "Pheromones, or whatever that chemical is in chocolate."

I shrugged like the cause was unimportant, so Alyse shrugged back and said, "Whatever. Sure, let's go to the Jew rally. But bringing the kids?"

"We have time to decide."

The whole flip reggae in my voice had my wife confused. She was going along with me, but I could tell part of her was also thinking I should be held for observation. Most wives, noting a change in their husbands, assume there's an affair going on. Maybe I should've been bugged that the possibility never seemed to enter Alyse's mind, but I wasn't. I started reading the paper, a sort of nonverbal cue that I was perfectly normal. Alyse headed upstairs to do something or other.

II.

Flipping through the paper, I caught an item about the cloned Australian Shepherd that ate the kid's finger. The animal shelter ran the odds of finding a new home for a dog with a rap sheet and decided to euthanize it, but PETA filed for an injunction.

If they were going to euthanize the kid, the PETA freaks wouldn't say boo.

The dog was remanded to the shelter pending legal maneuvers. I was blown away by the story, but again, Commie, I did not note the dateline. Clonegate was taking place somewhere in America. That's all I knew.

I bet when you were in law school, they didn't have classes in animal jurisprudence. Of course, when you were a public defender, you probably wished some of your clients would morph into family pets. I remember your telling me about that woman you represented who confessed to bludgeoning her husband to death because "he was an asshole." What did you try as a defense? Justifiable homicide because the guy really was an asshole? The judge must have loved that.

Actually, I bet he *did* love it, bored out of his mind as judges always seem to be. At least the ones on TV. Maybe the real life ones are more engaged. I don't know. The actresses they use on *Law & Order* for the DA's office, one's more gorgeous than the next. But whenever you see a public defender on the show, it's some roly-poly, bald guy oozing so much personality you want to dunk him in your milk. If you were an actor, Commie, you'd have never been cast for the job.

I can't really gauge attractiveness in men. Let me clarify that: I can't gauge attractiveness in *white* men. Black guys, I can look at and say, "Oh yeah, Billy Dee Williams, he must have to beat women off with a stick." Derek Jeter too. But white guys? Other than Johnny Depp or maybe Paul McCartney, I don't see it. And maybe George Clooney, though he looks like he has a huge head. But whenever women talk about some white guy as being really handsome—Tom Cruise, Sting, that Viggo guy—I'm like, "Really?" But, you know, girls are working on a whole other level.

That "six-pack" of girls in AEPHI asked me about you like eighty-five times—*What's he like? Does he have a girlfriend at home?*—before it hit me that they all were hot for you. Not that it was just that group of girls. SDT, DPhiE. I was like your press secretary. On that one account, your getting the boot from the frat was a blessing. Maybe it wasn't a coincidence that I got together with Alyse right after.

It probably wasn't a coincidence that you didn't meet her for a long time. Sorry about that. Yet another apology. Although it wasn't just you. At that time, I'd look at a fucking housefly as competition. Look, you know when I first felt like Alyse was truly mine? Not when we got engaged or married. When Esme was born. Having a child together at least made me know I was going to be a part of Alyse's life forever. In fact, here's another thing I've never told anyone: After each of Alyse's miscarriages, my emotions were split between grief over the baby and fear that there would be nothing holding Alyse and me together. Alyse would be sleeping off her sadness and I'd look at her, visualizing a bleak night in the future where she was on a third date with some senior buyer from Saks, taking a sip of her Perrier and saying, *Yeah, I was married once. Kind of a schmuck, but a nice guy. I sort of lost track of him . . .*

Alyse didn't know the extent of my insecurity, but she sensed some of it right from the start. She literally bent over backwards to reassure me.

She didn't *literally* bend over backwards. I hate when people say that. In fact, she was pretty subtle about it. At parties, she'd maintain light contact with my arm, air kiss other guys hello, little shit like that. Finally, one day when we were recounting our first seven or eight dates for the 30th time, she said, "I immediately knew you were exactly my type." I wanted to say, *Are you nuts*? I swear, Commie, even when I was about to propose, I asked myself:

You're going to ask her to spend her whole life with you? How arrogant is that?

So with all that off-the-meter insecurity, you can see why, consciously or unconsciously, I kept you at a distance. Not that I didn't tell her about you. I told her a lot about you. I remember when I told her you were kicked out of the frat for refusing to pay your room and board after the house rejected that black kid as a pledge. That impressed Alyse a lot. Too much. In fact she was so impressed, I remember kicking myself for telling her the story. Even after I told her that you paid the black guy to pledge, Alyse was still impressed. Believe me, it took me a few years before I got around to telling her how you wrote on your law school applications that you'd have to miss a bunch of classes if the Braves reached the World Series.

By the way, I've never told anyone except Alyse the whole black pledge story. You gotta give me that much credit: I can keep a secret. If nothing else, I'm one of the few people who has trouble telling a secret. Obviously. Why I didn't dump out of the frat with you . . . ? Jesus.

Esme woke up around eight-thirty, spilling out of bed and heading right to her laptop. An email from another of her friends, Sophie Malkin, inquired as to whether Esme wanted to accompany the Malkins to the Whitney. Being her mother's daughter, Esme replied yes first and *then* ran down the stairs to ask us if she could go. Maintaining at least comparable excitement levels between our two kids is a continual struggle for Alyse and me. Esme has her mother's gift of making anything she's doing sound like the coolest thing in the world. When Charlie hears the details of her adventures, he gets this look on his face like life is passing him by. Already. You don't have to ask where he gets that from.

At the end of our sophomore year at Maryland, I remember feeling heartsick that college was half over. That may not be exactly how Charlie feels, but it's definitely the same species of melancholy.

Anyway, we gave Esme the nod on the Whitney visit partly because it spared our having to ask her if she'd like to go to the rally and partly because it made the decision for us on Charlie since he was still a year or two away from being allowed to stay home alone for a few hours. Maybe that was another area in which we were overcareful. Charlie was fully capable of amusing himself alone and, if need be, picking up the phone and calling us on our cell phones. In fact, after the encounter with the police the night before, he was probably comfortable enough to dial 911. I almost said as much to Alyse but doubted my own motives. I wondered if I wanted Charlie to stay home on the off-chance that the Orthodox God would swoop down in the middle of the rally, point at me, and bellow, "J'accuse!" Then I wondered if God even spoke French.

Okay. I didn't wonder that. I just threw that out there for your amusement. You know, Commie, it would be nice if you'd give me a sign that I'm not wasting what I think are some funny lines on you. Your weirdly life-like eyelash flutters seem less and less encouraging.

I assumed Charlie had never heard the word rally outside of a sports context. *"Jeter started the Yankee rally."* To control his anticipation, we delayed telling him until just before we left.

The Malkins picked up Esme, Alyse went upstairs with Charlie, and I went online in the den. Just as I was about to check my email, a detour had me Googling the living shit out of Mossad Kosher Horseradish.

"Mossad Kosher Horseradish Brand, established in 2008 in White Plains, NY, is the finest hand-prepared, coarse-ground horseradish in the world! Its roots come from the horseradish capital of the world, Collinsville, Illinois, and are transported in seventy-five-pound burlap bags, dirt and all! Each root is washed, cut, and peeled according to kosher dietary laws under the supervision of Rabbi Hedrick Pearl. All retail outlets carrying the Mossad Kosher Horseradish brand are subject to rigorous background checks to ensure that no proceeds from this product wind up in the coffers of any group active in, or affiliated with, philosophies or attitudes contrary to the interests of Israel, the rightful homeland of the Jewish people."

My first thought was, who writes this stuff? People probably sat down and had meetings and arguments about that text. Then there were rewrites and re-rewrites. Amazing.

My second thought was, lawyers had to be involved in drafting the text. Why did they keep referring to the Mossad Kosher Horseradish *brand*? That word has gotten totally out of control. When did branding stop being something you did to cattle?

Third thought: Commie, you know I have no business acumen. But really, can a horseradish business turn a profit with overhead that includes paying for a rabbi's supervision and running background checks on potential clients? With my mind wandering around on its own, I surfed for websites about different kinds of glass. It seemed a little odd that the whole window shattered, as opposed to say, the bottle just flying through and leaving a hole. The shattering was certainly more dramatic than just a hole at the time of the incident, but was less so after. You know what I mean?

Come on, Commie. Picture it a second. Imagine if the next morning there was just a nice-sized hole in the window. You know what Uziel would have done. Exactly. Now we're getting on the same wavelength: He would have left the hole there in perpetuity, just like that deli in Paris with the bullet holes. The place would have been another stop on the landmarks tour of worldwide anti-Semitism. Dachau, the Paris deli, Nu? Girl Fashions Outerwear for Teens.

"Outerwear for Teens" isn't really part of the name of the place but, for the purpose of the tour, it sounds more tragic, don't you think? The right publicist could turn the whole thing into the Long Island version of Kristalnacht.

Reading about various types of glass and their properties was pretty fascinating, but I wasn't finding out much about the different ways they absorb damage. I was actually writing down a few of the manufacturers' phone numbers when the phone rang. My mother's name came up on Caller ID, so I waited for Alyse to get the phone.

It was—

Oh: If Alyse and I are home and my mother calls, it's Alyse's job to pick up. If her parents call, I pick up. After the calls alerting us to my father's cancer and Alyse's mother's broken hip from a fall in Florida, we set up that system, figuring we could do a more sensitive job of telling each other bad news. Whoever isn't holding the phone darkly says to the other: "Who?" The phone is hell. Alyse and I have aged parents. We know so much more than we care to know about Cumadin, stents, and Synthroid. Every ring of our phone sparks a hop of arrhythmia in both of us.

"I got arrhythmia, I got . . ."

Funny huh? You didn't know I could sing, eh?

Two minutes later, Alyse calls down and passes the call over to me. My mother, now living in a one-bedroom in Forest Hills, had read about the horseradish affair in the *Times*, which she somehow subscribes to at about a quarter of the price we pay for *Newsday*.

"Yeah, Mom. I read about it. In fact, the police questioned me because I was near the scene of the crime when it happened."

I explained how I was walking home and then I immediately dove headlong into a pack of lies, telling her I took the cab because I was cold instead of telling her about the ankle. I mean, really, who needs three weeks of two calls a day from his mother asking about his ankle? And she would too. Three weeks at least of her asking if I'd seen a battery of doctors. Shouldn't you have it x-rayed? Ba-da-ba-da-ba-da.

At that point, it dawned on me just how much explaining I'd have to do if, somehow, I wound up being arrested, tried, and convicted for my vandalism, or my malicious mischief, or wherever they would wind up throwing the book. After all, in a little over twelve hours, I'd lied to my wife, my kids, my mother, *and* the police.

Then I had another thought: If I get nailed, I'll just say, *Look, I hurt my ankle, got mad, threw a bottle through a window, fled the scene, and lied about it to everyone I know. Not my best choice ever. But it is what it is.*

Were you awake for *It is what it is?* That trash phrase has become the unimpeachable get-out-of-jail-free card for any offense you can name. If that phrase was around in 1953, the Rosenbergs would be living happily in Boca right now.

Besides being revolted by the idea of moving to Florida, the great thing about my mother is, I never know exactly where she's going to come down on any issue. She's a true wildcard. Like in the Clinton-Monica thing, my mother said, "I don't know why he didn't just say he had sex with her. That's why these men run for president, so they can have affairs. You think they want to give speeches and drop bombs? No, they want to cheat. Roosevelt, Kennedy, Eisenhower—they all took the job so they could cheat. And Clinton? When he was running, everyone knew that he cheats. All he had to do was say, 'Yeah, I had an affair with an intern from Beverly Hills. What of it?'"

Sure enough, on the issue at hand, my mother said, "I don't see what the anti-Semites hope to accomplish by throwing a bottle through the window of a clothing store. What do they think is going to happen? We'll throw up our arms and say, 'You win. I'll convert to Protestantism first thing in the morning?"

I told my mother about the rally and she said, "I don't see what a rally is going to accomplish either but go, enjoy yourself."

III.

Alyse and I decided to leave around 11:30 for the noon rally. These things never start on time anyway and, if we're late, so what? I did wonder how Nat Uziel could be on time. From the synagogue to the store is about a mile and a half, and that much walking would hurt his feet.

I didn't get into this earlier, but I did a pretty big job on his overlapping toe. It involved balancing the soft tissue supporting structures around the joint at the base of the toe which, in turn, included tendon transfers, joint capsule release, and ligament tightening. Plus, I had to cut through the bone, reposition it to the correct alignment, and stabilize it in place with screws.

You probably didn't need to hear all that, huh? I was showing off for you, but the truth is, I don't do surgery anymore. When I first started practicing, I went in on a surgical center with a slew of other guys and did several foot surgeries a week. Then, maybe five years ago, I dislocated my index finger playing hoops and couldn't do surgery for two months. I didn't want to take the chance of getting a malpractice suit for dropping the scalpel clear through someone's arches. To tell you the truth, I did previously dodge a bullet in that area. I started to operate on the wrong foot of a college kid. He actually played football for Hofstra. Punter. I went as far as making an incision on his good foot before it dawned on me, *I saw this kid play. He punts lefty. Shit!*

I broke into cosmic panic before somewhat calmly sewing up the incision and managing to focus on the original task at hand. Later, I sat down the kid and his family and came clean about my mistake. Somehow, I got lucky enough to fuck up with the right family. They correctly assessed that no harm was done and didn't press the matter.

Of course, I didn't charge them for the procedure. I took some solace in the fact that the kid graduated as the sixth best career punter in Hofstra football history. Last I heard, he's a mortgage broker. He probably wishes he'd sued.

Anyway, during the time of my dislocated finger, I took off from surgery and solicited business elsewhere to defray the loss of income. That's when I got the work at the three Assisted Living places, which turned out to be more lucrative than the surgeries. I know some podiatrists look down their noses at retirement homes/assisted living facilities but, really, someone had to do it and what more did I have to prove? I did surgery for a bunch of years, I'd proven I wasn't just some quack. So I stopped operating altogether.

I'll tell you what. Remember that book I mentioned about doctors reaching an age when they start losing it? Well, I'm bumping up against that age now, and just realizing that made me feel even better about giving up surgery.

Selling off my share in the surgery center also made for a handsome payday.

Long-winded point is, no matter how well the surgery went, Uziel's foot would hurt. Of course, considering his heart condition, the walk would be a good thing. So there you have it, good and bad in everything.

Maybe not everything.

I should have just spent the day with my ankle elevated on a couch, but I compromised. We drove about halfway there while all the Orthodox were still at services and then walked the rest of the way.

At around eleven, Alyse and I told Charlie about the rally. And, of course, he *did* know what a rally was outside a sports context because kids know everything. "So, because of what happened at the store where you told the police you didn't see anything, there's going to be a big rally? That's awesome. It'll be like the Boston Tea Party, right?"

"Yeah. Without the tea. And not in Boston. And not a party."

During our drive to the rally, Charlie asked why windshield wipers are called windshield wipers because they don't really have anything to do with the wind. I was about to say something about how the glass protects against the wind, but instead I said, "You're right, Charlie, it makes no sense. That's a fantastic observation."

Charlie shrugged and said, "Actually, I'm pretty surprised no one ever thought of that."

I think that was the kind of conversation that previously would have made me start worrying about my kids thinking I'm a schmuck. Remember I told you I used to worry about that? Even if that conversation had taken place a week earlier, I would have started thinking, *Jesus, his conclusion was more grounded than mine. Eventually he'll stop looking to me for explanations of life altogether. Being an unreliable source. That's where I'm headed.*

But that Saturday, I didn't feel like that. All I thought about was how lively and alert my kid's mind was. There he was, eight years old, and already he had an eye out for the little mistakes of the universe. Felt euphoric. *Look what's going on in my little offspring's head!*

In fact—and this is really great—not long after that, maybe a month, Charlie said to me something like, "Everything between midnight and noon is called morning, but after that the day is divided into afternoon, evening, and night. It's like morning is kind of greedy, isn't it?"

I swear, I wanted to pick him up and squeeze him like Haystacks Calhoun.

IV.

My ankle was kind of throbbing, so we drove through a couple of back alleys and managed to park a few blocks from Nu? Girl Fashions without being seen by the Yarmulke Squad. You'd think someone had declared martial law and we were driving after curfew.

Coincidentally, we hit Stratification at almost the exact point at which I'd gotten the cab the night before. I had a momentary thought of pointing to some tree root in the ground and telling Alyse, "That's what I tripped over." But, if I were caught, this particular lie would border on psychotic, so I said, "This is where I got the cab last night."

Alyse nodded without so much as a trace of piqued interest on her face. I noticed because, after she had a night to sleep on it, I was trying to see if anything in my story wasn't adding up for her. I don't know why it wouldn't have added up aside from my instinct to assign Alyse superpowers.

It wasn't surprising that we weren't the only non-Orthodox walking to the rally site. In fact, more than a smattering of non-Jews was present. I (cynically) put it down to a smart business decision, but I'm sure some people were genuinely concerned about our little town's sudden spike in crime. There had been some typical teenager hijinks, but I couldn't remember a felony within the zip code for at least six years. The Nassau County DA prosecutes something like thirty thousand crimes a year, but our little town? Nada. The last real case was an investment whiz a few blocks away from us who was cuffed in his home for embezzling a million dollars. And, let's face it, that's a pretty unambitious swindle by today's standards. Maybe he wasn't such a whiz after all. I presumed he was because he went to Wharton, which is ridiculous because, let's face it, the only thing MBAs learn in business school is how to run a meeting, right? At least I came out of grad school knowing my way around a human foot, for God's sake.

My westward limp on Stratification was fairly pronounced and

Charlie grew concerned. "Are you okay, Dad?" I assured him I'd been through this a zillion times and I'd be fine, but he persisted, "You'll be able to play hoops again?"

The question didn't surprise me. Charlie tells all his friends that his dad "has game." It's cool for him partly because his friends' fathers are all relegated to golf and partly because Charlie finds basketball impossible. He didn't inherit my hand-eye coordination or leaping ability. I give Alyse shit about that all the time because, obviously, it's her fault. She came from a long line of earthbound Hebrews. Seeing her father try to play tennis down in Boynton Beach—

Did I mention that Alyse's parents moved to Florida? We visit once a year. More than that would be carcinogenic. The first time we took the kids down there, we went to a restaurant near their condo and a seventy-five-ish guy at the next table pulled his pants down and shoved a syringe in his thigh. Right there in the restaurant! Esme, who was six at the time, said, "Eww, gross!" The guy looked at her and said, "It's not gross. It's something I need." At which point, Alyse walked over and whispered in his ear, "Trust me, my daughter only said what everyone else in the restaurant was thinking."

I think I told you before, she's got cojones.

Anyway, after assuring Charlie I was fine despite my limp, he started imitating my limp. I mean, he overdid it like crazy. He looked like Ratzo Rizzo in *Midnight Cowboy*. Alyse was laughing so hard we stopped for a second so she could get a grip. She didn't want to be seen giggling en route to such a serious occasion.

We actually sat on a bench outside the popular (and closed, of course) Belly Deli. When our giddiness over Charlie's limp passed, he asked if the detectives from the night before would be at the rally.

"That's a good question, Charlie," I said. "You know, they might come because sometimes a person who commits a crime likes to return to the scene."

Again I glanced at Alyse for her reaction. Nothing. Charlie, on the other hand, was flabbergasted. "Why? Wouldn't he be worried about being caught?"

"Well, he should—"

"Or *she* should," Alyse interjected, never wanting to shortchange the capabilities of women.

"Yes, he or she should be worried about being caught, but I guess criminals aren't as smart as you, Charlie."

So Charlie says, "That's why they're criminals."

I swear, Commie, you gotta wake the fuck up and meet Charlie. It would be well worth your while.

Among many other worthwhile reasons for you to wake up, of course.

Anyway, so, we wound up on the bench for 10 minutes. It was great, the three of us just sitting and jabbering away. When we got moving again, my ankle felt colder and creakier. I was hoping Charlie wouldn't start imitating my limp again when I turned and saw Nat Uziel with his wife, his ultra-Orthodox son Jason, and Audra.

A beam of *Oh shit* ran through me. Uziel skipped introducing his family and said, "The foot doctor is limping."

Charlie piped up, "He sprained his ankle on a tree root. He's on the DL from basketball for two weeks."

Audra looked at me and said, "That's a shame. You played so well Thursday night."

I felt Alyse look at me like: *What do we have here?* With my first tinge of guilt that day, I said, "Audra and her dad, Nat, are patients. She had an appointment yesterday, and she thought I looked like I had color, so I told her no, I'd just played basketball the night before . . ."

Alyse, enjoying my mini-squirm, said, "And you mentioned that you played well."

"Of course. I tell everyone when I play well. Patients, custodians, cashiers. They all know my stat line."

"It's nice to meet you, Audra," Alyse said with her warmest smile.

Audra looked at Alyse with what I took to be hero worship and said, "Likewise. Your husband is a really great doctor."

Alyse looked at me with the tiniest widening of her eyes: *This is the girl whose love life you thought you derailed?* Then she turned to Audra and said, "Thank you. This is Charlie."

Audra looked at Charlie and smiled. "Hey, Charlie."

"Hi."

Audra introduced her mother. The only introduction left was Jason, but she wasn't leaping into that rat's nest. Jason, with his pais and beard and black suit and tsit tsit, stood rigidly alert, eyeing my wife and kid as if they were Hezbollah. Sarah motioned to introduce Jason but Nat overruled her, "I appreciate all of you showing your support in light of last night's heinous act."

At that, he turned and walked away, his family dragging along behind him.

Heinous act. I flashed back to the cheeseburger incident. The over-the-top phrase that day had been *vicious barb.*

Alyse, thinking the same thing, said, "Boy, that guy must have the hysterical edition of *Roget's Thesaurus.*"

I nodded and Alyse added slyly, "But his daughter's lovely. Your type, kind of."

Too fast, my head turned to her. *Caught.*

"So, when you said 'looks are deceiving,' were you talking about us?"

Charlie said, "The guy with the beard was creepy."

Grateful for his input, I said, "No, he's just very religious."

"Still, he was creepy."

We started walking again and when Charlie skipped a few steps ahead, I said to Alyse, "I can't believe how easily you see through me."

"You were way too upset yesterday about what you said to her. I couldn't figure out why until now, when I saw her."

I shook my head, feeling sick.

Alyse said to me, "Honey, relax. It's alright. A young college girl adores you and you flirt. It's okay. Really, it's reassuringly human.

Of course, I'd rather you not pooh-pooh our marriage as part of your flirting, but—"

"Believe me, that's the part that's killing me. I know some dopey comment from a podiatrist isn't going to unhinge a smart girl like her. I just . . . I'm sorry. I'm an idiot."

"No, you're just rusty."

"Rusty?"

"You know," she shrugged, "when it comes to flirting."

"Jesus, stop saying that word. Besides, you can't be rusty at something you were bad at to begin with."

Charlie turned around with a "look-at-me!" look and started imitating my limp again. He was pretty good at it, I've gotta say.

Alyse nodded at Charlie (*Well done!*) and said, "Believing you were bad at flirting is what made you good at it, but I don't think we really need to get into that now. I mean, this is the first such conversation we've ever had. That's pretty amazing."

"Some people would find it weird." Then, "Do you find it weird?"

Alyse gave it a thought and said, "I don't think about relationships very much anymore. But I'd say the one thing I've decided in the last, I don't know, twenty-five years, is that a good relationship occurs when both people think the other is too good for them."

"What about when only one person feels that way?"

"I don't know. I have no experience with that."

You know, Commie? When I'm in a discussion like that, I'm not really thinking. Actually, I'm hardly ever in a discussion that actually touches on the deeper subjects of my life as it's being lived. But my point is, in the middle of it, I'm thinking, but I'm not—what's the word? realizing? deducing? those still aren't the right words—I'm playing ping-pong but only thinking about my next shot without seeing the whole game? How I got through the SATs with such shitty analogies is beyond me. The thing is, as I'm telling you this, I'm realizing how well Alyse handled that conversation. I feel like, if it's possible, she's gone way up in my book just over the course of telling you this whole story.

Really, you should think about opening a therapy practice right here in this room. You lie there and people just come in and talk like I am. I guarantee the epiphanies would come easier than with some shrink chiming in every two minutes. You could have a booming practice, scheduling patients twenty-four hours a day. You want a double session? A quintuple session? No problem. David Moscow, Doctor of Vegetative Psychology, can squeeze you in.

Just because you're not conscious doesn't mean you shouldn't be economically viable.

V.

Anyway, as we got close enough to Nu? Girl Fashions to see big clumps of people milling around, Charlie stopped limping. Like me, he only entertains for select audiences. He stopped and waited for Alyse and I before asking if either of us had a TicTac.

"You're concerned about the freshness of your breath?" I asked.

"I don't know. A little."

Alyse dug around her pocketbook for anything minty while I gave my standard passing thought to whether I'd one day look back at this moment as the first sign of my son having wicked OCD. Alyse pulled out a butterscotch sucking candy from 1982 and Charlie said, "That'll do."

As we were waiting at the last red light before the rally, Carl Penza, the Nassau County executive all dressed up in a boxy, grim suit, stopped beside us with a somber entourage of two men and a woman in their mid-twenties along with a uniformed cop so buff his badge looked like it was about to pop off his chest. Personally, I preferred when cops were fat and out of shape, like in Manhattan during the '80s. They seemed more approachable. Now they're all lifting weights, pumping pound for pound with the convicts they bust. They're scarier to me now than they were when I was a kid. Of course, that may also just be the criminal in me talking.

Carl shook our hands in a grave yet firm way, in a way appropriate for the occasion. He was in his mid-fifties but seemed a lot older than me. But then to me, all authority figures feel older than me. Not wearing a coat gave him a vigorous aura, like Reagan wearing next to nothing for his meeting with Gorbachev in Iceland. On the Island, Carl was a longtime political hack, but the only sign of the old days was his pinkie ring, which looked wrong on a finger that should have been a knuckle longer.

If Carl knew then that the next election would sweep him out of office, he probably would have stayed home and sent out some press release effectively saying, *Dear Jews: Fix your window and move on*, which would have been a good suggestion. But Carl didn't know he'd lose by fourteen points to a nervous, bony Democrat named Marcus King, so he made his virile appearance before a constituency that would soon help end his career.

Actually, Carl was indicted about a month ago, but I don't think I need to get into that now.

Jesus, it's twelve-thirty. How are you holding up, Commie?

Good. So as Alyse, Charlie, and I reached the crowd (which would be overestimated at "over three hundred and fifty" by *Newsday*), one of my Orthodox patients came over to say hello. I went into a mini-panic trying to remember his name, but all I could come up with was Infected Ingrown Toenail. I turned to Alyse and urgently whispered, "Denton Cooley!"

Okay, I'll explain quickly: Alyse and I were once discussing how there were no famous doctors anymore except Kervorkian. And then we got into how, when we were kids, everyone knew about Michael DeBakey and Christian Barnard and—we couldn't come up with the other big heart surgeon. Then, finally, we simultaneously said, "Denton Cooley!" Since then, that's been our code for when we can't remember people's names. Usually, we just introduce ourselves. But with Charlie there, Alyse got flustered too, and, just as Infected Ingrown came over, she said, "You know what? I'll take Charlie up front, closer to the action."

I said, "I'll find you," and they hustled off with only seconds to spare.

Covering both podiatrist and concerned citizen bases, I shook Ingrown's hand and super-sensitively asked, "Are you okay?"

"Yes, thank you. I just can't believe we're still dealing with this crap in the twenty-first century."

"So true, so true," I said, feeling truly full of shit.

"Even my shagetz lawyer said to me, 'It never ends, Jerry.'"

Jerry. Jerry Feinerman!

"Yeah, Jerry, he's right. It never ends, Jerry. Never, Jerry."

We went on for another minute about how the planet Earth was no place to raise kids, and then I wound through the crowd to find Alyse and Charlie. I nodded at some other Denton Cooleys before winding up face to face with Audra.

It never ends, Jerry.

Tapping away on her cell phone, she said, "Hold on one second."

"Audra, are you allowed to text on the Shabbat?"

Without looking up, she said, "No."

She finished texting and smiled, "Charlie's adorable."

"Thanks, Audra. He's a great kid."

She smiled as if cuing me for my next line.

"Look, Audra, I felt awful about what I said to you yesterday."

"About looks being deceiving."

"Right. I just—Well, let me be honest with you. The looks of my marriage are not deceiving. I just said that because I enjoyed talking to you and you've become so pretty and sophisticated—you were always sophisticated—but, whatever. Somehow something kicked in inside me and gave me the utterly insane impression that we were flirting. I know, it's the most idiotic thing in the world, and later I came up with the idea of the government handing out cards to guys like me officially pronouncing us out of the game. That's how . . . Anyway, I'm sorry and I hope I didn't disillusion you about the possibilities of true love."

Audra smiled, "Nice speech," she said. "But unnecessary. The truth is, I thought we were flirting too. I know *I* was."

"Audra . . ."

"The fact that you love your wife so much was kind of a turn-on. In fact, if instead of saying 'Looks are deceiving,' you had said, 'I'm crazy about my wife,' who knows what kind of fantasies I might have had about you?"

Jesus. Let me repeat: No one, but no one, sticks to the script.

I didn't know what to say, so I just said, "I had no idea you were into age-inappropriate relationships."

"How could you know?"

"Jesus, Audra, you're killing me."

"Well, don't be upset. Actually, at the moment, I'm into culturally inappropriate relationships."

"Culturally inappropriate? You mean you're dating a non-Jew?"

"Non-Jew would be an understatement."

"Audra, you came to my office a bunch of years ago with an apology for your family and I accepted. I hope you'll take my apology and just accept it to so I can live my life in some fucking semblance of peace."

Audra burst out in that killer laugh. "How did I find such an adorable podiatrist?"

"Your father fixed us up."

"Right. And speaking of my father, I better get close to him for the festivities."

"Is he alright?"

"Yeah. Righteous indignation agrees with him."

"Really. Does he know about your inappropriate boyfriend?"

"God, no. That he couldn't handle."

"You know, Audra, that's the second time you've told me about something you didn't think your father could handle, and this is the second time I'm going to tell you he may be stronger than you think. I'm getting the feeling you've always tried to live your own life, but to do it, you've had to be in the protection racket, shielding your father's feelings. And that's not fair to you."

That was the first time I said something that shifted the dynamic between us to where I was the adult and Audra was the kid.

Audra quietly said, "I wish you hadn't said that."

"Why?"

"Because you're right," she said, in a voice that sounded like it came from the future.

Audra looked at me and lifted her chin, her small goodbye, and walked off to the podium set up in front of her father's store. I watched her for a few seconds before setting off to find Alyse and Charlie.

VI.

Now, Commie, you must think I was in agony with having heard Audra say she was flirting with me. But I wasn't. I actually felt great. Knowing a girl like that could be attracted to me was enough. A great flirtation is better than sex. It's a monster ego boost without the mess. When I found Alyse, she was talking to a guy holding a reporter's notebook. He looked more like a better dressed, socially adjusted version of Bernard Goetz. Leather bomber jacket and chinos, mid-forties, but still kind of sallow.

As I got closer, I heard Alyse say, "I'm just not the person to talk to. I'm not religious really and, actually, I don't really even know Mr. Uziel. My husband—"

Right on cue, she glanced around and there I was. Alyse introduced me to Don Graydon, metro reporter for *Newsday*, and said, "I've been telling him I'm not a good interview subject for this story, but maybe you . . ."

Not to brag, but it made total sense the guy focused on Alyse. Graydon wasn't wearing a wedding band and found himself on assignment on a Saturday among people (mostly) dressed in the grave-side fashion of Orthodox Jews. Who would *you* zero in on?

Charlie said, "Dad, you want to be in the newspaper?"

"Only if they say nice things about me."

I shook Graydon's hand and said, "I thought all reporters used digital recorders these days."

"Yeah, they do," Graydon said, holding up his pad, "but my dad was a reporter for the *Times* and, I don't know, I'm just old school."

"No offense, but couldn't you get a job at the *Times*? Maybe as a legacy?"

"I actually worked there for a year and a half. It was a hell hole. The editors pitting everyone against each other. All these illiterate Ivy Leaguers thinking they'd bring down the next president like—"

"Woodward and Bernstein?"

"Yeah."

"Woodward was actually a pretty crappy writer. I was a journalism major at Maryland—"

"Maryland? I went to UVA."

Charlie perked up. "UVA beat Maryland in football this year."

I wound up telling Graydon about the cops interviewing me the night before and how they didn't really know much. Then, like Alyse, I told him I probably wasn't the juiciest interview subject since I wasn't Orthodox.

Graydon said, "Does an anti-Semitic act like this give you pause? Maybe rethink your religious convictions?"

"Look, we don't really know it was an anti-Semitic act. It could just as easily have been some bored, stupid kid getting a cheap thrill. It's not exactly on the level of shooting off mortars from the Gaza Strip. I mean, if you're truly an anti-Semite, couldn't you find a better way to express yourself than by throwing a bottle of horseradish through the window of a kids' clothing store?"

Graydon wrote fast, then said, "But the horseradish has that whole Zionist marketing concept."

With a little suggestive smile, I said, "Well, I'm not totally sold on that either."

"You're a major skeptic. I like that."

All jocular, I asked for his card and said, "Maybe I can help you out on deep background. We can break the case together."

Handing me his card, Graydon said, "Don't count on it. My source in the police department tells me they're close to making an arrest."

Oh shit.

Needless to say, I got less jocular. Reflexively, I looked around. I guess I was checking to see if any cops were scoping me out. I didn't see any, but then: *They wouldn't be uniformed cops. They'd be plainclothes. Detectives. How do you spot them in the middle of four or five hundred people? Wait! With all these Orthodox, it shouldn't be that tough to pick out a cop—*

"What are you looking at?"

It's amazing how you can be standing beside your wife and still go into such a personal panic that you completely forget she's there.

"Nothing really. I was just wondering if the detectives from last night were here."

"I can't believe they already have a suspect," Alyse said, more impressed than you'd expect. "That was fast. "

I nodded and glanced back toward Stratification. The cars parked on the street were the usual array of imports as opposed to the impossibly ugly American cars where you'd expect to see detectives sitting and drinking coffee on a stakeout.

"If they bring the guy here, these people would probably . . . what do they call it in the Mideast or in ancient times when they trot out a crook in front of a big crowd?"

"Stoning."

Another glance to see if there were any suspicious vans outfitted with zoom lenses and nosy audio equipment.

"Right. Stoning."

That's when I said to myself, *Are you nuts? Surveillance and undercover cops for a minor little vandalism case? The cops were probably sitting around laughing at the staff meeting this morning: "Men, put on a good show to make the Jews think we actually give a shit about this case."*

"It's been a while since Long Island had a good stoning."

"What's a stoning?"

Charlie's voice snapped me out of my fugitive head and back to reality.

"Mommy's kidding, Charlie. A stoning is when a mob of people throw rocks at a bad guy. It doesn't happen anymore, only in olden times. Today, the police take care of criminals, you know, like the two detectives we met last night."

"Oh."

Alyse looked up like she'd just remembered something. "Hey, isn't it funny that the cops were named Byron and Shelby? Almost like the poets."

Of course, having gone to Maryland, I never read any poetry. As if subconsciously proving my ignorance, I said, "Did you ever read Byron and Shelby?"

"Shelley. Byron and Shelley. And yes, I read some of their works."

"At Maryland?"

"Yeah. English 430. Junior year."

"Good school, that Maryland."

Charlie chimed in, "I want to go to Maryland!"

Alyse said, "Great. You'll study hard and go to Maryland."

"And we'll visit you."

"Go Terps."

Commie, can you believe how hard it is to get into Maryland now? Esme's friend Harley has a big sister who made Maryland her second choice after *Dartmouth*. She applied to the honors program and, frankly, I didn't know Maryland even had an honors program. Or I thought the honors program was called "the basketball team."

Kids sweat the application process so much these days you'd think they're trying to get onto an organ donor list. Charlie and Esme are younger than our friends' kids because of all the miscarriages, which is fine except for how we're always being told what's going to happen with our kids next. Like their kids are blueprints for ours. Alyse is sick of it too, but what can she say? *We're not worried about college because we intend to force them to join the military?*

"Ladies and Gentlemen, I don't want to take up too much of your time on the Shabbos . . ."

Carl Penza's pronunciation of "Shabbos" was flawless, his long years around Jews put to good use.

"The cowardly act that has brought us here today will not go unpunished, I assure you. We are using all of our resources to find the perpetrator of this senseless vandalism and, when we do, you have my word that we will prosecute the offense as a Class A felony."

People looked around. Class A. That's the worst, right?

I have to tell you, Commie, after a moment's thought, the Class A threat didn't scare me much. If I were caught, I'd fess up and they'd knock it down to a misdemeanor. After all, I'm a first offender. And a podiatrist.

"Good Yontiv."

Nat Uziel's appearance at the podium brought the kind of hush to the crowd that made you think you were about to hear from Mandela.

"In the annals of grievous acts perpetrated upon our people . . ."

Alyse whispered to me, "Ah, he switched it to *grievous*."

". . . the impotent gesture inflicted upon us last night may seem rather benign. But therein lies the danger. No act of prejudice, large or small, can be ignored lest its virulence be allowed to flourish and metastasize. The financial damage to my place of business is trivial, but that won't be the case if we turn the other cheek and simply move past the cultural and spiritual damage we have suffered. I, for one, will not simply turn the other cheek. I will pray to the Almighty that our community will be blessed with justice and peace."

And so much for the rally.

VII.

The crowd dispersed. Alyse, Charlie, and I gave everyone a head start before we walked to our car for the furtive drive home.

Charlie asked, "Do Catholic people have rallies too?"

"Sure." Alyse said, "if they have a good reason to rally."

"Are they the same as Jewish rallies?"

"Pretty much," Alyse said, "except at their rallies, they play Bingo."

That cracked me up. Charlie, prompted by my laugh, got that it was joke and laughed loud enough to make sure we knew he got it.

Laugh, laugh, laugh, laugh, laugh, laugh . . .

. . . and wait for the shit around the next corner.

This particular shit was detectives Byron and Shelby waiting in our driveway.

Yeah. So, after the *Newsday* reporter told us the cops had a suspect and the County Executive promised to prosecute a Class A felony—not to mention the fact that I was guilty of said felony—there were two familiar cops in my driveway. I immediately could feel that the good will from the previous night's coffee had worn off. I could also (almost) feel the Zoloft calling for a Code Red, capping my panic at, *Please don't cuff me in front of my son.*

Oh, and speaking of Zoloft, did I mention that, in my early forties, there was a month or so when I constantly thought I smelled something? No shit. I'd go, "What's that smell?" But no one else smelled anything, so I thought maybe it was the smell of my own body rotting away. Then I read a piece in the paper about how dogs could smell cancer so, for a while, I'd walk up to dogs and let them smell me to see if they got some edgy look on their faces, like, *Get to a hospital, pal.* But the dog reactions were pretty inconclusive.

Sorry. Bad time for a digression. I got two cops on my lawn and, out of left field, I tell you about another of my psychosomatic disorders.

Okay, so, the cops looked grim; I was anxious. For a second, I only remembered the name of one of the cops. Byron. In an effort to seem composed and unthreatening, I thought I'd just say hello to him. But my terror slipped out:

"Good afternoon, *Defective* Byron."

Alyse whipped her head toward me to make sure I wasn't making the most ill-timed joke of all time.

"*Detective* Byron. Sorry. That was a slip of the tongue. Not Freudian in any way."

Detective Byron stamped out a cigarette on the driveway which, I gotta say, was a little offensive. I mean, litter is litter, and this is my fucking home, you know? But, seeing as I was seconds away from having my head pushed down to avoid the roof of the unmarked car, I let it slide.

Big of me, huh, Commie?

"Charlie, you remember the friendly Detectives Byron and Shelby from last night, right?"

"Uh huh," Charlie said. "Did you guys come for more coffee?"

I had a thought that Charlie could be cute in the clutch, then I said, "That's a nice offer, Charlie. But why don't you let Mommy take you in the house while I talk to the detectives, okay kiddo?"

I glanced over at Shelby, the reasonable cop, and hiked my eyebrows into question marks. *You'll give me this one little break, right*?

Shelby didn't object, but he didn't give me any kind of reassuring look either.

Alyse put her hand on Charlie's head and said, "Why don't you use your key and go inside? Daddy and I should talk to the officers together."

Everyone looked down at Charlie and clearly he could sense the sudden tension in the air. He bit his lower lip, his telltale sign of edginess. Actually, I think I do that too. Heredity's some wild shit. Alyse motioned for Charlie to go inside and, after a pronounced swallow, he followed orders.

The door closed behind Charlie and I looked at the cuffs dangling from Detective Byron's belt, and the bulge of his gun under his jacket. Wow, I thought, so this is it. All those times I'd put myself in the position of a perp on *Law & Order*. The arrest, the Miranda reading, the fingerprinting, the DNA swab, the arraignment, the bail, the trial date, the media, the explaining of everything to my soon-to-be ex-wife. It all ticked off in my head with full visuals as if I were imagining my own life going to shit in the same way Steven Spielberg imagines a movie. *Farewell and adieu to you fair Spanish ladies.*

"We came back because we'd like to know why you failed to mention yesterday that you had a known anti-Semite in your home yesterday."

It wasn't about me.

Exhale, then a thought: *They'll never take me alive.*

Okay, honestly? I had that thought maybe twenty minutes later.

Of course, while I reveled in beating the rap, Alyse froze. She knew where this was going but looked lost as to how it got there. Detective Shelby caught her wobbling and said, "Your daughter had dinner at the home of a Gil and Janis Binder last night. During the course of the dinner, Mr. Binder says your daughter mentioned that a man at your home that afternoon had said to her . . ." Shelby checked his notes. "'You buffalo-nosed bagel-biters really know how to make money.' Do you recall that statement?"

I looked at Alyse sympathetically, now having no urge to add to her bad parenting guilt. "Neither of us were present when that statement was made," I said. "Esme told me about it over the phone. Although in her telling, she omitted the term 'buffalo-nosed."

"But by the time of our visit last night, you knew of . . ." another check by Shelby of his notes ". . . Mr. Radmonovic's anti-Semitism."

Alyse and I looked at each other: Radmonovic?

With full-throttled sarcasm, Detective Byron said, "He also goes by the name, You-ey Brushstroke."

Alyse, now marginally recovered from her initial shock, said, "Look, Mr. Brushstroke is a client of mine. He's an artist and, yes, he was here yesterday and, yes, we did later learn that he'd made that comment to our daughter, Esme. But, to be perfectly honest, neither of us ever made the slightest connection between his slur and what happened at the store. Maybe we should have, but I talk to Mr. Brushstroke all the time and I've never picked up any hint of his being prone to violence or rage or whatever it would take to have done what you suspect him of. Plus, in all honesty, he may have smoked a little pot on his way over here because he was really mellow. And hungry."

Again, the detectives gave no ground. Byron turned to me and said, "While you were in the taxicab last night, did you witness a man standing on the hood of a car removing a street sign reading 'Stratification Boulevard?'"

"No."

"Really?"

"Really, I didn't see anything like that."

"We find that odd since your cab driver says he not only saw that happening but insisted that he pointed it out to you."

Commie, remember when I told you to remember that the cab driver said, "What's this maniac doing?"

There you go.

"Detective Byron, I do remember him saying that, but at the time my ankle was throbbing and I was looking for a sheet of paper to write out directions to the highway for the driver. So I never saw what he was referring to. I'm sorry."

"And you didn't think to ask?"

Again, not an inch. In fact, he was talking to me like I was an idiot, so I got a little ticked off. "Detective, are you accusing my wife and I of somehow aiding and abetting in a hate crime against a religion to which we both belong?"

The grammatical structure of my question definitely gave off a whiff of condescension and I didn't care if it was obvious. For the first time in dealing with these cops, I was actually telling the truth.

Finally, Shelby eased off some. "Sir, there's no need to get indignant. We just find it odd that your child experienced an anti-Semitic slur in your home and yet you made no connection to an anti-Semitic act perpetrated shortly thereafter just two miles away."

Alyse said, "I guess we concentrated all of our focus on the impact the comment had on our daughter."

Shelby nodded, seeing the sense in what Alyse had said, but Byron cut right in, "Were you aware of the suspect's criminal record in the state of Rhode Island?"

Alyse nodded her "*It never ends*" look at me, so I said, "Are you going to arrest Mr. Brushstroke?"

"He's in the custody of Brooklyn NYPD and is on the way here as we speak."

Wow! I commit a felony and they not only arrest the wrong guy, but he happens to be a client of my wife to boot. That's as far as my thoughts ran at that moment. Really, the whole emerging moral dilemma didn't sink in for a few hours. For the time being, my instinct was to subtly poke holes in their case.

"So, you must have an eyewitness, huh?"

Shelby slumped a bit. "Someone who saw him throw the bottle through the window? No. We have no eyewitness." Then he smiled. "But we do have a woman who claimed the bottle of horseradish."

"What?"

"An elderly woman claimed that her grocery bag broke while she was getting to her car on that grassy strip across from the store. When she got home, she realized she hadn't picked up the horseradish."

Alyse tried to pick up on the humor of the moment, saying, "That should make for a real Perry Mason moment in court."

Shelby laughed and said, "Yeah, I bet."

Unfortunately, Alyse's effort to lighten the mood didn't have much staying power. Byron snapped the moment by adding, "The suspect was seen removing the street sign within a few blocks of the vandalism just over twelve minutes later. NYPD found the sign in his home when they arrested him. We have the anti-Semitic remark he made to your daughter and the other one he made to the NYPD when they cuffed him."

Alyse said, "The other one?" and cringed as Shelby rifled through his notepad.

"Oh, here we go. After being read his rights, Mr. Brushstroke said, 'I didn't do nothing. They're all Jews out there. It's another conspiracy. Just like the Holocaust.'"

"Oh God," came flying out of Alyse's mouth. "I can't believe I let that man in our home."

Right on cue, Charlie poked his head out of his bedroom window. "Mom? Dad? Are you coming in soon?"

Alyse turned around and said, "One minute, honey." While her back was turned, I caught Detective Byron eyeing her behind. This time, however, it wasn't a passing gaze like the night before with her midriff. Now I felt like he was leering. Then, as if to confirm my suspicion, he looked at me all snide, like, *Yeah, I'm checking out at your wife's ass. Problem*?

Alyse turned around. "Is it okay if we go inside now?"

Without taking his eyes off me, Byron said, "Yes. We're done here. For now."

Alyse said, "Thank you. Sorry we didn't make the connection last night."

Again, without turning, Byron said, "Forget it."

Alyse took my hand and started leading me back into the house. I hate to say I could feel Byron's eyes still on me, but I could feel his eyes still on me, so, as we got to the door, I turned to Byron and said, "Your case against this guy sounds pretty damn thin."

Byron stiffened in a way Shelby must have seen a hundred times before because he took his arm and said, "Let's go, partner."

VIII.

We got inside, closed the door, and Alyse looked at me like I was whacked. "Why did you say that? You totally antagonized the guy. He looked like he wanted to beat the crap out of you."

"Alyse, I said it because, when you turned to tell Charlie we'd be inside in a minute, *Defective* Byron made an incredibly obvious point of checking out your tush."

My wife dropped her shoulders about three feet.

"Alyse, he blatantly stared at it, then blatantly looked at me to make sure I knew he was blatantly staring at it."

"So what? Let him look at my ass! That's what it's there for. That's why I shlep that stupid yoga mat into town four times a week."

"Alyse, what he was doing had nothing to do with you. Not directly. It was all about intimidating me. I mean, first, he hints that we're covering for a rabidly anti-Semitic criminal, and then he tries to let me know he could rape my wife and get away with it anytime he wants? Fuck him."

"Rape?" Alyse whispered. "How did we get to rape?"

"Okay, I may have extrapolated a bit there. But still, I wanted to let him know I wasn't scared of him, so the best way of doing that seemed to be by highlighting his own lame-o incompetence. Bam! Hit him right where he lives."

"Honey, I think I'm going to have to lock you in a room for a week or so."

"I'd find a way out. Besides, we have dinner plans tonight."

"Oh, right. I'll try to remember to wear loose-fitting pants."

"Wear whatever you want, honey. I got your back."

You know, the first time Alyse met my parents, she was wearing a cowl neck sweater. We met at The Silver Star on 65th Street. First thing my mother says is, "Boy, that's some sweater." Alyse says, "It's a cowl neck." So my mother pulls from her pocketbook a notepad stolen from Brown's Hotel in the Catskills and jots down, *cowl neck*. A few days later, my mother got a package with a kelly green cowl neck sweater and a note saying, "Thought you'd look stunning in this. Love, Alyse."

My mother, bewildered by the concept of a gift for no occasion, said to me, "Should I accept the sweater?" After begging her to accept it, she looked around to make sure no one was listening and whispered, "This Alyse is a very refined girl."

It was as if she expected my girlfriend to be more along the lines of Squeaky Fromme.

I mentioned my family's underdog mentality, right? It was a full year later before I let Alyse see the apartment where I grew up.

Oh man, Commie, it's after two in the morning already. You probably need a break. I have one dopey seminar at ten tomorrow morning, and then I'll pick up the story where we left off.

Right, where *I* left off.

Jesus, Commie, when did you start grooming fleas?

SATURDAY NOW

I.

I know, Commie—I'm early.

Get this: A podiatrist named Richie Waddle—yes, a podiatrist named Waddle—was scheduled to give a seminar this morning entitled, "Interpretations of Jurisdictional Conflict in Foot Care." Put in plain English, it was a talk on who should treat what—podiatrists or orthopedists. I'd met Richie a bunch of other times. He's a nice enough guy from Philly who went to BU and then podiatry school in St. Louis. For at least four previous conferences, he'd submitted proposals for seminars, and this was the first time one of his ideas was accepted. In the last few months, he'd taken classes in public speaking and even hired a private voice coach. He called me twice to make sure I was coming. For the trip down here from Philly, he rented a Navigator so he could bring along his wife, his mother, *and* his four daughters. He has cousins in Chapel Hill which, as you know, is a haul from here, but he begged them to come also. On top of that, after reviewing the work of every videographer in Charleston, he hired a guy to tape the seminar. And he bought an Armani suit from Barney's. You'd think he was hosting the fucking Grammys.

In gratitude for their attendance/indulgence, Richie took his entourage to dinner at a steak joint, I forget which. Is there a Chart House here? Anyway, Richie sprung for a massive meal, then returned to the hotel, where he'd reserved a conference room so he could practice his presentation one last time before the big event.

I should say that the details I've got of what happened in the conference room are a little sketchy because they're totally based on a conversation another podiatrist overheard between Richie's wife and the EMT, who chauffeured Richie off for a thorazine night cap.

Apparently, in the corner of the conference room to one side of the podium where Richie was practicing his speech, there was a paper shredder with a blinking light. Richie kept angling his body to try not to look at the shredder. But, you know how once you tell yourself to not look at something, you can't not look? According to what was overheard, as the EMT was strapping him down, Richie kept saying, "The shredder was flirting with me."

Yes, that's what he said. The shredder was flirting with him.

I guess it was a pretty comely shredder because Richie took his entire speech, which was around twenty-five pages and, six sheets at a time . . .

When he was done, he started wailing like a dinosaur. A nervous breakdown always seemed to me to be more of a personal option than a disease, but this story has me rethinking that. Someone from Housekeeping passed by and called 911.

The world is too fucking sad.

Just the goddamn breakability between who you are and the wreck you can be. It's too much. I mean, I consider myself to be as sane as anyone can be. Maybe even too sane, too controlled. But I still relate to people who snap and shoot the guy who's tailgating them on the LIE. Is my grip on the social contract really so strong that I'll never lose it like that? I honestly don't know. My whole respectable, decent, low-impact, relaxed-fit, gluten-free world sometimes feels so shaky. I could be in the checkout line at Whole Foods behind any woman and have this thought force its way into my head: *All I have to do is move my arm a few inches forward to fondle this woman, and then my whole life collapses. That's how easy it is to undo everything.*

Sometimes I have to shudder or bite my hand just to push the compulsion back into its cave. I guess Richie couldn't push hard enough. When I think of the aftermath of this for him . . .

Should I go to the hospital to visit him? That's probably the last thing he'd want.

Maybe I'll send something.

Or leave a message on his cell.

The soap at the hotel is incredible. I took about five bars off the chambermaid's cart.

Anyway, I should get back into the story, if only to get my mind off Richie Waddle.

That afternoon was kind of an emotional stock market graph. That was actually the afternoon that Alyse called me a fucking idiot. Remember I told you about that? Whatever. I had to come down off my little conflict with the detectives. For a while, my parental responsibility head kicked in, so I played ping-pong with Charlie in the basement just to reassure him that nothing serious had happened with the cops. And I thought it was working until he asked me why it took so long for the conversation in the driveway to end. I gave him some Mayberry version of how the police operate and how sometimes they need our help as much as we need theirs and they're just doing their jobs as well as they can, ba-da-ba-da-ba-da.

Charlie seemed to accept it, but I guess I felt like he accepted it too easily, so I added, "Like anyone else, Charlie, there are really smart policemen and some that are less smart. Of the two you met, the short one with the mustache, Detective Byron, between you and me, kiddo? He's not that smart. I had to tell him a few things he should do if he had any hope of solving the case. The other guy, Shelby, he's quieter and does less talking and more listening. That's how you can tell he's smart. Really listening to what people say is something smart people do."

Charlie nodded fast like he'd been freed up to say something he'd been holding in. "Last night, I was thinking that I liked Detective Shelby more than Detective Byron."

"Why is that?"

"Detective Byron kept looking at Mom in a weird way."

How about that, Commie? My kid was onto the horny pig just like I was. On the other hand . . .

If I hadn't thrown a bottle through a window, I wouldn't have had this weird state of mind telling me to take my kid to a rally because there never would have been a rally and we would have just hung around the house and Charlie wouldn't have this haunting imprint in his little head.

I told Charlie not to worry about it, that cops are trained to observe people, and they wind up staring in ways different than normal people do.

Jesus. It was exhausting coming up with plausible ad-libs just to give Charlie the false illusion that adults aren't so vile.

Charlie picked up his ping-pong paddle and said, "The score's 11-8, I'm up. Your serve."

Apparently, my crap worked. After all, Charlie not only wanted to get back to ping-pong, but he cheated on the score. He was only up 10-8. One of the guys in my Thursday night hoops game constantly fudges the score by a point and he's one of my favorite guys in the group, so I decided: *Let the kid cheat.* He wants to win.

My body played a bunch of points while my head thought again about all these lies I was telling everyone. The amount of explaining I'd have to do if I was ever caught just kept growing and growing. Then my thoughts made their first turn to You-ey. *He's innocent and in custody. I'm guilty and playing ping-pong.* As my hand kept mechanically guiding the paddle toward the ball, I cooked up a stopgap rationalization, just something to hold me a while: *Let the fucking Holocaust denier rot in jail.*

Charlie put away the game-winning point with his rubbery-armed forehand, and I shifted right into off-the-meter enthusiasm. "Great shot, Charlissimo!"

Charlie did his hysterical impression of an NFL wide-receiver celebrating in the end zone. Then I told him I had to go to the bathroom and he says, "Mention my name. You'll get a good seat!"

That's a line my mother recently started saying to the kids. Where the hell did she come up with that?

On my way to the bathroom, I poked my head in on Alyse. She was working on her website. I was about to tell her Charlie seemed fine, and ask her if she had any theories on why Esme left out the words "buffalo-nosed" when telling me what You-ey said. But my eyes drifted to Alyse's neck and to the tufts of hair that escaped her sloppy bun, pulled up inside a purple scrunchy. I just gazed at that little spot on her neck, kind of amazed there could still be such aesthetic miracles for me to catch for the first time. I guess another fascination was that, zoomed in on the one spot, I could have been looking at a fifty-year-old woman or a sixteen-year-old girl.

I went with the sixteen-year-old girl because, I think, I always felt a little cheated by not knowing Alyse for the first nineteen years of her life.

II.

Oh, shit. Sorry, Commie.

"Hello? Oh, hi, Phil. What's up?'

"Oh. How is he?"

"Oy gevalt."

"There's nothing you can do."

"Actually, I'm visiting a friend at a different hospital. Well, it's not really a . . ."

"No."

"No."

"Okay Phil, I'll catch up with you later. Thanks for the update."

The great thing about not having a wife and kids would be the freedom to turn off my phone without feeling like a goddamn fugitive. Jesus, I remember when people started getting car phones. I used to say I'd never get one. Then I got one and said I would never walk around with a phone on my person. Now I'm tied to this fucking thing like you are to your colostomy bag.

Maybe a tad harsh on that analogy.

That was Phil Burton, a podiatrist from New Haven, an asshole I've met a bunch of times. He went to the hospital to see Richie Waddle, who is apparently delivering his seminar in an ICU psych ward without needing any notes.

Can you tell me why the fuck this Burton guy felt it necessary to call and tell me that? People love spreading bad news. I remember when Boris Yeltsin died. One of my patients blathered to me, "Did you hear Boris Yeltsin died?"

I said, "Yeah, I heard," and the guy actually looked disappointed.

Anyway, my mind-blown gaze at the back of Alyse's neck sent me to the bathroom with swirling thoughts.

Or, more accurately, it sent me to *my* bathroom.

For our twentieth anniversary, I had called Bennie Liotta, the contractor I mentioned before, and had him add on a separate bathroom for Alyse. It seemed like a great gift to her but, if I'm being honest with myself, it was a gift for me. I was reaching the point in life where my digestive system was starting to invent a whole new set of sounds and smells and, of course, I didn't want Alyse to know I had the same repertoire of disgusting bodily functions as everyone else on Earth. So, a few months of construction, and I was happily quarantined in the old bathroom, a safe distance from Alyse's brand new headquarters.

Again, my thoughts clicked off all I had to lose. All I had to do to ruin my life was follow the path my lifelong instincts would dictate: namely, wipe my ass, wash my hands, go to the police, confess my crime, and accept the life-toppling consequences. I could almost feel myself doing it, steeling my nerves, overriding my panic, and accepting my compulsion to be good. After all, how hard is it to do the right thing?

But then a weird, new feeling surfaced in me. You ever hear those stories about some guy who gets shot in the head and all the bullet does is change his behavior? In fact, I think I read about some kid who had that OCD thing, where he washed his hands ninety times a day, and then, when he finally couldn't take it anymore, he put a gun to his head, pulled the trigger, and woke up with his whole world intact minus the OCD. Wild, huh? Anyhow, without the hassle of putting a bullet in my head, the human instinct of resentment resurfaced in me.

Suddenly, I'm sitting there staring down at the Turkish Kilim throw rug on the blue and green tile floor: *Fuck it. I'm not throwing over my life for this. So I chucked a bottle through a plate glass window and someone else got blamed for it. The someone else is a rabidly anti-Semitic Holocaust denier. Let him have his karma shoved up his ass. What do I care?*

See? When it's convenient, I can really get into being Jewish. Another funny thing is, you don't tend to feel as bad about screwing over some Eastern European as you would if he was black or Latino or Asian or even Arab. At least no one can accuse you of being racist. Those Slavs and Serbs provide a big service. They supply everyone else a guilt-free victim.

The phone rang while I was on the toilet which, for some reason, I find incredibly invasive, exacerbated by Alyse letting it ring three times before grabbing the phone two inches away from her. I heard the words, "Oh my God," and turned the water on in the sink.

My definition of "a moment's peace" gets narrower and narrower.

Anyway, the second I got out of the bathroom, Alyse appeared to tell me that Meri Katzen had called.

"What couldn't wait for dinner tonight?"

"She had some news."

"Of course she did."

"Word got out about You-ey, and a bunch of Orthodox were waiting at the police station for the cops to take him in. When they pulled him out of the police car, they started chanting 'Never Again! Never Again!'"

"Oh my God. It was *one store window*—that's it!"

"Apparently, someone threw a bottle of horseradish at You-ey."

"Mossad?"

"Stop grooming fleas. I didn't ask the brand."

"Did they arrest the guy—or woman—who threw it?"

"They took someone into custody for like ten minutes."

"I'm sure the synagogue will deal with the perpetrator in its own way. Throwing things on Shabbat has to be some kind of infraction, don't you think?"

That's when a look came over Alyse that I'd hardly ever seen. Her left eyelid shuddered on its own, her facial muscles ticked to atrophied places. Her complete control over her world was wobbling for the first time in forty years.

On the other hand, I felt calmer than I could remember. Flat and fluid, I asked, "What's wrong, hon?"

"I don't know. You find all this funny, but I'm a little freaked. All this stuff is happening; cops, arrests, riots."

"Riots? Alyse, I don't know what Reuters said, but it doesn't sound like what happened at the police station was a riot."

"If a bunch of people get together and chant and throw things, then it's a riot."

"Come on, Alyse. Rodney King was a riot. This is . . . it's nothing."

"It's *not* nothing. It might be nothing if we weren't involved, but we are. We're part of this, this incident, whatever, and it feels like it's getting bigger and bigger and closer and closer."

"You're really taking this too personally."

"I can't help it! I got off the phone with Meri, and it all just came rushing down on me. Cops are showing up at our house, questioning us, making accusations, scaring Charlie. Esme hears her first anti-Semitic slur. The slur comes out of the mouth of my client, who makes everyone in this whole quiet town suddenly out for blood. These things start swirling around and, I'm telling you, this is how innocent people get . . ."

Without a wisp of concern in my voice, I said, "What? Get what? Put in jail and finally exonerated eighteen years later because of DNA evidence? No, Alyse, it's not going to happen to us. This isn't Mississippi in the '50s. We're not going to wind up in 'To Kill a Kosher Mockingbird.' We live in Long Island, where people like us run things. This is nothing, and it'll all fade away before you know it. Just take it easy."

At this point, Alyse lost it. I mean, she went into uranium-enriched yelling: "I don't want to *take it easy*! I want all this to stop! I don't like what the fuck's going on! Since you got home Friday night, the whole world has flipped over. You, the one who was getting panic attacks from the sight of the Grand Central Parkway, are suddenly Mr. Calm when there's a real reason to panic. Is this the new you? Your middle-aged Zoloft phase where nothing bothers you anymore? Well, I'm sorry. It's a little late for you to be test-driving new personalities, and I don't want any part of them. I'm scared shitless about everything's that's going on, and it's sure as hell not helping me to know that I'm totally alone now."

Alyse started crying in a spastically pained way I'd never seen before. Alyse doesn't cry much, and so it was doubly affecting. Seeing her so, I don't know, pathetic . . . right then and there, I switched gears and confessed to Alyse that I threw the bottle through the window.

III.

Jesus, Commie. Can I at least get a lifted eyebrow on that twist of the story?

If you would just raise your eyebrow out of some tiny nod to our presence on this Earth and how surprises keep happening even when your life is built around the concept of "the same old shit," then I'd be more willing to tell you the truth: I did not tell Alyse that I threw the bottle.

I told you I never told this story to anyone right from the get-go and I haven't. I don't even know why I told you I told Alyse the truth. Maybe just to throw in a left turn that would blow the whole story for you and make you wake up and tell me to get the fuck out of your hospital room. Or maybe, in my own head, that moment of Alyse, crying in my arm, was the one moment when I could have or should have shared this secret with her instead of just shlepping it around with me all alone for the rest of my life.

So, I repeat, Commie: I did not tell Alyse I threw the bottle. You still have the exclusive.

Instead, I just told her to cry. "It's okay. Go ahead and cry. Let it out. Just keep on crying. It's okay, it's okay, it's okay, it's okay."

It's rare that my first instincts are correct, but that was an inspired choice. Alyse hugged me in a way more desperate than I could have ever imagined, her head in my chest, her hands flush on my back, frothing tears.

I tightened my grip to assure her I wasn't the emotionally flatlined zombie she accused me of being. In a weird way, the biggest emotion I was feeling at that moment was—well, I felt kind of good. Remember, I told you how great it's been to know this secret that no one else knows? How it makes me feel vaguely above it all? Holding her like that was the first time I really felt it. The poised superiority of *knowing*.

When we finally let each other go, Alyse seemed a little embarrassed by her, what? Outburst? And who could blame her? It wasn't a role she was used to playing. With little pleats in her face I'd never noticed before, she apologized and said that she didn't "mean what I said about the middle-aged Zoloft phase." I, of course, told her it wasn't necessary to apologize and then I apologized "if I sounded flip about your feelings." And she said, "Flip? You even have a new vocabulary." And I said, "Alyse, I'm not—"

She cut me off, saying, "I'm kidding. You've said 'flip' before, and even if you haven't, I'm just a little hyper-everything right now, and I think I'll take a bath." I told her to take her time. She smiled and, as she walked to her bathroom, she said over her shoulder, "We should have lived in Louisville."

You wouldn't get the Louisville reference but, you know what? I'm gonna get back to the Louisville thing a little later. Let me just take a second here to talk about Alyse crying. It seems to me, and this is something I've noticed for a long time, that ninety-nine percent of the time an adult cries, it's all about time gone by. You're crying because you miss those days when the deceased relative was hale and hearty and filling out his or her airspace on this planet. Maybe you wish you'd appreciated them more. I hug my kids sometimes, stop and look at them, and try to feel the moment, try to appreciate the greatness of that one totally ordinary second and, I gotta say, I never feel what I think I should feel. I mean, smelling the roses or sharing a perfect sunset with the ones you love just never gets me where I want to go or where I think I ought to be going. If you told me I had a week to live, I wouldn't have the first clue what to do. Maybe I'd just want to die sooner so I wouldn't have to torture myself over wasting the last week of my life.

Anyway, what I wanted to say was, Alyse was not crying over a long lost past. She was crying about the present, which I found really refreshing. You know, she's just really alive. That's one of the big things I love about her.

IV.

Oh. I almost forgot to mention something. While taking my dump, I had a thought: *How fast would you have to throw a bottle of horseradish for it to shatter a glass like the one at Nu? Girl Fashions?* If you remember from intra-frat softball, I had a fairly strong arm. Not overly accurate—my throws home from center field tended to tail up the third baseline—but I could zing it. So even if my arm was only seventy-five percent of what it was thirty years ago, I could still put some mustard on a throw. And—and!—let's assume some of the speed I've lost on my throws was made up for by the adrenaline rush I felt as I threw the horseradish. My point is, I figured I must have whipped that bottle at least sixty miles an hour.

Well, it turns out, it's altogether possible I threw the bottle in the low seventies. After Alyse's meltdown and bath, she took a nap—which she's really good at—while I dropped Charlie off at Ari Weprin's house. So, instead of coming straight home, I decided to take a drive. I went south, then west, then north to avoid the yarmulkes, and stopped at a batting cage called "Blew By You Baseball." Without a thought, I had ended up driving fourteen miles to get to a place maybe three miles from the house. The batting cage is a pretty amazing facility where kids can work on their skills all year round with private instructors. Then again, what the fuck *don't* kids have private instructors for these days?

I went there and talked to guy who runs the place, a weathered chunk of humanity named Pete Preston.

"What can I do for you, sir?"

Not wanting to arouse any suspicion, I went into another boring story.

"I was watching some old baseball game on the Classic Sports Channel and I felt this weird nostalgia for baseball. I played as a kid and I wasn't Reggie or Catfish Hunter, but I wasn't bad. So anyway, I've had this hankering just to hit and throw a few pitches."

"Just so you can tell yourself that you played baseball again after the age of sixteen?"

"Something like that."

"Don't feel weird. I get lots of guys in here like you."

Wow, I thought, *my ability to come up with good lies is starting to seem like a hidden talent.*

The place was fairly empty—just four or five kids getting hitting instructions from their coaches. Every kid had the exact same stance and swing. They teach the kids to hardly stride at all nowadays. With my ankle throbbing, I didn't do much striding either.

I got in the batter's box and hit against one of those pitching machines. I'll just tell you that if you ever thought you could get a hit in a hundred at-bats in the Major Leagues, I assure you, you couldn't.

"Don't feel bad, sir. You actually made more contact than most guys your age."

Then I pitched. I threw easy for a while, coming down lightly on my bum leg. The pain was manageable, so I picked it up, putting more heat on my pitches. The target was a tarp hanging off the back of a cage with a taped strike zone. At my request, Preston clocked my pitches with a radar gun. About ten minutes in, I rocked back and let loose with one that really went *thwap!* against the tarp. Caught the outside corner too, I might add.

"Whoa!" Preston said, looking down at his gun. "Sir, you hit eighty with that one."

Of course, my first thought was: *Really? I figured that one was at least 95.*

Preston said, "Eighty is awesome. Most guys top out somewhere around sixty- five."

I shrugged and said, "You don't even get pulled over for that."

Preston squeezed out a *Yeah, like I've never heard that joke before* smile. But I was happy for that reaction. I didn't want to stand out in this guy's my mind. Otherwise, I could just see the court scene: "The defendant came to my batting range and insisted on my using a radar gun to clock how fast he could throw. So, yes, I did have a sense that, in the days prior, he had thrown a small bottle through a rich Jew's window."

Commie, I assume you've gleaned where I'm going with all this.

Jesus, do I have to spell it out for you?

You-ey Brushstroke is Eastern European. He's probably never played baseball in his life and, hence, probably throws like a girl. If I could find out the minimum speed it would take to heave a bottle through that window, I could prove that he couldn't do it, and then he'd be off the hook. That dick cop would have to start all over.

Yes, Commie, I realize it was a little dicey of me to put out any effort toward exonerating You-ey. I thought about that too. I came up with a way of doing it on the sly. If I found exculpatory evidence, I would leak it to Don Graydon at *Newsday*, off the record on deep background. A privileged source! Nothing could come back to me.

Yeah, I know. But that's what I thought as I left the batting range. That and, *Jesus, my arm is killing me*. Then, *Jesus, my ankle is killing me*.

Commie, I'm aging at a breakneck pace.

Before heading home, I stopped at my health club, where I sat by the side of the hot tub with an ice pack so I could ice my ankle before dunking it into the scalding water. Over and over. That's the way they treat these things now. Hot, cold, hot, cold, hot, cold. They also use ultra-sound. I have one in my office, but I wasn't about to go there to treat myself. I mean, I'm middle-aged. It's not like I have to get myself ready for a fucking NCAA Tournament.

The health club locker room is pretty peaceful on Saturday afternoon anyway. Guys draped in towels, sitting in the steam room, or the Jacuzzi, mindlessly gazing at the toll the week took on their bodies before weighing themselves, shaking their heads and scouring the room to see if everyone else is decaying at the same pace. A bald guy used to sit on a chaise lounge right at the nexus of the Jacuzzi, the steam room, and the showers, and somewhat discreetly watch naked bodies walk by. I figured he was gay but, really, I didn't give a shit. Of course, not everyone at the gym agreed. After a few complaints, the guy was given a warning by management and I haven't seen him since. The one time I'd caught him checking me out, my only reaction was to wonder, *If a gay guy finds you attractive, should you be flattered*? I brought it up with Alyse and she said, "Why not? They're shopping the same aisle as straight women."

I grabbed another bag of ice and plopped down in the empty steam room, spreading out on the tiled ledge along the back. The image of a crying Alyse bubbled up in my head and, Commie, I had the weirdest thought: *Other than the miscarriages, this is the only time I've ever seen her unflappable nature broken.* I know that may not seem like such a weird thought to you, but it was for me. I don't usually analyze things on such a basic level. And, if I do, it usually comes weeks or months or even years after the event. And, after that thought about Alyse, my head went even more basic: *What does Alyse want out of life?*

Don't you think that's a pretty incredible thing, to actually contemplate what your most intimate partner in life truly wants from this world? It's really mind-blowing. For the first time in twenty-something years of marriage, I was actually really considering what my wife wants. Of course, I got so caught up in the wonder of actually asking myself the question that I didn't even get around to trying to figure out the answer. The closest I came was allowing myself to think: *Wouldn't it be amazing if the main thing she wants is me?*

V.

Then the door to the steam room flew open. Usually, I hate when guys have conversations in there, the tiled acoustics pumping up their voices to a million decibels. But I'd had enough deep thoughts for one steam and, as it happened, two guys entered in mid-conversation about "the vandalism on Stratification Boulevard." They sat up front, a blinding blanket of steam standing between them and me.

"With my wife being a shiksa, I felt like I had to seem concerned, you know, just to keep the home fires burning. But I'm not so sure it was anti-Semitism."

"Well, the fact that it was a bottle of horseradish . . ."

"So what? Everyone eats horseradish. Mormons probably eat it."

"But it was that Mossad shit."

"Still, that's a long way from spray-painting swastikas."

"But the guy they busted for it—"

"See, even that sounds fishy to me. He comes here all the way from Brooklyn for the first time in his life just to smash a window and go home?"

"Yeah but, A) He also stole some street signs and B) The guy whose window he smashed is a big deal in Jewish circles."

"Whatever that means."

"How did you know it was the suspect's first time here?"

"Jennifer's brother's a cop. So I'm not totally talking out of my ass like I usually do."

The two guys burst out in laughs that sounded like they were break-dancing off the walls, and the tumult went straight through my eardrums. Still, fairly certain they didn't know I was even in there, I didn't make a sound.

"So this cop, he doesn't think they got the right guy?"

"He's uh, well, between you and me, he's got his doubts."

Commie, you won't believe what I decided to do next. I'm somewhere between a limp piece of spaghetti and a prune by the time the two guys leave the steam room, but then I barely wait a minute before flying out of there to try to find them. I grab a shower stall across from the two they're in—mind you, they're still talking throughout their showers—and then I follow them to their lockers. I should explain: When you get to the locker room, you hand the attendant your membership card and he puts it in a cubbyhole with a number on it. Then he takes a key from the same cubbyhole and gives it to you. From the voices, I figured out which of the guys was the one with the brother-in-law who's a cop, and so I nonchalantly checked out his locker number, went to the attendant, asked him to get me a few band-aids from the back, went around the counter, found the number of the cubbyhole, grabbed the guy's card, looked at the name, reached up to put the card back in its cubbyhole—

"What the fuck are you doing?"

The attendant was lanky, maybe 19, kind of white trash-y. He held the box of band-aids in front of him like a Glock. Maybe because I'd just been playing baseball, my first thought was: *Kid looks like Randy Johnson.* I don't know if you remember, but looking like Randy Johnson without actually being Randy Johnson is not a good thing.

"Are you stealing ID's? I'm getting the manager. He's gonna kick your ass out of this club so fast. He'll probably call the cops as well . . ."

Kids don't say "too" anymore. They say "as well." Like, for this one tiny tic of the English language, I'm going to sound really British. "So I hooked up with that skank ho . . . *as well.*"

The fear of being busted finally rushed through me and I went out of body again, hearing myself say, "Look, I'm sorry. It's not what you think."

The kid just looked at me, the band-aid box still trained on my chest.

"I've been a member here for a long time. You've probably seen me around. I saw a guy, another member, who I've seen a million times and I couldn't remember his name. It was driving me crazy. Believe me, when you hit my age, you'll understand how nuts your lame memory can make you. Anyhow, I happened to know about what locker he was at and I just was so fixated on getting his name, and I was standing here waiting . . . So, I did what I did. It was a totally uncool thing to do, but it was innocent. I mean, really, I have my own ID, so what reason would I have to steal someone else's?"

The kid slackened, pondering my question.

"Actually, forget I asked that question. Your job is to protect the members and their property so you shouldn't have to figure out my motives. The truth is, you're right. I deserve to be busted. But I'm telling you the truth and I'm asking you to give me a break this one time. I'm sorry. I guess I'm just a little . . . brain-damaged."

The kid almost smiled, handed me two band-aids, and grunted, "It's cool. Forget it. But don't do it again."

You know those old over-told stories about adrenaline allowing mothers to lift cars to save their kids? I think, for me, adrenaline just turns me into a really good liar.

Anyway, can you believe I did that? Sneaking around and grabbing the ID? It was like *All The President's Men,* when Bernstein got rid of the secretary to barge into the office of that guy in Florida who had all the Committee to Reelect checks written to the Watergate burglars. Only Bernstein was taking down the President of the United States and I was trying to exonerate a two-bit Jew-hater.

You know, I'm starting to feel a tiny bit guilty about the number of "Jew" references I'm throwing at you. It's like, whenever I want to say something funny to you, I throw in the word "Jew." I should stop doing that. It's the same as in college when anyone could get a laugh just by saying the word JAP. *Hey, great idea for a TV show: Jappy Days.* It's just . . . it's cheap is what it is. And, for what it's worth, it *is* our religion. Besides, you're not laughing. So, what's the point?

Maybe in lieu of laughing, you're wondering what I planned to do with the guy's name. Which, by the way, was Greg Pompian. Or maybe you already knew that.

I went into the gym's "quiet room" and Googled the living crap out of Greg Pompian on my BlackBerry. Like most people you Google, his most cyber-worthy achievement was finishing third in a 5K race, followed by a tiny wedding announcement from *Newsday*, October 16th, 1988.

Jennifer McNeill and Greg Pompian were married October 16 at Temple Israel of Tenafly. She is an accountant for Blitz Advertising Inc. of Sands Point and is the daughter of Jack and Eileen McNeill of Summit. The bridegroom is the chief financial officer of Amherst Corp. in New York and is the son of Herbert Pompian of Littleneck and Denise Kramer of Boca Raton, Fla.

Another search turned up Detective Chris McNeill, also gracing the pages of *Newsday*, curtly commenting on the raid of a photography supply facility that, in lieu of matte paper and stop bath, housed just over 12,000 marijuana plants. "We've watched the place a long time. That's all I'll say."

The Internet is totally amazing, but if I were a reporter today, I think I'd feel like it's cheating. Twenty-five years ago, this information would have taken some real digging. Now, it's all just there, waiting to be found. It takes a lot of the fun out of it.

On the other hand, if you're an investigative journalist with a podiatry practice, a family, and maybe three free hours a week, it's pretty great.

I took Don Graydon's card out of my wallet and emailed him. In the subject box, I wrote: "Deep background from Deep Throat." Underneath: "Nassau P.D. Detective Chris McNeill has serious doubts about the guilt of their chief suspect."

Upon hitting "send," I was now taking an active role in trying to clear You-ey. But I convinced myself that Graydon would assume I was a bored family man getting off on playing journalist. That was certainly more reasonable than his assuming I was a bored family man who committed the crime myself.

Chris McNeill. Wasn't that the name of the character in *The Ex-*

orcist?

Whatever.

As I put the phone in my pocket, it rang loudly, knocking another three days off my life. Did I mention that my ring tone is the beginning of *The Perry Mason* theme? You're supposed to turn your phone off in the quiet room, and a guy lying there with a towel over his head jolted up like Raymond Burr had hit him over the head. He peeked out, rolled his eyes at me, and then burrowed back under his towel. I guess he thought I was an asshole, but what can you do?

"Honey, where are you?"

Quietly, I said, "Just leaving the gym. Ankle rehab."

"Oh. Long rehab session."

"Yeah. You feeling better?"

"Uh huh. I don't know what happened. I'm so sorry. I'm just sick that I said what I said. I know your panic attacks were a purely physical thing, and for me to make a snide comment like that about it was just horrible. I can't believe I did that."

"Alyse, you're entitled to lose it on occasion."

"Yeah, well, I don't like cracks in my armor."

"You can cover them with a scarf before we go to dinner tonight."

"That's a good idea." Then, "Oh, and by the way, I heard there was another chant by the mob waiting outside the police station when they brought You-ey in."

"What?"

"They were chanting, 'No Justice, No Shalom!"

"You're joking."

"Yes. I'm joking. I just thought of that. Funny, isn't it?"

"Yup. I'll probably steal that line."

"I know you will."

"Look, I gotta get out of here."

"Okay. I love you."

I hesitated.

Alyse said, "Guess you're not alone, huh?"

"No. But you're a really good person."

It was good to hear Alyse laugh. While driving home, I thought it was also good to see Alyse cry too. Occasionally, I need to view my wife as a mere mortal. Between us, Commie? Sometimes, when Alyse goes to the city, I picture millions of people passing her on the street without being the least bit affected by her presence, and I wonder who's crazy, me or the world?

Maybe in your state, you're freed from such dopey thoughts. I hope so.

I got home, showered, and got ready for our triple-date dinner. Yes, another shower. I think the gym shower leaves me smelling chlorine-y.

VI.

"I'm sorry if I'm a little fablunged."

"What's wrong, Meri?"

"Our sitter . . ."

"Are you still using Marissa Prager?"

"Uh-huh. She's been Emily's sitter for two years. Always responsible, a good role model. Until tonight. She comes in, leans over to hug Emily, and I see this giant tattoo over her tush."

"So what? It doesn't mean she's a degenerate."

"I'm getting rid of her. Who do you use, Alyse?"

"Chelsea Gotbaum."

"Oh."

"What?"

"Nothing."

"Meri!"

"It's just that I did Rita Gotbaum's den and guest room and Chelsea had a bit of a problem."

"What?"

"If you must know, she refused to poop."

"Excuse me?"

"Chelsea would do anything to hold it in. Sometimes Rita would give her a pill to induce diarrhea. She was four at the time."

"Meri, she's sixteen now."

"Yeah, I'm sure she's over the problem. Look, I shouldn't be talking about diarrhea at dinner. Besides, every kid goes through a difficult pooping period."

"Not my kid. Every time I saw one of his shits, it was so perfect, I felt like scooping it out and taking it to a fucking taxidermist."

That was pretty much Arnie's first contribution to the evening's dinner conversation.

Diagonally to my left, Meri Katzen looked at Arnie like he was Bin Laden. Alyse, to my immediate left, doubled over laughing. Meri's Civil War freak husband, Ira, blinked on Meri's left, a silent partner in his marriage. To my right, Arnie was looking pleased with the image he'd put out there. To Arnie's right, Fumi, not wearing her surgical mask (the psycho-pharmaceuticals kicking in?), gazed off at the exposed kitchen of The Peace Pipe Grill.

The restaurant was a pretty groovy place, copper-colored with an open kitchen and exposed beams. When it opened in '97, Alyse got the idea of re-naming it, The Meeskite Grill, where ugly girls get the best tables. Funny, no?

Anyway, that night—you remember Greg Weinstein? He was in Phi Sig Delt? Oh wait, of course you remember Weinstein. You kicked his ass in an early round of the one-on-one tournament. Oh, and his best friend was Greg Kolker. We used to call them, "The Gregs of Society." I caught his eye. We nodded hello and I scanned the rest of the room. So many of the guys there struck me as lost. Dressed too hip for their age, wearing shirts from Abercrombie, those yellow LIVE STRONG bracelets, growing late-breaking soul patches, fumbling with half-moon glasses so they could see the menu. I actually felt moved by that, like there was something touching in how people try so hard.

Of course, for all my feelings of superiority, I still filled my role of making everyone at our table comfortable again after Arnie's taxidermy line: *Meri, Arnie's humor just takes a little getting used to. Anyway, if you need a good taxidermist, I'm sure Arnie can recommend one. So Ira, is it more fun to be on the Confederate side or the Union? Fumi, I'm so glad you're here. I need to read more and you're always in the middle of a book. What do you recommend?*

It's too easy to charm people. The tiniest bit of interest in their lives disarms. Even the art world people I met when Alyse worked at the gallery in Chelsea were affected by my methods—one genuine-sounding question about their lives and they were all, *Gee Alyse, your husband's such a cool guy.*

At the restaurant, however, Arnie made charm and diplomacy trickier.

When Fumi recommended a book by Joan Didion, Meri said, "I

saw her on TV. She's stick skinny!"

So Arnie said, "I think she won the Pulitzer Prize in the featherweight division."

When Ira mentioned the Dalai Lama, Arnie said, "That Dalai Lama's so full of shit. He's spent so much time hanging out with Richard Gere and all those hot actresses that, if they freed Tibet, he'd be like, 'Wait, I have to go back to that shithole?'"

Alyse laughed hysterically at everything Arnie said, which pleased me to no end. I wanted her to know why I liked Arnie so much. But I got the feeling Meri was annoyed by how Alyse enjoyed Arnie's jokes. And, maybe I'm extrapolating a little too much here, but I think she was just trying to reel Alyse in with a sobering conversation topic, when she asked, "So, this client of yours they arrested today. What kind of art does he do?"

Alyse took a sip of her wine before replying, "What do you mean?"

"Does he do classical paintings or what?"

Alyse took another sip. "You mean like classical impressionist paintings that always have titles like, *Girl In Green Dress Sitting In Garden Drinking Nectar Moments After Hearing Her Lover Has Chlamydia*?" Another sip. "Uh, no, Meri. You-ey Brushstroke doesn't do classical."

"Jesus, Alyse. I just asked a question."

"I'm sorry. He's my client and he's in jail, so I'm a little touchy."

Meri was about to add something (stupidly) when the waiter broke in. He was skinny with what my mother would describe as "some head of hair," a beard, and an incongruous diamond stud in his nose that looked to me like a preemptive strike against Nerdom. Everyone's their own image consultant these days, you know? As he ticked off the specials, Alyse leaned over and whispered to me, "Meri's getting on my nerves."

"Hey, it took thirty years for her to get on your nerves. That's a world's record."

Alyse smiled. Gave me a little kiss. It was nice.

Everyone ordered, the waiter made a show of not writing the orders down ("Uh-huh, very good; uh-huh, excellent choice"), then sped back to the kitchen. Arnie watched him, then said, "Fucking waiter looks like Ted Kaczinski."

"Excellent call!" I said. "He does look like Kaczinski, just not when they first busted him."

"No," Arnie agreed. "When he made his first court appearance."

"I'll tell you, when they cleaned him up, Kaczinski looked kinohura terrific."

Everyone laughed, which made me feel good. Alyse gave me a little nudge like, *Good one!*

Arnie shook his head and said, "Amazing how a total math genius like Kaczinski could wind up killing people with exploding packages sent from a frozen shack in Montana."

Meri, infected with psycho-Dr.-Phil-babble-bullshit, said, "His parents must have traumatized him early in his upbringing."

Arnie said, "His brother who turned him in grew up in the same house and he wasn't sending out bombs by express mail."

Ira said, "Well, you know, Aristotle said something about how the right trauma can turn any man into a monster."

"You know, just because Aristotle said something doesn't mean it's true," I said, though with a dash more aggression than I'd intended (of course, if I'm being honest, it did feel kind of great). Alyse leaned back and away to see from a better angle.

At their silence, I quickly added, "I'm just saying I don't see why there had to be some trauma that turned Kaczinski into what he became. Isn't it possible that, for all his math genius, he was also just an asshole?"

That felt pretty good too. So, I just let my mouth continue on, on its own:

"It's like we need some concrete cause for everything. I mean, look at all of us with our kids. If they're not perfect angels with tons of friends, high test scores, and straight A's, immediately we're looking for a reason. They're ADD, PDD, they have Asperger's, there are hormones in their milk, mercury in their tuna sandwiches, they're brain-damaged from polio shots—I don't buy it. I think there are still *some* kids out there who are just flat-out stupid. And that's nothing to be ashamed of. We need stupid kids. Without stupid kids, you can't identify the smart kids."

There were smiles and chuckles around the table, but I was getting all my pleasure purely from my spewing.

I exhaled. *So that's how it's done: You have a thought and you just say it aloud. Fantastic!* The fact is, I never considered myself overly opinionated. I'd always been happy to hear Daniel Schoor's opinion on NPR and adopt his views as my own.

This was a whole new me.

VII.

The reaction around the table, like a movie audience suddenly seeing an actor in an unfamiliar role, made me realize that my reputation for laid-back tactfulness was deeply deserved. Ira didn't look the least bit offended. In fact, he seemed like he'd just heard a highly enlightening critique that could actually make him reassess his position. Meri's face lost its usual clench and eased into the look of some co-ed all ga-ga over a professor. Even Fumi surfaced from her chemical haze with a wan smile and said, "I think that is a very . . ." She looked around the room for two more English words ". . . good theory." Arnie elbowed me in a *My man!* way. I glanced last at Alyse. She was smiling but looked a bit thrown, blinking a lot. I always found her hyper-batting of lashes totally adorable until that moment when it was I who'd caused the blinking (my standard reflex to a moment that could in any way tweak my wife's image of me).

Or maybe I was just reading way too much into things.

Chances are, if my (let's face it) incredibly mild diatribe caused any tension or nerves at the table, it was, most likely, mainly my own. As I said, I was new to outspokenness.

Anyway, the moment of silence following my little outburst was quickly broken by Greg Weinstein, who stopped by to say hello on his way out. A little too hurriedly, I introduced him to everyone at the table.

"Oh man," Greg said, morphing into all of our fathers. "The booze, the spicy pasta, heavy desserts . . . I can't eat like this anymore. But you know, it's all good."

It's all good. I glanced at Alyse, expecting her standard eye-roll. It didn't come.

Then Greg said, "I saw you guys at the rally this morning. It was so crowded, I didn't try to call out to you. But that was something, huh?"

"Yeah, it was a pretty unusual—"

Apparently, Greg was one of those cheerfully chatty drunks, unable to even let anyone else finish a sentence.

"My neighbor growing up owned the store that used to be where Nu? Girl Fashion is now. It was a bedding place back in the day. Ah, well, it's all good."

It's all good. Glance at Alyse again. Still, nothing.

Meri bubbled, "I remember! *Sleep Tight Bed and Mattress.* I used to say they were so overpriced I'd rather stay awake."

Ira laughed and gave Meri a playful nudge. I tried to remember if I'd ever seen a moment of affection pass between them before. For some reason, it bugged me.

Then I caught Weinstein saying, "The second floor of the store was all brick. When Uziel made it into a place for pre-teen sluts, he tried to make it look bigger, so he replaced the bricks with glass. If he'd kept it the way it was, that bottle of horseradish would have shattered, and not his window. Go figure."

Go figure. I didn't glance at Alyse after that one because I was too focused on what Weinstein said. *Find the architect Uziel used and ask him about the strength of the glass . . .*

"Greg! I've been waiting for you in the car, you fucking idiot!"

Weinstein's wife Cheryl blew in on a cloud of industrial strength perfume, her copper-dyed hair sprayed to a tsunami-proof hold. "It's freezing in that car."

"Okay, honey. Okay. I just stopped to say hello."

The Weinsteins marched out and Meri said, "I designed their kitchen a hundred years ago. She had a case of postpartum depression you wouldn't wish on your worst enemy."

I glanced at Alyse again, who was now staring darkly at Meri.

Arnie elbowed me and said, "You know, I must say, if your friend Weinstein gets home tonight, beats his wife to death with a ball-peen hammer, hacks her up, stuffs her body parts in clearly-marked Ziploc bags, puts them in the freezer, and then serves them to his kids for dinner tomorrow, I would still testify on his behalf at the trial."

I turned left as Alyse snorted out her latest sip of wine from laughing so hard, and then turned right as Fumi, who laughed as well, fell back from her chair and hit her head upon the floor.

Arnie jumped off his chair. "Oh, shit!"

He pulled open one of her eyes, put his face next to her mouth, looked up at me, and calmly said, "Call 911."

VIII.

Arnie, Alyse, and I followed the ambulance to the emergency room. (Meri offered to come as well but Arnie, instead of just saying "Thanks but it's not necessary," threw a few bills in her face and said, "No. Just go home.")

Alyse called Chelsea, our sitter, who immediately told Alyse not to worry, she'd stay as long as necessary. Pretty responsible for a girl who wouldn't take a crap at four years old, huh?

At the hospital, it was determined that Fumi hadn't fallen over from laughter, but from an overdose of her medication (which apparently had been her secret side dish throughout the meal).

Arnie, Alyse, and I sat in the waiting area, all of us having reached an age when hospital vigils were nothing new. An EMT swept in with a teenager on a stretcher, the poor kid's hand wrapped in bandages, a small version of a picnic cooler sitting between his legs.

Arnie broke a long silence. "I can't tell you how much I appreciate you guys coming here with me."

I waved it away and said, "It's nothing, Arnie. What's a hospital vigil among best friends?"

"Don't you have, like, a million best friends?"

"No. Alyse is the one with all the friends."

Alyse nodded, "Yeah, I have a lot of friends. None that I like, though."

Shit, did I say that line to you before as if I'd made it up myself? Somehow I think I said that to you at some point. Hmm. Truth is, I've stolen that line from Alyse a million times since she first said it. I actually steal a lot of her lines. I've even unknowingly co-opted her lines right in front of her. Later, she'll give me shit, threatening me with a plagiarism suit, but I still do it anyway. She's full of great one-liners.

"Your friend Meri is kind of . . ."

Alyse finished Arnie's sentence, "An asshole?"

"Well, I wasn't going to go that far."

Alyse gazed off and said, "It's weird realizing that the only thing you have in common with some of your friends is that you're friends."

"Hey," Arnie said, "you make these friends in high school and college, and thirty years later, you're supposed to feel the same about them. What the fuck?"

I'd thought a lot about this very subject and said, "Actually, I have no friends left over from high school and just a few from college, the closest of whom lives in South Carolina. And he couldn't even make it to my wedding."

"Why not?" Arnie asked, seeming genuinely miffed on my behalf.

"Well, he had a good excuse. He'd just graduated from law school and was doing volunteer legal work for the World Hunger Foundation. So, considering he was in Sub-Saharan Africa at the time, it was a little tough for him to make it to Long Island for the wedding."

Commie, you came up in conversation that night. You must feel good about that.

"Of my friends who *did* make it to the wedding, I'm in touch with maybe five. There are three or four I just cut off altogether."

Alyse said, "I've always been amazed at how you've done that."

"Really?"

"Yeah. Like that guy from your frat house who used to hang around us a lot?"

"Oh, Doug Maitz. Jesus."

Okay, Commie, I guess it's not as flattering that your name came up when you hear that Doug Maitz's came up too. Oh well. Sorry.

"Arnie," Alyse said, tapping his arm in a way I'm sure Arnie found adorable. "This guy Doug never dated anyone in his life, but he was, you know, a nice guy. As harmless as can be, really. Anyway, after college, he lived in New Jersey back when we still lived in the city, and we'd see him once in a while. What was he, a sales rep?"

"Yeah, for a company that manufactured slim-cut, bulletproof vests."

Arnie held his hand up, "What?"

A snort/laugh escaped Alyse, "Oh God, I'm sorry. But it's the truth. Bullet-proof vests that didn't fit all bulky."

"Form-fitting flak jackets," Arnie mused. "Sure, why not look thin while taking a slug from a .45?"

Again, Arnie made Alyse giggle and, again, I didn't feel at all insecure about it. I thought I'd mention that again.

"Of course, Doug had no money," Alyse went on, "so we'd treat him to an occasional day in the city like it was some kind of backward version of the Fresh Air Fund. And then one day . . ." Alyse turned from Arnie to me. ". . . Doug left a message that he was coming to town and you just said, 'You know what? I've had it.' You ignored the message, then a few more, and that was it. We never saw the poor free-loader again."

"I probably saved us enough to pay off a year's worth of college tuition."

Arnie laughed aloud, which was fairly amazing considering that we were sitting there waiting for the results of his wife's stomach pump. "Man, I have so much more respect for you now than I did before hearing that story."

Alyse laughed too and said, "Yeah, that's my husband's version of the Atkins Diet. Instead of carbs, he cuts out people."

Now we were all laughing, which must have been a highly unusual sight for the chief resident of the ER, Dr. Felix Chang.

"Everything went fine," Chang said, putting his hand on Arnie's shoulder. "Your wife is resting comfortably. We're gonna keep her overnight. She's a little woozy, but if you want to look in on her, you can."

With surprising urgency, Arnie said, "Yes, thank you. Please, I do."

Dr. Chang said, "Of course. But it's best that only one of you go."

Arnie turned to Alyse and me, "I'll be just a minute. I just want to see her."

Alyse and I gave take-all-the-time-you-need nods and Arnie followed Dr. Chang to the action. Sitting across from us about fifteen feet away was a Latino couple quietly arguing in tense Spanish. The Israel part of Park Israel Hospital seemed pretty superfluous in that ER. I guess it's no different at Columbia Presbyterian Hospital or the Lutheran Trauma Center. Medical emergencies cloud all religious preference. If there were a place called Long Island Atheist Hospital, I wonder what kind of business they'd do.

"Their son was shot in the neck with a nail gun," Alyse said in a whisper, nodding toward the Latino couple. She listened more. "He was conscious when they brought him in." More talk. The woman said something as her voice cracked. Alyse didn't say anything.

"What did she just say?"

"'So much blood.'"

Did I mention that Alyse is a language savant? She spoke fluent French after three classes at Maryland. My mother's bugged her for twenty years to get a job as an interpreter at the UN. God forbid a talent isn't used to make money. Alyse laughs every time that comes up. She still gets a huge kick out of my mother. It's nice.

I was in love with my freshman Spanish teacher. She was the first woman I knew who called herself "Ms." and who never wore a bra.

"Makes you feel a bit trivial to be in the Emergency Room waiting on a Paxil overdose," Alyse said, taking her eyes off the Latino couple. "Heroin, okay. But this? Eh."

I smiled and said, "That was a funny thing you said to Arnie before about having so many friends but no one you like."

"I was only half-joking. It's not just Meri, who was a total jerk tonight. I was already mad at Gil Binder."

"What did he do?"

"Esme had dinner at the Binders last night. Esme mentioned You-ey's anti-Semitic comment because she's at an age where she can't keep anything to herself. Then the crime happens and Gil decides to call the police and mention Esme's name. Couldn't he just leave it at, 'One of my daughter's friends told me she had an anti-Semite at her house at about the time of the crime?'"

"Alyse, to follow up on the lead, the cops needed Esme's name."

"Not necessarily. I guarantee Esme mentioned that the guy's name was You-ey Brushstroke. Gil could have just told them his name and left Esme—and us—out of it. Then we wouldn't have had cops coming to our house, scaring the shit out of Charlie and enraging you by staring at my ass."

"I'm over that," I lied.

"I'm not. I mean, I'm not over your reaction to it. But that's beside the point."

I had a flicker of a thought: If it was all so beside the point, why did Alyse mention it again? But she went back to her main point before I could fully process the thought.

"Sometimes I really *do* hate my friends. I can see why you like Arnie so much. He's the complete opposite of everyone else we know." For an unprecedented second time in one day, Alyse's eyes misted over. This time, she fought back full-on crying and just said, "We should move back to the city."

"Really?"

"I don't know. This probably isn't the best moment to decide."

"We can talk about it some more."

Alyse took a tissue out of her bag and blew her nose. The Latino couple looked at her.

"Sorry." For such a feminine girl, she sure can pump out some volume blowing her nose. I suppressed a laugh, and Alyse smiled and said, "I have to go to the bathroom."

Like a perverse bedroom comedy, Alyse exited and Arnie entered. I stood up.

"How is she?"

Arnie shrugged and said, "Alright, I guess." He threw up his hands in that international you-just-can't-win kind of way.

"What's wrong?"

"I was thinking about how I wound up in this situation. Not the hospital. The marriage. You know, when I was, let's say, between marriages, I was totally obsessed with girls. It was sick. Every time two girls passed on the street, my mind would immediately decide which one I'd do if I had the choice. If there were twenty-five girls, I'd run my own little NCAA tournament in my head to decide the winner. I saw a shrink for about a month because that's what you do after a divorce, and he said I needed to get to the bottom of my 'preoccupation with fornicating.' Jesus. Fornicating. We don't have enough words for screwing without coming up with another that sounds so scientific? *Photosynthesis leads to fornicating within the plant's stamen*. Anyway, at some point, I decided that having a wife and family was an insane way to go through life. I'd look at random couples on the street and wonder: *Why don't they get divorced*? I'd hear people talk about how hard divorce is on the kids and think: *Still*? You'd think kids would have evolved to the point of being used to divorce. The stable family is what seemed to me to be hardest on the kids. So, that was my state of mind until I had that skiing accident in Steamboat."

"The separated shoulder. You couldn't work."

"For a month! I was just stuck at home. I couldn't do anything. Suddenly, I had this overwhelming feeling that I needed a wife. I needed people around me. Kids. You name it. I realized that the future was only going to bring along even more debilitating ailments and I needed to be taken care of. I *wanted* to be a burden on others! I did a total attitude U-turn. The only thing I can compare it to is that moment you're watching a movie and realize that you won't be spending your life with Halle Berry. As sick as it makes you feel, it's a relief too. You can move on. Get married to a woman—a human woman. Well, I may as well have stood on the corner trying to hail down a wife. The first woman to slow down and pull over was Fumi and she seemed perfect. I'd heard somewhere that Asian women are really devoted to taking care of their men. And here I am, taking care of her."

Arnie paused. "Anyway, you asked how Fumi is. Well, she can't even talk between whatever anesthesia they've got her on and whatever the tube did when they stuck it down her throat. But the second she saw me, she was trying to tell me something, so I gave her a pen and a pad. She writes down, 'They cut my dress.'

"They cut her dress? Oh, you mean the doctors. They just cut through clothes when they're in a hurry—"

"Exactly. And it was a Junya Watanabe dress. It cost like a grand."

"Oh, sorry, I didn't notice."

"Of course you didn't notice. You're a guy. But it was a Junya Watanabe dress and Fumi's writing like a lunatic on the pad that she can't replace it, they don't make it anymore, it's her favorite dress, and then, get this: She wants me to call our lawyer Monday morning and sue the hospital for the cost of the dress plus emotional pain and suffering."

"What?"

"You heard me right."

"Jesus. Must be some, you know, dress."

"It's a Junya Watanabe."

It was about then that Alyse came back and said, "Am I hallucinating or did I hear you two talking about Junya Watanabe?"

We explained the situation and Alyse, trying desperately to show some sisterhood with Fumi, said, "It is a shame they'd cut through such a gorgeous dress. They couldn't just slip it off her?"

"Oh, hi. Back on your shift, huh?"

"Yeah, I'm back. Boring Commie to dea—I mean, tears."

"Oh, in college we called him Commie. You know, his last name is Moscow, so . . . It's not important. Let me grab my jacket and I'll take a walk so you can tend to him."

"Really? I don't know . . ."

"Oh, okay. I guess."

"Oh man . . ."

"No, it's just . . . Commie used to do 200 sit-ups a day so . . . Forget it."

"Yeah, you too. Have a good one."

Seems like a pretty competent health care professional, Commie. Anyway, let's see. Oh: Another kid was wheeled into the ER then. He'd flipped his car, but he was still conscious, and I overheard one of the EMTs say, "Probably just whiplash."

Arnie hugged Alyse and me. We left. And I guess that's it for that day.

What am I saying? There is one more thing.

IX.

Driving home, we stopped at a light. It was about one o'clock. I know because I had WINS playing low on the radio and, at the top of the hour, they led with an item about the cloned dog that bit off the little kid's finger. It was the report saying how the local pet shelter had finally been green-lighted to put the dog down until, at the last second, two teenaged Latino kids came forward to adopt it. As you know, the guy at the shelter suspected the kids were gang-bangers, so the kids called a lawyer, who called another lawyer, who called a third lawyer, and that's when everything was put on hold until a judge decided what would be best for the dog: Latinos or death. I remember thinking, *Fucking case will probably wind up in the Supreme Court. The kid's pinkie will have grown back by the time those embalmed judges make a decision.*

At the end of the report, I caught the correspondent say, "Reporting from Hilton Head, South Carolina, I'm . . ." And it crossed my mind then that Clonegate was happening in your neck of the woods but, you know, so what? I just shook my head and was about to tell Alyse I'd been following this dog story, when I saw that she'd fallen asleep. She looked good in the red of the stoplight—sweet, you know? But, as I looked at her, I realized that not all of the red was from the traffic light. Looking around, I found that, from the headlight of a SUV waiting across from us, there was this laser beam that had zoomed in on her face as she slept in the passenger seat, all curled up—her mouth was even hanging open and a droplet of spittle was shining on her lip. I just froze for a minute. This girl I'd spun my entire adult life around was ambushed by a halogen spotlight at the most unattractive moment of her life and I swear, she just looked so goddamn beautiful, I got choked up. That was really big for me, just being in that moment and knowing I was feeling something I was supposed to feel.

Shit. I mean, don't you think that, for most guys our age, the deepest feeling of love we feel anymore is, I don't know, the love we feel for someone who pulls out just when we really need a parking spot?

Did I mention that I drive a Saab station wagon now? I like it. It's a non-statement car. I don't need to have a car that says something about me. *I'll* talk. Let the fucking car shut up and drive.

Anyway, that moment in the car with Alyse sleeping is a moment I go back to a lot now. It steadies me, tells me I'm kind of emotionally healthy. Or, at least, emotionally intact. In a weird way, that moment for me has become something like the one when I saw Jenji's nipple at the pool—the fifty-year-old's version.

The radio didn't wake Alyse, but her eyes popped open when my cellphone's little text message alert started beeping.

She asked, blearily, "Who's texting you at this hour?"

Turns out it was Don Graydon, the *Newsday* reporter, saying, "Your doubtful detective was helpful/interesting. Thanks for the tip. I owe you one."

Without looking at Alyse, I told her the text was a wrong number.

SUNDAY THEN

I.

Horseradish Incident Sparks Protest; Suspect Held
By Don Graydon

Commie, I don't know if you've ever seen *Newsday*. It's a somewhat hifalutin tabloid, but a tabloid nonetheless. The front page has the obligatory headline trying to out-scream the other tabloids, and the local news doesn't start until about page 20. Graydon's story was buried at the bottom of the first local page. It wasn't a particularly long piece, but it felt like forever until it mentioned anything new, like that the police had delved into You-ey's computer. "Despite an unusually high amount of time spent online, no visits to any anti-Semite-oriented websites were found in his browser history."

One police officer—clearly Chris McNeill—anonymously said, "It's unusual for someone committing a hate crime to not frequent like-minded websites."

The only other interesting tidbit was that a seventy-six-year-old woman, Elsie Koppel, had stepped forward to say that she'd dropped a bag of groceries at the scene of the crime around four o'clock and, upon arriving home, had realized she was short a bottle of horseradish. Mrs. Koppel apparently tried to reclaim the bottle and had to be told by police that the condiment to her gefilte fish was evidence in a criminal investigation.

We had three kids for breakfast that morning. Chelsea Gotbaum had ended up sleeping on the couch. Esme and Charlie asked why she spent the night and, without going into too much detail, Alyse recounted the events of the night before. As Alyse generically described the ER scene, I grabbed the phone. The all-seeing Alyse said, "Honey, maybe you should wait before you call Arnie. It's only ten and he had a long night." She was right, of course, so I held off even though I was excited to call him. My entirely new, actually social, best friend role was giving me a big kick.

We get the Sunday *New York Times* and so I picked it up (which used to take some effort, though now it's way thin and the pages are smaller and depressingly manageable). We get an edition with a separate section devoted to Long Island and, apparently, they sent a reporter to the rally:

Anti-Semitism Finds Chi-Chi Shopping Mecca

Playing up their angle, the story cited (another) anonymous cop quoting You-ey's "buffalo-nosed bagel-biters" line. I glanced at Esme happily eating a bagel with cream cheese and nova. Laughing, she grinned in the faces of Chelsea and Charlie, and exhaled: "Don't you love my fish breath?"

This sweet little girl's first in-person brush with the endlessly nasty adult world made our national newspaper. *Damn*, I thought, *just give me one little variety of grown-up poison I can keep my kids shielded from. Just one.*

Alyse noticed my jaw clench, so I gave her my well-established not-in-front-of-the-kids look. "More coffee, hon?" she said, and got up without waiting for my answer. She grabbed the Krups and poured while reading over my shoulder. If it were a movie, she'd have poured the coffee all over my lap.

"What's wrong?" Charlie has hair-trigger anxiety sensors. A tickle of tension in our house and his head whirls like a radar dish.

"Nothing, kiddo. Why?" I grabbed the sports section. "Huh. The Knicks didn't even sell out last night for LeBron."

"Who wants to see losers? And Dad, you know, even with LeBron, the Cavs aren't such an exciting team. There are teams in the West who won't even make the playoffs and they're more fun than any team in the East. Don't you think, Dad?"

Charlie already knew the defusing value of sports. Whenever the shit gets too thick, talk sports. It's the demilitarized zone for the American male.

Then Chelsea piped up: "My dad talks about sports whenever I want to talk about . . ."

That's when Chelsea saw me stab her with stop signs in my eyes. She did an admirable job rerouting herself. "Well, you know, movies and stuff. Whenever I want to talk about movies or TV shows, my dad wants to talk sports."

Charlie went for it: "Your dad's into sports too? That's cool."

Chelsea gave me a little smile like, *Kick-save and a beauty!*

But then Esme picked up on Chelsea's angle and said, "Sports are the sandbox of life."

Charlie shot her a look, then turned to me for help.

"Ezzie," I said, "you know what's the sandbox of life? The beach."

Okay. One of my lamer parental moments.

When breakfast broke up and Chelsea went home with $200 in her pocket, Alyse shook her head and said, "Between Charlie's sensitivity and innocence and Esme's growing rebelliousness and false sense of sophistication, this whole balancing act is getting pretty shaky."

"Yeah," I said, "we have to watch every word we say."

"I guess."

"You guess?"

"Maybe we'd be better off just going with the truth. Then they won't be so shocked when the rest of the world just blurts out stuff."

"You might have a point there. I mean, just stopping myself from saying fuck or shit in front of them is exhausting."

"I'd rather they hear it from us. Or at least with us present. Maybe we should just sit them down and have them watch *Taxi Driver*, *Clockwork Orange,* and *Last Tango*. Just throw them in the deep end of the sex and violence pool."

"Gee, honey, you really should write a parenting book."

"At least with *Last Tango* they'd learn some French."

"Maybe you're experiencing some kind of right brain rebellion."

"That's the crazier side of the brain, right?"

Alyse smiled through an exaggerated exhale.

I had a thought. When changes are gradual and expected, Alyse, like most people, can handle them with ease. But the sudden ad-libs of life are not her thing.

Actually, that thought hit me later, after the main events of this story were long over. The alarm on my cell phone chimed in then, a daily reminder to take my Lipitor and Zetia. I have a mental block against taking all these pills, so I need the reminder. Anyway, it dawned on me that, since we'd gotten home so late, I hadn't recharged my cell. I checked out the battery strength and saw Graydon's text again. As I hit delete, I noticed it'd been sent at 1:30 AM. That made me wonder, when did he interview that cop, McNeill? Did he meet him in a parking garage, like Woodward and Deep Throat? But, mostly, I thought about how some people—not many, but some—live for their jobs. They sleep and eat just so they can work more.

You hear these soft rock stations on the radio sell themselves by saying, "We make your workday go faster." That's most of the world: people just trying to get through another work day so they can get to whatever it is they like doing. How do guys like Graydon get so possessed? Maybe they don't have families, so work becomes their whole lives. Come to think of it, Woodward and Bernstein were both divorced during Watergate. Still, even if that were my situation, I'd hate to think of what I'd do with all that solitary time. Or, more to the point, what I *wouldn't* do with it. I guess what I'm saying is, I just don't see myself joining Podiatrists Without Borders.

Going off and tending to the feet of freedom fighters in some Third World hell hole? I don't think so. Maybe in college I would have been appalled to know that I would one day be content in a less-than-thrilling life. Even now, when these wars break out in Iraq or Afghanistan, I get a tinge of envy seeing photographers and correspondents reporting from the front. Then they get taken hostage by fanatics with Russian AK-47s who, if they don't chop their fucking heads off, move them around from one dump of a safe house to another for God knows how long before releasing them thirty-five pounds thinner, and for what? *So they can go right back to work.*

What drives these people to take these risks? They act like dying is just another way of re-inventing themselves. Tell me: What makes someone believe their work is worth dying for? Even if they explained it to me, I don't think I'd grasp it on any kind of meaningful level. I can't convince myself that death is any better for Martin Luther King Jr. than it is for my father or Ted Bundy.

So, that's what I was thinking about that morning. Which was what made me think of you. Which was what led me to call you that morning. The second-to-last time we spoke.

Or the second-to-last time I spoke and you responded.

I always thought you lived your life like those kind of people, totally into your work. And, at least for that little chunk of time, I felt similarly neck-deep in something. I know it wasn't my job, but it was something. I was talking to cops, investigating different kinds of glass, tracking people on the Internet. Of course, I didn't tell you anything about that on the phone, but at least that feeling was in me. In some small way, I felt like we'd finally be operating on a similar level of passion.

I'm not explaining this well, but I just felt like calling you.

And it's funny, because two minutes into the conversation, you said to me, "Hey, you sound great."

That made me feel great. And when you told me that Nick was an awesome nine-year-old b-ball player and we started laughing about having a father-son two-on-two grudge match, it was great. Just catching up and giving each other shit. It was a hell of a lot better than walking around College Park sniffing for memories of a previous life.

I asked you what you'd been up to work-wise and that's when you told me you'd just gotten involved in a case in which you were representing a cloned Australian Shepherd. I have to say, I felt great that I was so up on the case. Then you told me that lots of law schools had classes in "non-human animal" rights.

The only bummer of that conversation is that I wasn't totally focused on the details of the case you were making on behalf of the dog. And it had nothing to do with your telling me that you could be disbarred for divulging so many details. I was just totally focused on how excited you sounded talking about it. I mean, fifty-whatever and still into it like that.

I remember thinking: *Wouldn't it be great if enthusiasm really was infectious?*

It reminds me of when you won that moped in a campus-wide raffle and then won $400 in the frat NCAA pool. Everyone told you to buy a lottery ticket because you were on a hot streak, so you bought a ticket but ripped it up on the day of the drawing and never checked the winning numbers, all because you were worried that if you won a million dollars, you'd lose your motivation to accomplish all the things you wanted in life. Everyone thought you were nuts. I thought you were nuts. But now I'm thinking, maybe that's what genius is: thinking stuff at nineteen that most people don't know or think about until they're forty or fifty or whatever age is too late.

II.

Anyway, it was a fun conversation we had. Remember we were talking about all the guys from college who were on their second and third wives? You told me that Jeff Silver's wife dumped him after she caught him doing a black girl, and I said that if you cheat with someone from a different race, it shouldn't count as adultery and you cracked up, saying, "Only you would say that." That stuck with me. *Only I would say that?* I didn't know you saw me as having a unique point of view. It's funny how you can spend your whole life without a clue about your own personality. It felt like the best compliment I'd gotten in a long time. I was so happy I'd called you.

I'm sorry we never got the families together in the Cayman Islands. It would have been great. I meant it when I told you I was definitely up for it. I even told Alyse about it. Yeah. I think I'd have done it.

Anyway, you should just know that our phone conversation affected me and the story I'm telling you.

Maybe fifteen minutes after we hung up, there was a knock on the door. Alyse and I got to the door at the same time. I opened it. Nat Uziel, looking more robust than he had since I'd first met him, stood there with his long coat open in the cold weather, holding a bunch of papers on a clipboard.

"Nat, what a surprise. You met Alyse at the rally."

"Yes. I recall thinking that my foot doctor had such a pretty wife. Who knew?"

"Yeah, I get that a lot."

Alyse shook Uziel's hand and said, "It's nice to meet you. I'm so sorry about what happened at your store. Our daughter Esme drools whenever she looks in the window at your clothes."

That wasn't really true and Alyse smiled at me as if to say, *Yes, I know that wasn't really true.*

"Yes," Uziel said, "The young girls love my store. Sometimes I don't know if that's such a good thing. But who am I to say?"

"Gotta make a living," I said in a jocular tone I never knew I had.

"Yes, that's the rationalization I use."

I thought that was a pretty revealing comment. Uziel's Orthodoxy conflicted with the whole Lolita aspect of his business. But then, Jews never really worry themselves much about promiscuity. I think that, so long as you say shtup instead of fuck or screw, you're pretty much in the clear in the eyes of the Jewish Lord.

"As you probably have guessed, I've come regarding the incident at my store."

Alyse nodded and said, "Well, please come in. Would you like some coffee and a bagel?"

"A salt bagel would be nice."

"Oh, we only have plain, poppy, or bialy."

"Besides," I said, all professional, "shouldn't you watch your salt intake, Nat?"

"If I watched my intake, as you put it, I'd be eating nothing but spinach and Jell-O."

"Maybe a decaf coffee, Mr. Uziel?"

"That would be nice, Alyse. Thank you."

I looked at Nat, giving him an opening to say, "Oh, and Alyse, please call me Nat." You'd think after coming over unannounced, requesting a salt bagel and then accepting Alyse's offer of decaf, the least the guy could do was give her the security clearance to call him Nat. But he didn't, and it bugged me. I think I was feeling so good after the phone call with you, Commie, that there was a little more attitude than usual flowing through me.

I said, "Come on in," as if ordering around a guy from Allied Van Lines.

Uziel followed me into our unused living room. "Lovely home."

I gave him the most perfunctory, "Thanks," imaginable. I don't know if he was picking up on whatever tinge of defiance I was feeling or not. Remember when we used to listen to that Richard Pryor album over and over? He had that routine about being convicted of tax evasion and, feeling all defiant, he said, "The judge is gonna sentence me, but he ain't gonna get my dick 'til he kiss my ass." That routine was actually in my head as we sat down. I led him to the squishy sofa and I sat on the arm of a leather club chair, making myself a couple feet higher than him.

Richard Pryor . . . damn.

As I was about to ask Uziel what he wanted from me, my kids came hurtling down the stairs.

"Dad?"

"In the living room."

Charlie flew in, breathless, "Dad, is douche a dirty word?"

Esme, shaking her head, said, "I called him a douche and he got all whacked. I told him it's a perfectly good word. Right? I saw it on the cover of a magazine. There was an article called 'Don't Be a Douche Bag.' I think it was in *Details*."

"It is a word, but Esme, it's not a nice word to use—especially not in front of *company*."

That's when Esme noticed Uziel. "Oh, hi."

"Esme, Charlie, this is Nat."

Not Mr. Uziel. Nat. You like that?

"Nice to meet you both," Uziel said, staring at Esme.

The kids did their standard, bored hellos.

"So," Uziel said, "you're the young lady who was unfortunate enough to hear that terrible anti-Semitic comment on Friday, right?"

I swear, Commie, I don't know if my blood froze or boiled. I shot Uziel a look like: Shut the fuck up. But he didn't.

"It's a shame there are people like that in our world, but there are. So we must remain vigilant."

Esme got a faraway look. She turned to me. Then Alyse walked in with the cup of coffee and felt the blowback of awkwardness in the room. I went over to Esme, gave her a hug and a kiss on the cheek, and said, "Ezzie, Mommy and I have to talk to Nat. It won't take long. You and Charlie go upstairs and I'll be up in a minute or two, tops. And try to cool it on the douche thing."

"Okay, Dad," she said with a mixed-up smile as she turned to leave. Charlie followed her, both thrown for another loop by the adult world.

Alyse put Nat's mug on the coffee table and said, "Is something wrong?"

"Nat, it was way out of line for you to bring up the anti-Semitic remark with my daughter. You have absolutely no idea how Alyse and I, as her parents, decided to deal with this matter. For all you know, we successfully talked it through with her and it was over and done with. Why would you bring that up within two seconds of meeting a young girl?"

"I'm sorry if I upset her. But, frankly, I doubt that whatever bromides you used to explain the situation would, as you seem to imply, so completely alleviate the trauma she's suffered."

"Bromides?" I said, struggling to reel in my composure. "What do you call, 'We must remain vigilant?'"

Like the day in my office after my dispute with his pious freak son, Uziel seemed impressed by my point. "Yes, I suppose that would also qualify as a bromide."

I was ready to move on, but Alyse said, "You-ey's comment . . . ?"

"Yes, I brought it up with your daughter and perhaps that was a mistake. Although it was bound to happen because people in town do know what was said and to whom it was said."

Alyse closed her eyes and slowly shook her head. "Mr. Uziel, we are, for the most part, bringing up our children as non-believers."

"You can't be a non-believer in anti-Semitism. It exists."

"That doesn't mean we have to instill fear in our children. If we feel they need to know more about anti-Semitism, we'll invite Elie Wiesel over and let him teach them how to 'remain vigilant.'"

All men are unnerved by sarcasm from a pretty woman, but Uziel did his best not to seem flustered. He murmured, "I'm sorry if I spoke out of turn."

Without openly accepting his apology, Alyse excused herself. I watched her leave, then said, “Nat, what brought you here today?”

He lifted the clipboard. “Nassau County is planning to prosecute Mr. Radmonovic with a grade-one felony. We are circulating a petition to urge the powers that be to prosecute the case as a federal hate crime. That way, if the case is botched in any way, the federal government can retry it.”

I know what you’re thinking, Commie: After the whole discussion about what he said to Esme, this guy still had the chutzpah to hand us his petition? That was my thought too.

“Nat, Mr. Radmonovic hasn’t even been indicted yet.”

“It’s important to get out ahead of these situations.”

“You may not even have a situation. As you probably know, detectives have talked to us a couple of times now. Frankly, they have a very thin case against Mr. Radmonovic.”

“They’ll strengthen the case. They always do when it’s someone who is so clearly guilty.”

How much did I want to tell him right then and there that I was guilty? *It was me! I crashed the window of your store*. What I really wanted to say was: “You know what you should do, Nat? You should change the name of your store from Nu? Girl Fashions to ‘Young Pussy Fashions.’” I guess I was still in Richard Pryor mode.

“What are you smiling about?”

I couldn’t help it. I was smiling. Enough for Uziel to notice.

“Nothing,” I said. “I just had a funny thought. Nothing relevant to our discussion. Anyway, I can’t sign your petition.”

Uziel paused.

“Nat, I’m not really as sure as you are of Mr. Radmonovic’s guilt and, in any case, calling this a hate crime seems like a real stretch to me. If the bottle was thrown through the window of a synagogue, okay. But the perp in this case could just as easily be some normal guy who, I don’t know, tripped over the bottle and got so angry that he picked it up and threw it through the window without thinking.”

“What kind of person throws a bottle through a window without thinking?”

“I have no idea.”

III.

Closing the door behind Uziel, I had a great feeling of suddenly having switched sides from the Joint Chiefs of Staff to the Anti-War Movement. Not that I have ever heard of anyone in history who had made that move. But I did feel like I was suddenly on life's fun team.

I pulled back a curtain to see Uziel turn right to, presumably, hit up our next-door neighbors. Gail and Jonathan Herman were perfectly thoughtful, reliable neighbors who, upon sending their morose, pimply twins off to BU, declared war on each other. Every few weeks, they had monster fights. Their house may as well be miked by roadies for *Deep Purple* the way their livid voices carry through the neighborhood. Rage, bottled up for the sake of the kids, needed only the spark of college acceptance letters to ignite the Hermans.

Alyse and I don't want to hear the fights—too creepy—so we crank our TV volume up hoping that, during lulls in the hysterics, the Hermans might hear those two music strings on *Law & Order* and not feel awkward the next time they saw us. Sure enough, sometimes we'd see them on a "morning after" and they'd act like nothing ever happened. One time Gail even called Jonathan to come say hello to us. "Hon? Come on out a sec!"

I remember exactly one time when my parents had a fight. I have no idea what it was about. All I remember was my father's voice cracking at one point and then, at an especially high-pitched moment when I was about to barricade the door to preserve my family, this fat, asshole jeweler down the hall, Mr. Bratton, knocked on our door and, without waiting for it to open, called out, "Hey in there: Can you cool it with the heavies?" My parents both came to the door and told him to shove it up his ass, which must have unified them because the "heavies" died down pretty fast.

Alyse and I have never had a major blow-out. Some people say that's unhealthy, we're in denial, we're headed for the same hell currently occupied by the Hermans. We've been out with couples where one spouse says, "Marriage is hard work," and the other nods like: *You said a mouthful, honey!* Think about that: They openly talk about how labor-intensive marriage is in front of a couple who never fights and *we're the unhealthy ones?* This whole compulsion about putting everything out in the open? It's crap.

Of course, that was a needless digression in the story because, as it turned out, Uziel didn't go to the Hermans. He got in a Lexus driven by his son Jason. It wasn't a door-to-door petition. It was targeted.

I took off a few minutes before going upstairs for another bout of crisis management with the kids. Back in the living room, I saw Uziel's untouched coffee still sitting there. I picked it up and drank it. Fuck him.

Yeah, I know, Commie. Not much of a fuck-you gesture, but I was new to acting on my moral outrage.

If only Esme had called Charlie a douche bag a little earlier, they would have run downstairs before Uziel got here and never would have had to hear about being vigilant in this sick world . . .

Up in Charlie's room, Alyse was almost done dealing with the kids. As I entered, she was saying, "Remember Friday night when we were talking about inner lives? A lot of people have empty inner lives, so they gossip about other people. Ezzie, you did nothing wrong. You were at dinner with the Binders on Friday night and you mentioned a pretty important thing that was said to you that day. Mr. Binder was wrong to tell your story to other people, especially the police, and I'm going to let him know. As far as You-ey is concerned, he may have thrown the bottle through the window. Then again, maybe he didn't. He's not a dangerous person, and he's definitely no one to be afraid of. I'm just sorry Mr. Uziel brought the whole thing up. But again, that's not your fault. He should have known better, but he has an empty inner life, so he says things he shouldn't."

Charlie chewed this over a second and said, "You should never buy clothes at his store again. It could be like, you know, a protest."

I loved that. "Sounds like a good idea. What do you think, Ez?"

"That's a good idea, but you know what else we can do? We could buy *tons* of clothes there and always return them a day later. Store people hate it when you return stuff."

Commie, everyone talks about how great their kids are, but, really, can you believe how much *better* my kids are than everyone else's?

Things leveled out at chez moi for a few hours. The kids went ice skating, Alyse went up to take a long shower, and I—

Well, I don't know if you need to hear this. Probably not.

I'll just pick up the story later in the afternoon. I was doing more research on the web. I tracked down the architect who remodeled the mattress store into Uziel's joint. Turns out . . .

IV.

Okay, Commie! Jesus, let go of my arm. I'll tell you what I left out: the kids went ice skating, Alyse took her shower, and I went to the basement, sprawled out on a couch, and did my thing with Jenji. I imagined doing her on the ping-pong table. It sits on a pool table, so you just move the net out of the way. It's no big deal, okay?

You know what? I'm sick that I told you that. On principle, I'm just nauseated. I'll tell you why I'm nauseated. I can't stand people talking about sex in any way.

I'm not being cogent here, I know. Look, the thing is, even when I go to the movies and see sex scenes where the guy pounds the girl up against the wall and she's digging her nails into him and he's biting her lip and she's tugging up his head by the hair and he's flipping her over and she's cursing and grabbing an ice pick from a credenza . . . it all just bugs me. It seems less like sex and more like some kind of freak show.

I hate turning everything into a theatrical command performance. Or maybe I don't want to see through the window of people's secret perversions. Or maybe I'm just repulsively wholesome. Maybe I'm scared of obsession in all forms. Or maybe I'll go so far as to say that wild sex just scares me. Okay? There, I said it. On the other hand, when I watch a nature show on lions, ducks, click beetles, horses, dolphins, and elephants, they all mate in their one way every time.

But humans, with our oversized brains and endless capacity for boredom? No. It's not enough to complete the staggering feat of getting a girl into bed. You also have to be creative. And the more creative you are, the more demand there is for variety! And if you run out of creativity, you bang headlong into the Emasculation Proclamation: You're boring in bed. I mean, otherwise, how the hell would seemingly normal couples wind up having anal intercourse?

I have nothing against societal advances, but when the vagina becomes a victim of job obsolescence, something's very wrong. And,

and! With all that going on, you have these religious nuts pushing the concept of intelligent design! If God had a lick of intelligence and gave a shit about families, he'd have made us physically capable of screwing in one position and one position only. A simple edict: *Here's the way you're going to do it. If you're not happy with it, tough shit.* And maybe, in all His wisdom, He'd throw in a reluctant blessing on oral sex, you know, just to keep the peace. But that's it. No more crazy ass shit. Don't you think that would have made the world a better place? All He had to do was keep the possibilities for longing to a manageable number and He could've had a much easier time selling all the rest of His bullshit. You with me here? Just think about it a moment.

You wanna hear something really insane?

I can't believe I'm telling you this one.

Once, while whacking to Jenji, I tried spicing things up with a little dirty talk. Nothing raunchy. I just said something about "your great tits." And Jenji says to me, "Ugh! You're disgusting!"

That's right. She scolded me in my own fantasy. Two seconds later, I'm lying there apologizing to her!

You can bet I didn't try that again.

You know what? I gotta get off this subject. Enough already.

Where was I?

After I checked out the architect on the web, I called Arnie to see how he was doing as any dirtyful friend would. Dirtyful? I meant *dutiful.* Jesus.

I caught Arnie just as he was about to pick up Fumi from the hospital. He sounded whipped but managed to slip in one great thought, "You know, when you ask a woman to marry you and she says yes, all it does is give you the confidence to think you can get other women. I'm telling you, man, you just can't win."

Now that I think of it, that kind of dovetails with what I was just talking about.

Anyway, just before we hung up, Arnie wondered if he should buy a stomach pump for home use. How funny is that, Commie?

Next order of business. I texted Graydon with my theory that a non-baseball-playing artsy Eastern European most likely couldn't throw a bottle hard and fast enough to bust through a dollhouse window, let alone a window like Uziel's. I included the contact info of the architect, Preston Lomeli, and:

Ask about the glass he used and what it would take to shatter it.

Best, Deep Throat

Less than a minute later, Graydon texted back, "*Hey, Hal Holbrook.*" That gave me a chuckle. Then,

Good idea. I'm on it. BTW: charging Radmonovic w/ felony Monday or Tuesday. Asking 50G bail.

Best, Ben Bradlee

To tell you the truth, that wasn't the first moment I thought of bailing You-ey out. Right after he was busted, part of me wanted to bail him out just to stick it up everyone's asses, especially that of Uziel and that pig cop, Byron. Another part of me wanted to spring him because, well, I *am* the guy who committed the crime. I mean, you know as well as anyone that I have an over-developed sense of guilt. In this case, my guilt was pretty much justified by the fact that I was guilty.

That's another symptom of our times: People express guilty feelings but never admit guilt. The closest anyone comes to copping to anything is saying they "made bad choices." These senators suck the marrow out of the state to pay for hookers and they "made a bad choice." Mike Vick disembowels a pack of pit bulls? Bad choice. Really? Is that what it was? Just once, I want to hear someone say, "I did it because I'm a horrible human being."

Or here's a conversation I'd like to hear: "Gee, I feel responsible for your father's death."

"Why?"

"Because I shot him."

Dream on, huh?

The point is, no one actually speaks anymore. No one just says the words. I don't know exactly when the English language went from being a way of communicating to a way of deflecting. Watch a tape of Nixon's dopey "Checkers Speech," and he seems sincere next to what you see now. Today, everyone in America talks like a spokesperson with an arsenal of meaningless buzz words or hedging phrases. *Wow, he handled that well.* We've just accepted this Teutonic shift toward stonewalling. In fact, we admire it. I hate getting up on a soapbox again, but—

Oh my God. Did I just say '*Teutonic* shift'? Yikes. I'm really starting to lose it here. Or maybe it's just yet another pre-Alzheimer's tip-off. I meant *tectonic* shift. Obviously. You're not an idiot. I'll tell you, I'm glad you've been out of it for these tongue slips. The shit you would have given me . . .

Although, cut me a little slack. This is definitely the most I've ever spoken in a concentrated period my entire life. Which is pretty cool, you know, setting a new personal record at this age.

Wouldn't it be funny if there was a God, but all He did was keep statistics? You die, you go up or down to wherever. God doesn't make any judgments or dispense any universal wisdom. He just gives you the stats of your life: You ate 36,452 slices of pizza. You drove 5,306,911 miles. You sneezed 123,968 times. You said the words, "I'm sorry," 97,455 times, 62,122 times of which you meant it. You spent $336,977 on restaurants and left $57,286 in tips, an average of 17 percent. You'd probably get a better idea of how you lived your life through those numbers than by hearing some pompous, snotty recap from that condescending dick, St. Peter.

The Statistical God.

I think we're coming up with some pretty good philosophies of life here, Commie. I really do.

V.

I didn't really know if fifty grand was a lot or a little for heaving a bottle through a window, but I did know that You-ey didn't have the money. I'd started doing a little research on bail when the phone rang. Alyse was up in the bedroom and I was downstairs in my little office, so I didn't hear any of her conversation. But it wasn't long before she came down.

"That was Meri."

I turned to Alyse and saw her you-won't-believe-this look.

"You won't believe this. She says to me, 'So, I hear you guys didn't sign the petition.'"

"What? How did she hear that?"

"She heard from Claudia Belkin."

"Who's Claudia Belkin?"

"A friend of a friend of a friend of the mother of a kid who knows Nat Uziel's son."

"That bony freak has friends? Amazing. Did Meri sign the petition?"

"Oh, yeah."

"Was she shocked that we didn't?"

"I don't know. When she told me she signed it, I called her and Ira 'mindless sheep' and hung up on her."

"Get out."

"Not good?"

"Very good. I'm proud of you. Fuck Reuters and her Jefferson Davis husband. You know, in his quiet way, he really is a moron."

Alyse laughed. Then she said, "Hon, I'm not going to get hysterical again, but something is changing around here. Just since Friday night. I don't know."

"Is that necessarily bad?"

"That's what I've been asking myself. I was thinking that I can't really remember ever feeling scared in this way before and maybe I shouldn't assume the worst. I don't really know what I'm saying."

"It takes time to process these things."

"You seem to be doing it more easily than I am. I may have just ended a thirty-whatever-year friendship and I don't feel what I think I should feel. I don't know if that's good or bad."

"Without knocking your past or your friends, feeling the way you do could be a sign of—I don't know—growth? Not that you *needed* to grow. But it's good to evolve a little, I would think. As long as you don't wake up tomorrow and decide to move to Rwanda."

"I don't think I want to live in Rwanda. Although, since we talked about the city, it's been on my mind. Getting away from all this oppressive tact and gossip to a place where you can see your neighbors and not even have to say hello sounds kind of civilized to me."

Shit, Commie. Didn't I tell you before that ignoring neighbors in New York is the peak of civilization? I think I did. Well, if so, I stole that from Alyse too.

The thing that stuck with me from that conversation was that Alyse was now following my lead. It seemed like a role reversal, but maybe it wasn't. I'd always felt like this was Alyse's world and I was lucky enough to be along for the ride. But that didn't mean it was true anymore. Maybe it hadn't been true for years. The impressions that pockmark your brain are hard to shake. And frankly, I guess I wasn't overly intent on shaking them. I like Alyse World. But now I was having that wisp of a thought that maybe I'd become more than just a mid-level executive in my own life. Maybe I was controlling things more than I thought. Talk about your tectonic shifts!

As Alyse turned to go back upstairs, I said, "What would you say to taking the kids to the Cayman Islands over Passover?"

"The Cayman Islands? Why the Cayman Islands?"

"Commie invited us down." Alyse kind of smiled through her confusion, so I added, "I called Commie before." Alyse nodded, no less baffled. "I just felt like calling Commie. It was great talking to him."

"This is what I mean about things changing," she said, "All of a sudden, you're connecting with friends and I'm dumping them."

"Role reversal. I don't know what that's about. But Commie's got a place in the Caymans."

"Isn't that some pricey real estate for a do-gooder lawyer?"

"His kid brother owns it. He was an arbitrageur in the '80s and, according to Commie, he green-mailed his way to insane amounts of money. Now he's a venture capitalist—whatever that means—and he took his whole family to Shanghai. They're living there for a few years. And, besides, Commie's not a public defender anymore."

"I didn't know he was a public defender. I remember he worked with that non-profit outfit."

"The Southern Poverty Law Center. That was before the public defender's office, which was after The World Hunger Foundation, which was after Save the Children. Now he's with a big firm. Of course, he's in charge of all pro bono work, so it's not like he sold out. In fact, at this moment, he's representing a dog."

Alyse looked at me.

"Yeah, he's the attorney for a dog."

"What did the dog do?"

"Don't ask."

Alyse didn't ask. Instead she just said, "You know what? We should give your friends a shot. Arnie's a blast, and Commie's always been this mysterious Christ-like figure in your life. Fine. Let's go to the Cayman Islands."

Alyse turned to go upstairs, but this time she stopped herself. "Oh, by the way, Hanukkah is Tuesday night."

"It is?"

"I figured you didn't know. Hanukkah is the most elusive holiday in the world. You never know where the hell they'll decide to shove it on the calendar."

"Why can't they just decide on a day? Just pick one. Independence Day is July 4th, Hanukkah is December 10th. Every year. Is that so hard?"

"You should bring it up with Pope Alan Greenspan."

"Yeah. I know Esme is past it, but is Charlie over the eight crazy nights phase?"

"I think so. One crazy night ought to do it."

"I'll buy him something tomorrow. You handle Esme?"

"Deal."

That was a mild relief. I wouldn't know what to get Esme. The tastes of her demographic group change every twenty minutes.

I decided against telling Alyse my thoughts about posting bail for You-ey. *Enough*, I thought. *Give her a break.*

And the rest of that Sunday passed without incident.

Oh, one tiny thing: When the kids got home from ice skating, Esme said to Alyse and me, "You know, Chuckster is a really, really good skater."

Charlie reacted as if he'd been sainted. Esme smiled at him with something like real love for her little brother and said, "You should play hockey. You'd be great at it!"

"Maybe I will!"

Even though hockey's a moronic sport, it looks kind of fun to play. Right then, I decided to get Charlie full hockey gear for Hanukkah.

Another decision out of the way.

MONDAY THEN

I.

On Monday morning, maybe fifteen minutes into my solo time in bed, Alyse came running up the stairs and jumped on my side of the bed.

"Wake up."

"What? Is everyone okay?"

"Yeah, yeah. Everyone's fine."

"Then what's going on?"

"I just went on my website and there are six bids for one of You-ey's pieces and four bids on another. The asking price for each was four hundred and they've both been bid up to over eight hundred."

"Holy shit. A bidding war? How did that happen?"

"That's what I was wondering. Then I noticed that two of the bidders had email addresses ending in 'AllWhiteMeat.com.' So, I Googled it and AllWhiteMeat.com is a white supremacist group."

"Jesus Christ."

"Exactly."

"How did they find out about You-ey?"

"Their website had a link to *The New York Times* article from yesterday. The 'buffalo-nosed bagel-biters' phrase was highlighted along with You-ey's line about the Holocaust conspiracy. What should I do?"

"Did it say where these nuts are located?"

"They're based somewhere in Oregon, but they offer on-line memberships so people can hate from anywhere. They offer all these photos on their website of guys in fatigues with rifles. They have bomb-making lessons—you name it. And the weird thing is, they also have recipes on there."

"Recipes. For what?"

"Butterscotch pudding. Shrimp cocktail sauce. French onion soup."

"I used to order French onion soup every time I went out to dinner during college."

"I remember."

"That's not important right now."

"No, not really."

"Alyse, these are scary people. This may sound extreme, but you might want to call the FBI. Commie used to prosecute these hate groups. He told me that between the weak economy and a black president, they're sprouting up so fast, the FBI can barely keep track of them anymore."

"I don't think it's extreme at all. I think it's a great idea."

"Oh, good."

It wasn't until I was in the shower that it dawned on me I was (so far) an unsuspected fugitive who had just willfully suggested bringing the FBI into my life. And yet, in what was becoming a pattern, I just shook my head and smiled. Craziness was starting to feel normal.

Not thirty seconds out of the shower, Alyse was back upstairs and going on about the Feds.

"So, I looked up the FBI. They list a field office in Manhattan serving the whole area, but there's also something called a resident agent on the Queens/Nassau border, so I called that number."

"Good," I said, drying my back. "Think globally, call locally."

"I explained to a receptionist why I was calling and, in no time, she connected me to a FBI agent *at his house* in Baldwin. He's dropping by."

"He's dropping by?"

"He wanted to come at 8:15, but I asked him if I could get the kids off to school first, so he said he'd go out to breakfast and be here around 8:45. Can you—?"

"I'll call Sylvia and cancel my first appointment. No big deal."

Commie, among the admittedly more obvious reasons why I chose you as the one person I would tell this whole story to, I think you can now understand why I thought it would interest you. Granted, it took me over two days to get to the white supremacist aspect. But you spent all that time at the Southern Poverty Law Center nailing white supremacists. You told me how they spread like weeds after Obama was elected. This shit's right in your wheelhouse.

I woke up the kids a bit earlier and with more vigor than usual.

Did I mention that Charlie has a fish tank in his room? I only mention it now because, when I went into his room that morning, the light in the tank went on right as I opened the door. It's weird how fish look when they wake up, glassy-eyed and stoned just like people. I also noticed there was a build-up of algae on all their plastic plants. I remember thinking that was so weird. You have plastic plants. Then algae grows on them, making them look like real plants. It was like the botanical version of Pinocchio. *Look, I'm a real plant now!*

I don't know why I even mentioned that. I guess, with all that was going on, irony was suddenly popping up everywhere in my field of vision.

"Hey, kiddo, you gotta clean your fish tank one of these days."

Funny, my kids have never asked for a dog. If they'd asked, I'd have probably done it. Not that I feel one way or the other about dogs. I've never had one. Sometimes I think it might be nice to have something around the house that's aging even faster than me. But otherwise, I can take 'em or leave 'em.

"Maybe we can get a bigger tank soon, Dad."

"Maybe."

"We have to get a bigger tank if I buy a silver arowana."

"A silver arowana can grow to be a foot long. He'll eat all your other fish."

"I know. They're so cool. I read that, in the wild, arowanas can jump out of the water and eat small monkeys."

I pulled the blanket off him. "You're a small monkey, and it's time to go to the zoo we call school."

As I said, it's warm in Charlie's room, so, instead of pajamas, he sleeps in Allen Iverson basketball shorts. By the time he turned eight, I found myself stealing glances at his ankles to see if any hair was growing in, always hoping there wasn't. It was as if I wanted him to stay the exact age he was, dreading the day he'd turn into another adult with unsavory hormones and hidden motives. On that morning, his ankles were smooth and innocent, temporarily freeing me to worry about all kinds of other stuff beyond my control.

You know what, Commie? Nothing happened at breakfast. We ate and they went to school.

II.

My image of a FBI agent is Efrem Zimbalist Jr. So, when Alyse and I opened the door for Lester Horton, I felt like asking for his ID. As it happened, he showed his ID on his own and we welcomed yet another law enforcement official into our home. Horton was in his early forties, jowly, with a comb-over, gray pants, blue jacket with brass buttons—the kind of guy who always played the father in the high school play.

Alyse gave him a cup of coffee, which he absently sipped while scanning her website. He then whizzed around her computer in such a blur that the hard drive must have been thinking: *What the fuck*?

In no time, he leaned back and asked Alyse, "Do you have any other pieces of Mr. Brushstroke's artwork that you can post on your website?"

Alyse, appropriately baffled, said, "Actually, I do. He brought over a few that I took shots of, and haven't posted yet, and he emailed me photos of three others."

Horton reacted in a way that was both pleased and grim. "That's good," he said.

Alyse and I looked at each other, lost. Horton was probably used to this kind of reaction, so he explained things in a firm, even-paced way that even mindless civilians could grasp.

"First off," he began, "you need not worry about these people. I've investigated and taken down white supremacist groups for years."

My glance at Alyse was less than a glance. But Horton caught it.

"I know I don't look the type, but that's part of why I'm so good at it. "

Alright, sir.

"Now, not all supremacists are rural auto mechanics. Some are middle class, even upper middle class, from metropolitan areas. They post gun-toting photos and bomb-making instructions on their websites, but that's just a smokescreen. They want you to believe they're like all those whacko militiamen in Northern Michigan."

"They're bourgeois neo-Nazis," I said.

"Right," Horton said with light impatience. "So bourgeois that they collect what we call 'hate art.'"

Alyse was compelled to say, "You-ey's work isn't really political."

"Doesn't matter. He made the anti-Semitic remarks. They just assume his work reflects that. These guys are more insidious than others of their ilk because they hide their identities and they have money. So, while they don't get their hands dirty, they give money to groups that do. They let the militia idiots—that's how they often refer to violent white supremacists—do their bidding. That's how some band of schmucks who do lube jobs all day can get their hands on grenade launchers. These money guys are the ones I've been focusing on. You can help me find them."

Alyse looked at me, seemingly resigned to watching her life permanently spin into surreal places. I put my arm around her and nodded at Horton. *The FBI can count on us, sir.*

"I want you to post five new works by Mr. Brushstroke and start the bidding higher than you're used to. At least $1,500 per piece. I'll be on an FBI computer and get in on the bidding. We'll keep bumping the price up to see who stays in the game. Then we'll let them win and follow the shipment of the art. Get the picture?"

By that point, I could have easily imagined the jowly, bald Horton ripping off his clothes, igniting rockets in his Cole Hahn shoes, and flying through our chimney to intercept a Soviet cruise missile.

Instead, Horton said, "We'll be monitoring your computer closely, so, if you're in the habit of exchanging sexually explicit messages, you may want to refrain from doing so for the time being."

No problem, sir.

"I want to thank you in advance for your cooperation." He handed Alyse his card. "It has all my numbers on it. Day or night, don't hesitate."

Like one of those kids begging for Trident in the old commercials, I said, "Can I have one too?"

I got a card too, and then the first federal agent ever to grace our abode ambled out the door to fight crime.

After briefly contemplating our new life of counter-terrorism, Alyse looked at me and said, "I feel like I've been serving a lot of coffee lately."

I opened the closet to get my coat, then turned to Alyse, "I meant to ask, did you ever ask Esme why she left out 'buffalo-nosed' from the 'bagel-biters' description?"

"No. I figured she just didn't want to hurt my feelings."

"What?"

"You know, my nose."

"Alyse. A) You have a slight bump on your nose and B) Your slight bump is among my top 65 favorite physical traits of yours."

"I have 65 physical traits?"

"At last count. And your nose is beautiful. It should be part of the Whitney's permanent collection."

Driving to work, at the red light where I turn left onto Stratification Boulevard, a thirty-ish guy wearing a yarmulke stopped beside me in his Acura. Every time one of the Orthodox looks at me, I assume disapproval, which may or may not be paranoia. It probably is. But this time, I met eyes with the guy and found myself contriving my face to look innocent. *Just act natural.*

See, Commie, it's tricky to be simultaneously a criminal and not a suspect. The criminal in you says you're a suspect, while everyone else looks at you as just another guy in the world. When the light turned green and the non-confrontational confrontation ended, I started thinking about the likelihood of having driven beside a serial killer at some point in my life. Chances are, I've exchanged glances with a guy in the next car who had strangled nineteen total strangers in the previous three years. I may have even treated some homicidal maniac's feet. Imagine getting a guy back on his feet so he can kill some more. If you watch that show on Channel Two, *Criminal Minds*, you realize sociopaths are all over the place. I probably sat at a Mets game and high-fived Son of Sam after Tom Seaver struck out the side.

Actually, that was before the high-five was invented.

Sometimes I watch that *Investigation Discovery* channel. All true murders, all day. Ninety-five percent of the murders take place in small towns where the residents say, "A father drugging his wife and kids, then burning them alive in the guest room is the kind of thing that just doesn't happen in a place like this." The truth is, that's exactly where that kind of thing happens. You know where those kind of things don't happen? New York City. That's where.

III.

I strode into the office and realized I wasn't limping. The ankle felt weak, but I had it wrapped and wore black cross trainers that can pass for office shoes in a pinch, if no one looks too closely. Covering up or disguising my steady but unpredictable influx of ailments has become another preoccupation. Soon my whole wardrobe will be designed by doctors.

Sylvia informed me that she had moved around two of my morning appointments and then handed me a phone message from Audra Uziel. I figured she wanted to apologize for her father again. No doubt she'd heard that I didn't sign the petition and, more importantly, that her father gave Esme his lecture on vigilance. But Commie? I didn't feel like talking to Audra. Maybe my thing for her had run its course, like some middle-aged virus. It's not that I wasn't going to call her back. I just wasn't in a rush. The rush, in all its forms, was gone. Then I had a tiny thought: Maybe Alyse wasn't as cool about my flirtation with Audra as she let on, and that was what had sparked her emotional shakiness that weekend. But you know what? I didn't want to start analyzing it. I just wanted to ease back into the friendly confines of my life. Let's face it. I hardly ever come to a firm conclusion on anything anyway.

My first patient was Sam Kipnis, an unusual Orthodox in that he has no problem making jokes about God, Jews, or anything. The first time he came to my office, he asked me what it's like to have lights on in my house on Friday nights. I was cautious at the time, even wondering if it was some kind of trick question or a test to see whether I was a suitable choice of podiatrist. I said, "Excuse me?" Sam laughed and said, "I'm just kidding around. I wanted you to feel comfortable with me, seeing as you're not observant and I'm a fanatic." Still not sure it wasn't a trap, I just said, "Thanks. That's very considerate." But Sam said, "What's on TV on Friday nights? Am I missing anything? I won't even set my TiVo for a show airing on Shabbos. It feels like cheating, although maybe it's a perfectly legal loophole. I should talk to the Rabbi."

Eventually, I accepted Sam's sense of humor as unsquelchable by piety. I liked seeing him. He'd first come in with garden-variety corns, but now fleeting pain buzzed the metatarso-phalangeal joint of his big toe. Every time he played tennis, the pain would radiate from that spot the first time he ran, and then it would recede into a dull but tolerable ache. I put on my rubber glove and moved the toe this way and that, gauging his reaction. I concluded he was in the early throes of arthritis. "Ha!" Sam said, way too loud. "That's exactly what I thought it was. When I was a kid in summer camp, I stubbed my big toe into my cubby and, I swear, it's never felt perfect since. Could that have led to the arthritis?"

"It's possible," I said, "combined with the pounding you take playing tennis. It's a cumulative thing."

Sam asked if I still play basketball and, when I unconvincingly said yes, he said, "I hear you have a lot of game."

"Really? Who told you that?"

"Kenny Victor. He works at my wife's brother's law firm."

"Oh, Kenny's great. Good player."

A white lie. I score at will on Kenny Victor and throw his jumper back in his face all the time even though he has three inches on me. But it was nice of him to speak highly of my game.

I told Sam to get an OTC arthritis pain med and to keep me up to date on the pain. If it got worse, I'd recommend someone to implant a prosthetic joint (a procedure I used to do myself) to alleviate the pain and increase the range of motion—and off Sam went.

Okay, Commie. I'll come clean: I only told you about Sam Kipnis so you'd hear someone testify that I can still play ball. It was a cheap trick, although my cross-over dribble *is* better now.

Alright. I'll spare you.

My second patient, Beverly Kay, an orange-haired shrew in her mid-sixties, didn't show up for her appointment. Good. I could escape her fat pedicured toes and charge her anyway. Paying for missed appointments is a strict policy for patients I can't stand. I was telling Sylvia to bill her when Arnie popped by.

"Hey," he said, "I just got in from bringing Fumi home from the hospital."

"How's she doing?"

"Who knows? The shrink who prescribed the pills came, spent some time with her, and offered two suggestions you won't believe."

"Oh God. What?"

"He told me Fumi has to stay on the pills if only to avoid a very uncomfortable withdrawal. But since he doesn't trust her to take the right dosage, he assigned that to me. I have to keep the pills 'on my person' and dole them out to Fumi as prescribed. Next thing you know, I'll be running a fucking methadone clinic out of my garage."

I tried to squelch a laugh but couldn't. "I'm sorry, Arnie. I couldn't help it."

"It's okay. I was trying to be funny."

"So, what was the second recommendation?"

"Well, after talking to her, he decided that her overdose was not a suicide attempt. Apparently, she just wanted the pills to work faster."

"When he first prescribed the pills, didn't he explain to her that this isn't like an upset stomach? That it takes weeks to take effect in your system?"

"I asked myself the same thing, but it didn't seem the time to raise the idea of malpractice."

"No, I guess not."

"So, anyhow, he says she's not suicidal, but, just to be sure, he encouraged her to pursue a lawsuit against the doctor and the hospital for ruining her Junya Watanabe dress."

"What?"

"Yeah, he thinks a lawsuit would give her something to occupy her mind and look forward to. Can you fucking believe that?"

"So it's like litigation therapy?"

"Exactly! Well put."

"You know, Arnie, it's kind of comforting to know that you and

I aren't the only health professionals flying by the seat of our pants. This guy's a psychopharmacologist—med school, residency, the whole shebang—and he doesn't know what the hell he's doing either."

"Throwing shit against the wall and hoping for the best. That's all any of us are doing. So, what's up with you?"

I recounted the story about Alyse's website and the neo-Nazis. First, Arnie said, "Well, if you're not part of the final solution, you're part of the problem." I did my "*that's so sick*" laugh, then told Arnie about the stuff on the hate group site.

Arnie mulled everything over, then said, "Neo-Nazi websites have shrimp cocktail recipes?"

Leave it to Arnie to fixate on the most tossed-off aspect of everything I said.

"Yeah, Alyse saw it on their website."

"I love shrimp cocktail. I had it as an appetizer Saturday night. In fact, I make it at home. And the sauce. From scratch. "

"I once made hard-boiled eggs from scratch." Arnie laughed, and I added, "Actually, my mother used to make shrimp cocktail sauce because my father would always bring home shrimp but no sauce."

Arnie nodded and—this is the relevant part of all this—he said, "The key to cocktail sauce is the horseradish. It's gotta be the white stuff. The hotter the better. I bet if those red-neck white supremacists could get past the whole Jew aspect, they'd love that Mossad shit. It's the hottest I've ever tasted."

My mind started whirring.

"I should have stopped at the shrimp cocktail on Saturday. That mushroom and asparagus gnocchi had me so gassy I swear I had a contrail coming out of my ass."

Arnie waited for me to laugh, but thoughts kept filling my head.

"Write down the website for me," he said.

"Huh?"

Arnie shrugged. "I'd like to see their recipe."

At that moment, Sylvia knocked on my open door and told Arnie he had a patient waiting.

"Oh shit . . ."

I went over to my computer and clicked onto AllWhiteMeat.com, and there it was—a detailed recipe for shrimp cocktail submitted by Margot G. of Hurley, Oregon. I scanned the list of ingredients and, well, you won't believe this. At the end of the list was: "My secret ingredient: one quarter tsp of Kick 'em All Out Extra Hot Horseradish."

I was like: *When did horseradish become the marketing vehicle of choice for the lunatic fringe?*

Without even thinking, I Googled "Kick 'em All Out."

"Kick 'em All Out Extra Hot Horseradish Brand is the finest hand-prepared, coarse-ground horseradish in the world! Its roots come from the horseradish capital of the world, Collinsville, Illinois, and are transported in seventy-five-pound burlap bags, dirt and all! Each root is washed, cut, and peeled by the members of our family—an American family that proudly dates back to the 17th Century. All retail outlets carrying the Kick 'em All Out Extra Hot Horseradish Brand are subject to rigorous background checks to ensure that no proceeds from this product wind up in the coffers of any group active in, or affiliated with, philosophies or attitudes contrary to the interests of ethnically pure, TRUE Americans."

Sound familiar, Commie?

Almost the exact same wording as on the Mossad Horseradish website. Same typeface too. Same sun-drenched photo of roots sticking out of seventy-five-pound burlap bags.

Instead of texting Graydon, this time I called him. I started by saying I didn't know how this would affect the stuff he was reporting on, but it would definitely be a fascinating sidebar to the main story. When I told him that the horseradish producers were double-dealing Jews and white supremacists, Graydon was blown away.

"How the fuck did you find this out?"

"I'll tell you, but this is all off-the-record."

"Jesus, listen to you. Okay, off-the-record. What?"

I told him about the bidding on You-ey's art.

"Holy shit."

And about the FBI agent coming to our house.

"Holy shit!"

"So, you see Graydon, you can write what you want about the horseradish, but it's crucial you sit on the rest."

"Don't worry. Just because I'm not Jewish doesn't mean I'm a fan of neo-Nazis."

"Imagine my relief."

Graydon laughed and said, "Oh, I looked into the window. You'd only have to throw the bottle about sixty miles an hour to shatter the glass. In fact, a bird flying that fast might shatter it."

"Sixty miles an hour is faster than you think. Most people couldn't throw a baseball that fast."

"Well," Graydon said, "I don't know where that's gonna go."

I said to Graydon, "You know what you should do? Tell You-ey's lawyer that you doubt You-ey is physically capable of shattering the window. Then, maybe at the arraignment, he can set something up where he throws, like, a tennis ball to You-ey. If You-ey has a pathetic throw, then you got something, right?"

Commie, I don't know where ideas like that were coming from. It was like my thoughts were imported from somewhere else.

Graydon hesitated, so I backpedaled immediately. "I guess getting in bed with a public defender to exonerate his client wouldn't exactly be ethical journalism."

"Not really. Although the idea is tempting."

"Maybe I could do it. I'm a podiatrist. What do I give a shit about ethics?"

Graydon burst out laughing and said, "You really should have been a reporter. You have the head for it. Of course, if you had, you would have been denied a life of prosperity. But still, you're good at this. Really good. You got anything else?"

"Yeah. The walrus was Paul."

I guess admiration for my reporting skills was in the air because I called Alyse and told her the whole Neo-Nazi/Zionist horseradish story and she said, "Nice investigative journalism. Maybe we really should have moved to Louisville."

IV.

Oh.

You know what, Commie?

I meant to follow up on the last time Alyse mentioned Louisville, but I don't thing I ever did.

I'll zip through this fast:

Remember I told you about that spring break when I decided to be a journalist and find work on a small town paper, then taking Alyse out to dinner and totally selling myself out? Well, I neglected to tell you that I'd actually gone as far as listing a bunch of possible newspapers and sending out some resumés. Then, at about the same time I was about to be "accepted" into podiatry school, I got a letter from the managing editor of the *Louisville Courier Journal* offering me a job on the metro desk. I remember reading the letter and getting a sick feeling. I'd put the whole idea of journalism out of my head in a totally voluntary case of denial. Then I get a job offer and it was like those people who see something that triggers a repressed memory of being fondled by an uncle when they were eight. That's a bit much, but you get my point. And, by the way, the *Courier Journal* was a highly regarded paper, which only made matters worse.

I threw the letter in the back of some drawer, an out-of-sight, out-of-mind move that worked pretty well. Maybe too well because, after graduation, when Alyse and I were packing up our stuff, she found the letter. I kind of spastically told her I'd sent out a resumé just as an experiment to see if professionals would think I was a good writer. Lame, I know.

Alyse, God bless her, said, "Hon, do you want to be a reporter? I mean, would you want to move to Louisville and pursue a newspaper career? Because, if you do, it's fine. We can talk about it."

Once again, I must point out that life refuses to stick to your script. Crossroads don't show up in the distance; they fall from the sky and land on your forehead. I don't have to tell you the rest of the story, do I? You know me: I danced around my feelings without identifying what they were and reassured Alyse that I had no desire to live in Kentucky. As Woodward and Bernstein used to say, "another non-denial denial."

So, now, Alyse brought up Louisville for the second time in forty-eight hours. I guess, after all these years, she was as aware of that crossroads moment as I was. I took it as an opportunity to say, "I don't know. Journalism is fun when it's a hobby and your livelihood's not at stake, but I can also see how it can wear you out. If I'd gone into journalism after college, I'd have probably burned out by 40 or 45. So, I'm quite happy to be just dipping my feet in it now, knowing I can jump back into our real life at will."

"I'm glad to hear that," Alyse said. "You know, we never really talked about it all these years."

"Yeah. It never really bothered me or popped into my mind with any, you know, regularity. Hardly ever, in fact. Still, now that we've talked about it, I'm glad. Because I wouldn't want you thinking it's a major regret or whatever. Certainly not for me, so . . ."

Even though I was being pretty honest, I also really wanted to change the subject. The older I get, the more I believe that facing facts head-on hardly ever does anyone any good.

Sylvia—God bless her oppressive competence—knocked on my open door and, with a smile, whispered, "Someone in the examination room needs a podiatrist."

"There's a patient. Gotta go. I love you."

Freed in mid-squirm.

I had a run of three straight patients and then Sylvia handed me a message saying that Rico, the guy from the assisted living place, had called.

I went to my office.

"Mistah Feets! Wassup, my man?"

"Not much. How are you, Rico?"

"I'm good, man. Good."

"How is everyone over there?"

"You know, the same."

"Is Ruth improving after her mini-stroke?"

My normal tendency would be to avoid having Rico think that Ruth occupied even a tiny spot in my mind. But now, I just didn't care. Constantly monitoring everyone's opinion of me suddenly felt pointless and stupid. I guess it was about time I realized that people are going to think what they think. You can't influence their views and why waste time trying? It just shocks me how long it takes to reach such a simple conclusion. I couldn't have figured that out at nineteen? Whenever I do finally grasp a basic life lesson, I always think I'll pass it on to Esme and Charlie to save them years of doubt and insecurity. And I do try and will keep trying. But, more and more, I'm convinced everyone has to learn these things for themselves. Considering how critical good parenting is in a kid's life, it's amazing how you, the parent, can be so superfluous.

"I guess Ruth's head cleared up some 'cause she asked if she did anything to embarrass herself when you was here. She had no clue! That mini-stroke knocked a whole week out of her head. Gone."

"What did you tell her, Rico?"

"Shit, man, I told her she didn't do nothing embarrassing, that she acted like, really nice, you know?"

"She buy it?"

"No, man. I think she knew I was lying my ass off. But what could I do? Tell her that she told us she never sucked a dick?"

"No, Rico. I think you were smart to leave that out."

"Yeah, I think so too."

"So, what did you call me about?"

"Carolina asked me to ask you if you would give him a call."

"Is he okay?"

"He's good. But he's going blind, so he can't see the numbers on the phone too good and, by the time he dials right, he's made like ten wrong numbers."

"It's frustrating for him."

"There you go."

"I'll call him right now."

"You da man, Mistah Feets."

After I tell you about my call to Carolina, I'll try not to go off on any long tangents. I'll fail, but I *will* try. I just think you'll find this little thing about Carolina interesting.

V.

After minimal small talk, Carolina said to me, “I lied to you on Friday about something. I don’t want you to feel singled out because it’s something I’ve been lying about my whole life. But, after you left on Friday, I started feeling bad about it. You’ve always been a good listener. So lying to you just didn’t sit right with me.”

“Carolina,” I said, “you’re killing me with suspense.”

“Sorry about my—what’s the word?—preamble.”

“Preamble. Okay.”

“The thing I lied to you about was when I told you I was never married. The truth is, I was married in 1962, in Texarkana. The marriage lasted three months.”

“Three months can be a long time.”

“Thank you. Most people would laugh at me when hearing that: ‘Three months! That don’t even count!’ But it counted for me and I appreciate you supporting me in that feeling.”

“Sure.”

“Her name was Esther. Pretty, pretty girl. For me, it was love at first sight, so when she got pregnant, I married her. She was morning sick for the first month or so, but when she got over that, she started going out and shopping and doing whatever she did. She was kind of new in town, so she didn’t have any friends that I knew about. I was working for my dad at the time, so I wasn’t too sure what she did with her days.”

“Uh huh.”

“This one day, I come home from work and she’s not there. I don’t think much of it. But, when it got around seven and eight o’clock, I started worrying. Like I said, she didn’t have any girlfriends. Down in Texarkana in 1962, a black man didn’t call the police and report a missing person.”

“I can imagine.”

“I walked around for hours looking for her—another thing a black man had to think twice about doing. Then I came home hoping she'd come back, but she didn't. I called a few of my friends and they hadn't seen her. I didn't know what to do. So, I gave it some more time and decided I'd go to the police if she wasn't back by morning. In daylight, going to the police was at least a little less intimidating."

"Uh huh."

"I slept maybe two hours and, come daybreak, I walked to the police station. On the way, I passed a newsstand and there on the front page is a picture of Esther." Carolina paused for about ten seconds to gather himself. "Seems Esther was arrested because she happened to be present when the police raided this house where a woman was running an abortion business."

"Oh, God."

"Yeah. And even worse, she was there just resting because she'd already had her abortion. They also arrested two white women who were waiting to get fixed up. Everyone knew about this abortion lady. She was open for business every Tuesday afternoon. And one day, I guess the police decided to shut her down."

"Boy."

"But, my friend, it gets worse. Because Esther's picture was in the paper, three other men—one from Galveston, one from Lubbock, and one from somewhere else—came forward and claimed they were married to Esther."

"Oh, Carolina. I'm so sorry."

"She'd stolen all kinds of money from them. I didn't even wait to hear the particulars of the scam she was running. It all just came clear to me that I had to pack up my things, take whatever money I'd saved up, and go somewhere far, far away. And that's how I ended up in New York."

"That's some story."

"And, like I said, you're the first person I've even told it to."

"Does it feel good getting it off your chest?"

"Not sure. I'll get back to you on that."

"Can I ask you one question?"

"Shoot."

"You said there were two white women arrested while waiting for their abortions. Were their pictures in the paper too?"

Carolina chuckled. "No way, baby. They slipped the white girls out the back and let their husbands deal with them their own way. But Esther, they made a public example out of her."

"I admire how you just quietly left town. I'd have wanted to kill someone."

"Yeah, well, you wouldn't have lasted very long as a black man."

The Statistical God: You spoke on the phone to a black person 92 times in your life, of which 23 were black people you knew, 54 were customer service representatives, 15 were civil servants . . .

After the conversation with Carolina, I putzed around with a few hundred dollars' worth of feet, then called Alyse. She wasn't home, so I called her cell. No answer.

I figured she was at a yoga class. The thought of calling Audra back crossed my mind. But I still wasn't in the mood. Instead, I walked out to Sylvia and asked her if Arnie was seeing a patient. When she said no, I popped in on him.

Turns out, he was asleep on his couch.

"Sorry, Arnie."

"No, no. I'm just wiped out. It's cool. Besides, I don't want my next patient to see gobs of sleep snot in my eyes. It's unprofessional."

I told Arnie about the double-dealing horseradish company.

"A marketing strategy that exploits people's hatred. That's fucking brilliant!"

"I guess."

"Hey, we should order a few bottles of the Nazi variety. At the very least, they'd be good conversation pieces."

And so then we (I assume) became the first New York Jews to place an on-line order of Kick 'em All Out horseradish—the Nazi variety. Actually, Arnie placed the order. On his credit card. Six bottles shipped to the office. As Arnie completed the transaction, he looked up at me with total sincerity and said, “Should we subscribe to the mailing list?”

Before I could answer, my cell rang.

“It’s Alyse. I should go talk to her.”

I walked back to my office. Alyse was calling from the car.

“Where are you, honey?”

“Hempstead. On my way home. You won’t believe from where.”

“Where?”

“I visited You-ey in jail.”

“You’re kidding me.”

“I know it sounds nuts.”

“No, it doesn’t sound nuts. I’m surprised, but you do have a relationship with him. And with all the innocent-til-proven-guilty stuff, there’s nothing wrong with continuing to be a friend to him.”

“I guess. The truth is, I haven’t really sorted out why I did it. I know the concrete reason but not the emotional ones.”

“What was the concrete reason?”

“Gil Binder called me and said, ‘So, I hear you hung up on Meri.’”

“What is he, a yenta girl?”

“I know. I dated the guy forty years ago and I’m still paying for it.”

“So what did you say?”

“I said, ‘Gil, I just didn’t feel like taking shit from Meri Katzen for not signing some idiotic petition.’ So, you won’t believe what Gil said.”

“I’m sitting.”

“Gil says, ‘Meri should have known you wouldn’t sign the petition.’”

“What’s that supposed to mean?”

“That’s exactly what I said. What’s that supposed to mean? And Gil says, ‘Let’s face it, ever since you stopped belonging to a synagogue, you’ve been headed in that direction.’”

“What direction?”

“Again, that’s exactly what I said. What direction? And Gil says,

'Well, to be perfectly blunt, the self-hating Jew direction.'"

VI.

Commie, these are the kinds of moments that make me a guy who favors gun control. At that moment, all it would have taken is someone a smidgen less sane than me to grab a gun, drive to Gil's mock-tasteful-modern style house, kick open the front door, take aim at him as he's sipping his green tea, and empty a clip into his fat, Billy Joel-loving, St. Bart's-vacationing ass.

But that's not me, Commie. Even though I truly believe that if I were given a license to kill five people a day, I could make this a better world, I also believe in "thou shalt not kill." So, instead, I said to my beautiful wife, "That is so fucked up, honey."

"Tell me about it."

"What did you say to him?"

"I said, and I quote, 'I'm not a self-hating Jew, I'm a you-hating Jew.'"

"Whoa. I like it."

"I'm getting pretty good at this shedding friends thing."

"So you hung up on Gil."

"And I was so angry and resentful, I thought, *What can I do to really stick it to them?*"

"Uh huh."

"I have to admit, I'd thought about contacting You-ey before that. In fact, not contacting him all weekend made me feel a little guilty. I'm like his only friend. I was actually a little surprised I wasn't his one phone call."

"Maybe with all the anti-Semitic stuff, he was embarrassed to call you."

"That's exactly why he didn't call me. He told me so."

"I'm somewhere between appalled and impressed that you went to see You-ey in jail."

"I know. I feel the same way. And, even though I'm feeling a little shaky about it, I think I'll look back on it as an interesting experience. Not one I'd want to have again, but interesting."

"How did you know how to go about, you know, seeing him?"

In a sing-song-y, don't-get-upset tone, Alyse said, "Well, honey, the truth is, I called the police and asked to talk to Detective Byron."

"What? Why that prick?"

"I figured since he was so taken with my ass, he'd be more helpful."

"Jesus, Alyse."

"Sorry about that. But I didn't even see Byron. I got him on the phone. He sounded like he was in a real pissed-off mood. He just told me about the detention center and that was it."

"So, how was You-ey?"

"Devastated, actually. He was so upset, he swore up and down that he didn't throw the bottle, but that wasn't the thing that upset him the most. It was the hate crime thing that was eating away at him."

"Did you ask him about what he said to Esme?"

"Yeah. And he was really honest about it. At least he seemed honest. He said that when he came over, he started feeling sad because he didn't think he'd ever have a home like ours with a wife and kids. And he said that it looked to him like Esme and I seemed so natural in our upper-middle class lives that his sadness turned to jealousy and he just said something he shouldn't have said."

"Yeah, but that doesn't explain the Holocaust denial line he said when he was busted."

"I asked him about that too. All he said was that he didn't know why he said it."

"He probably said it because he believes it."

"Maybe."

"Not that it's any excuse, but half the country believes it. The Holocaust, the moon landing—all bullshit. I'll tell you, Alyse, since all the stupid people learned the word 'conspiracy,' there's been no hope for this country."

"Yeah. Look, You-ey was so depressed I felt like I had to say something to make him feel a little better, so I told him that you thought he was innocent. I hope you don't mind."

"You couldn't cheer him up by telling him his art is suddenly worth something?"

"I could have. But then I would have had to tell him that all the interest in his art was coming from neo-Nazis."

"Good point. And no, I don't mind. I *do* think he's innocent."

"Still?"

"Yeah. Do you?"

"I don't know. I think I just want to think he's innocent."

"Have you been driving throughout this whole conversation?"

"No, I pulled over."

"Oh, good. So, are you worried about people hearing that you visited You-ey in jail?"

"Um, no. Not really. In fact, I've had thoughts about going one step further."

"I'm listening."

"What would you say if I told you that, after You-ey is arraigned, I've been wondering if I should bail him out?"

Commie, at that point, I decided not to tell Alyse I'd already thought of bailing You-ey out myself. When you think of Alyse bucking up and going to a jail to talk to a possible convict, it's so amazing. It was like, suddenly Alyse and I were back on the same wavelength, albeit a whole different wavelength than we'd ever been on. On Saturday, she'd been hysterical about how all this shit was suddenly going down in our lives, and when you columbine with how I—*Columbine*? Jesus, I'm losing it. When you *combine* that with how I seemed to be enjoying the tumult, it's understandable that she was upset. But now it was Monday and she'd caught up to my state of mind. As if we'd stepped out from the upholstered life You-ey wanted for himself and crossed into a world of intrigue. Not that I'm saying we morphed into some suburban, less-witty version of Nick and Nora Charles, but we were kind of working the case together. You know what I mean?

Anyway, I thought it best to let Alyse think the idea of bailing out You-ey had never entered my mind. You know, let her continue getting her feet under her.

The truth: Do all guys who've been married for over twenty years still ply all these strategies to bolster their wives' confidence? I don't think so. At this point, most guys have long ago shifted into manipulating their wives, if not outright playing them for saps. And vice versa. Most couples are bored magicians. She pulls out the rabbit, he takes four aces out of his ass, and they both yawn. How do people go on like that?

"I have no problem with bailing him out," I said. Then, to make me seem appropriately surprised by her question: "I mean, you know, on first reaction, I don't think I have any problem."

"We'd have to put down, like, ten percent. It's like going into escrow on a possible convict."

"Yeah. So, I guess you researched all this already."

"No, I just asked someone at the desk after I left You-ey."

I said, "Aside from doing your jail time, how's the rest of your day going, hon?"

"Totally awesome, sweetie. You?"

"Just terrific, darling. I've been working hard, making a lot of money, and just, you know, doing my part to help the Jewish people continue to control a disproportionate amount of wealth in America."

"You once told me that it seemed like every time I talk to you, I apologize for something my family did. I swear, this is going to be the last time I apologize. I'm sorry. And I'm so glad you steadfastly refused to sign the petition."

Before going to lunch, I figured if my wife spent her morning in a prison visitation room, I could return Audra's phone call before lunch. What one thing has to do with the other, I have no idea. But that's what I thought.

VII.

Audra's voice sounded even more resolute than usual over the phone. None of the hedging "likes" and "you knows" that cripple the sentence structure of every other American kid. None of the declarative statements ending in a vocal question mark.

Come to think of it, I say "like" and "you know" a lot. Well, screw it. Mangling the language keeps me young.

"Audra," I said, "not to nitpick, but I didn't 'steadfastly refuse' to sign the petition. I simply said, "No, thanks." If your dad wants to circulate a petition, it's his right. Just as it's my right to decline to sign it. Yes, I completely disagreed with him. But there was no hostility. At least, no open hostility."

"Was there under-the-surface hostility?"

"Oh, Audra."

"What?"

"Nothing, Audra. I guess I find it annoying how hard it is for me to lie to you."

Commie, can your primitive nervous system flirt on its own? I called Audra as if it were a chore. But in two seconds, intimacy slipped out on its own.

"You're probably a shitty liar anyhow."

"I'm getting better at it. The truth is, when your father told my daughter that she must be vigilant about anti-Semitism, there was a part of me that wanted to snap his head off."

"He told your daughter *what?*"

I should have known she wouldn't have heard that part of the story. I recounted the omitted section of the conversation with Nat and, over the phone, could feel his daughter's nervous system cranking up to Def Con One.

"I don't believe he said that. I do not believe he said that!"

"Audra, please. Alyse very clearly explained our point of view on this, so there's no need for you to lay into him."

Commie, you notice how many times I say the word "Audra"

when I talk to her? That's another kind of flirting, isn't it? I always liked it when girls spoke to me and said my name. That, and when they'd make a point of touching my arm. Greatest things in the world.

"Audra, I hope you're not planning to confront your father over this. It's not worth it, believe me. My wife and I already made him feel bad enough about it. Just let it go."

"Okay," Audra said. "I won't say anything about it. But the only way I can do that is to make some excuse for not showing up tomorrow night for Hanukkah, because, if I go and see my father, I don't think I'll be able to keep my mouth shut."

"Audra, I think you're old enough to miss the lighting of the Hanukkah candles."

"Yeah, probably. I wonder if I'll get to a point in my life where I can convince myself to 'let it go.' Every quote-unquote adult is constantly saying that to me: *'Let it go.'*"

"Well, Audra, hopefully that's one of the few things we're right about."

"If you decide in the next 24 hours that you're wrong," Audra said, "please let me know. Email or text me and just write, DON'T LET IT GO."

The call lasted maybe five minutes. The second I hung up, a text beeped for my attention.

Talked 2 pinkie-less kid. Admits he held Bose headsets over dog's ears, cranked 'Holla Back Girl.' Dog freaked, bit pinkie.

Commie.

I texted back:

That's a great song. What's the fucking dog's problem?

You texted back:

Only u would say that. Gotta run 2 court. Late 4 hearing.

I loved that you remembered me as having a unique point of view. It just made me happy. I immediately went to Sylvia's desk and asked her to call my kids' schools and find out when spring break was so I could start looking into flights for the family to Grand

Cayman.

So long as we're on the subject of me and you: The second I looked down at my phone and saw the text was from you, I had this weird little rush of memory. It was as if all of my old familiarity with you came back through Verizon, because, before I even read the text, I thought that if you were contacting me in the middle of the day like this, it must be something really good. And, sure enough, it *was* really good. As much as I watch cop shows, I never saw the kid's confession coming. Anyway, just sensing that your text would be a doozy says something, doesn't it? Maybe all it says is that I remembered that you've never been boring.

Even now, you're more interesting than most.

(Another lame joke.)

Yeah, I know. I never run out.

Of course, now, in retrospect, it's the last line of that final text you sent me—*Late 4 hearing*—that sticks with me.

If I had typed my text a tiny bit faster or used the shorthand that everyone else uses, maybe Commie would have gotten to court a few seconds earlier and the hearing would have started a few seconds earlier and ended a few seconds earlier and he would have gotten out of court a few seconds sooner and . . .

I know, I know. It's just a reflex: an obsessive, useless, morbid, self-destructive reflex. I wish I could get a prosthetic nervous system. Just order up a whole new set of instincts.

Seems unlikely. What can I say? I ain't no Harlem black girl.

I left the office at 12:30 to eat and to buy Charlie's Hanukkah gift. The stores would be packed, I knew, so I downed two slices of pizza as quickly as I could.

Beat Down Sports Gear was less packed than I'd expected, but it still maintained a packed attitude. Shoppers grabbed at merchandise without a trace of holiday spirit. Or maybe that *is* the holiday spirit. *Get yours before it's someone else's.* The only evident good cheer was the store's physical decorations—menorahs and dreidels under blue and white lights fighting it out with Santas and plastic trees under red and green lights.

Did I mention that I hate holidays? Not just *the* holidays, but *holidays*, as in all of them. Any day that feels out of the ordinary makes me edgy. I'm at peace with the boredom of everydayness. In fact, I'm pretty much at peace with boredom. Boredom implies that everything's okay. No crises going on; no one in bad health; no festering dilemmas. What's bad about that? Sometimes I'll be reading a book and, when I realize I've been staring at the same page for a half hour, I feel great. My mind's been given free rein to float, and it's taken full advantage. Those glazed reveries are when I have my best thoughts. Not that I have any major use for those thoughts. A lot of the stuff I've been throwing out to you has come out of those mental space walks. Of course, you may not necessarily agree that's an upside.

I went overboard on buying hockey stuff. Pads, sticks, jerseys, masks, gloves, pucks—you name it. The teenage sales clerk must have been working on commission because, every time I said, "Okay, I'll take that," he'd grab it up and say, "Sweet!" He did an impressive job of hauling all the merchandise in one trip over to check-out. As he reached out to start entering his employee ID number into the computer, his sleeve rode up his arm to reveal a tattoo that read, in blue, Times Roman Bold, Italic, 18-point, all capitalized letters:

OH SHIT!!!

Were we ever that openly profane? We said every word in the book, sure, but permanently etching them into our skin? I don't think so.

Jesus, listen to me. I sound like Fred Mertz.

Did I ever tell you that during my junior year of high school, I worked in a women's shoe store on Main Street in Flushing? The place was owned by a widow in her early fifties named Blanche Diamond. She'd come in once or twice a week to look things over. Mostly it was just a thirty-five-ish manager named Ted Something, a sixty-ish salesman named Sam Something and, in the afternoons, me. Ted was my first contact with unbridled raunchiness. He'd look outside the store to check the foot traffic and report back, "Motherfucker, there's not a swinging dick on the street." When Blanche would stop by, Ted would watch her leave, then turn to Sam and me, and say, "Jesus, did you catch the smell of Blanche's box? Someone's gotta tell her that even if her old man kicked off, she's still gotta wash out her box when she takes a fucking bath." Sam would cough out his Lucky Strike laugh. I'd try to smile like I was one of the boys even though I was usually somewhere between horrified and disgusted. You spend all those years in elementary school, junior high, and high school sitting in classrooms, your mind drifting out through the huge windows and imagining what wonders are going on in the outside world. But when you finally get to experience a sample of it, it's appalling beyond your darkest dreams.

Next to the shoe store, college was a relief. Scuzz Lehman used to stick his head out the window of the frat and yell, "Yo, Snatch!" at girls passing by. Nice. And, at the first mixer I ever attended—in fact, the first time I'd ever even heard the word "mixer"—I heard our semi-sadistic pledge master, Bonk Berger, say to a girl, "Well, Barbara, if you're not gonna ball me, I'm gonna mingle." That was somewhat eye-opening. Otherwise, I don't remember things being overly gross. Even the standard misogyny was pretty mild. "I wouldn't fuck her with your dick" was a little rough. But mostly it was stuff like, "I wouldn't throw her out of bed."

"The expression is, 'I wouldn't *kick* her out of bed.'"

Really? Kick her out of bed? Oh yeah . . . I guess you're right, Commie.

Commie?

Holy shit!

You're out of it? Can you open your eyes? Say something else!

Oh, shit! Is there a button to push?

I'll get the nurse and be right back!

Oh—don't tell anyone about Jenji McKenna and my whacking . . . okay?

Nurse!

SUNDAY NOW

I.

Hey, I'm back. How you doing?

Mm. I spoke to Alyse last night and, God bless her, she thought it was great that I'd blown off the seminars yesterday to hang with you. Then, just from listening to me, she sensed that I hadn't eaten. Can you believe it? Over the phone, she knew I was light on basic human nutrients.

I spoke to the kids. Esme was going bowling with friends. She started liking to bowl only after I bought her bowling shoes of her own. The idea of renting shoes already worn by a thousand other girls grossed her out. So, I guess being the daughter of a podiatrist *has* had an impact.

Charlie, who has tons of friends, was staying home with Alyse and trying to make sense of math. He's been having a rough time with it and it really bugs him. Alyse goes with total honesty and tells him that some subjects come easier than others and that, for the tougher ones, you just have to put in more effort. Then Charlie gets that worried look on his face (the one he inherited from me) and Alyse will call his teacher and ask her not to give Charlie the impression that her teachings are overly important.

Alyse is tough. And funny. She said this morning, "Someday, Charlie's gonna go to college and graduate Omega Cum Laude."

That cracked me up. Then Alyse said, "Get something to eat."

"I will."

"I love you."

"I love you."

I went to Chamberlain's Seafood Bistro all by myself. Usually I'd be self-conscious about eating dinner alone in a restaurant, but

I think I went in too self-conscious to be self-conscious. I'm sure you've been to Chamberlain's. It got a strong Zagat rating and the people eating there seemed like they could be friends of yours. Some definitely fit my mother's description of Charleston's "very active" Jews. The service was lousy. Amazing how waitresses develop that ability to look past you when you want their attention. It took a half hour to get my entrée, which was a trout with its head still attached. Trying to be cool, I pointed at the fish and said to the waitress, "Look, it's a classic fish-out-of-water story."

I think humor is more important to people in New York than in the rest of the country.

I got back to the hotel around 9:30 and drifted into the bar. I don't know why. The first person I saw was Phil Burton, the guy who'd been so hot to give me updates on Richie Waddle's nervous breakdown. Phil was hitting on a woman who reps Prince tennis racquets. Phil Burton, a guy who looks like a slightly more mobile version of Steven Hawking, gets a weekend away from his uptight pigeon of a wife and he thinks he's got a shot with some tall, ex-varsity doubles player from Knoxville. Remember my idea for government-issued "YOU ARE OUT OF THE GAME" cards?

Phil should have gotten his card at 12.

"Hey! Where have you been? You missed all the seminars today."

Phil introduced me to Darby Hinkle, his wet dream girl.

"I was with my friend in the hospital."

"Wait. You were with Waddle?"

"No. Waddle's back in Philadelphia having cheese steak with a side of thorazine."

Darby Hinkle laughed. It was nice. I made a girl laugh.

"I was with someone else at a different hospital. My old college roommate. He lives down here. He's in a persistent vegetative state."

"A what?"

"He's in a fucking coma, Phil."

Darby laughed again. Maybe she just found it funny that I was zinging this little twerp who'd had the nerve to hit on her.

Anyway, Commie, I didn't know why I was giving information about you to this douche bag and the tennis girl. But I got a glass of Pinot Noir and told them even more.

I told them about what happened earlier in the day.

"Oh my goodness," Darby said, all wide-eyed. "That's intense."

Burton sniffed, clearly put off by the shift in Darby's attention. "Sounds pretty nuts to me."

Without taking my eyes off Darby, I said, "No. A doctor assured me it's common for someone who spends a lot of time talking to a coma victim to imagine the other side of the conversation, then reach the point of believing the coma victim has responded. It happens to the very sanest of people, like me."

After a hush, Darby asked how you got in the coma.

I said, "From watching ESPN."

I just didn't feel like talking anymore.

I knocked off my wine, threw some cash down, and said good night to Burton and Darby.

Looking back, I think I could have fucked her.

Just kidding. Christ, she was like 5'11" with legs up to here. She'd have probably snapped my helmet right off.

If you woke up now and said, "I wouldn't kick her out of bed," it would be really funny.

Didn't think so.

You know, last night when I thought you talked? As I ran out to find a nurse, I thought that maybe I'd found the cure for Persistent Vegetative State and I was going to win the Nobel or something. *For his discovery of the Bore-the-Crap-Out-of-the-Coma-Victim Remedy, we honor . . .*

Of course, part of me thought your awakening was too good to be true. But usually all of me thinks things are too good to be true, so I was still pretty excited.

Look, my flight is in a few hours and, even though last night took a little of the starch out of my story-telling desire, I don't want to leave you hanging.

Where was I?

Oh. Beat Down Sports Gear. Jesus, the whole economy is so in-your-face. There's that other big sportswear brand now: Under Armour. Their commercials make it look like you're supposed to suit up to kill Catholics at Shea Stadium.

Whatever. The place was convenient, so I took my Amex for a spin and bought Charlie all that hockey stuff.

You know, I believe in advertising even less than most people seem to. The only commercials that ever worked in my eyes were for Charmin toilet paper—Mr. Whipple changed the face of ass-wiping. But now? Paying for thirty seconds on shows that everyone TiVo's? It's got to be a con game between the TV stations, the ratings people, and the advertisers.

And, speaking of economic bullshit, I went on the Internet back at my office. I Googled Hilton Head to find a local newspaper and see if there was a verdict in your dog case. I was about to call you, but then I thought maybe you were in the courtroom and I imagined your cell going off and the judge getting pissed off, disbarring you and ruining your career. That's how thoughtfully paranoid I am. *The Hilton Head Island Times* site had nothing new about the case. They did have a lead story about the late Indian summer that drove the local temperature into the 80s, breaking a record set in 1932. It hadn't been that hot in over 70 years *That. One. Day.*

It's too much to even think about.

I surfed off the *Island Times* and back to the main AOL page, where there was a photo of an actress in an "unflattering" bikini. When Alyse and I lived in the city, sometimes we'd go to a newsstand and browse. That was the evening's activity. We'd talk and laugh about the articles. It was so much fun. We called it Rag Night.

"What are we doing Saturday night?"

"I thought maybe we'd just do Hunan Balcony, then a Rag Night."

Around 1982, at the newsstand on 72nd and Broadway, there was a total Yuppie-fied guy with an Akita, and a homeless guy said to him, "Hey man, you got an Akita." The Yuppie ignored him and kept reading *Fortune*. But the homeless guy went on and on about how Akitas are from Japan and they're real expensive and they weigh 150 pounds, until, finally, the Yuppie walked away and the homeless guy screamed out, "*Akita!*"

The dog freaked, jumping and spinning around. And the homeless guy said, "They know their names too!"

Man, what a great city. I can't believe you never lived in New York, Commie. You'd have loved it. Of course, you spent time in Beirut, Johannesburg, Sarajevo, Berlin, and Bhopal. Every time you told me you were in one of those places, I'd think to myself: *Does every hotspot need American lawyers?*

Anyway, I guess I'm stalling a little before telling you one of the more disturbing or scary moments in the story.

Hey, remember I told you that Meri's Civil War freak husband quoted Aristotle about how trauma can make a man a monster? I looked that up last night. Aristotle never said anything close to that. The guy put phony quotes in the mouth of a Greek philosopher! I almost admire it. Such a nervy way to sound smart. And you can do it constantly.

As Plato said, "Maybe I should wear a sweater."

Oh: I also Googled Ted Kaczinski. Turns out he once looked into getting a sex change. So there you go.

Alright. Here we are, onto the tough stuff.

Just as I was looking at my schedule and saw that I had a patient coming in 15 minutes, Sylvia poked her head in and said, "There's a detective Byron here to see you."

You never get over that fear of cops from when you were a kid, but the shiver I felt seemed justified.

"Just him? No partner?"

"That is correct."

Jesus.

"Sylvia, I want you to tell him I'm just wrapping something up. I'll buzz you in about a minute, then you can send him in."

Sylvia caught my anxiety and nodded like, *Roger that, sir.*

You won't believe what I did next. I buzzed Arnie on the intercom. He picked up and I said, "Remember that cop I told you about who was leering at Alyse?"

"Yeah. Why?"

"He's here."

"What does he want?"

"I don't know, but it can't be good. I'm a little freaked. I was thinking maybe if I start feeling a little threatened, I'd buzz you."

"Don't buzz me. Call me on your cell now and stick it in your shirt pocket. I'll stay on the line and listen in. If anything sounds bad, I'll casually drop by."

"That's a great idea. You're the man, Arnie."

I called Arnie on my cell, put the phone in my shirt pocket, and went out to the waiting room to bring in Byron personally. He was standing over Sylvia's desk, tapping his feet, with poor Sylvia cowering like a hostage.

II.

After the toe-tapping, the first thing that struck me about Byron was that he wasn't wearing the jacket and loosened tie that make up the standard TV detective uniform. Instead, he wore the kind of Members Only black jacket you see on sex offenders in *Law & Order SVU*. My instant Members Only/Megan's Law profile, accurate or not, started to unnerve me until I remembered from TV that maniacs like this feed off fear. *Don't look scared*, I told myself. I looked Byron in the eyes and waved him wordlessly into my office.

He looked around like he'd just stepped onto a crime scene. Habit, I guess. Now get this, Commie: His eyes stopped on the Intra-Fraternity One-on-One Basketball Tournament trophy I keep on a small shelf behind my desk.

"What, did your kid win a basketball trophy?"

"No, Detective, *I* won a basketball trophy."

"Somehow I can't imagine that."

That crack sent me flying from scared to pissed. My head went right back to the stick-it-to-him attitude I'd had in my driveway.

"You don't have to imagine it. You want to go to a gym right now and play some one-on-one?"

I visualized Arnie in his office hearing me say that and thinking, *Holy shit!*

"I'm not here to play basketball."

"That's good. The game wouldn't be fun for you."

"You're pretty ready to play for a guy who claims to have hurt his ankle Friday night."

He kind of nailed me there.

I tried to recover by putting my foot on my desk, pulling up my pant leg, and showing him the still multi-colored swelling. "I didn't claim I'd hurt my ankle. I stated it as a fact. As a podiatrist, I can assure you this is how a severe ankle sprain looks after two days. Maybe I should take a photo of it in case I wind up needing to mount a defense."

"Maybe you should," Byron said, keeping his foot on the gas. "Then you can post it on Facebook."

"Facebook?"

"I noticed you were on Facebook. I'm on it too. I like to post gruesome crime scene photos."

Byron was clearly trying to freak me out and truthfully, it was working.

"Where's Detective Shelby?" I asked.

"He's got a cold."

"Don't you get assigned a different partner for the day?"

Byron smiled and said, "I forgot. You watch a lot of cop shows, so you know all about my job. Well, I'm not on duty right now."

At that point, I started to feel creeped out. An antsy cop visiting me on his own time—this was personal.

"Have a seat," I said, trying to seem relaxed.

Byron sat on the other side of the desk and tapped his fingers. I noticed his nails were bitten way down, receding into stubby, fleshy fingers. My first thought was: *How the hell does this guy open a soda can*? My second thought was about Jerry Orbach's character on *Law & Order* saying something about adult nail-biters having major psychopath potential. All in all, everything going on in my office was highly nerve-wracking.

I felt for the outline of my cell phone inside my shirt pocket, and asked, "So, what can I do for you?"

"I got flat feet."

"Sorry, can't squeeze you in. I have a patient in 10 minutes," I lied, then quickly, "Actually, less than 10 minutes."

"I had a suspect cuffed to a chair at my desk this morning and just as I was about to squeeze the details of how he made eighty grand selling baseballs signed by Lou Gehrig with a Sharpie, guess who phoned me?"

"My wife. I know."

"Yes. Your wife."

"So?"

"Well, with my forger hovering around my desk, I was tied up, so I told her what she needed to know and then hung up."

"She appreciated your help."

"I'm sure she did. But a little while later, I wondered: Why would she choose to call me, of all people, for information on the penal system?"

"You and Shelby may be the only people connected to the criminal justice system that she's ever met."

"That's possible. But then, I thought, why would this high-class babe want to visit an anti-Semitic convict in a scummy joint like county detention?"

Babe? This is not good.

"What did you conclude?"

"I'm still working on it."

"Well," I said, standing up, "when you figure it out, be sure to let me know. Now, if you'll excuse me."

"Why? It's only been a minute or two. Your patient's not here yet. I gotta say, business seems a little slow. You sure you can support Alyse in the manner to which she's accustomed?"

Now he's calling my wife Alyse.

"I appreciate your concern, Detective, but my practice is quite healthy."

I was holding my own, clinging to my flat, casual demeanor. But, at the same time, I was kind of hoping Arnie would decide it was time to come to my rescue.

Byron smiled and said, "You Buffalo-nosed bagel-biters know how to make money." Before I could respond, he said, "Maybe that's what you're up to. Maybe it's all about money. Trying to drive up the price of that whack-job's art. Jailed artists are almost as valuable as dead artists. Whatever. I'll find out. You and Alyse will be seeing me again."

Every time he said "Alyse," I got both livid and terrified. The terror was starting to win out. Shakily, I said, "I don't want to see you again."

"I bet you don't," he said. Then he leaned forward and almost whispered, "Maybe we can make a deal."

"What? A deal? What kind of deal?"

"I can offer to get out of your life. And what do you have that I might want? Oh, I know! I really like Alyse's ass. Can you give me a piece of her ass?"

I wasn't prepared for that. Not prepared at all. That moment kicked off another Teutonic shift, an inevitable quake of dread and agonized regret about everything that I'd done over the past three days.

If only I'd just allowed myself to call the cops and confess the second after I threw the bottle through the window, I'd have been set back a few grand but none of this would have happened and I'd have never fucked around to the point of putting my wife in the cross hairs of a rapist cop. Oh my God Oh my God Oh my God Oh my God Oh my God . . . Yeah, Commie, once again, I conveniently found religion. Hiding my terror became a finger-in-the-dike kind of totally impossible thing. Byron was eating it up.

"You know what?" he said. "Forget it. That's not really a good deal for me. You know why? Because you don't have to deliver Alyse's tight JAP ass to me. I can just grab it up myself."

I specifically remember feeling Charlie in my face at that moment—the pleading, helpless look he gets when something makes him feel his world is about to disintegrate. For the first time in years, my emotions slipped past the Zoloft guard gate. The peach pit in my throat, the popping sweat, the racing heartbeat, the dizziness—the whole deal. My mouth opened.

Feebly, "You stay away from my wife!"

Commie, I can't even replicate the tone of my voice when I said those words, so you're not getting the full effect. And frankly, I'm glad I can't replicate it. I sounded like a fucking weasel, a sniveling little sissy laughably defending the honor of his mousy little sweetheart. When Byron laughed at me, I felt like I didn't have a bone in my body. I'd turned into everything an American male is supposed to hate. The cowering little pussy getting sand kicked in his face. I know it sounds like I'm exaggerating, but I'm not. In fact, here's another thing I've never told anyone in this whole wide world: When Byron stopped laughing, he said, "Yeah, that ass bent over the couch in the den with that nice TV. It's just waiting for me." Well, you know what I did when he said that? I'll tell you, and only you.

I peed in my pants.

III.

Please, Commie, of all the confidential things I've told you, that one is the secret I most need you to keep under your hat. Getting into podiatry school without applying, whacking off to Jenji McKenna for 30 years, throwing the horseradish bottle through the window—you can tell anyone any of those things. Just not the peeing in my pants thing. Not even your wife, okay?

"Hey, what's going on?"

Apparently, Arnie decided that Byron's reference to "Alyse's ass" was his cue to launch into my office.

Byron looked at him and said, "Who the fuck are you?"

Arnie had no pee in his pants. He stiffened to his full 6'3" and said: "Who the fuck am I? I work here. Who the fuck are you?"

"I'm a Nassau Fucking County detective."

"Wow! That means you must have had almost a 1.5 grade point average in high school. Do you think that gives you the right to say 'Who the fuck are you?' to anyone who comes into this office?"

Byron answered, "No, I'd have that right even if I wasn't a cop."

Arnie, in full condescension mode, said, "Actually, it's not illegal. But there is a difference between liberty and license."

"What the fuck are you talking about?"

"The difference between liberty and license. For instance: If you come into my friend's office—his property—and act menacingly toward him or me, I have the liberty to beat the living shit out of you. But since this is a civilized society, I probably don't have the license to beat the shit out of you. Which is kind of a drag because I have this black belt I've always wanted to use to, you know, fuck up a guy like you."

Arnie seemed like he'd waited his whole life for this moment. After all the petty little confrontations of life, Arnie finally found the real deal. He was eating it up.

I wasn't.

All I remember thinking at that point was, *I gotta call Alyse and tell her to grab the kids, buy a disposable phone, drive to her sister's house in Pound Ridge, and hire private security*. I felt like a jittery little bird. I actually asked myself, *I wonder if this ever happened to Jack Bauer*?

Anyway.

Byron calmly said to me, "Gee, I guess I should be scared of your office-mate and his black belt."

Arnie said, "That's true. But there are other considerations that should be scaring you even more right now."

"Really. Like what?" Byron pressed.

Arnie dropped his head toward his shoulder with an air of empathy and said, "I'm sorry, I can't tell you that right now."

I looked at Arnie, wondering what the hell he was talking about. If anything, I thought he was bluffing, making it seem like he had the goods on Byron. Cops like Byron probably have enough dark shit in their closets to get pretty paranoid.

Sure enough, Byron got a glazed look. Unconvincingly, he said, "I got nothing to be scared of from a dick like you."

Arnie shrugged and said, "Maybe not. But you probably should go now. Just in case a dick like me is in possession of something that would make you look really bad down at the station."

It dawned on me that Byron could reach for his gun and that would be that. But then I thought, no. Because if he killed Arnie and me, he'd have to take out Sylvia and then wipe down the front door and my desk, kill my next patient, steal some stuff to make it look like a robbery, throw a bag of some stranger's DNA on all the dead bodies, and grab up all the footage off the security cameras hanging in the lobby and the elevator. Cops are good at covering up their own felonies, but they're not that good.

As if he knew that I'd peed in my pants and wanted to see if he could squeeze a few more drops out of me, Byron shot one more spine-tingling smile my way and said, "Best to Alyse," then walked out of my office at an exaggeratedly relaxed pace.

Arnie and I were frozen, listening for the sound of the front door opening and closing, the elevator arriving, opening, closing, and dropping to the ground floor. Arnie looked out the window and saw the unmarked car pull out and drive off.

Then Arnie turned to me and said, "Motherfucker parked in a handicap spot—can you believe it?"

IV.

I wanted to laugh but couldn't. Sensing my fallen balance, Arnie added, "What a douche!"

I nodded lamely.

"I'm not sure I got that whole thing right about liberty and license, though."

I dropped my head and shook it to make it seem like I was laughing along with him. The truth is, my head was all I wanted to move because of a (possibly) irrational fear that I'd set free a whiff of the urine in my boxers.

Then Arnie said, "Hey, man, do you smell piss?"

Okay, he didn't say that. I'm just kidding. I don't know why I thought that would be funny. It wasn't funny.

Arnie said, trying to prop me up, "I can't believe you told him you'd kick his ass in hoops. That was fucking great!"

Finally, I spoke over my gag reflex. "It felt great when I said it, but it was pretty stupid from where I'm sitting now. I'm a fucking mess, Arnie."

Arnie lowered his voice, "Look, pal, you couldn't have been ready to hear him say that stuff about Alyse. It was totally beyond the pale. You'd have to be dead not to be majorly shaken by a threat like that."

"Thanks, but what am I going to do? I mean, I'm really scared this guy's gonna stake out my house."

"Don't worry about it."

"Don't worry? We can't go to the police. They got that whole blue wall or whatever they call it. If I claim that Byron threatened my wife, it'll be my word against his."

That's when Arnie got this huge grin on his face.

"What?"

Arnie pulled out his iPhone and hit the touch screen. It coughed out a few seconds of static, then:

"What, did your kid win a basketball trophy?"

"No, Detective, I *won a basketball trophy."*

"Somehow I can't imagine that."

"You don't have to imagine it. You want to go to a gym right now and play one-on-one?"

Arnie tapped his iPhone, stopping the recording, then said, "I got the whole conversation right off my speaker phone."

"You're a fucking genius, Arnie."

"I'm always ready for things that hardly ever happen. It's the shit that goes on every day that catches me by surprise. Oh, wait." Arnie stuck his head out my door. "Sylvia! Can you hang up the phone in my office?" Then he turned to me. "You got any booze in here? I could use a shot of tequila."

"Sorry."

"No problem. I got a patient soon anyway. All he has to do is smell booze on my breath just as I'm about to crack his fucking back."

I didn't respond, but Arnie knew where my mind was. "So, I guess the question is, who do we let listen to the tape? I don't even know who the boss is at a police station. The Lieutenant? Captain?"

"There would be a lieutenant in charge of detectives, but I think I have a better idea."

"What?"

"I know someone with the FBI."

Before I tell you about my call to Agent Horton, I think I should say a few words about having someone threaten to rape your wife.

I've always had this secret theory that no one really puts anyone ahead of themselves. I know it's kind of an inhumane thought, completely lacking in empathy. It's more of an objective conclusion that I'd always hoped I was wrong about, but still always believed on a purely scientific level. It's somehow connected to the survival instinct, I think. It was this idea that, no matter what afflicts other people, even the ones you love, it's still *not happening to you.* Horrible, right? I hated that I believed that, but I believed it anyway. Maybe Byron did me a favor, because he kicked the hell out of that theory.

When Arnie left my office, I had ten minutes to myself before my next patient. I immediately—and I mean *immediately*—went to a closet where I always kept an extra set of clothes just in case of . . . whatever. I'd certainly never imagined *this* whatever. As I replaced the pants hanger, I remembered my lie to Charlie about my being a bed-wetter when I was a boy. I wondered if this was karma, but I decided to use the same lie if I had it to do over. It worked for Charlie and that's all that matters. That led me into another realization—I would be willing to die in exchange for Alyse not being subjected to—

Well, you know. Along with Arnie's tape, that thought took a little of the edge off my anxiety. It was just nice to know that someone else's well-being could be more important to me than my own. Any sign that you're not a piece of shit is reassuring, don't you agree?

Kind of a major disclaimer there, huh?

Funny about my willingness to die. To be honest, I used to have doubts on both sides of that question: whether I'd be willing to die for something or someone, or whether I'd be ferocious enough to survive a catastrophic event. Like when that crazy tsunami hit Southeast Asia, there was that supermodel on vacation who wound up clinging to a tree branch for hours before being rescued. I wondered if I had it in me to hold on like that. The survival instinct in animals makes sense because they think they're going to live forever—but us? Fighting like hell for another day of putting on shoes and deciding where to have lunch? Sometimes it seems like, if I reached the end of my rope, I might be the kind of guy to decide, a little too early perhaps, to let go.

Lately, I've been trying to think the best of myself and believe that I'd buck up and survive. I guess that's progress too.

V.

Agent Horton didn't sound overly surprised when I told him about what had happened with Byron. Not that he knew Byron. But on cop shows, the FBI always has disdain for local cops.

"I don't want you to worry about this. I promise, I won't let anything happen to your wife. As you might imagine, I have selfish motives. Your wife is helping me in an investigation."

"I appreciate that, Agent Horton, but my selfish motive has me worried that this Byron guy can drop by my house any time."

"I understand. First, I want to tell you that, judging from what you told me of your conversation, Byron was simply trying to scare you."

"He succeeded."

"I know. And he knows. He has too much to lose by carrying out his threat. He's a detective. He knows he'd be caught. But he went right for your greatest vulnerability—your family. That said, I will do two things immediately: one, I will post a man on your house. Check that: I'll post a woman. Agent Francine Brooks. She's top notch. She'll maintain surveillance as discreet as possible."

"Discreet? You could put nine agents on my lawn with a bazooka and I'd be fine with it."

"With all due respect, no, you wouldn't. I won't tell you how to conduct your marriage, but it would be a mistake to tell your wife what Byron said. There's no point in terrifying her. Like I said, the odds of Byron following through are minimal. You'll have to trust me on that. I am authorized to post an agent at your home because of the hate group investigation. Tell your wife that. I've already e-mailed Agent Brooks. She'll be at your home within a half hour."

"That's wonderful. Thank you so much."

"My pleasure."

"You mentioned there were two things you were going to do."

"Right. I'm going to look into this Byron fellow and make sure I have my ducks in a row if I decide he needs to be neutralized."

Neutralized? I'm sure Horton thought Alyse was a great girl. But now, even I felt he was going to mysterious lengths to protect her. I said, "Really?"

Horton paused as if having a momentary argument with himself. Then, he said, "I can't get too deeply into this. One of the bidders who showed interest in Mr. Brushstroke's art is tied to a group that's financing another group that's been trying to get their hands on some pretty serious—"

I screwed it up. Feeling so close to getting a classified national security briefing, I eagerly said, "Serious what?" Horton stopped. In his pronounced exhale, I could hear my security clearance drop below zero. Horton simply said, "You did me a big favor by calling me. I'm grateful. That said, these kind of investigations have a way of being derailed by the most unforeseen snags. Detective Byron could easily become such a snag. And I won't let that happen."

I was disappointed to fall out of the loop on top secret information. But still, I was impressed. In fact, I said, "You're so thorough, Agent Horton. It's almost surprising how badly you guys fucked up 9/11."

Chill, Commie. I didn't say that.

Actually, I said, "Jeez, Agent Horton, you should have your own TV show."

"I think I'll pass on that. By the way, if you have an old-style mini-cassette player, make copies of the conversation your chiropractor buddy recorded. Give one copy to Agent Brooks, keep one in your office, one at home, and one in a safety deposit box."

"And one to leak to the media?"

Surprisingly, Horton didn't dismiss the idea out of hand, and I'd only meant it as a joke!

VI.

When I called Alyse, I followed Horton's suggestion to lie to her about the FBI agent posted near the house. I spoke fast to hide any leftover terror in my voice.

Alyse—boy, she can cut to the chase—said, "Why did Horton call you at the office rather than calling me?"

I tap danced with a bit of truth, "Actually, I called him," and a big chunk of lie, "I just wanted to know more about the hate groups."

Alyse said, "You sound a little weird."

"I do? Maybe. I had a Coke at lunch. Sugar, caffeine."

My last patient of that day was Brian Singer, a guy I play basketball with. Good player, nice outside shot. Knows how the game is played. Great guy. Under normal circumstances, this would be a fun, chatty office visit. I did my best to pretend these were normal circumstances and I guess I pulled it off.

Actually, Commie, Brian has a decent game, but I do blow by him pretty easily on the offensive end. Just so you know.

Brian started feeling pain in his right Achilles tendon a few months earlier. Now, with the pain increasing, he worried about the possibility of having to endure surgery and months of rehab. I fiddled around with his tendon, gauging his response. It was a piece of cake diagnosis.

"Relax. Tendinitis, my friend. Here's the game plan: We'll start you off with a series of small injections of a sclerosant to ease the pain. We'll get you into some orthotics, and you can do the physiotherapy yourself. It's just a fancy term for calf stretches."

"Awesome."

"How old are you?"

"Thirty-four."

"Right. About the age when all your shit starts falling apart. I can't predict which body part will betray you next but, as far as your Achilles is concerned, you'll be splashing jumpers again in no time."

I said exactly what Brian wanted to hear, which is, let's face it, a huge part of my job. He was thrilled. Still, seeing a health care provider whom you know in regular life? I wouldn't do it. I'd only leave my health up to a total stranger, someone I could mythologize to the level of off-the-charts genius.

Hey, remember when Farrakhan had heart surgery performed by a Jewish doctor? *Say, Lou: Before I crack open your fucking rib cage, you care to clarify your remarks about Judaism being a "gutter religion?"* That was a big victory for the Jews. Up there with The Six Day War and Caroline Kennedy marrying that Schlossberg guy.

My mother always wanted me to marry a Jewish girl, but she was willing to give me a waiver if I could bring home Caroline Kennedy. Another reason Judaism makes occasional sense. It leaves room for ad-libbing.

Actually, you want to hear something unbelievable? A while ago, a kid in my neighborhood, Jared Horowitz, started dating a Catholic girl. But how did I hear this described? He was *caught* dating a Catholic girl. Like he'd knocked over a fucking CitiBank branch. Jared was the varsity point guard at the Mordechai Lehman School, the girl was a cheerleader at Saint Whoever's Sacred Heart, and somehow they hooked up. When his parents found out, their faces went all Picasso (as Alyse described it). They were like: *This is it; the end of the Jewish people, and it's all* our *fault. We, Aaron and Jackie Horowitz, will go down in history as having spawned the child who led to the demise of our people.*

So crazy. We've been around for five thousand years! Even if the religion does die out, we've had a pretty good run, right?

Anyway, I don't know what happened to Jared and Mary Theresa Whatever, but I pictured them stealing moments together, whispering, *We gotta get out of this town.* Of course, in the movies, that "town" doesn't have a train going to Penn Station every half hour. But the same problem pops up everywhere. How do you rescue kids from adults?

After taking care of Brian, I poked my head out and heard Sylvia on the phone saying, "I'm sorry, Mr. Washington, but we will have to charge you for the missed session."

Clarence Washington played hoops for Hofstra about thirty-five years ago, then got cut by a few NBA and ABA teams. Whatever. His feet are a mess (his big toenails split horizontally, like he's got two-ply nails).

You know what? I think I've told you enough about Clarence's toenails. More relevant is that, like most ex-jocks, his life after hoops has been a downer of an epilogue—bouncing between sales jobs and "community outreach" stuff, whatever that means. To me, it meant he could use a break.

I snapped my fingers to get Sylvia's attention.

She covered the phone and said, "Mr. Washington got pulled over for speeding, so he won't be making his appointment."

"Tell him he won't have to pay for the missed appointment."

"Are you sure?"

"Yeah, Sylvia. I'm sure."

"Mr. Washington, never mind. We'll just reschedule, and don't worry about the fee."

Sylvia hung up and said, "He sounded relieved."

And I said, "Goddamn cops."

Sylvia—did I mention she goes to church *every day*?—looked at me like I was Satan. I give a guy a break and, two seconds later, I'm the devil incarnate. No good deed, huh?

"I'm sorry, Sylvia. I'm just tired and cranky."

As I said that, I thought I was just making a lame excuse. But I *was* tired and cranky. I went back to my office, slumped into my now piss-ruined chair, and realized I'd hit a wall. All the stuff going on—cops, reporters, hate groups, Audra, FBI—I'd had enough. The whole devil-may-care high from throwing a bottle through a window had worn off. That school's-out feeling of spouting off at the mouth had lost its potency. Apparently, three days on a tightrope is my limit.

VII.

In a new twist on my usual nutcase ruminations, I started trying to remember what was on my mind before my conscience developed a rap sheet. *What the hell was filling my head at this time last week?* For the life of me, I couldn't remember. I began trying to retrace my life—what was going on with Alyse, the kids, me—before simply making the smart choice and stopping the whole exercise. After all, what if I tried to retrace beyond a week earlier and couldn't pinpoint any prevailing mind-set at *any time in my life*? That would suck, right? A lifetime of utterly disposable thought? Yikes. Instead, I just shook my head and thought, *I want my boredom back.*

Sylvia buzzed me to let me know that Alyse had called during Brian's appointment. "I'm sorry, I forgot to mention it."

"No problem, Sylvia. And, again, I'm sorry for my language before."

Fifty fucking years old and still apologizing for using bad words.

I picked up the phone and, a bit more raggedly than I'd meant to, said, "Hi, honey, what's up?"

"The bidding. That's what's up."

"Really?"

"Oh, yeah. I posted one of You-ey's untitled pieces and had a thought: What if I make up some kind of name that sounds a little provocative to people who hate Jews and blacks? So, I called up Horton and asked him about it and he thought it was a really good idea!"

Alyse had an all-new excitement in her voice. Just as I was flagging in my propensity for intrigue, Alyse was growing in hers.

"So what name did you come up with?"

"You won't believe it. You ready?"

"Ready."

"The piece has a big 'DO NOT ENTER' sign You-ey stole from an off ramp of the 59th Street Bridge. He graffiti-ed the sign with the stenciled words 'THAT MEANS YOU-EY' and posed puppets of a man and a woman—you only see the backs of their heads—over the sign. Then he photographed the whole thing and framed it in a stained glass window he stole from a church in Brooklyn. It struck me that it was like a church telling everyone to keep out. So, I called the piece 'F-asterisk, ALL Y'ALL.'"

"F* All Y'all?"

"You like it?"

"It's not very subtle."

"Why not? I used an asterisk. Besides, you want to be subtle with Neo-Nazis?"

"Good point, honey."

"I started the bidding at $24,000."

"Jesus. That's higher than Horton suggested."

"I know. But the last bid was $46,000."

"Holy shit. When do you cut it off?"

"That's up to Horton. He's been goosing the bids like he said he would."

"Okay, here's a dopey question: Do you get the commission?"

"Why's that a dopey question? I asked Horton the same thing."

"And?"

"He kind of ducked the question."

"So, he didn't say no outright."

"No, but he definitely didn't say yes either."

"Gee, we could get a year of college tuition out of this."

"Or the down payment on a co-op in the city."

"How great would that be?"

"So great."

"So, did the FBI woman show up to watch the house?"

"Yup. She introduced herself. Seems really sweet."

"That's nice."

"Are you okay, hon?"

"I'm a little tired. I'm gonna come home soon."

"Good. Come home."

"Okay. I love you."

"I love you too. And, by the way, I was very impressed you said it in front of your patient before."

"Yeah, I'm making great strides, don't you think?"

"Absolutely."

You know what? I don't like hearing, "I love you *too*." That "too" makes it sound obligatory, don't you think*? He said it, so I guess I gotta say it back.*

How are we on time? Shit. I gotta move it along here.

Arnie, God bless him, made five dubs of my conversation with Byron. He kept one, plus the original on his phone. I looked around my office trying to figure out where to hide two of them. It was like hiding a key outside your house. You look for a spot that burglars or, in this case, cops wouldn't think of. Then you realize that if you thought of it, someone else could. So you look for a spot that wouldn't be the first place anyone would look. Half the time, a week later, you've forgotten where you put it.

I wound up putting one in Brian Springer's file. No one would look there unless they had hours to search the place, plus seeing Brian at hoops every week would remind me of where I'd put it. It's good when you can reduce someone to a mnemonic device. I wrapped the other tape in plastic and put it in the bottom of an unused anti-bacterial soap dispenser. Then I got out my Blackberry and made a new contact entry: Jack McCoy. (Yeah, as in Jack McCoy the prosecutor from *Law & Order*; what of it?) I put in a fake phone number, right down to the 555 exchange, and under the heading of "spouse," I wrote down where I'd hidden the tapes.

Maybe I had a touch of a taste for intrigue left in me after all.

I grabbed one more cassette and got in my car. As soon as I pulled out of the garage, my cell rang.

You.

VIII.

"Commie! If you're calling, something really good must have happened with the dog."

"Actually, I'm walking it right now."

"You? How did you wind up with it?"

"All the sides of the argument got so out of control, the judge didn't know what to do, so I volunteered to take custody of the dog while everything got sorted out. The judge just wanted to get the case off his desk. So he said, 'Fine, Mr. Moscow. Take the dog.'"

"Well, the dog *is* your client."

"It's actually a really great dog. I wouldn't mind keeping it permanently."

"Well, while it's in your custody, you can always clone it."

"Great idea! Two more clones and I'll have Cujo."

"I can't believe I've been following this story since it broke and you're right in the middle of it. It's so weird."

"I know. It's totally bizarre."

"Before I first heard about the dog, there was a story about gang-bangers in Cincinnati car-jacking Priuses so that their drive-bys would be quieter."

"That's going on all over. I heard about that from a DA friend. A guy driving a Prius in Atlanta was killed during a jacking."

"Jeez."

"Yeah."

"Hey, if you murder someone who drives a Prius, do you get both the gas chamber and the electric chair?"

I heard you totally lose it on the other end of the line—that you spit out a mouthful of coffee from my joke. I just wished you lived here. If I could have my family hang out with you and Arnie, that would be enough. Most of the boxes of life would be checked off and I'd spend less time drumming my head with horseshit thoughts.

I'm not explaining this well.

I considered suggesting that Arnie would be a great addition to our week in the Cayman's, but I thought maybe it would be a bad idea to invite people you didn't know to your vacation place. More horseshit thoughts, huh?

Anyway, then you asked me what was going on with me.

"Actually, Commie, I've had some pretty tasty intrigue in my life lately as well. Something's been going on—I've been dealing with cops, FBI agents. It's too much to explain right now. I'll tell you about it soon, when there's time."

If only I'd told him just part of the story, just the part about throwing the bottle through the window, maybe he'd have slowed up his walking or just stopped to listen long enough to have missed . . .

"You're not in trouble, are you?"

"Nah. Probably not. It's an unbelievable story, though."

"You're killing me with suspense."

"I know, but the story requires focus. Where are you with the dog?"

"I thought it would be great to walk him on the beach. Hilton Head is freakishly warm right now—like 85 degrees."

"Global warming is really underrated. Unfortunately, it's cold as the Yucatan here."

"The Yucatan is in Mexico."

"Oh, right. Jesus. I meant the Yukon. I always mix those up. What I'm saying is, it's cold as hell."

"Yeah, I got your drift."

"Isn't it weird how you can say it's cold as hell or hot as hell? I mean, really, what's the goddamn weather like down there?"

You laughed again. "I miss your insane thoughts."

"I'll store some up for the Cayman Islands. In fact, maybe I'll sit you down and tell you the meaning of life."

"No, no, no. Don't leave me hanging. What *is* the meaning of life?"

"Well, if you have to ask . . ."

After we hung up, I looked down to see how long the call had lasted. Eight minutes. It felt longer, but in a good way. Like we really covered some ground. I checked the time on my dashboard just to see if the phone time was off somehow. It wasn't.

The time was 3:34.

IX.

I pulled up to my house and quickly picked out the FBI car occupied by Agent Francine Brooks. *Francine Brooks?* I thought. *Sounds kind of Jewish.*

Agent Brooks couldn't be less Jewish. For one thing, she was black. For another, well, that's enough. She was black.

"Agent Brooks?"

"Yes, sir. Nice to meet you."

"How are we doing?"

"Don't worry about a thing, sir. Agent Horton has been looking into this Detective"—she looked down at her notes—"Byron. Recently divorced, rumors of drug use, and a few complaints of intimidation. Other than that, he's actually a superb cop."

"Somehow that's not very comforting. The other cops, the ones over him, will tell him the FBI is looking into him, right?"

"The Nassau police have no idea we're looking into him."

"Then how did Agent Horton find out all that information about him?"

Expressionless, Brooks looked at me. I widened my eyes like, *Was that a bad question*? Brooks held her flat look. I took the hint. This was on a need-to-know basis and, clearly, I didn't need to know.

"Wow," I said lamely, breaking the moment, "Agent Horton is something else, huh?"

"Yes, he is," Brooks said, her features loosening. "He may look like Charles Kuralt, but he's an amazing agent."

"Charles Kuralt. So weird you said that. I told Horton he should have his own TV show."

"He gets that a lot. By the way, if you want, you can give me the code to your security system."

I guess I reacted like I'd been told the FBI had picked up chatter about a terrorist attack on my family, because then she added, "Oh, no! Don't be concerned. It's just a precaution. I'm sorry."

"No, I'm sorry. Guess I'm a little edgy. Sure, the security code is—"

I stopped myself thinking it would be weird to tell this FBI agent that our security code is:

G-O-Y-S.

Alyse and I came up with the code after figuring out who we were trying to keep out. It was funny at the time.

"Let's see. The code is . . . 4-6-9-7. It's a date, April 6, 1997. Something happened. It's a long story."

"I got it."

"Anyway, I'm happy you're here. You want to come in for coffee?"

"Oh, thank you. Not right now."

"Well, all you have to do is knock."

"Another agent, Ken Foreman, will be replacing me here at about seven. Here are our cell numbers. Call us if—" Then, glancing at her passenger side mirror, she said, "Your daughter is coming."

I turned and saw Esme trudging home as if her backpack was filled with bricks. Being on a need-to-know basis, I didn't bother asking how she could identify my daughter at fifty yards in a mirror that makes things look even farther away.

"You should go greet her."

One look at Agent Brooks and I took her meaning. No point in Esme knowing her home was under surveillance by the most powerful law enforcement organization in the world. Really, how do you explain that to your kid?

I jogged over to Esme and was a little surprised she hadn't noticed me talking to a black woman in a strange car. She's usually way too on top of that kind of stuff.

When I reached her, I knew instantly why she hadn't noticed me outside the FBI car. She had that look on her face kids get when they're frozen out of a party or when they learn their conception was an accident.

"Ezzie, what's wrong?"

"I don't want to talk about it."

There, there, honey . . . accidents happen.

As we walked to the house together in silence, Esme kept her head down, but I caught her sneaking sidelong glances my way every few steps. She wanted to talk, but clearly it was a discussion that needed her mother to make it official. I put my arm lightly about her shoulders, guiding her toward our house and nudging her away from the middle of the street.

Alyse, with her radar for knowing when family members are approaching, opened the front door for us and instantly noticed Esme's look. Ezzie flew up to her room in her I-don't-want-to-talk-to-anyone-but-you-so-you-better-come-talk-to-me-right-now way. Alyse, wearing a Yankees cap with a pony tail out the back—a look I love to no end—said, "Should we go upstairs to see what's wrong with her, or just head to JFK and flee the country?"

That was a nice lull before the next wave of rage swept in.

Esme started by shouting down the stairs at us, "Why do I have to be Jewish just because *you* two are?"

In hindsight, not a bad question. But at the moment, I flashed to Nat Uziel's vigilance speech from the day before. And, in no time, I had about a thousand pinched nerves in my neck.

Heavily, Alyse and I kissed our JFK dreams goodbye and hiked up the stairs. After a little prodding, Esme told us that her social studies teacher had decided to throw out the day's original lesson plan to instead discuss the "horrible anti-Semitic crime that occurred over the weekend."

I know.

Exactly how many ways was this one thing going to bite me in the ass?

By the way, her teacher's name is Jennifer Sturdivant. The kids call her Jennifer. Not Mrs. or Ms. Sturdivant. Jennifer. I always think Jennifers are going to be hot but, at the October parent-teacher conference, this dream was shattered as Alyse and I sat across from a pasty, gray-eyed, farina-haired, thirty-five-year-old woman with a slight lisp. She spoke about Esme with an enthusiasm so over the top you couldn't even feel good about it.

Anyway, Esme said Jennifer was acting "like really super offended" about the Nu? Girl Fashions vandalism. Alyse and I looked at each other, both thinking this Jennifer woman was talking through the kids and straight to the Jewish parents who paid her salary.

A hundred whatever years in America, and we go from being totally discriminated against to being sucked up to in the most blatant and annoying ways.

When Jennifer asked the kids for their reaction to the incident, Harley Binder raised her hand. Esme inhaled and went on.

"So Harley like, stands up and says, 'The guy who threw the bottle through the window called Esme an anti-Semitic name!' I couldn't believe she said that. Everyone in the class was totally staring at me like I was supposed to say something, but I didn't know what to say. So, I just said it wasn't a big deal and I, like, said what you guys said yesterday about You-ey not having a good inner life but that he isn't a dangerous person?"

"Uh huh."

"Well, like the whole class was like, 'How can you say he's not dangerous? He threw a bottle through a window—hello?' I mean, like, they were attacking me! And then Jennifer asks everyone if they signed Mr. Uziel's petition, and when she got around to me, I was so freaked, I just lied and said yes. But then Harley says that her father told her that we didn't sign the petition and I lied. So I just started crying."

Alyse glanced at me, conveying some guilt because she had told Gil Binder we didn't sign the petition. Me? I couldn't register any guilt because no one could know just how guilty I truly was. Under different circumstances, I probably could have enjoyed that dynamic.

"Honey," Alyse said, "you have nothing to feel bad about. Harley has a big mouth and I'm going to have a talk with Jennifer. The only thing I wish you hadn't done was lie about the petition. I told you why we didn't sign it, and you agreed with us, so you've got to stick to your guns."

Esme was getting her first taste of doing the right thing, her first taste of a Rosa Parks moment.

And, hey, did you ever hear that there was another black woman who sat in the front of the bus before Rosa Parks? I heard it on NPR. Not that it lessens what Rosa Parks did, but it would be nice to know that at least one thing we learned as kids is totally true. I mean: Rosa Parks was second with the bus thing, Columbus didn't discover America, and JFK's story about the PT-109 is a little shaky. Next thing you know, they'll do some kind of carbon dating and figure out that Jesus was an April baby.

X.

Anyway, as I told you, I have a fixation with Rosa Parks, and with anyone who has a moment of truth and does the right thing. So I brought her up with Esme and gave her a quasi-inspiring pep talk on trusting your beliefs and being willing to accept some heartache in defense of your principles. Esme actually nodded and, I don't know, steeled herself.

Finally, a bit embarrassed, she said, "I hated how everyone in the class was staring at me."

And I said, "I'm sure lots of them just stared because they were too scared to say they agreed with you."

"Agreed with me about what?"

"That the You-ey thing was no big deal." Esme looked doubtful, so I added, "Or maybe they stared at you because you're nice to stare at."

Full eye-roll and, "Ugh, Mom, how come you married him anyway?"

Of course that deflated me. After a wonderful family drama, Esme makes a sarcastic crack about Alyse's choosing me, and boom: a blue haze blows in through my ears. My inevitable awkwardness was broken by the sound of Charlie barging in through the front door and motoring up the stairs. He flew into Esme's room: "Guess what? I won a free-throw shooting contest!"

All three of us did our best to downshift about thirty emotional gears.

"Mrs. Rhodes made everyone in our class shoot seven free-throws and like, I got really hot and made four! More than anyone else in the class! So afterward, Trevor Blank whispers to me, 'You got lucky,' but Mrs. Rhodes saw him and said, 'Trevor, stop talking. The champion doesn't wish to be bothered.' How awesome is that?"

"That's so great."

"That is awesome."

"Way to go, Charlie."

"Hey, why is everyone in Esme's room? Is something wrong? What's going on? Tell me what happened—"

There you have it: my son. From glory to off-the-meter worry, zero to sixty, in no time flat. Sometimes you hear how parents can choose their kid's gender or eye color? I always think, *Fuck eye color. Can you do something about the chromosome responsible for runaway dread?*

"No, Charlie, nothing's wrong."

"Everything's fine."

"We were just chatting."

Charlie was convinced. Or, more likely, he just let himself be convinced because he's a kid who desperately wants to believe everything is fine. Watching him root around for a relieved look to put on his face, I knew our days of being able to so easily snow him were winding down.

After we all drifted out of Esme's room, I super-casually told Alyse I was going to veg out in the den for a while. The truth was, I didn't want her to see how pissed off I was. Maybe Alyse was pissed too. Maybe she was on her way to call her ex-boyfriend, Gil Binder, to tell him to find his daughter and tell the little pubescent cunt to go fuck herself.

I guess you can see how pissed I was. When have you ever heard me refer to *anyone* as a cunt, let alone a twelve-year-old?

When I got to the den, I pulled out my Blackberry and accessed my patient list. I scrolled to Audra Uziel, found her phone number, pushed *text message*, and typed in: DON'T LET IT GO.

Fuck it, I thought. What do I care if Audra rips into her father? Look what he's done to my daughter.

I pushed "send," and felt better. Sometimes, one little impotent gesture works wonders.

The Statistical God: "You made 14,393 impotent gestures in your life, of which 4,891 made someone think you were an asshole, one that had an indirect effect on someone's health . . ."

I shoved my Blackberry back into my pocket and flopped down

in front of a TiVo-ed rerun of *Law & Order*. TNT runs about thirty reruns a day, so I had a nice backlog. It was a pretty good episode focusing a lot on that insanely gorgeous ADA. I can't remember the actress' name. She married that guy who was a number one draft pick of the Giants, but then he got hurt and never panned out. I can't remember his name either. But this girl just kills me. I think she's from Texas, or is it her character that's from Texas? Whatever. She's tall and lean and dark-skinned, huge black eyes, great lips. Jesus, if I ever saw a naked picture of her in some magazine, I'd have to consider cheating on Jenji.

XI.

Sehorn! Jason Sehorn. That's the name of the football player she married. Guy tore up his knee pretty bad, but, on balance, he's pretty lucky.

Alyse came in and plopped on the sofa next to me. She missed the first ten minutes of the show but still picked out the alleged killer before I did. I asked her how she knew, and she said she'd recognized the actor from a lot of other shows, so, despite his airtight alibi, he wouldn't have taken the part if he wasn't going to be the killer. Even though it was cheating, it was still some pretty good armchair detective work.

Esme and Charlie were upstairs dutifully wrapping up their homework. One of the perks of Judaism is that there's a better chance of your kids being studious. One of the downsides comes later, when you have to explain how good grades have no impact on your life. Anyway, Alyse and I watched another TiVo-ed *Law & Order*, this time with the short-haired ADA. I can't remember this actress's name either, but the character's is Jamie Ross. She doesn't knock me out like the Texan, but if there were a Miss American Bar Association Beauty Pageant, she'd be a major contender for the crown. Alyse and I, happy to shoo aside all the craziness in our lives, immersed ourselves in the case of a woman who jumped (or was pushed!) off the Brooklyn Bridge.

And, as the verdict was coming down, I had this thought that, if there were a janitor or something in Nu? Girl Fashions who got killed by my bottle of horseradish, it would make a really good *Law & Order* episode.

"You want to watch one more?" Alyse sounded like a teenager proposing a day of playing hooky, so what else was I to do but say, "Okay."

"Oh, good."

Hey, Commie. Maybe watching *Law & Order* with your wife is the meaning of life.

Alyse had stopped checking how the bidding was going on Youey's art, I had stopped glancing out the windows to see if Byron had slipped past our FBI agent, and we just sat there together. It was the kind of scene that makes America great: husband and wife cuddled up on the couch, all warm and cozy, with our FBI detail just outside. We playfully commented on every twist in the stories, Alyse made cracks about the ADA's cleavage, I pretended not to notice—it was the best. Life felt familiar again. God knows how many episodes went by. Just as Jamie Ross was being swatted down by a judge for requesting absurdly high bail for a defendant against whom the case was seriously circumstantial, we heard Esme say, "Uh, are we perhaps planning to have any nourishment tonight?"

We looked up and saw her and Charlie looking at us like we were a pair of slack-jawed truants. The foremost job of children is to make sure no precious moment goes uninterrupted.

I hate to say this, but I think I prefer the dependent, vulnerable Esme to the budding wise-ass teenager Esme.

I guess I'll get used to it. I hope so.

That was about when I announced to the kids that we'd be going to Bongo's for dinner. It's a fun family place with gorilla-sized portions and milkshakes dense as mud baths. Charlie was thrilled out of his mind. Esme said, "Oh, I guess I'm getting the Chinese chicken salad then," the one somewhat healthy dish on the menu. Every other entrée should come with an angioplasty on the side.

I also should be happy my daughter eats well, but I worry there's something joyless about that kind of discipline. Or any kind of discipline. Children scarfing triglycerides at McDonald's – isn't that what makes America great?

The kids went to bundle up and I said to Alyse, "We should tell the FBI we're going out, right?"

I may have made the suggestion too quickly, or maybe my tone had a smudge of urgency to it, because Alyse looked at me and said, "I guess. But, to tell you the truth, I don't even understand why they're here. Why do they have to stake out our house? The neo-Nazis are a thousand miles away, and they have no idea where we are. Is there something going on with this that I'm not quite grasping?"

There are lots and lots of moments in a marriage when it's important to pull off a convincing white lie. Sometimes I wonder how many white lies it takes to qualify as someone living a lie. Is the answer black and white? Aren't you either living a lie or you're not? Can you be merely living a fib? More unanswerable crap.

I answered with a lame joke to make it seem as though I wasn't worried about anything. "Alyse, this family is crucial to national security. Clearly the FBI knows that."

"Really. What are they going to do, taste our food before we eat it?"

"I doubt it. But Horton put the agent out there, so I'm just thinking we should let them know."

"If we don't, will they think we're trying to sneak out?"

"It's the FBI. Who the hell can understand what they think? Their job is to be paranoid so we don't have to be. We are cooperating with, I guess they call it 'an operation.' So, let's not look at it with suspicion."

"How should I look at it?"

Commie, I came up with a good answer here, if I must say so myself: "Why don't you look at it this way? Tonight will be the safest night we've ever had in our own home. The FBI is looking over us and nothing bad can happen."

Alyse bought it. "I like that." Then, "I don't know how you come up with such baloney, but I like it."

Of course, nothing bad did happen to us that night. Nothing. Bad. To. Us. Nothing. Bad. In. Our. Home. But even the FBI couldn't stop the phone from ringing.

I'm getting ahead of myself, which I really don't want to do.

I looked out the front window, saw the bland no-name car across the street with the silhouette of a man inside, and I quickly jogged out.

Agent Foreman had taken over for Agent Brooks. He looked

more like my conception of an FBI agent—dark, steady eyes, a certain calm edge to him.

Actually, he looked like Lou Piniella.

I told him we were going out to dinner. He asked where, then said, "Enjoy your meal."

I grinned and said, "So, you're not going to tail us?"

Foreman didn't crack a smile. "No. Leave your cell on. You have my number if you need anything."

At the left turn lane onto Stratification, we pulled up behind a Maxima with a nasty slalom course crack down the middle of its rear window. From the back seat, Charlie said, "What kind of fish is that?"

No one knew what he was talking about for a second, and then Alyse saw the Jesus fish above the Maxima's right taillight. "It's a symbol for Jesus, Charlie."

"Why would a symbol for Jesus be a fish?"

"To be perfectly honest, I don't know."

"Maybe it's for good luck. Like Jesus is protecting your car."

"That's a really good guess, Charlie. You're probably right."

Then Esme says, "Jesus didn't do a very good job. Look at the crack on that window. It's majorly ugly."

"Maybe they put the Jesus fish on the car after the accident."

Esme, like an encouraging third parent, said, "You're probably right, Chuckster. They had the accident and decided they needed help."

The light turned green and the Maxima pulled out, then made a u-turn a block later.

Charlie said, "What do Jews put on their cars for protection?"

I said, "Well . . ."

But Esme interrupted. "Jews put on the Mercedes logo."

Alyse couldn't help laughing, and said, "Ezzie, that's a little cynical."

"Mom, do you ever see a Jesus fish on a shiny new Mercedes?"

"No, I guess not."

"Maybe," Esme said, pausing to collect her socioeconomic thoughts, "maybe religion is mostly for poor people."

Charlie said, "Mr. Uziel isn't poor and he's super religious."

"Good point, Chuckster."

Not a bad family discussion. It carried us most of the way to Bongo's. Alyse and Esme ordered their Chinese chicken salads, I had a hot open-face turkey, and Charlie got a bacon cheeseburger "well done." That order has some relevance. I'm not totally throwing shit out just to bore you to tears, although some tears at this point would be—

Before our orders came, my cell rang. I looked down and whispered to Alyse, "It's that *Newsday* reporter. I'll be right back."

I walked toward the restrooms and Graydon supplied me a great little tidbit: "So, I was at the courthouse waiting for You-ey to be arraigned, but they got jammed up and had to push it back another day. But, on the way out, I chatted up You-ey's public defender, who told me he was going to talk to You-ey later in the day, and then he mentions that the jail is so chaotic and crowded, he's going to have to confer with his client in the prison recreation area. So, I told him he should take a tennis ball and see if You-ey can throw."

"That was my idea!" I said, stupidly excited.

"I know, I know. That's why I'm telling you. Anyhow, he has a witness come along with him and he videos the throw off his cell phone and, sure enough, You-ey is a total spazz. He couldn't throw a horseradish bottle through a wet paper bag from ten feet away."

"Why didn't You-ey say that? That he can't throw?"

"For the same reason he can't throw—he never played sports. He has no idea of his capabilities. Or lack thereof."

"Wow, that's great."

"I've got to write this up. And I'm also working on the racist horseradish company story. That'll probably come out Wednesday."

"I'm making you into a star, Graydon."

"I know. Of course, the big question now is: Who *did* throw the bottle through the window?"

"God only knows."

"Someone other than God must know."

"Sure," I said, "the guy who did it knows."

XII.

I hung up and, on the way back to our table, I cursed myself for saying "the '*guy*' who did it knows." I imagined Graydon leaning back in his chair and thinking, *Hmm, why did he say* guy? *How does he know it was a guy*?

The food was on the table, the kids gobbling away.

"What did the *Newsday* reporter want?"

"I'll tell you more later, but, suffice to say, the case against You-ey is getting weaker by the moment."

"Good," she said, though, on second thought, she added, "If You-ey is really innocent, just imagine the person who really did it. Whoever he or she is, they're just sitting back and laughing."

Jesus. Even Alyse went gender-neutral. What an idiot I am. Luckily, I'm not a paranoid idiot. That two people wondered about the true culprit of the crime within a minute of each other might have led a less stable person to break down and confess. Not me. I chose to focus on being a high-functioning idiot and ate my dinner, over-tipped, and went along on my merry way.

We piled out of the restaurant, Charlie with a giant jawbreaker pushing out his cheeks. In the parking lot, I watched an old couple negotiate their way into their Lexus 3-series. The wife got behind the wheel, grim-faced, and obviously on a mission. The jack-knifed husband slumped in the passenger seat, helplessness dotting his face like the mumps. Job obsolescence to go along with all the other obsolescence. It just got to me.

Alyse, omniscient as ever, took my hand and, with a ribbing smile, said, "You drive, honey."

"You don't miss a thing when it comes to me, do you?"

"I've been a little off my game lately, but I feel it coming back."

"Good."

Actually, I can't exactly pinpoint what about that scene had gotten to me. I can't say the sight of that—what's the right word? *Vanquished*? I can't say the sight of that vanquished man was something I could relate to or foresee for myself. Not any time soon, anyway. And it wasn't that the whole scene instilled me with a sense of dread. It was just strange that the kind of depressing sight I can usually look away from and delete from my hard drive altogether was suddenly haunting me. Even that's too strong a word. It wasn't *haunting* me. It was just there. Remember the music in *Love Story*, when Oliver is walking the streets after the doctor tells him Jenny is dying? Weight-of-the-world music. Sometimes I feel that music, a low bumping rhythm. I felt it on the way home.

Alyse studied me as I drove and turned on the satellite radio to '70s pop as if hoping that it would repel whatever was settling inside me. That all sounds like syrupy melodrama, I know. In hindsight, I'd probably like to go even further and say that I had a sense of foreboding. But that would just be morbidly melodramatic.

Before we pulled into our garage, I saw Foreman sitting in his car. I wondered if he saw this as one of his lamer assignments. And, if so, did he resent it or did he welcome the relative safety of the mission? What did he do in that car? What did he think about? Did some random sound from outside make him realize he'd been dozing off for the last half hour? Trying to get inside Foreman's head based on my observations of fictional detectives suddenly made me feel a little sick about how many hours I'd spent watching *Law & Order*.

The Statistical God: "You spent the equivalent of 27 days of your life watching Law & Order, *1.5472 times more than you spent reading books . . ."*

Actually, without God telling me the exact number, I'd say ninety percent of my lifetime news-watching took place before I hit thirty. The news now, with all those baritones who know just enough to be ignorant, shouting their opinions at each other . . . I can't even stand listening to people I agree with anymore.

Walter Cronkite, buddy. Still the only guy with a mustache I ever trusted.

After we all got inside, the kids ran upstairs to finish their homework. I thought about grabbing Alyse and watching more *Law & Order* but, you know, you can't force the magic. So, as I imagine it's become with most American nuclear families, Alyse and I meandered to our separate computers and did whatever we do on them. I still don't totally get the recreational value of the Internet. Surfing from site to site, buying stuff without getting out of your chair, reading blogs—isn't blogging just for people who can't get paid to write?

Alright. That was when it happened.

XIII.

I'd met Danielle a few times, but I never knew her maiden name was Lyonne. Later in our conversation, she told me that some of the cases you'd worked on at the Southern Poverty Law Center made it unsafe for her to use your last name—hence the dummy surnames. And, no offense, but she got the better deal there, I think—Lyonne beats the crap out of Moscow.

So, when my cell rang and the Caller ID read "Danielle Lyonne," I drew a blank for a second until I noticed that the area code was the same as yours.

Commie, Danielle apologized profusely for calling me with the news, but there was no need for apology. About the only thing less than cataclysmic about the call was when she said, "David was going on and on the last two days about how happy he was that you'd called and how you two were laughing like old times...and I just couldn't reason out the protocol on whom to call at a time like this, and so, when I looked at his cellphone and saw that you were the last person he'd spoken to, I . . ."

I got the feeling Danielle was recounting what had happened, to the best of her knowledge, as much for herself as for me. I swear, my heart palpitated when she told me that the local news noted the time you were struck as 3:37. Just three minutes after we'd hung up.

If only there hadn't been a big bang, then there wouldn't have been any planets, any America, any dogs, any money, any Hilton Head, any horseradish, any ESPN, any BMWs, or any reason to rewind the tapes of a day to find moments that could have been edited down or dragged out in order to have nudged the non-existent universe into sidestepping one Godless, freak tragedy . . .

Danielle told me everything the doctors had said. She described them as being "agonizingly forthright." That word *forthright* sounded so genteel.

Your odds of surviving a plane crash are _____ times better than being hit by lightning.

Your odds of winning the lottery are ____ times better than being hit by lightning.

Your odds of being hit by lightning while walking a dog in December and being knocked into a bottomless coma, combined with the dog being utterly unharmed and running off without ever being seen again, are roughly equivalent to . . .

I snapped back into full focus on Danielle's voice when she said, "I got the call from the police as I was teaching my last class of the day. The Dean of Arts and Humanities quite kindly assigned a campus police officer to drive me down to Hilton Head with the sirens on and everything. Nonetheless, as I was entering the hospital, there was already a klatch of reporters hovering about, and one of them asked me if I thought David's being hit by lightning had anything to do with his having married a black woman."

"Oh, God, Danielle, I'm so sorry."

And then, Commie, you want to laugh? Your wife said, "Oh, no need to be sorry. Believe me, I'm used to these meshugenuhs."

Remember when you got engaged and I kept kidding you, asking, "What kind of gorgeous black girl with a Ph.D. would volunteer to convert for you?" Jesus.

Alyse was on her computer. She looked up. None of our parents had ever called us on our cellphones, and the house phone hadn't rung. And yet, Alyse still said, "Who?"

"Commie."

Alyse's face threw off disjointed question marks: *Commie? What could have . . . Commie? Something happened to . . . What?*

I was about to give her the headlines of what happened and nothing more, knowing we'd be dealing with getting the kids to sleep before long, and so it seemed like it would be best to wait for a solid chunk of time before sinking too deeply into the subject. Tragedy. Grotesquery. Whatever. On cue, Charlie came in. His dinner had left him too logy to notice his parents' distress. "I'm going to sleep now," he said.

We didn't even ask him if he'd brushed his teeth or washed up.

We just followed him to his room. He oozed into the comfort of his Serta offset coil mattress.

Charlie fell asleep before we closed the door to his room. Alyse took my hand and we walked down the hall from Charlie's room to Esme's. That little touching of flesh kept the bad news both present and at bay while we put up a just-another-night front for the kids.

Unfortunately—in the what, five-step walk down the hall?—Alyse's cellphone also rang. I don't know who said that thing about "fresh hell" whenever the phone rings, but Jesus Christ!

The caller was Janis Binder. Remember I told you that with all her previous-life wackiness, I really like her? Well, now she went up another notch because she was calling to profusely apologize for "my fucking idiot husband." She went on about how "the douche bag" had had no right to mention Esme to the police and even less right to "call you a self-hating Jew." She said, "I'm just mortified."

Alyse said, "Janis, you believe in reincarnation, so feeling mortified shouldn't be so bad."

Janis cracked up so loud, Alyse held the phone out toward me so I could hear.

I took the phone and said, "Janis, we totally appreciate the call and we both think you're a great girl."

Commie, if we hadn't found out earlier about your being waxed by lightning, we'd have probably felt some very deep satisfaction from Janis' gesture.

XIX.

By the way, Janis and Gil are still married. Amazing, isn't it? I mean, once you refer to your husband as a "fucking idiot" and a "douche bag" with no hint of insincerity, how do you stick together? Then again, it probably wasn't the first time Janis had called her husband those things, and it certainly wasn't the first time she'd thought them. When she married him, I'm sure he was more palatable than he is now. Alyse had dated him once, after all, so he must have been okay at some point. That's what I tell myself anyway. But to turn into what he is? That's a mystery. He did pretty well in custom electronics during the '80s. Through some snaky connections, Gil wound up handling all home entertainment systems for Bon Jovi. Every time we'd see Gil, he'd be going on about how "Bon said" this, "Bon has a gig in the Meadowlands," "Bon ba-da-ba-da-ba-da . . ."

I wanted to tell him, "You know, Gil, wiring Bon Jovi's TiVo to his plasma TV is not the same thing as actually *being* Bon Jovi."

Maybe he realized that on his own, and maybe that's what made him become Orthodox? I don't know. The guy turned into a complete tool. Let's leave it at that.

The funny thing is, when I talk to people from Maryland I haven't seen in a long time, I almost always like them much more than I did when I'd first met them. I bumped into Rickie Strumpf in the city once and it was nice talking to him. We had a drink, we laughed, and I almost forgot that the guy had been a vile, nebbish prick in college. It produced one of the few reassuring thoughts I've ever had about humanity: Often, people turn out okay.

Esme was wrapping up her biology homework. On the top of her notebook page was the name Gregor Mendel, with a double underline. All the genetics stuff with the fruit flies and the peas and the recessive genes—I'm just happy they're still teaching it and not telling kids that God decided that brown eyes, baldness, and manic depression should be passed on from generation to generation.

(Alyse once said that if God was smart, he'd have made pregnant women lose weight.)

Esme takes homework dead seriously. Her wrist, thin as fettuccine, tenses up as she writes in her notebook. Talk about recessive genes. I swear, entire years passed when she never asked me for help with her homework. Perhaps that's why I was worried she'd think I was a schmuck.

As Alyse and I sat with Esme on her bed, I mentioned that I'd gotten the only perfect score in my class on a genetics test in the eighth grade. I didn't mention that I'd cheated off Joey Annunziata on at least five of the 25 multiple choice answers. (Yes, the same Joey Annunziata who'd felt up two girls at my Bar Mitzvah a year before, but that hardly evened the score in my book, but that's neither here nor there.) The funny thing is that—and it's amazing how you can delude yourself—at Maryland, I'd signed up for a class in genetics as if I'd had some true aptitude for it. My chutzpah lasted less than a week. By the end of the second class, I'd already begun the process of dropping the course and signing up for that gut class on the Baby Boom.

"Why were you two holding hands when you came in?" asked Esme.

Daughters. One thing out of the ordinary and they're on it.

Alyse said, "Do we need a reason to hold hands?"

Esme gave the question due consideration before replying, "No, but if you were holding hands outside at night, and there was like, lots of ice on the ground, it would make a lot more sense."

I said, "Ezzie, nothing about love makes perfect sense."

Ezzie widened her eyes for a second, as if she'd found a quote in Bartlett's that she really liked, before snapping back to the blasé attitude her station in life demands. "Gee, Dad, a few more lines like that and you can write a song for Britney Spears."

"Yikes, that hurt."

"Not a Britney fan, Dad?"

"My answer should be 'no,' right?"

Ezzie cracked up at that one, which gave me what would have been a great feeling of paternal bliss, Commie, if I weren't shlepping around thoughts of your lying in a hospital after taking the equivalent of 25 electroshock treatments all at once.

Esme needed a little prodding to close her books and go to sleep. Maybe twenty minutes later, Alyse and I were huddled in our own bed. I finally told her what had happened to you.

There was a stretch of silence until I added, "Boy, Commie being hit by lightning really fucks up our trip to the Cayman Islands."

After that, the main thing we discussed was what your hair looked like after the lightning bolt. You always had a thick, somewhat unruly, mop. It seemed a natural thing to focus on. Did it straighten your hair? Did it make you look like a white Don King? Alyse said she knew a lot of girls who used curling irons in high school, but "that's probably not the same thing." And I wondered if maybe the lightning had changed your hair color from light brown to something more charcoal-y, like, I don't know . . . Jerzy Kosinski's? Alyse seemed to think that was a plausible theory and added that the electricity would have probably stimulated your scalp and strengthened the follicles, so maybe there was a considerable upside to the whole thing. Or, picture Roger Daltrey around, say, 1982.

Okay.

Enough.

That's not true, Commie. I didn't say the thing about the Cayman Islands. Alyse and I didn't discuss the effect of a lightning strike on your hair. But, to recount what was said about you between Alyse and I, it would just be too maudlin to repeat.

Alyse snores sometimes. It's a light, almost dainty snore, if that's not a contradiction in terms. She started snoring at about 1:00 AM and I probably listened until 4:00.

TUESDAY THEN

I.

Alyse popped up and out of bed for her self-inflicted 5:30 wake-up call. If one gray can be grayer than another gray, that was the grayest day ever. Sometimes it's hard to figure out what makes people live anywhere other than Hawaii. Manhattan makes some sense because weather isn't even a factor there; it's just another speed bump in the greatest city on Earth. But what the hell makes anyone in possession of a few adult dollars want to keep living in Indianapolis, Kansas City, Milwaukee, or Cincinnati? At least in San Diego or Oahu, you can check off weather and move on to dealing with all the other things that depress the hell out you.

I got out of bed and took three Advil purely on principle. In the middle of the night, I'd pondered the not-too original thought of how quickly your entire world can go to black, how beyond your control it is, and how, if there are 12 billion people in the world, 11.9999 billion of them probably deserved a bonk over the head by lightning more than you do, Commie. On an objective level, helplessness against bad luck is generally manageable—or, let's face it, how dead would I be by now? But hopelessness weighs so much. And forget about feeling bad for yourself. By unwritten rule, that's not allowed. The second you feel like life blows, someone will be there to tell you, "Hey, just imagine if you were living in Rwanda."

That argument always pissed me off. I mean, really. That's my choice? Feeling down about my suburban life *or* living through the Rwandan genocide? That's it?

You feel bad about your coma? Hey, just imagine if you were living in Rwanda.

Oh, wait. That's actually a tough choice.

Downstairs, I kissed Alyse, and she stared at *Newsday* without reading it. She had a Joni Mitchell CD playing on volume level three. All the girls from *back then* love Joni Mitchell. I never got it. Really, I never got it with a lot of the singers girls liked in the '70s. Boz Scaggs? Peter Frampton? That dreary Jackson Browne?

They all loved Cat Stevens too, but he was someone I was actually on-board with. His stuff was really good. So good that when he went Muslim and gave up music, I was kind of pissed for a time. Another shred of pleasure in the world given up for God.

Alyse sang along quietly with Joni.

It was somewhat amazing that I could focus enough to catch some of the lyrics coming out of Alyse's wobbly little voice.

We were both feeling numb, but Alyse doesn't give into numbness as easily as I do. After the song ended, she said, "I was trying to sort out exactly why I'm feeling so totally depressed about Commie. I don't know him too well. But then I realized there's not much to sort out. It's just about the saddest, craziest thing that's ever happened."

I didn't know how to answer. Too many thoughts filled my head to actually allow any thinking. You know how when you picture the Great Depression in your mind and it seems like the whole world was in black and white? That's how I felt. Everything in the kitchen looked vaguely washed out. They talk about how events can *color* your outlook on life. That morning, events un-colored my outlook on life.

I trudged upstairs to wake up the kids. At the top of the stairs, I saw Esme walking to the bathroom.

"What are you doing up already, Ez?"

"I don't know. I'm just up."

Okay.

I went into Charlie's room without any of my usual, lame military bluster.

Charlie sat up and said, "I don't feel good."

"What's wrong, kiddo?"

"My stomach. I have to go really bad."

Shit, I thought, *he's not faking*. His face was sallow and he was sweating.

I scooped him up in my arms. Esme was in the nearest bathroom and, even in an urgent situation, there was nothing that was going to make me barge in on her. I raced to my bathroom and got Charlie about three feet from the toilet, when the poor little boy's intestines just evacuated.

"It's okay, Charlie. Good job. You needed to do that. You'll feel better. Just sit here for a few seconds and I'll run the bath and we'll have you good as new in no time."

As the hot water filled the tub, Esme popped in.

"Why were you running down the hall?"

"Charlie doesn't feel well."

Esme looked down at the diarrhetic pool on the floor. "Ewww."

"Yeah, eww. Ezzie, can you do me a favor and go downstairs and get the mop and a bucket?"

She took two steps, then turned around. "Maybe on that well-done bacon cheeseburger, the bacon wasn't so well-done."

"Maybe, Ezzie. Go."

Of course, it was Alyse who wound up bringing the mop. Charlie was already in the tub, limp as a jellyfish. Alyse kneeled over and kissed him. "Good morning, sunshine."

Charlie managed to eke out a smile, which was more than Alyse or I would do that morning. The good news was that any gloom in our general demeanor could now be falsely attributed to Charlie's digestive tract protestations.

"Alyse, I'll handle the mopping."

"You sure?"

"I'll be fine."

By the time I finished bathing Charlie, putting him back in bed, talking him to sleep, mopping the bathroom floor, and spraying twenty gallons of all-natural deodorizer (that doesn't work nearly as well as the shit with all the toxic chemicals), Alyse had fed Esme,

taken her to school, and returned to the kitchen.

There wasn't even time to sit together and catch our breath. Podiatry called.

Alyse and I hugged like we were mutual life rafts, and then I went to work.

Let me tell you something, Commie. The troubles of two people *do* amount to a hill of beans in this crazy, mixed-up world. The problems of two people are a goddamn Kilimanjaro of beans.

I'd completely forgotten about our FBI detail until I pulled out onto the street and saw two generic cars parked on the curb, bumper to bumper. Agent Brooks (back on the job already!) got out of the first car and hailed me down. When I pulled up alongside them, Horton scrambled out of the back car with a huge green and white golf umbrella.

Horton asked, "How are you, sir?"

"Well, my kid just had diarrhea all over the floor, my oldest friend was struck by lightning yesterday, and I am still scared to leave my wife alone knowing that freak of a cop is still out there somewhere. Otherwise, I'm fine."

"Really? Struck by lightning?"

"Really."

"Where?"

"South Carolina."

"Sorry to hear it."

"Thanks. What's up?"

"Well, I'm going to talk to your wife about the hate groups and all the online bidding. That's all going fine. In fact, better than fine."

"Okay. And what do you want to talk to me about?"

"It's nothing urgent. I wanted you to know that we've been keeping an eye on Detective Byron. He was at a bar in Jericho last night."

"You have a tail on him?"

"No."

Before I could ask another question, Horton said, "Around noon today, Byron will be randomly drug tested by the Nassau County

PD."

"They told you that?"

"No."

FBI agents must practice their blank looks in the mirror. My need-to-know status had tapped out again.

"Boy, you've been busy," I said.

"Yes. I also know that Byron's not going to pass that drug test." He put his hand up, "Don't ask me how I know."

"Agent Horton, I don't doubt that you have good reasons for telling me just so much, but I have to tell you, I don't like this feeling I have."

"What feeling is that?"

"Like there's a ping-pong game going on over my head."

"There is, and I'm sorry about it, but you'll have to trust me that you're better off not knowing everything."

"In this circumstance or in my life as a whole?"

Horton allowed himself a microscopic *touché* smile before replying, "The most important point is that, very soon, Detective Byron will either be fired or suspended indefinitely. That should ease your mind some."

I thought about that a second, and then just looked at Horton, scrunched up against the cold, rain dripping off the front of his umbrella.

"It doesn't ease my mind."

Horton turned his head.

"Agent Horton," I went on, sighing, "down the road, are you sure Byron's removal from the force makes him less of a threat to my family rather than more of a threat to my family?"

That was the first time one of my questions caught Horton off guard. "In all honesty," he said quietly, "it could go either way."

II.

For the first quarter of a mile of my drive to work, I thought of picking up my family and moving away as fast as possible. It wasn't just the Byron thing. It was everything. Swirling, swirling, swirling, swirling thoughts. The Advil couldn't even begin to beat back the pulsing in my head, and the Zoloft was on red alert.

The traffic light was out at the corner of Stratification and Seaview Avenue (never mind that, to view the sea from Seaview, you'd need a mile-high periscope). The back-up was huge and the progress slow. No one honked or tried anything tricky. The day was so gray and depressing, everyone just seemed resigned to, even at home with, misery.

The blocked path of my day gave me time to settle myself and prioritize the disasters in my life. No offense, Commie, but the situation with Byron was the one that worried me most. Everything else was a distant sound. It seemed to me that an unhinged detective on suspension would be worse than an unhinged detective whose day was filled with work. Neither option was great, of course.

When I was about twenty-five feet from the intersection, a BMW turning left collided with an Acura going straight. Guess whose fault it was. Civility broke down. Horns honked. Heads popped out of windows. Impotent curses flew from mouths. Cars drove up on the grass that divided the east and westbound roads to make muddy U-turns. The town beautification freaks were not going to be happy.

I waited, thinking about Byron. I have no idea what a Zen state is actually like, but I was in some kind of dark but clear-headed meditation. If anything, it was directly opposite to the nothing-to-lose euphoria I'd felt while throwing the bottle through the window. This was a nothing-to-lose calm stemming from depressed worry.

Another five minutes passed when, with a plan in my head, I got through the intersection with the help of a cop in an orange slicker. The second I was in the clear, I picked up the phone and called Sylvia.

"Sylvia, are there any gaps in my schedule this morning?"

Without hesitation, Sylvia said, "You have 20 minutes between 10:10 and 10:30."

"Good. Thanks, Sylvia."

I hung up and pulled out my wallet with its recently boosted inventory of business cards.

Either Byron saw my name on his Caller ID or he greets everyone by saying, "What the fuck do you want?"

"I want you to meet me in the garage of my office building at 10:10."

"Why the fuck would I do that?"

"What if I promise you that you'd be making the biggest mistake of your life if you don't?"

There was a pause, which I took as a good sign.

"Why the fucking garage?"

I left out the part about what a big fan I am of *All The President's Men* and said, "I didn't want you thinking I was going to have my chiropractor friend waiting around to come in and save my ass again."

A longer pause. It kind of dawned on me right then that cops know what motivates crooks, but with law-abiding civilians, they're a little lost.

"This better be good, asshole."

III.

Commie, you're not looking at me like I'm crazy, but I know you're thinking it. Yes, I know what I said—that I'd hit the wall on adventurousness the day before. And that was true. But my mental state in the car had given me a kind of grim resolve that probably stemmed from a feeling that the entire world was going to shit. Maybe it was that nothing-to-lose attitude. Since that time, I've also considered the possibility that I had a need to atone for peeing in my pants the last time I'd met with Byron. Whatever. My son was sick, my daughter was being attacked in class, my wife was being eyed as sexual prey, the world was a dismal gray, and you were hit by lightning.

You may find this overdramatic, but maybe this was my cushy, suburban, bourgeois version of a Rosa Parks moment. Just stand up and fucking do something.

Alright, wise-ass. Rosa Parks *sat down* and did something.

You really do have that annoying law school attention to detail.

But at least you're listening.

Three patients were scheduled before the 10:10 time gap. I freely admit, I treated them all on auto-pilot. One, oddly enough, was nine-year-old Sophie Wanderman, who came in with her father and a case of plantar's warts just like Audra Uziel had at that age. Unlike Audra's first appointment, however, I didn't put the Pine Scent air freshener around my neck to make anyone laugh. I was in no mood. I ran through the treatment like a stone-cold professional. I think I was no less effective than any other day, which is a little comforting in the sense that, let's say on the morning you're going to have an operation, your surgeon finds out his or her kid is turning tricks and hooked on amyl nitrates, there's still a good chance the procedure will go without a hitch.

No, Commie, I don't really know if you can get hooked on amyl.

Jesus.

I don't even remember the second patient. After he or she left, I remember looking down at my watch, saw it was 9:20, and thought: *In an hour from now, I'll be ten minutes into my appointment with Byron.* The third appointment was with another Orthodox Jew, Irwin Cole. Irwin is some kind of computer programmer. He was a decent, unassuming diabetic. (I told you before about Carolina having diabetes and its impact on the feet, so I'll spare you a recap on my treatment of Irwin.)

I will tell you that, uncharacteristically, Irwin confided something in me that morning. I say "uncharacteristically," because people don't often confide in their podiatrist. Maybe, in dealing with their feet, we're too far from their heads. Who knows? In strangely formal tones, Irwin simply said, "I'm having an extra-marital affair with a woman from the yeshiva."

When I repeated that to Alyse, she referred to the yeshiva as the Theological Inseminary.

If I hadn't been so preoccupied with my own life, I might have found Irwin's story interesting. But the only tidbit that registered was that he'd met the woman in a Talmud study class.

I know what you're thinking, Commie. It's like being in law school and cheating on an ethics exam.

All I said to Irwin was, "Gee, Irwin, I hope things work out."

I gave his feet a more superficial inspection than usual. Nothing I'd live to regret and nothing he'd notice. I just wanted him out of my office by 10:05. I needed a second to collect myself, grab some things from my office, and go to the bathroom.

On my way to the elevator, I told Sylvia I'd be back in time for my 10:30. She must have heard doubt in my voice, though, because she asked if I had my cell with me. Good employee, huh? I tapped the elevator button nervously because I wanted to get away before Arnie happened to come out and see me. If he did, I didn't know if I could resist the safety net impulse to tell him what I was up to.

IV.

The garage has three levels. The bottom is reserved for people who work in the building, and the top two are for visitors. I went down to the bottom level, where there would probably be no one pulling in or out in the middle of the work day. Rain oozed down the ramp through a grating in a corner of the ceiling, leaving a gunk of stained wall like in a cave. What do they call that, a stalagticite? Whatever. The place was dank and looked vaguely green in the fluorescent light.

I, ridiculously, decided not to wait in front of my car—as if Byron couldn't find out what I drive if he'd wanted to. Instead, I leaned against a Buick Regal which, I think, belonged to a receptionist for an endocrinologist on the second floor. It seemed like a neutral car, not too suburban and not expensive. I wanted to give Byron the impression I was a man of the people. It was idiotic, sure, but then again, it's pretty fascinating to see what goes through your mind in these situations.

When it got to be 10:13 and Byron still hadn't arrived, my thoughts started going to bad places. *What are you doing here? Are you nuts?* Byron's being three minutes late was all it took to discombobulate me, all it took for me to picture the cops looking for defensive wounds on my hands; finding my wallet missing and misdiagnosing my murder as a robbery gone bad; grimly walking to the front door of my home and then leaving with the words, *We're sorry for your loss*; and Alyse spending the rest of her life wondering '*What was he doing in the garage in the middle of the morning*?'

I then projected the fatherless lives of my kids: Esme turning 13 and going Goth with black clothes and thick mascara; Charlie developing a love for killing small animals, and sticking cherry bombs in the ass of the neighbor's cat; both kids reaching their late teens, their only thing in common being how much they hate their new stepfather. Or, even worse, how much they really like him. That thought was enough to make me take two steps to my left toward a door with an exit sign. But then I heard an aggressive *vroom*, and I knew it was Byron.

Apparently, he did already know what car I drive because he pulled right up to the back of my Saab. Then he let his car lurch a bit, clanking my bumper with his grill.

"Oops," he said, getting out.

To which I said, "I guess we should exchange insurance information."

Can you believe I said that, Commie? It was just like when Uziel confronted me that first time in my office and I joked with him that he could pay at the front desk. This latest joke came out of me from God knows where.

Anyway, Byron wasn't laughing. In fact, I think he was pissed because the joke made it seem like I wasn't intimidated even though I was beyond intimidated. He said, "How's Alyse?"

"She's okay," I said. "She feels safe because of the FBI detail outside our house."

Well, that backed him up some. That was the first part of my plan: mention the FBI as fast as possible. Then Byron would at least have to listen.

"FBI? What the fuck are you talking about?"

I took a deep breath and launched into a badly under-rehearsed speech:

"Look, Detective Byron, you and I got off to a bad start and, for whatever part of that is my fault, I'm sorry. And, as a way of making it up to you, I'm here right now to basically save your life."

Okay, that was a little over-the-top. Stupid. I still shudder about that. Byron took his hands out of his pockets. I'm sure he was this close to beating the crap out me.

"You fucking little—"

"Just hear me out. If what I have to say doesn't have any impact on you, then you can just beat the shit out of me and rape my wife and there's nothing I can do about it."

I tried not to beat the shit out of myself for what I'd said, and instead chose to simply talk faster.

"Detective, because my wife sells the artwork of You-ey Brushstroke and he made some very public anti-Semitic remarks, neo-Nazi hate groups started bidding on his work. My wife's computer was filled with bids from whack-jobs all over America. We didn't know what to do, so we called the FBI and they immediately got on the case. An Agent Lester Horton—you can look him up—posted a security detail outside our home. Alyse thinks the detail is out there to protect the operation from the neo-Nazis but, the fact is, it's there to protect the operation from you because I told Agent Horton about your threats to my wife."

Byron stared at me fiercely, then threw me a hanging curve ball. "Try fucking proving I threatened your wife."

I pulled out a mini-cassette recorder, hit *play*, and let it roll for maybe twenty seconds of the conversation between Byron and me.

In the slow-motion of my terrified state, I noticed Byron's Adam's apple bob. I took that as a sign that shit was sinking in. "Detective, my chiropractor friend recorded our conversation over his phone. After you left, I told Agent Horton about you, and he advised that we make several copies. My friend has a few, I have a few, there are some in a safety deposit box, and there is one that will go to Agent Horton if anything happens to me."

V.

Okay, those last two were lies. Horton already had the tape and there weren't any in a safety deposit box. I don't even have a safety deposit box. What the fuck would I put in a safety deposit box? The savings bonds I got for my Bar Mitzvah?

Hey, did I ever tell you about the Bar Mitzvah gift I got from one of my parents' best friends? This will only take a second, I promise. My friend, Scott Pfeiffer, had had his bar mitzvah in February and, since the Pfeiffers were such close friends, my parents splurged and wrote him a check for fifty bucks. His mother kept saying how she couldn't believe how generous the gift was. But, when it came time for my Bar Mitzvah in September, did the Pfeiffers reciprocate in kind? Oh, no. For a gift in honor of my becoming a man, the Pfeiffers, knowing I was such a Knicks fan, gave me four shares of stock in Madison Square Garden, selling at five and a quarter per share. Can you believe that? Not even an even five shares! To this day, I try to imagine the strategy sessions between Ken and Estelle Pfeiffer as they tried to figure out the most elegant way of being cheap pieces of shit.

Okay, back to the garage.

Byron looked down and swung his head left and right. It seemed as if he was sure he'd find a way out of this, but didn't have an immediate plan. I said, "Detective?"

He looked at me, and then I was sure he was trying to figure out what he'd do after he killed me.

"Detective," I pressed on, "in a few hours, you are going to be given a random drug test."

Byron grabbed me by my jacket and threw me up against the Buick Regal.

"What the fuck?"

I guess he was confused and a physical impulse was all he had. I felt lucky that he hadn't decided to shoot me, so I started talking fast again.

"Detective, I told you when you first came down here that I wanted to talk to you to save your life. And, the fact is, I'm here to help you in the hope that, if I do, you will in turn leave me and my family alone."

"I'm totally fucked. How the fuck do you know I'm gonna be tested?"

"If you repeat this, I'll deny it. FBI Agent Horton told me so. He's a computer whiz, so my guess is that he hacked into the department's computer. And he also knows that you're not going to pass it."

"Jesus fucking Christ. Well, that's it. I'm fucked."

"Not necessarily."

This is kind of funny. I started to reach into my inside pocket, then flashed to all those *Law & Order* perps who freak out the cops by reaching into their pockets. I said, "I'm not pulling out a gun, okay?"

Byron tilted his head up at me like, *Go ahead.*

From my pocket, I pulled out a long, thin vial full of my own pee.

"You can hide this somewhere on your person and fill the urine test cup with it. It's my urine, and it's a lot cleaner than yours. There's no reason for anyone to frisk you beforehand because they know of no way in the world you could know in advance that you'd be tested."

I have to tell you, Commie, Byron's reaction registered with me as one of the greatest, if not *the* greatest, moments of my life. I know I'm supposed to say the best moment of my life was when my kids were born, or the first time that I made love with Alyse, or my wedding, but those are moments that happen for someone twenty thousand times a day. To find yourself in a horrible situation and devise a plan that leads to a predatory cop dropping his tensed-up shoulders, widening his eyes, and looking like, like—I dunno, a grateful human being? It was the best moment of my life.

Another thing I never told Alyse, so . . . you know the drill.

You know the drill. Another expression coined and popularized for exclusive use by idiots.

"You put a lot of thought into this, didn't you?"

I took it as another good sign that Byron managed to get out a sentence without using the word *fuck*.

"Actually, I came up with the whole idea when I was stuck in traffic this morning."

"Really."

"Yeah. And it wasn't easy because I had a lot on my mind. Not only did I have you to worry about, but my oldest friend was struck by lightning yesterday and is now in a coma—not to mention that Charlie woke up sick as dog today . . ."

"He's a cute kid."

"Thanks, though hearing that from you makes me a little more appalled that you'd threaten to sodomize his mother."

Well, I really pushed my luck there. I guess I started feeling too comfortable. Byron tensed up, and I thought I'd blown the whole thing, but then he dropped his head.

"I caught a fifty-four-pound striped bass and brought it to a taxidermist," he said, "I had him hollow it out and put a removable square in the gut. While I was working one morning, my kid—he's five—he climbed up on the couch and knocked the fish off the wall. My stash of ecstasy and Oxycontin, all wrapped and labeled by the guys in the evidence room, flew out on the floor. By the time I got home, my wife had taken my kid to New Jersey."

"Were you selling or using?"

"Both." He said it with a look of, *I'm such a fuck-up*. Then he looked at me and said, slowly, "My ex-wife is gorgeous. Thin and tan with dark eyes."

He paused to make sure I made the connection.

"Of course, she's Italian."

Even though Byron's solid-state rage had all but dissipated, I didn't like this part of the conversation. You know, I just didn't want to talk about girls. So, I handed him the vial of urine. My end of a trade: I give you clean pee, you don't rape my wife.

"Look," Byron said, "I appreciate this."

"I have a good rapport with Agent Horton. So, I don't think it'll be a big problem to tell him we had a good talk and worked things out ourselves."

Byron put the vial in the crotch of his pants. Smart move, to keep it warm. Then he said, "I thought you were an asshole from the first second I met you."

I said, "Well, now you know: I'm just a schmuck."

Byron shook his head, almost laughed, then put his hand out for a shake.

VI.

Look, even in your coma, I appreciate your restraint in not telling me that what I did was unbelievably stupid and risky. I know I said that this moment in the garage was the best moment of my life, but I avoid thinking too much beyond that. It was a good moment. The whole thing worked out. But now that I'm solidly back to my annoyingly sane self, the whole scene in the garage makes me shudder. To be perfectly honest, if it's raining when I go to work, I'll slip the garage attendant a twenty to let me park in a visitor's spot on the first floor. Unlike the campus at Maryland, I don't seek out memories in that garage.

You know, listening to myself, I'm a little bummed about all these mentions I've made about "the best moments of my life." Isn't it a little early for that? It's not like I'm ninety, sitting in a rocking chair with nothing left in my life but retrospect. Maybe I should merely hope for two or three moments per year that I remember at all. Jesus. Have you ever seen someone who can lower his expectations faster than me? This aging business is relentless.

I got in the elevator and pressed two to get back to my office, but it stopped at the lobby and my next patient got in. I'd only had one previous appointment with him, so, combined with being over-juiced on adrenaline, I couldn't even remember his name (George Hershey) or what I was treating him for (heel spurs).

"Getting in a little late today, Doc?"

Doc. I was in an elevator with Bugs Bunny.

"I had to go down to my car."

"What for?"

I couldn't stop my neck from turning my "*Are-you-fucking-kidding-me?*" face toward him.

"Sorry, Doc. I was just kidding."

I guess I'd run out of personality. The elevator ride was a shade longer than it takes to get to the roof of the Chrysler Building. When the door opened, I said, "I'll see you in five minutes."

I drifted past Sylvia, who whispered, "Everything okay?"

I nodded and glanced down at her appointment book. George Hershey. Heel spurs.

Mr. Hershey, you can stop walking for the rest of your life or I can amputate. Try to make up your mind fast. I'm in no mood for delay.

I closed my office door. Finally, a second alone to digest all that had happened in that leaky garage. You would think some of the weight would be off my shoulders. And, in a way, it was. Just not in a way that had me shoot my fist in the air and go, *YES*! Quite the—well, oh Jesus. The truth is, actually, I just, you know, quietly lost it.

Commie, it's moments like this that make me glad there are euphemisms like, "lost it." You get the point. We can move on, right?

O. K.

VII.

I broke down. I sobbed. Head in hands, quivering, snot, phlegm—the whole deal. I'm not ashamed to admit it. Actually, I'm totally ashamed to admit it. But, in the spirit of full disclosure, coupled with your unconscious state—

The normal thing to say is that "I cried like a baby" but, in the rare times I've thought back to that moment, the description never seemed apt. Really, it was much more pathetic than that, much sadder. Isn't it always sadder when an adult cries? The only thing I can compare it to is the way Kevin Kline breaks down and cries in the car at the end of that movie about all the couples with waterbeds in the '70s dropping their car keys in a fish bowl and swapping wives.

I never remember the title of that one.

I splashed my face and took another sliver of time to pull myself together. That was nixed by the little ping of a text message: *Thanks. I WON'T let it go.*

It was from Audra. It took me a few seconds to figure out what the hell she meant. The "Don't let it go" text I'd sent her the afternoon before felt like five years ago. Part of me wanted to answer with a screaming text back to her: *With the horrible things that have happened since yesterday, you expect me to give a shit about your puny problems with your father?*

Don't worry, Commie. I didn't do anything stupid. At least not anything else stupid. I didn't respond at all. It was no time to be dealing with Audra. I had no clue what she planned as part of her not-letting-it-go strategy, and I didn't want to know. Even with Audra's sophistication, let's face it: The smartest nineteen-year-old in the world is still a moron.

I treated Hershey without lopping off his foot at the ankle. On the other hand, I should mention that he blew off his follow-up appointment and never came in again, which is fine by me. I hope he found another podiatrist who appreciates his sense of humor. I also hope he took a trip to Arizona, walked around barefoot, and was stung on the heel by a scorpion. I am human, after all.

I drifted over to Arnie's office. I should mention that you didn't get the exclusive on my session with Byron. This wasn't like the bottle-throwing thing, where I kind of had to keep it secret so as not to wind up in jail. I had to tell *someone* about Byron because A) it was too much to keep to myself, and B) it had to be Arnie because, for obvious reasons, I couldn't tell Alyse. Truthfully, I didn't think I should talk to Alyse at all for a couple of hours. All I needed was for her radar to pick up some jitter in my voice.

Actually, that should be sonar, right?

I poked my head in Arnie's examination room and he mouthed the words "Two minutes" while monitoring a fairly attractive woman suspended in traction. I hovered around Sylvia in the waiting room and decided to head off a call from Alyse by texting her.

How's Charlie?

Ten seconds later: *Resting comfortably. How r u?*

I'm so slow at texting, I was sure Alyse would think something was wrong based purely on my delayed answer. Then again, she knows I'm a technical pea brain.

K. Trying not 2 think 2 much, I managed.

The moronic cheerfulness of text shorthand felt all wrong in light of the emotional g-forces of the day. It reminded me of the day after my father died. I was at the funeral home going over all the arrangements with one of those guys who must have studied grief at Yale Drama School. Every word was so delicate, every hand motion so deliberate and rounded off. The whole world felt solemn and severe, yet I couldn't help thinking that there were millions of people just outside Browning Funeral Home who were riding and walking and sitting and gossiping their way through another blissfully forgettable day. How could they not be aware that this moment in time was no joke?

Then again, let's face it, that question is small potatoes. Maybe the real brilliance of humanity is our ability to totally ignore our own survival instincts. Some stymied corner of our brain is trying to tell us we should worry about living through the day, but it's outvoted by the rest of our brain telling us to worry about parking spots and credit ratings. By now, it probably sounds like I enjoy contemplating stuff like that, but the truth is, it gets me frustrated. My capacity for it has pretty strict limits.

Luckily, Alyse cut off the texting with, *Charlie calling. Gotta run.* (By the way, we relaxed the rules on "I love you's" when signing off text messages. Enough is enough already.)

Arnie's patient emerged from his examination with a real bounce in her step. She was a lot of woman, tall and solid like an Olympic swimmer with a big, pretty face, and long, dirty blonde hair in a loose ponytail. Come to think of it, Olympic athletes do seem to get more and more attractive all the time. The shtupping that must go on at those Olympic Villages.

Arnie saw me watch her get on the elevator. The second the doors closed, he whispered, "Former plus-size model. Imagine getting wrapped up in that."

My smile was feeble.

"You okay?" he asked.

"I've got a sick story to tell you."

"You wanna grab lunch?"

"Oh. Okay. But not around here, where I'll see people I know."

"How about that place in the Bronx where Michael Corleone took out Salazzo and that crooked cop?"

I laughed because it was funny coming from Arnie, but I'm not a *Godfather* freak like every other guy in the world. Something about the way you're supposed to root for these thugs who are passed off like they're trustees on the board of Chase Manhattan just rubs me the wrong way.

We went to a Chinese place in one of the economically depressed towns located closer to the beach but not close enough. You know what I told Arnie already, so I'm not going to go overboard describing lunch. If you want to pop up now just to say, "Thank God," and go right back under, that's fine with me.

For the most part, the conversation with Arnie went like this:

I'd say "This morning, ba-da-ba-da-ba-da," and Arnie would say "Get the fuck out!" And I'd say, "After Byron plunked my car, ba-da-ba-da-ba-da happened," and Arnie would say, "You're fucking kidding me!" And, eventually, I said, "So, in the end, ba-da-ba-da-ba-da."

Arnie leaned back and said, "Holy shit. You took a pretty insane chance there. I mean, you pulled it off and I'm glad you did, but why didn't you at least tell me, so I could hide behind a car and leap out if things got out of hand?"

"I guess I just didn't want a safety net this time. I pretty much needed to feel unsafe and hope Byron would see that I was scared. That way, at least he'd have to be somewhat impressed by the fact that I had the guts to face him."

Actually, I hadn't thought of that until I said it to Arnie, but it made sense.

"Dealing with him one-on-one was the only way I could really get him out of my life."

"You know," Arnie said, "you could get in a lot of trouble for supplying the clean urine. I mean, you could lose your license."

"I know, but Byron's pee test will come up negative and that should be that. They can't give him a random test and not trust the results, right?"

"Yeah, you're right. And, look, even if they didn't trust the results and Byron broke down and said he'd gotten your urine, he can't prove it. You just deny it, then play the tape of him threatening Alyse. Not that any of that's going to happen anyway."

"Yeah, let's hope it doesn't come to that."

Arnie nodded thoughtfully before saying, "So, even if this all works out perfectly forever, I hope you're not going to tell Alyse about it."

"Don't worry."

"Good," Arnie said. "Because women have a real bug up their asses about rape."

I choked on a spring roll, and that was pretty much lunch.

Wait. Of course, I did also ask Arnie how Fumi was doing, and Arnie told me about the doctor who suggested to his wife that they hire a Filipino nurse to take care of her while she convalesced.

I looked at Arnie like, *huh*?

"Filipino nurses have a reputation for being really great. And they speak English so they're especially good."

"Oh. I didn't know that. So, did Fumi go for the idea?"

"Fumi liked the idea of a nurse, but not a Filipino. See, the Japanese are totally racist against all other Asians."

"Another thing I didn't know."

"I didn't either, but Fumi explained, and I quote, 'For Japanese, it's simply tradition for us to look down on other Asians.' So, I said to her, 'Well, that's perfect. The Filipino nurse would be your servant. You can look down on her all you want.' But still no dice. There was no way Fumi was going to have a Filipino in our home, so I just dropped it, but not before saying something really stupid."

"Uh oh. What?"

"I said, 'You Japanese gotta lighten up on your traditions.'"

"What's stupid about that?"

"Well, you know they also have a whole suicide tradition, and that's what Fumi thought I was implying. She got all crazy, crying and telling me that she didn't attempt suicide at dinner, that she had just wanted the pills to work faster."

"Wow."

"Yeah. I eventually convinced her I wasn't implying that she attempted suicide, and that I was guilty of a poor choice of words."

"Is she still pursuing the lawsuit against the emergency room doctors who sliced up her dress?"

"Oh, yeah," Arnie said, nodding helplessly. "I'll tell you, from the second America's idiots and/or nutcases discovered litigation, there was no hope for this country."

We talked about that for the rest of lunch. How there's no hope for this country or this world. It was reassuring to hear that Arnie was, like me, too freaked to even contemplate what his kid would see in life. By the time we covered dirty bombs, biological weapons, global warming, over-population, Jesus-freaks, and swine flu, we agreed that we were pretty lucky to have lived during the years we've lived.

I grabbed the check from Arnie, paid for lunch, and said, "You know, it's impossible."

"What?"

"All of it. Everything in the world. You name it, it's impossible."

"Yeah, well," Arnie said, "no one said it was going to be easy."

It was rare to hear Arnie spout such a *Readers' Digest* line. Maybe that's why I thought to myself, *Really? "No one said it was going to be easy?" But someone must have said it at least once. I couldn't have gotten that impression out of thin air.*

Arnie and I drove back to the office and repaired to our separate examination rooms. I felt even keeled after muscling through three patients, and I called Alyse, confident my voice wouldn't give anything away.

"Your timing's perfect. Charlie just fell asleep."

"How's he feeling?"

"He had one more round of diarrhea around noon, but not that long after, he sat up in bed and started chatting up a storm."

"What was he chatting about?"

"Becoming a vegetarian."

"What?"

"The thought of meat pretty much grosses him out right now."

"You know, Alyse, most of the vegetarians I know are actually pretty fat."

"I know!" Alyse said, laughing. "I've noticed the same thing!"

"What are they getting fat on?"

"Mac and cheese."

"That must be it. Their diet is so limited they think that anything they can eat must be good for them."

"Exactly. I love mac and cheese, but I have it maybe once a year."

"I think they eat a lot of nuts, too."

"And nuts are also fattening. In fact, a lot of veggies are fattening. Avocados—you can totally blimp out on them."

"That's kind of unfair. They should make a law that all plants are healthy."

"That would be a great law. You could run for president on that."

"I think you're right."

"If I were president, I'd make a law that the gas tank has to be on the same side of every car."

"Oh, Alyse. That is brilliant. I've had my car for four years now, and I *still* can't remember which side to pull into a gas station on."

"No one can, honey."

You could say it was some kind of testament to the human spirit that Alyse and I, on that particular day, were able to veer into a conversation that had us laughing over the phone. We kept it going a few minutes more. I think we ended on the idea of passing a law that would abolish the death penalty except in the case of people who clip their nails on the subway.

Just as I felt a hairball of guilt about laughing so much on such a shitty day, Alyse came through with her typical mind-reading. "Honey, Commie wouldn't want you to feel guilty about having a good laugh."

"Even over the phone, you picked that up?"

"Even over the phone."

"Well, you're right. Commie was never into guilt trips."

Then I sensed that Alyse took a second to gather herself. I was right. She told me Agent Horton had spoken to her in the morning after he left.

"He told me he was going to talk to you. He said everything with the bidding was going well, right?"

"Yeah. Horton said that they've tracked three separate groups doing most of the bidding and one he'd never heard of before. He said that he checked up the guy—his name is Ezra Panchen—and he's super-loaded. He compared him to—remember that billionaire who spend all that money trying to destroy Clinton?"

"Yeah, vaguely. I think he had three names?"

"Horton mentioned the name, but I don't remember it. Horton also compared him to another bazillionaire whose money was behind the swift boat thing with Kerry."

"In other words, wealthy right-wing crazies."

"Exactly, but this Panchen guy's a wealthy right-wing, Neo-Nazi crazy. So wealthy, that by the time Horton closes the bidding on the nine pieces up on the site, he expects it to cap out at about $800,000."

"Get out."

"I know. It's crazy."

"And, eventually, because of this, Horton will hopefully nail this guy, right?"

"I guess. And he also confirmed that we can keep our share of the commissions."

"Wow," I said, and then, like a dipshit, I thought aloud: "Twenty percent of $800,000 comes to—"

"Don't get into the math, honey."

"Oh, no?"

"No. I started thinking about how I'll feel to know we made all that money off American hatred."

"Oh, fruit of the poison tree."

"Well put."

"I guess we'll have to discuss this."

"We have time. Horton has to close the bidding, the Nazis have to send the checks, we have to wait for them to clear, then ship off the artwork."

"Don't forget dealer prep and destination charges."

"Right."

"We'll have time to think. That's good."

VIII.

When I said "good," I meant it. I'd been making some pretty snap decisions lately, so it was a relief to be able to settle back into the comfort of procrastination. You know, sometimes I think the most beneficial thing I learned in college was how to effectively put shit off.

I'm not complaining. It's a good skill.

When Alyse and I hung up, I felt pretty much okay. I mention that because you might remember what I said when I started this story—what? 55 years ago now: I told you that it bugged me when Alyse said she had a feeling, "I'm gonna make a fortune" off You-ey. Well, during the phone call, she kept saying "we" instead of "I." Horton confirmed that *we* can keep the money. And *we* have to wait for the check to clear. One little word change and I didn't feel threatened anymore. We were in this together, and why not?

I'm justifying myself here, and it's totally ridiculous. Jesus. To start doing an archeological dig into every thought or emotion I have is so pointless.

Let's not groom fleas here.

I felt good. Let's accept that and drop it. Okay?

Actually, after my next three patients, I mentally added up how much money I'd made from office visits that day. It felt a little paltry next to the numbers Alyse was throwing around. It didn't bug me. A nano-second of a twinge, and that was all. I felt good.

The skies were clearing.

Before leaving, I put in a call to Graydon at *Newsday*. He told me his piece on the horseradish company would run the next day and that his editors had been pretty thrilled with it.

"Well, that's great," I said. "Maybe you'll get a Pulitzer."

"Maybe."

I'd been kidding when I said that, so Graydon's saying "maybe" was pretty surprising.

"If I win, I'll be sure to send you a bottle of Champagne or something."

"If you win a Pulitzer, you owe me at least dinner and Champagne for me and my wife."

"You're right. I thought I'd try to lowball you."

Of all the stuff that happened, one of the more enjoyable things was the give-and-take I had with Graydon. We had a really good rapport. After telling me You-ey would definitely be arraigned the next morning and that some of the people at the DA's office were thinking the case was pretty shaky, Graydon said to me, "You know, I have a theory about this case."

"Really?" I said. "What's your theory?"

"I haven't really thought it through very much yet, but I was thinking maybe *you* threw the bottle through the window."

Maybe our rapport was too good, I thought.

Commie, knowing me, you have to assume I totally panicked when he said that. Not my pee-in-my-pants panic, but pretty damn close, right?

Wrong. Calm as can be, I said, "Hey, that's a fantastic theory."

To which Graydon said, "I'm half-serious."

To which I said, "I can see why. It would be a perfect crime. Who's gonna suspect a Jew of anti-Semitic vandalism against a store owned by a big Jewish macher?"

"*Macher*? What's that?"

"Oh, it's Yiddish. It means a guy who's a big deal. Something like that. Yiddish is tough to translate. On the other hand, the macher and his daughter are my long-time patients, and I didn't steal anything from the store. So, I think your problem is motive."

"Yeah, I don't know why you would have done it. And, if you did, I'm not exactly sure why you've been doing all this stuff to clear that You-ey guy."

I exhaled in a way that sounded as if I were disappointedly agreeing.

"Like I said, I haven't really thought it through."

At that point, I wanted to quit while I was ahead and get off the phone, but I also didn't want to sound suspiciously abrupt, so I said, "Well, I watch a lot of *Law & Order*, so I pretend like I know about this stuff. So, I'd say, next time you face a situation like this, you should think things through more before confronting your suspect."

To which Graydon said, "Yeah. The theory hit me because you seemed more interested in the case than the average person. But I like you, so I took the lazy route and thought I'd just throw it out there to you and listen to hear if you went speechless or, you know, puked."

"I haven't puked in, like, fifteen years."

"Well, I guess I should apologize for even thinking it, but, then again, you went with my theory so happily, I get the feeling you enjoyed it."

"You're right. No apology necessary. In fact, any other theories you want to run by me, don't hesitate."

"Thanks. How are your wife and kid?"

"Kids. We have two. They're fine, but this was a rough day. My oldest friend was hit by lightning yesterday and now he's in a coma."

"Oh, Jesus, I'm sorry."

"Yeah, it's horrible. I don't want to think about it."

"I bet."

Sounding reluctant, I said, "Well, I guess I should be going. It's Hanukkah tonight so the kids are going to want me home."

Graydon wished me a happy holiday.

Click.

It was pretty surprising that, on a whim, he came up with me as the perp, and I guess I was pretty lucky he didn't have much confidence in the theory. But that wasn't what I thought about after we hung up. Instead, I thought about the number of times that I'd told people that "my oldest friend was hit by lightning." There's no denying I was using your tragedy to get sympathy or to soften people or to swerve out of dicey conversations. Even though I felt you wouldn't mind, it still seemed a little skeevy. I did the same thing in the weeks, or even months, after my father died, and I decided he wouldn't have minded either. My father would have said, "Hey, I'm dead. If you can benefit from it, be my guest."

One time at basketball, a few of us were talking about all the post-traumatic stress victims coming back from the war, and one of the two guys I didn't really like in the game said something like it's impossible to kill someone and not be traumatized, even in war. So, I said my father told me he shot a few guys in World War II and never regretted it for a second. It wasn't true. I just wanted to nix the guy's point because he got on my nerves.

One nice thing about the dead—you can misquote them with impunity.

IX.

Did I ever tell you about my father in the war? I don't have much time, but in the short strokes: My father was there for the invasion of Normandy on D-day. He was on one of the LST boats, and he got so seasick that he couldn't get out of the boat. All the other guys charged the beach while my father lay nauseated on his back. The guy who was at the helm of the boat had been killed, so it just floated there. My father was lying so still, with his eyes closed, that he figured the Germans thought he was dead. When he finally picked up his head, I guess he was in calmer waters because he had his equilibrium back and was able to get out and hit the beach.

By that time, the Germans weren't shooting at guys in the water because all the soldiers were either dead or on land. My father ambled out of the water onto land and found a bunch of GI's huddled behind a huge rock. In the next few days, he said he fired his rifle a bunch of times but was pretty sure he never actually shot anyone.

And that's how he survived the invasion of Normandy and lived to meet my mother and produce yours truly.

When I get into my usual habit of mentally retracing the steps of what led me to whatever fix I'm in, you'd think I'd go back to that. But I never do. I guess that's Existentialism. Whatever. Another thing I can only take so far. I mean, I'm on the planet Earth because my father basically slept through the bloodiest battle of World War II. What the hell am I supposed to do with that?

At about 4:30 that afternoon, I was getting some paperwork out of the way. (Don't get me started on insurance forms.) But, at the moment, I was happy to occupy my mind with busy work.

Midway through an explanation of why Blue Cross was only going to cover 60 percent of a bunion, Sylvia buzzed me. I assumed she was letting me know she was shoving off, but instead she said, "I have a Detective Shelby here to see you."

I wasn't overly worried because Shelby had been the good cop through everything, but my immediate thought was, *"God, it never ends."*

I was even less worried when Shelby came in with a smile, holding a gift-wrapped box.

"Detective Shelby, how are you? I heard you were a bit under the weather."

"No big deal. I get about ninety colds a year." Shelby lowered his shoulders like: *Enough small talk,* and said, "Well, first, I wanted to thank you for what you did for Byron."

He looked at me in kind of a friendly/conspiratorial way, and I guess my cop show instincts kicked in because I said, "I don't know what you're talking about."

Shelby laughed and said, "You're a smart guy. I promise you, I'm not wired."

I smiled and said, "I still don't know what you're talking about."

He handed me the box. "Byron wanted to return something to you, and he wanted to give Charlie a gift for Hanukkah."

"That's very thoughtful."

"Open it."

The lid of the box was separately wrapped, so I pulled it off and saw the tube I'd given to Byron, cleaned and dry like a commercial for Cascade.

"What's this?" I asked, knowing exactly what it was.

"I don't know," Shelby said grinning, "but it's yours for you to do with however you wish."

"Alright, sir."

The other item in the box was a kid-sized, navy blue windbreaker, which I unfolded and turned around. On the back it said, NASSAU COUNTY SWAT.

"Oh, Charlie's going to love this."

"We usually save them for kids who've been crime victims or whatever. But Charlie seemed like such a great kid and you helped . . . Well, let's leave it at Charlie being a great kid."

"Thank you. Really, that's very nice of you guys. And, not that it isn't a pleasure to see you, Detective Shelby, but why didn't Byron bring it himself?"

"He didn't think you needed to see him again today."

I nodded, trying to look as appreciative as possible.

"Byron's not a bad guy. He's gone a bit off track and . . . But hey, he's my partner, you know?"

Again, I nodded, now trying to look as understanding as possible.

Finally, Shelby warmly wished me and my family a "merry Hanukkah," shook my hand, said, "You're a good man," and left.

You know, I shouldn't have even mentioned that he said "merry Hanukkah." It bugs me that we'll hear a thing like that and have a big laugh about the "dumb goyim." Like I said before, Jews barely register on the chart of world population. How the hell should anyone know that we don't do "merry?"

On the other hand, he *is* a cop in New York.

Jesus. I'm so sick of being someone who looks at both sides of a question.

Before I left the office, I called Danielle. We only talked for a few seconds because she was on her way to the ICU, but she didn't sound so hot. Things must've been sinking in. I didn't even ask Danielle what the doctors were saying. But, even with all of that weighing on her, she still wished me a happy Hanukkah and thanked me profusely for calling. I didn't have the words lying around to tell her how unnecessary it was to thank me, but I did manage to stop myself from wishing her a happy Hanukkah. I guess she could've had a happy Hanukkah if you popped awake sometime during the holiday and said, "Wasn't I just on the beach?" But from the sound of her voice, it didn't seem likely.

I hung up and closed my eyes for a second, then looked at my watch and saw it was time go.

Sylvia wished me a happy holiday on my way out and, in an uncharacteristic display of human personality, she said, "Did you get any exciting gifts for your children?"

I told her I got ice hockey stuff for Charlie, and Sylvia said, "Oh," in a way that made it seem like I'd gotten him a subscription to *Penthouse.*

"Not a hockey fan, Sylvia?"

"No, it's . . . nothing."

"What, Sylvia? You can tell me anything. I won't be offended."

"No, it's just that ice skating is very dangerous. It's easy to fall and the ice is very hard."

Okay, folks. And now for our next guest on the "Thank God, She Doesn't Have Kids" Show . . .

It was still raining when I drove home. On the satellite radio's '70s rock station, I caught some jazzy Steely Dan, a little campy Queen, and Bruce. I always thought it amazing that you were into Springsteen before anyone had even heard of him. I've never been ahead of the curve on anything. Well, maybe Prince. I liked him pretty early. Anyway, it was nice to drive in the slop singing along with *Thunder Road.*

But I remember when Alyse and I saw him in concert about two years earlier. He still sounded amazing, but, truth be told, Alyse and I both thought it was a little weird to hear this bazillionaire still singing about juvenile delinquents in New Jersey. I don't know. I guess he's got to make the fans happy with the oldies, but I couldn't help thinking that, by now, the words must fly out of his mouth by pure muscle memory, the same as the gibberish Hebrew came out of my mouth at my Bar Mitzvah. *Baruch atah adonai, you ain't a beauty, but, hey, you're alright.* In a way, I found the whole thought comforting. Even Bruce Springsteen has this day-to-day existence with obligations that go on and on, year after year. Even with 20,000 people watching, chores are chores.

Alyse and I tried to get the kids into Bruce. We even thought about taking them to the concert, but the tickets were pricey for two, let alone another two for kids who'd probably pass out during *Jungle Land.* As it happened, halfway through, a lot of the audience looked like they were wondering why the hell they blew off their own bedtimes for Bruce. Fat couples in tented tour t-shirts, passing binoculars back and forth, writing down the set list, smoking joints, flicking on lighters for encores . . . oy. It was like updated Thomas Wolfe. You can't go nubile again.

Agent Foreman was back on his shift in front of my house. As I had that morning, I was waved over to a Chevy by a federal agent. Foreman told me that Horton, twenty minutes earlier, had closed the bidding on Alyse's website.

"So, he's got all he needs?"

"Yes."

"So, you don't really have to monitor our home anymore?"

"No. But Horton wanted me to tell you to lock up your house as securely as possible, keep on a lot of lights, and keep his number close by."

"I appreciate that. The fact is, I had a one-on-one meeting with Detective Byron today, and I feel confident that we settled things."

Foreman looked at me a little cross-eyed. "How did you come to have a one-on-one meeting with this guy?"

"I called him and told him to meet me in the garage of my office building."

"Sir, with all due respect, that was an incredibly stupid thing to do."

"Oh, I have no doubt of that. I can't believe I did it myself. But it worked out. Seriously. He even sent over a gift for my kid."

"If you don't mind my asking, what did you say to him?"

It struck me as a bad idea to tell an FBI agent that I'd tipped off a rogue cop about an impending drug test.

"Well, if you don't mind, Agent Foreman, I've got you on a strict need-to-know basis."

That was the first time I saw Foreman crack a smile. As I said before, people in law enforcement just don't know what the hell to make of civilians. In his amused confusion, Foreman said, "Have a happy Hanukkah, sir."

He started up his car. Onto other criminals.

X.

You know, something just dawned on me. During the entire Tuesday I've been describing, four people wished me a happy Hanukkah and only one of them was Jewish. And she had converted.

I got home to my Jewish-by-birth family and Hanukkah commenced, albeit exclusively in Charlie's room because the diarrhea left him too limp to get out of bed. Esme was atypically enthusiastic about her new boots, a new sweater with a penguin logo, and a new Edit Pro computer program so she could make her own movies that I'd be highly reluctant to see. Charlie was pretty thrilled about the hockey stuff until Esme said, "Chuckster, you're going to be such a great player," at which point Charlie was over the moon.

When Charlie opened the box from Byron, I said, "That's a gift from the two nice detectives you met." Charlie and Alyse looked quizzically at the jacket, and then at me. "They just enjoyed meeting you, Chuckster." He didn't need any help getting juiced over the NASSAU SWAT jacket. By April, he was wearing it every day. After I gave Alyse a tell-you-later look, she nodded and went downstairs to bring up a bushel of latkes.

We blow off the menorahs and dreidels and prayers, but we draw the line at latkes.

In no time, there we were, all sitting around Charlie in bed, sprinkling the latkes with sugar and dunking them in applesauce. A happy family. I assumed Esme didn't have any blowback from the previous day's classroom discussion of anti-Semitism because she was in great form that night. The fact that she was wolfing down latkes was enough to thrill me, since I'm endlessly worried about her winding up like one of those women you see in restaurants pretending to enjoy hummus.

Charlie wondered if his tropical fish would eat latkes, so I took a few crumbs and sprinkled them in the tank. The four of us peered in as all the angel fish took the crumbs in their mouths and immediately spit them out; the school of neon tetras batted the crumbs between them like a hyper-kinetic soccer game. When the crumbs landed on the teal blue gravel, the albino catfish came over and hovered over their Hanukkah meal, tasting it, spitting it out, smelling it, tasting it again. Esme put herself in the head of the catfish saying, "These latkes smell good, but I don't like them. Why don't I like latkes? I know I'm not a kosher fish because I eat crap off the bottom of the house, but still, there's no reason I shouldn't enjoy some latkes. They smell good and they're chewy, but I just don't like latkes. Look at all those people outside the tank: they like latkes. So, what's wrong with me? Why, God? Why? Why do I keep spitting out these latkes?"

Charlie was laughing so hard I was pretty sure he was going to get sick again, but we were all laughing too hard to stop him. Esme was like our own little—Who's that short comedian who shouts with his eyes closed? He's on Howard Stern all the time? I can't remember his name, but you know who I'm talking about. Esme was like the female pre-teen version of that guy. Only she ad-libbed the whole thing!

I guess I can hype the wonders of my kids as much as everyone else. But just because I do it doesn't mean I can't hate it when other people do it.

Anyway, that was, at least for the time being, the best Hanukkah we ever had. Just the four of us sitting together in Charlie's snug little room, laughing and eating and opening gifts. I mean, when you think about it, is that really a somehow less holy observance of the holiday than anyone else's? How exactly is lighting candles while saying a prayer a more religious experience than watching tropical fish eat latkes? I know that sounds funny, but I really mean it. I honestly think Esme's doing her catfish/latke routine was as meaningful or even more meaningful to my kids than if they were rocking back and forth at the Wailing Wall asking God to bless our home. Those laughs blessed our home more palpably and creatively than God ever did.

There. I said it.

You know, I think that's the first time I used the word "palpably" in a conversation. I remember from high school, some guy in a Shakespeare play said it. "A hit. A palpable hit."

Whatever. Another word now mine forever.

"I think I heard the doorbell."

Charlie, in his perpetual vigilance, sat up in bed. We all went quiet and heard nothing for maybe fifteen seconds.

Finally, Alyse said, "I just heard the bell, too."

We don't get many solicitors in our neighborhood, and being targeted by one was even more unlikely on Hanukkah. Of course, someone just popping over without calling—well, a law against that could be another policy you could ride to the White House.

Alyse and I went downstairs.

In one of the rare times when I've felt called upon to play the male role in our relationship, I strode ahead of Alyse and intoned, "Who's there?"

A familiar voice answered and Alyse looked at me like: *What the shit?*

XI.

I opened the door and there was Audra. She held the metal end of a closed, black umbrella on the floor under the roof of our porch. Despite the umbrella, she looked smaller and more washed out than I ever remembered seeing her. But that might have had something to do with the fact that just behind her stood a hulking six-foot-five black man with long dreadlocks, dark sunglasses, and, hanging around his neck, a cross big enough to anchor a Carnival Cruise ship.

It's amazing how quickly long-cultivated open-mindedness can scurry away for old-school racist bullshit. My instant read was that Audra was a hostage, her body screening my view of the gun being held to her back.

If only I didn't give a shit about being warm and comforting to my patients, I'd have never made any impression on Audra, and she wouldn't be here with Cinque from the Symbionese Liberation Army.

I looked out at the street knowing the FBI cars were gone.

"I'm so sorry to disturb you," Audra said. "This is Winnie."

Alyse, Audra, and I all tilted our white heads up toward Winnie.

"How do you do?" Winnie said with a warm Caribbean lilt in his voice.

He removed his glasses and extended his hand. I shook it, already embarrassed and in the throes of one of my worst self-inflicted guilt-trips by my initial racist reaction to him. Maybe it would be best if you don't tell Danielle this story. I don't want her to think I'm some kind of closet John Bircher.

Regaining my head at last, I blurted out, "Audra, how did you know where I live?"

Alyse gave me a look: *Why would you ask that?*

"The petition my father brought here. It had your address."

To stop me from blurting out something really off-the-wall, Alyse stepped forward and asked, "Audra, are you alright?"

"My father's in the hospital."

Tears leaked down Audra's cheeks. I had a thought that I'd now seen the full gamut of this woman's emotions.

Alyse—God bless her—didn't go right to, "*Then why the fuck are you here and not at the hospital?*" No, Alyse put her hand on Audra's shoulder and said, "Is it serious?"

Audra coughed out, "I don't know. It's his heart."

Alyse and I glanced at each other. Winnie quietly added, "Audra believes she caused her father's heart ailment."

"It *is* my fault. That's why I didn't go to the hospital. I was scared he wouldn't want me there and I'd make things worse. I didn't know what to do, and you're the only normal people I know around here to ask."

Kind of a nice compliment, don't you think, Commie?

Alyse calmly said, "Then you did the right thing."

Alyse being so magnanimous left me both blown away with admiration and mildly insulted. Any other wife would have taken the whole thing to mean there must be something more going on between her husband and his hot little patient. I guess being oppressively reliable is both a blessing and a curse.

Alyse ushered Audra and Winnie off the porch and into the foyer. I softly closed the door, not wanting the kids to hear.

Alyse took Audra's umbrella and put it in a two-foot high glass—I don't know. Jug?—that was painted with pictures of toppling skyscrapers by one of Alyse's artists about an hour after 9/11 happened. It was a gift.

Audra stood around waiting for the next directive from Alyse when I said, "Audra, no matter what you did, your father loves you. It can only help him if you're with him at the hospital."

Audra looked at Alyse for confirmation. After my *how-did-you-know-our-address?* line, I could hardly blame her for seeing Alyse as the coherent thinker of our household. Alyse nodded her solemn agreement, before saying, "Audra, did you walk here?"

"Yes."

Alyse turned to me: “Honey, you should drive her to the hospital.”

Okay, Commie, you want to know just how clutch Alyse was that night? How tactically and tactfully brilliant? I'll tell you: Before I even got the chance to agree to drive Audra to the hospital, Alyse turned again and said, “Winnie, I'll get you some coffee and you can hang out here with me and my kids for as long as you need to.”

“That's very kind of you, but I do not wish to impose, especially not on such a sacred holiday.”

Alyse smiled and said, “The only sacred holiday in this house is Super Bowl Sunday.”

I threw in, “We have a Super Bowl party every year to justify the price of our plasma TV. It's our big religious event.”

Apparently unversed in secular Judaism, Winnie said, “Thanks so much, but I can just go to the train and get out of your hair.”

“Bad idea,” Alyse said. “You'll want to be nearby for a while in case Audra needs you.”

XII.

Audra folded her bulky overcoat and put it in the back seat of my Saab. As we drove to the hospital, she recounted all the events that Alyse had figured out on her own. Angry at her father and, I may add, emboldened by my text message (*DON'T LET IT GO*), Audra had decided the first night of Hanukkah would be the right time to introduce her family to the jazz pianist she'd been dating for two months. Later, I learned that the relationship was the first thing Alyse had pegged. ("As soon as she introduced Winnie, it was obvious they were dating." "Really? 'Cause I definitely didn't pick up on that.")

Maybe that's why Alyse wasn't suspicious about anything going on between Audra and me. She already knew Audra had a boyfriend. Yeah, that must be it. Alright. Everything makes more sense to me now.

Audra made certain to arrive home as close to sunset as possible, ensuring that her whole family would be there when she and Winnie made their entrance. Alyse had also visualized the rest: Nat Uziel opening the door, looking down at Audra's hand around Winnie's waist, looking up at Winnie, grabbing for his heart, and doing a bug-eyed swoon to the floor.

I mean, don't get the wrong idea, Commie. Nat's a good enough person, but there are just some things you don't expect, like racism to kick up in you big enough to stop your heart (especially after all his railing against anti-Semitism at the rally and with the petition. Hypocrisy really does catch up with us in the end, I guess).

As Audra remembered it, an EMT was packing Nat into the back of an ambulance in what seemed like less than a minute. She said that, even in all the chaos, she noticed how cheerful the EMT was, like someone gaily working on an assembly line, her father just the next widget to be inspected, wrapped up, and shipped off to the repairs department.

In that thin sliver of time between Nat's clutching his heart and the EMT's arrival, Jason Uziel used the words "slut," "whore," and "animal" several times, but got off "baboon" only once. Not that Winnie punched him out or anything. Audra had prepped him about Jason on the Long Island Railroad. Simply by removing his sunglasses, Winnie put a cork in the flow of epithets before Jason could pull out "the N word."

("The N word" is another expression I hate, by the way, but what choice do you have?)

Jason wanted to go in the ambulance with Nat. But, according to Audra, her father made a motion indicating that he didn't want Jason there. I thought maybe that was a wishful perception on Audra's part, but I didn't call her on it. So Jason and his mother got into the Lexus to drive to the hospital. Audra said she'd made one step toward the car when her mother said, "Dear, I think it's best you and your boyfriend don't come to the hospital."

"Boyfriend." It must be one of those woman things: Mrs. Uziel also sniffed out Audra's relationship in no time. Audra told me she felt a wave of love for her mother upon hearing the word "boyfriend," which, of course, made her a thousand times sicker about what she'd done. "Not that I ever thought that bringing Winnie home would cause my father to have a heart attack," she said.

I thought to myself: *The man did have a heart condition. And it's not like you weren't aware of his hypocritical hang-ups.*

Hey, did I ever tell you my hitchhiking story from Maryland?

I'll be quick. This is worth it. For maybe a month during my senior year, I was working a few hours a week at Jeans West in PG Plaza. Eddie Fleck, who had graduated already, was managing the store and asked me if I wanted to make some easy extra money. I thought it'd be good to have some funds so that I could escort Alyse on slightly more glamorous dates, and so I took the job. Really, it was incredibly nice of Fleck to offer. But then, Eddie was always a nice guy. I wouldn't cheat off his test paper, but he was a nice guy.

I took a bus to get to the store, and one day I missed it by a second, so for the first time in my life, I stuck out my thumb. A black guy in a pea green Gremlin stopped and asked, "Where you going, man?"

I said, "PG Plaza."

He said, "Hop in." He leaned over to open the passenger door and just as it flew open, his elbow knocked over a huge bucket of Kentucky Fried Chicken.

We looked at each other, frozen. I mean, come on! I'm three feet from this black guy, separated by a flock of fried chicken. I tried to be nonchalant while thinking maybe I could even up the stereotypes by having a wad of bills pour out of my coat. That's how awkward it was. And then, out of nowhere, we both started cracking up. In unison, the whole comical absurdity landed and we both doubled over. It was fantastic.

Of course, in retrospect, thank God that he laughed too. Knowing me, I'd have tried to break the tension by saying something idiotic like, "So, how about that George Washington Carver fellow?"

But he turned out to be a really good guy, a tour guide at the Air and Space Museum. We even exchanged phone numbers, but, you know, I never called.

Anyway, after Audra told me what had happened, all I said was, "You don't know your father had a heart attack. It could have just been angina or palpitations."

I felt myself become distant toward her in the car. Maybe it was because, only a half-hour earlier, I was warmly aware of being in the middle of one of family life's rare, memorable times. Alyse and I still talk about that Hanukkah night, how great it was to huddle up together in Charlie's room. So can you blame me if I was thinking: *Who needs this shit*?, while sitting in the car listening to Audra talk over my windshield wipers rather than at home enjoying the holiday with my kids?

On the other hand, maybe just this once, I felt like skipping out on my guilt. Obviously, it wasn't too tough to see myself as an unindicted co-conspirator in Audra's crime on account of my text message.

Audra must've sensed my iciness, because she went silent halfway through the drive. In all the time I'd known her, it would have been hard to imagine ever discouraging her from talking to me. Just three days earlier, she'd admitted to flirting with me. Now I was in a car with her, just the two of us, in the basic setting that has led millions of American men to shtup their baby sitters. But me? I was pissed at Audra, feeling protective of Audra, puzzling over Audra, and periodically peeking at the shoulder strap of the seat belt running over her sweater, dividing her breasts and making them appear fuller than I'd remembered.

U. G. H.

An un-conflicted moment. Or only two thoughts in conflict. Is that too much to ask for? Making matters worse, I thought it was possible Audra caught the tail end of one of my peeks. Somehow, my general annoyance over the whole night allowed me to skirt my usual self-torture. So she may have seen an older guy checking out her chest. What was I supposed to do about it after the fact?

You know, not long ago, Alyse was paying some bills and I was telling her about one of my patients. I described her as "a bit of a ditz." Alyse didn't react, so I silently thought about what a funny/great word that is. "Ditz." Then, in one of those times when your thoughts cross over into words, I said aloud, "I love ditz."

Alyse spun her head around and looked at me as if I'd admitted to editing a kiddie porn site.

Less slow on the uptake than usual, I said, "Ditz. I said, *I love ditz*. The word ditz. Beginning with a D as in David."

My wife of a thousand years was genuinely relieved.

Jesus. If I get off on another tangent like that, just smack me or I'll wind up calling you from New York and telling you the rest of the story over a speaker phone.

XIII.

Not far from the hospital, with Audra staring out her window, we approached a railroad crossing. Naturally, about fifty yards from the tracks, the lights went red, the bells rang, the metal arms started slowly dropping. Just wanting this night to end, I gunned the car about twenty yards. Audra whipped her head around toward me and I slammed the brakes.

In a muted tone, I said, "Sorry."

"It's okay," Audra said. "I'm sure you'd like to get back home."

I said nothing as the train approached.

"Wow," Audra said, "that could have been a close call."

"I said I'm sorry."

Audra smiled in a way that gave me a chill and said, "That would have been the perfect capper on the night. I get killed by a train, my body is taken to the same hospital where my father is, and, when he has to identify my body, he realizes that I can't be buried in a Jewish cemetery."

"What are you talking about?"

Audra just looked at me.

"Oh, what? You got a tattoo?"

Audra could have just said "Yes" or "Uh huh" or "yup," but why just answer my question when in two smooth motions you can simply lift up your sweater, unsnap your front-fastening bra, and show me the tattoo reading "God?" in flowing script just above the surprisingly expansive areola on your high, perfectly rounded right breast?

Again, a no-one-keeps-to-the-script moment. Like, what am I supposed to do with that?

The weirdest thing about it, though, was what kept me from reaching out and copping a once-in-a-lifetime feel. I didn't hold myself back out of any sense of propriety or guilt or fidelity. No, not me. I held back because it just seemed like too much work to take off my left glove, place it down, and reach out. Fuck, Commie. Don't ask. Instead, I just took a long look at her breasts, making no effort to hide it. It was like seeing a naked actress in a movie and suddenly thinking, *Holy shit! I can stare all I want!* I must have gazed for five or ten seconds, silently. When I heard Audra say, "Go ahead," I finally looked up at her. Maybe I managed some kind of perfectly executed cut-the-shit look, because shame suddenly coated her face. I felt instantly relieved at not having to say something so dusty as, "Audra, do you really think it's appropriate to be baring your breasts in front of me, a married man, when you're father is in the hospital and your boyfriend is with my wife?"

I've always been amazed at how fast women can navigate bras. On and off and on again. Like nothing. The train hurtled by, the noise doing a brilliant job of dispersing Audra and my thoughts about what had just happened.

We got to Park Israel Hospital and went right to the emergency room. Turns out, my diagnosis was correct. Nat didn't have a heart attack. It was just palpitations or angina or whatever else they stick under the heading of CARDIAC EPISODE.

Nat was already resting comfortably in a private room, no doubt one of the perks of being "prominent in the Jewish community."

I gave Audra a hug that was pretty chaste on the $E=MC^2$ scale. Is that the right physics analogy? Does $E=MC^2$ even have a scale? Whatever. When we disengaged, I saw her face go from relief to dread. Now she'd have to face the music. Actually, much worse—she'd have to face her family.

It was no surprise that Nat was in the "amenities unit." But you wouldn't believe the room itself. Picture a suite at the Four Seasons, fully stocked with Perrier and heart monitors. The second Audra and I entered, I zoomed in on the king-sized bed with a Chippendale backboard. The only patient you'd expect to see lying limp in such grandeur was Sonny Von Bulow. Instead, it was Nat Uziel, tucked under a bazillion thread-count sheet wearing plush pajamas and his yarmulke. I flashed to my father dying in the semi-private room he'd shared with a jaundiced, cirrhotic Korean War amputee from Levittown, and said to myself, *"motherfuckers."* I don't even know why I said it or who I was saying it to. Just a general principle *motherfuckers.*

A nurse outside Nat Uziel's hospital room asked Audra and me to take off our shoes and put on paper-y foot covers. The door was cracked open and we pushed through into a suite so grotesquely spacious that Audra and I had already taken a few steps in before anyone noticed us. Mrs. Uziel had her back to the door and Jason sat across from her in country modern club chairs, chest-high at Nat's bedside. We passed the shabby-chic sofa along the wall perpendicular to the door and the knotty pine coffee table with back issues of *Vanity Fair* and *Architectural Digest.* And, even then, we were a good seven or eight steps from the bed. The room had to be 700 square feet. When the bedside threesome finally looked at us, you could tell they didn't know quite what to make of my presence. I swear, it could have easily been the set of a campy musical, with Mrs. Uziel and Jason breaking into a song called, *What Is He Doing Here*?

Actually, for me, it was more like a cheesy sci-fi movie where I'd been mistakenly and tragically beamed from the happy family around Charlie's bedside to the ostentatiously morose Uziel bedside. Where Charlie's fish tank should have been, there was a brushed slate metal cart holding a really, really tasteful defibrillator and an electrocardiogram, presumably made special by Restoration Hardware. Where Esme should have been hilariously dropping latke crumbs into the tank, Jason sat in maximum agitation, nervously fidgeting and clunking his right elbow into the side of the medical cart. Unobtrusively placed on the side of the bed was an emergency call button encased in rounded wood. Also knotty pine, I think. I gotta say, whoever designed that room did an amazing job of dancing around the inescapable morbidity of the project.

But, you know who wasn't morbid? Nat. He seemed like the only lump of peace in the room. In fact, he immediately smiled at me as if he was really happy I'd tagged along. I'd entered with the dark view that, "When the revolution comes, you and this 'amenities unit' are first to go," but Nat turned my attitude around pretty quick.

"I'm here for my heart, not my feet," Nat said in a jocular tone.

"Audra was upset and came to me for help, so—"

Jason interrupted me, "How the hell are you going to help her? What are you going to do—teach her how to eat a cheeseburger?"

Mrs. Uziel gently said, "Jason, don't be rude."

Audra went over to her father and hugged him and kicked off a medley of apologies that's probably still going on today. Nat surprised everyone by saying, "It's okay, honey. It's my fault and I apologize to you."

"What do you have to apologize for?" Jason said. "She's the slut who brought that monster to our house and caused your heart attack!"

"Jason," Mrs. Uziel said, "your father didn't have a heart attack. And please keep your voice down. And watch your language."

You could see the pattern developing: Jason spits out bottomless rage, his mother chastens him, he slumps in simmering rage for half a minute, at which point the next trigger sends him back over the edge.

Audra sat on the bed beside her mother and to her father's right. Jason scowled at the nerve of his sister to get so close to Nat. I didn't know where the hell to be, so I just stood at the foot of the bed. Really, all I wanted was to get out of there. Another family's dynamic is something no outsider needs to see.

After maybe twenty seconds of silent bedside vigil, Nat smiled again and said, "Boy, I used to love a good cheeseburger."

Jason lurched in his chair, but before he could get off his next blurt, Nat looked at me and said, "What kind of cheese do you like on your burger? Cheddar?"

"Actually," I said, "I prefer American. After all, it is our national cheese."

Nat laughed, and said to his family, "I have some humorous podiatrist, no?"

"Yeah, he's a friggin' riot."

"Jason!"

Jason looked up at his mother, down at his father, across at me, and refused to make eye contact with Audra.

"Good old American cheese," Nat said, all dreamy. I was getting the impression that the second he was alone in the room, he'd order in a half-pound bacon cheeseburger from Peter Luger.

As it turned out, I wasn't far off.

Jason hunched his shoulders and muttered, "Jesus fucking Christ."

This time, Mrs. Uziel glared her admonishment, which seemed to have more bite than her words. As for me, I was starting to welcome Jason's outbursts. They were preferable to the interim periods of killer silence.

"Good God," Mrs. Uziel said, looking over the credenza through the picture windows that were probably fitted for curtains by Laura Ashley herself, "the rain just never lets up."

Audra turned toward the drops rolling down the glass with the pitch black of western Long Island spread out below. Jason shook his head until there could be no question that his mother noticed. Nat gazed at an empty space somewhere over the middle of the room, peacefully zoned out. I watched the sheets over his chest slowly rise and fall, and marveled at how his organs kept chugging away. This reverie ended when Jason cleared his throat with Richter Scale force. Nat's eyes swung toward his son and quickly back to the vacant space somewhere out there. I had an odd thought then, wondering if, given the chance, Nat would take back that one microscopic sperm that became the noxious son beside him.

XIX.

During that particularly long hush, you could practically hear Mrs. Uziel and Audra flipping file cards around in their brains for a neutral conversation topic. Coming to the rescue was my job that night, so I said, “You know, Nat, there’s going to be a big exposé in the paper tomorrow about the makers of Mossad Horseradish.”

“An exposé?” he said, genuinely interested. “What kind of exposé?”

“Apparently they package it under different labels in different parts of the country and market it according to regional prejudices.”

“I don’t understand,” Nat said, sitting up.

“Around here, they target Jews by saying they won’t sell their product to anyone who’s anti-Israel. In other parts of the country, they promote their horseradish to white supremacists with thinly veiled slurs against all non-Christians.”

Nat wasn’t at all taken aback. He was fascinated. “So, they’re pioneers of hate-based marketing.”

I nodded and said, “That’s very well put.”

Nat smiled again. “I guess there’s a certain perverse genius in that.”

“Genius! How’s that genius?” said Jason. “It’s pure, unadulterated, rabid anti-Semitism! *That’s* what it is!”

On cue, Mrs. Uziel piped in, “Jason, keep your voice down. This is a hospital.”

And, weirdly, it was helpful to be reminded of that.

Nat said, “I wish all of you would stop hovering over me. The doctor said I’m fine, and you’re all acting as if I’m on my deathbed.”

The other members of the Uziel clan looked around, trying to decide if that was their cue to leave. I certainly took it that way, but not wanting to seem as if I couldn’t wait to bolt, I said, “You know, Nat, this would make a pretty spectacular deathbed.”

Nat smiled and said, “I could do a lot worse.”

For the first time, I was genuinely liking Nat. Suddenly, he was a normal guy, someone you could kibbitz with. So, in the spirit of kibbitzing, I said, "Some mattress company ought to come out with a line of deathbeds. They could call it something like The Sealy Extinct-a-Pedic."

Nat pulled up his knees and slapped his thigh, laughing. So, I kept going with the idea:

"We at Sealy believe everyone should die well-rested. That's why we've introduced this new line of deathbeds, so you can pass on in firm, ergo-dynamic comfort that continuously adapts to the individual contours of your lifeless body."

Nat hooted, "I love that! Never mind Sealy. You and I should start our own mattress company."

"Count me in," I said, feeling pretty good about myself. After all, it's a known fact that laughing is good for the heart. I read that somewhere.

"Who knew my podiatrist was such a card?" Nat said, smiling.

Jason just glowered because, you know, that's what he does. Mrs. Uziel—whose first name I don't know to this day, by the way—was smiling, probably because her husband actually (finally!) looked like he was having fun. Audra looked like she wanted to smile, but wasn't entirely ready to let herself that far off the hook. She just curled up an inch or so more onto the bed. Nat looked at her and gave her a really sweet wink. He was crazy about his little girl no matter what form of shock value she brought home from college. It was a nice moment, but I still just wanted to get out of there.

Nat blew out a big sigh and said to me, "Does your family observe Hanukkah?"

I smiled and said, "Yes, but we observe from a distance."

Nat let out a, "Hmm," without any disapproving, holier-than-thou tone.

"We give the kids gifts—not many—eat tons of latkes, and that's about it."

Jason said, "And you have the temerity to call yourself a Jew?"

I'd noticed that the word "temerity" seemed to have caught on with the Orthodox community. The two Orthodox patients I mentioned earlier—Irwin Cole and Sam Kipnis—had both used that word in my office. I think I mentioned that I like both Irwin and Sam, but they did seem to have that somewhat obscure word right near the top of their vocabulary list.

Imagine the temerity . . ."

"Then he had the temerity to insist . . ."

Unlike Irwin and Sam, Jason had adapted the speech cadence you hear among hyper-observant Jews. That choppy rabbinical reggae. I can't even imitate it.

I said, "Jason, as I told you the first time we met, I'm not a Jew according to your definition. But to answer your question, I've been Jewish for over 50 years, so it doesn't take much temerity to call myself a Jew."

As soon as I said that, I regretted it. I had no business getting into it with Jason. His mother was doing the job just fine.

Backpedaling, I said, "I'm sorry, Jason. This is a difficult night for you and your family. I was wrong to take any kind of a tone with you."

Nat waved his hand as if to say, *No apology needed.*

Audra, probably emboldened by her father's wink, said, "This is America. Everyone's free to worship as he or she sees fit."

Well, that was like a Molotov cocktail thrown into Jason's combustible head. "And how do *you* worship, Audra? By purposely trying to kill your father?"

"What?" Audra said, "You think I wanted this to happen?"

"I don't think, I *know*. You'd have to be an idiot to not know what was going to happen. You know your father has a heart condition and, on the first night of Hanukkah, you bring that monster to our door? You're probably disappointed it didn't kill Daddy."

Mrs. Uziel held up her hand and said, "Jason, calm down."

"I will not calm down! Listen, Audra, you talk about everyone's rights as an American? Fine. I have the right to protect my family from harm. And that's just what I'm going to do."

Audra got off the bed and stood up in what looked like a dramatic gesture to look down on Jason. "Oh, really? What are you going to do, Jason?"

"I've already done it."

Nat, who had been trying to stay out of the fray, got a look of dread on his face and said, "What have you already done, Jason?"

"You want to know what I've done? I'll tell you what I've done. While you were being examined, I called the police and told them my sister must be arrested for attempted murder."

Mr. and Mrs. Uziel said, "Oh my God," in perfect unison.

"I'm meeting with an officer tomorrow morning," Jason said, leaning back and looking self-satisfied.

Mrs. Uziel said, "You mean, you're going to try to have your own sister arrested?"

"And convicted and imprisoned, hopefully."

Another round of "Oh my God's" swept around the room. I considered comforting Audra by calling up my *Law & Order* expertise to let her know there was no chance that she would even be arrested, much less put on trial, but I restrained myself. The exact phrase that ran through my head was: *This isn't my peace to negotiate.*

The various scenarios and implications of Jason's actions swam silently around the room. Audra's jaw clenched. She looked out the window as if ready to parachute out. Mrs. Uziel stared at her son, her eyelids batting as if she were communicating in Morse code. Only Nat seemed unruffled, returning his gaze to the non-spot in the air above him.

And me? I was telling myself that no one would hold it against me if I politely got the fuck out of there. And I was right. I could've just left. Nat probably would have thought, *I'd leave too if I could.* Mrs. Uziel would've likely just been relieved of her agonized embarrassment at having a stranger witness her secret family insanity.

I guess I stayed for Audra. In my office, she'd always seemed like someone who had the world all figured out. Just seeing her so—I don't know—so *reduced*, standing there, biting the inside of her cheek . . . it just killed me. I tried to get a handle on her state of mind and got as far as realizing that Audra was about the same age as Alyse was when I'd met her. She was another girl. Another smart, cute girl. A smart, cute girl in crisis. I couldn't leave. Because really—well, I just couldn't.

Jason sat upright and alive like he owned the moment. At 23, he looked almost young.

Nat took an exaggerated breath through his nose and opened his eyes.

"Jason," Nat said, "I have contributed to and therefore have very strong ties to the Nassau County Police Department. The moment I tell them that your allegations against your sister are ridiculous, they will send you off on your way like they do with all citizens whom they regard as crackpots."

The vitality visibly drained from Jason's body. "But you won't tell the police that."

"Yes I will, Jason."

"How could you, Daddy? Audra is guilty! She brought that animal into our home with a cross hanging from his neck. She tried to take advantage of your heart condition and send you to an early grave!"

Nat paused to look upon his son so his words might sink in. "Jason," he said, "I have failed you as a father. My self-righteous, vengeful bullying—that's what I've passed on to you. And for that, I'm sorry."

Jason tried to interrupt but Nat talked over him. "You see, Jason, in the ambulance, speeding to this hospital with the sirens and the lights and whatnot? I had a moment to consider how I'd gotten there; to ponder how the events of the last few days had led me to that gurney, my body connected to machines. That's when I knew: all of my ruthless, pernicious, and unforgiving . . . *shit?* It was time to let it go. To forgive and forget. All of it. Finally. And Jason? You must let it go too."

"No, I will not let it go."

"Jason—"

"No. Never."

Commie, in response to that, Nat Uziel closed his eyes again—this time for a full ten seconds—then opened them and looked coldly at his son. Jason looked stricken, as if he knew something big was about to happen. And he was right.

XX.

Nat slowly lifted his left arm from under the blanket, raised his hand to his head, and gently removed his yarmulke, softly dropping it on the night table inches away from Jason's face.

"Son, you have to let it go."

I'm pretty sure I have the things that happened next in the right order:

When the enormity of Nat's gesture had sunk in, Jason wailed the word, "No!" in a pitch so gutturally tortured that the attending nurse barreled into the room with a CODE RED urgency that caused her to drop her *Don't Mess With Texas* coffee mug. The mug shattered on the floor and caused Audra to step back and wheel around just as Jason, in a blind rage, grabbed the closest possible object he could find to hurl across the room and into the wall: the defibrillator.

But I guess Jason hadn't counted on the paddles separating from the machine, because one of those paddles caught on the edge of the mattress, causing the machine to waft like a whiffle ball over Nat's waist and flutter just over the edge of the other side of the bed, where it picked up gravitational speed and landed on Audra's hospital sock-covered foot, causing disruption of the soft tissue envelope, the oblique spiral comminuting fractures of the second, third, and fourth metatarsal bones, not to mention the kind of nerve compression that can make a delicate nineteen-year-old girl pass out on the floor from pain.

XXI.

I got home around 8:45.

There was no point in my staying at the hospital. The surgery on Audra couldn't be done for several days due to the swelling. And, anyway, even if the surgery could be done immediately, it wasn't like I was going to supervise the thirty-two-year-old, let's-hit-the-beach orthopedist who eventually performed the procedure magnificently and even wound up dating Audra for three months before she got past her gratitude and went back into her quasi-avant-garde pool of guys from the Meatpacking District.

When I opened the front door, I heard singing upstairs. I checked to make sure I was in the right house and, you know, it was indeed my stuff that was everywhere, so indeed I was home.

A show-off-y spray of electronic music pumped out, undoubtedly Winnie playing the computer keyboard we'd bought for Charlie two years earlier (one of our bigger wastes of money in recent memory).

Alyse, Esme, and Charlie screeched out the chorus to "Yellow Submarine" in creaky harmony with Winnie's Caribbean baritone, and I thought: *Well, things seem to have worked out well back at the ranch.*

By nine, I was back in the car. Winnie was in the front passenger seat, Alyse and the kids squished in the back. I didn't go into detail about what had happened in the hospital with the Uziel family, but just mentioned that Audra had gotten her foot broken, and that she'd be okay. That didn't stop everyone from trying to fill in the huge gaps in the story. The whirring minds in the car were practically buzzing. I said to Winnie, "So, this will be a night you won't soon forget, huh?"

"Man," Winnie said, half-smiling, half-shell shocked, "my consciousness is all over the place."

It had finally stopped raining when we got to the train station. Alyse and the kids all piled out to hug Winnie. The few straggling commuters who had worked late and looked like hell, literally or figuratively, rubbed their eyes at the sight of four of their generic townsfolk warmly bidding adieu to a massive, jet-black Rastafarian. I really loved that moment. It was like a small sticking-it-up-the-ass to the neighborhood. Conveniently forgetting my initial racist impressions of Winnie, I felt cool.

Alyse asked Winnie for his contact information and promised to invite him to our Super Bowl party. Winnie hesitated to accept the invitation, but Charlie and Esme cheered, "You gotta come! Please!"

A guy I'd seen at the gym who, as far as I could tell, limited his workouts to reading the *Wall Street Journal* in the sauna, walked out of the train station and stared at Winnie, then us, then back to Winnie, who looked right back at him. Alyse said to Winnie, "That guy will be at the Super Bowl party."

Winnie laughed and at last agreed. "I can't wait."

Maybe a quarter of the way home, with Alyse back in the passenger seat, I turned to my family and said, "Let's take a drive and look at some Christmas lights."

The suggestion was weird enough to make everyone shrug and say, "Okay."

We rolled north toward the WASPy rich areas along the Long Island Sound. People living there had an obligation to be tasteful, so we were spared the lawns with three-bedroom crèches beside obese plastic Santas—you know, the ones with the demented smiles like you see in the other less monied, kitschy, wishful thinking towns of Long Island. The festooned homes we cruised past looked stunningly beautiful. At one point, Esme made me stop the car outside one particularly killer house—a craftsman style, according to Alyse. It was huge and woodsy with gigantic windows rimmed by amber lights. "Wow," Esme said. "I'd sell Charlie to the terrorists to live in that house."

God help the guy Esme marries. Kid has expensive taste.

We drove maybe ten miles an hour up and down winding streets (the ones that are too exclusive to be laid out on any grid), with the kids ooh-ing and aah-ing at the beauty and sheer elaborateness of their Christmas decorations. It was like watching fireworks on July 4th without all the garish, blistering noise.

Along a street called Leatherstocking Lane—no, seriously: *Leatherstocking Lane*—I lost focus for a moment and drifted my right tires onto a previously flawless lawn, plowing a Goodyear radial rut into the soaked grass. The kids laughed. I said, "Oops," and kept driving. Oh, well. Another brush with being a fugitive.

After a while, the kids fell asleep in the back. All we needed was *Silent Night* to complete the sweet peacefulness of it all. We drove some more, wordlessly, one array of festive lights after another reflecting in our eyes. Finally, we reached a Mediterranean-style villa on a sprawling, manicured lawn that led right into the Long Island Sound. Wrapped around the entire home were blue and red lights set parallel to each other with dripping snow-like white lights suspended between them. The precise, God-like elegance was so spellbinding that I felt divinely compelled to look at Alyse, my life's work, and say, "Honey . . ."

She turned to me.

And I said, "You know, the people in the world outside of this car . . . they're all out of their fucking minds."

Alyse tapped my arm. "Yeah, they're a pretty unruly bunch."

About the Author

After graduating from the University of Maryland, **Peter Mehlman**, a New York native, became a writer for the *Washington Post*. He slid to television in 1982, writing for *SportsBeat with Howard Cosell*. From 1985-90, he returned to forming full sentences as a writer for numerous national publications, including *The New York Times Magazine*, *GQ*, *Esquire*, and a multitude of women's magazines due to his advanced understanding of that gender.

In 1989, he moved to Los Angeles, where he bumped into Larry David, whom he'd met twice in New York. David, developing "a little show with Jerry Seinfeld," invited Mehlman to submit a sample script. Having never written one, Mehlman sent a humor piece he'd written for the *Times Magazine* and got an assignment, which became the first *Seinfeld* freelance episode, "The Apartment." Over the eight-year run of the show, Mehlman rose to executive producer and coined such *Seinfeld*-isms as "yada yada" "spongeworthy," "shrinkage," and "double-dipping."

In 1997, Mehlman joined DreamWorks and created *It's like, you know . . .* a scathing look at Los Angeles. In recent years, he has written screenplays, a novel, and humor pieces for NPR, *Esquire*, *The New York Times*, *The Washington Post*, and *The Los Angeles Times*, several of which were published in his collection, *Mandela Was Late.* In addition, he has also appeared on-camera for TNT Sports and the Webby-nominated *Peter Mehlman's Narrow World of Sports*, while also starring in his short film *Blank*, for which he won best writing at the Los Angeles Comedy Festival.

He lives in Los Angeles. This is his first book of fiction.